COLD HARD CASH

TREVOR DOUGLAS

vinci
BOOKS

By Trevor Douglas

The Bridgette Cash Mystery Thriller Series

Cold Comfort

Cold Trail

Cold Hard Cash

The Cold Light of Day

Out In The Cold

Hot And Cold

This book is dedicated to David Kenneth Laverty.

An exceptional young actor and performer who took his final curtain call way too soon.

Vinci Books

vinci-books.com

Published by Vinci Books Ltd in 2025

1

Copyright © Trevor Douglas 2019

The author has asserted their moral right to be identified as the author of this work in accordance with the Copyright, Designs and Patents Act 1988. This work is a work of fiction. Names, characters, places and incidents are the product of the author's imagination or are used fictitiously. Any resemblance to actual persons, living or dead, places and incidents is entirely coincidental.

All rights reserved. No part of this publication may be copied, reproduced, distributed, stored in any retrieval system, or transmitted in any form or by any means, including photocopying, recording, or other electronic or mechanical methods, nor used as a source for any form of machine learning including AI datasets, without the prior written permission of the publisher.

The publisher and the author have made every effort to obtain permissions for any third party material used in this book and to comply with copyright law. Any queries in this respect should be brought to the attention of the publisher and any omissions will be corrected in future editions.

A CIP catalogue record for this book is available from the British Library.

Paperback ISBN: 9781036702014

Printed and bound in Great Britain by Clays Ltd, Elcograf S.p.A.

Part I

Wednesday - 10:30 A.M.

Bridgette tightened her grip on the side railing of the small police runabout as the boat plowed on through choppy water. She did her best to focus on the large rocky outcrop they were headed toward as the boat rose and fell on the swell. Although technically an island, the rock mass in the middle of the bay had no redeeming features. About the size of a soccer field and covered with spindly trees that survived among the rock crevices, the island's only residents, a small colony of cormorants, ignored them as they approached.

She wiped the salt spray from her face as she looked back across the bay toward the shoreline and wondered what the residents of the prestigious bayside suburb of Stone Bay would think when they read their newspapers in the morning.

Her thoughts were interrupted by Officer Danny Canning, who was piloting the boat. "I'll get you to move into the middle of the boat and slide down, Detective Cash.

We're going to enter the cave shortly, and its entrance is very narrow."

Bridgette complied and shifted to the center of the boat as Canning gently maneuvered the boat through the swell toward the cave entrance.

The young officer, who she had only met half an hour ago, added, "You'll need to keep your head down too—the swell is a little unpredictable, and we've got very little headroom."

She didn't fancy being knocked out as they entered the cave and flattened herself out as much as possible as the boat slowly approached what looked like a split in the rock face at the northern end of the island. She had learned from her conversation with Canning on the way out from the jetty that the split hid an entrance to a cave that was only accessible at low tide and at certain times of the year. As the boat moved forward, she could see a small amount of light reflecting off the waterline and marking the entrance to the low-set cave entrance. She knew this light was coming from the floodlights set up by the forensics team inside the cavern and took a deep breath to brace herself for what was to come.

Canning throttled back the outboard motor and deftly guided the runabout through the tiny entrance and into a small tunnel. Bridgette did her best to remain relaxed as the pungent smell of death began to surround her. From her prone position, she looked around at the cold and damp surroundings. She could have reached up a hand and touched the roof, and she marveled at Canning's skill as he maneuvered the boat around a sharp bend.

The tunnel opened up into a cavern, causing Bridgette to shield her eyes from the floodlights as she stared around the underwater cave. She guessed the space was about thirty feet wide and twenty feet deep. She barely noticed Canning kill the engine as the boat drifted toward a rock ledge as she studied the scene before her.

Four people currently occupied the cave—two living and two dead. She ignored the coroner, Doctor Ray Warner, and his assistant and focused on the two bodies that were propped up against the far wall of the rock ledge. One was little more than a skeleton, the other the bloated and putrefying remains of someone who had died recently. It was in an advanced stage of decomposition; she could tell it was the body of a man but not much more.

Her thoughts were interrupted by Ray Warner as he made his way to the edge of the ledge. The friendly, fifty-something medical examiner had worked a case with Bridgette several months earlier and said, "I'll give you a hand to get out of the boat, Bridgette. The ledge is slippery, and we don't want you falling."

Bridgette responded, "Thanks, Ray," as she gripped Warner's outstretched hand.

"Are you flying solo today?" asked Warner as he helped her out of the boat and up onto the ledge.

Doing her best not to gag, Bridgette nodded. "The chief had to go to a funeral this afternoon, and I don't have a new partner yet, so it's just me."

Warner motioned for her to follow him into the center of the cavern. "It won't matter much if he misses today. We've only got about another fifteen minutes' work time here before we have to abandon it for today. Once the tide starts to come in, the boat won't fit back out through the tunnel, and I for one don't fancy spending the night in here with these two."

They turned as one and stared for a moment at the two bodies that were slumped side by side on the back wall.

Warner handed Bridgette a surgical mask. "We've been here a bit over an hour and haven't done much more than set up floodlights and do a preliminary examination of the cave."

He waited until Bridgette had the mask fitted before he asked, "So what have you been told already?"

Bridgette took a moment to compose herself. At twenty-seven, the rookie homicide detective still struggled with the smell of badly decomposing bodies. When she was confident she wasn't going to vomit, she replied, "The chief gave me a short briefing before I drove down. Two bodies were found here early this morning by divers who were trying to salvage a boat that sank nearby. Apparently, they discovered the cave by accident."

Warner nodded. "That about sums it up. One of the diving crew led us out here earlier and showed us the spot. He's local and has lived here for over thirty years and had no idea the cave existed."

Bridgette tore her eyes away from the bodies. As she looked around the cavern, she said, "So we're above sea level, somewhere inside the northern end of the island?"

"You got it. Rook Island is essentially one large rock, although it's not as solid as everyone thought." Warner nodded toward his forensic partner who was busy laying out several pieces of electronic equipment. "Robert and I spent half an hour going over every square foot of the cavern once we got the lights set up. There's no way in or out except through that tunnel which is underwater most of the time."

Bridgette returned her gaze to the bodies. "Have you had time to examine the bodies?"

"Not really. We're still setting up, and we need to leave

soon. All I can tell you is both bodies are male, probably Caucasian, and slightly under six feet in height."

Bridgette took a few steps toward the bodies and then stopped. As she crouched down to get a better look, she asked, "How long have they been here?"

"The skeleton has been here a long time—I would guess ten years at least, but we'll confirm that back in the lab." Warner paused as he pointed at the remains and then said, "Originally, he was propped up against the wall like the other body is now. The collapse is just the natural result of the body breaking down over time."

"Do you think they were killed here?"

Warner shook his head. "My guess is no. I can't see any sign of blood spatters or anything else to suggest they were killed here, but I'll know more tomorrow. Even though this is a damp cave, if there are bloodstains here, we should find them."

Bridgette moved slightly closer and studied the skeletal remains of the man in more detail. He had been reduced to bones covered with just a few shards of blackened skin and clothing. The remains had collapsed over the years but were still largely intact. She pointed at a small hole in the middle of the man's skull just above the two eye sockets. "Bullet hole?"

"Almost certainly." Warner came and squatted beside her.

"Well, that rules out death by natural causes." She turned her attention to the bloated body of the other man. The man's skin had turned black, and the body barely looked recognizable as a human being. She could see clumps of the man's dark hair had started to fall out and wondered whether that was just part of the decaying process or whether maggots and insects had hastened the process as they fed on his remains.

While she studied the body, Warner said, "This body has only been here for a month or two. He's currently in stage four of the decomposition process, but because the cave is sealed most of the time, it slows down the process. I'll need to get him to the lab before I can give you a more accurate time of death."

Bridgette nodded. "Any idea how he died?"

"Not yet."

Bridgette moved closer to the body and was thankful for the mask as the putrid smell threatened to overwhelm her. Without taking her eyes off the body, she pulled a pen from her jacket pocket and gently moved a large lock of hair on the man's forehead slightly to the left. She pointed at a small divot in the man's forehead. "What do you make of that, Ray?"

Warner moved forward. "I'll be damned, he's been shot as well." Warner shook his head. "So how did you spot the bullet hole?"

Bridgette shrugged. "I didn't, really. I figure if they were killed and brought here by the same person, there was a good chance his latest victim was also shot…"

Warner stood up. "Why would he bother bringing them here after they're dead? Wouldn't it be easier just to go a little further out to sea and feed them to sharks?"

Bridgette moved back to the center of the cavern. She responded, almost absently, as she scanned the interior of the cave, "I think they're important to him. Maybe he even comes here to visit from time to time?"

Warner frowned. "I know Chief Delray has a lot of faith in you, Bridgette, but finding whoever did this isn't going to be easy…"

Bridgette nodded. "I'm sure the chief will want it handled like any other murder investigation—we break it down into small steps."

"I'll take DNA swabs from both victims before we leave. I'm reasonably confident it won't take us too long to figure out their identities."

"Once we know who they are, hopefully it will help us answer the next question."

"Which is?"

"Is there a link between them? If they're just two random strangers, finding the killer will be like looking for a needle in a haystack…"

"But if they're connected?"

Bridgette stared at the bodies again. "Then we're one step closer to finding the killer."

Wednesday - 6:20 P.M.

Felix Delray stepped out of the elevator and onto the plush carpet on level four of the Vancouver Metro police complex. He walked toward an empty reception area furnished with leather lounges and a coffee table he guessed would have cost him more than a month's salary. It was well after six p.m., and all of Commissioner Underwood's reception staff had left for the day, so Delray kept walking. He paused in the doorway to the commissioner's spacious office, replete with original oil paintings, two couches, and a conference table for six, and knocked lightly.

Underwood looked up from a file he was studying on his desk. "Come on in, Felix, and close the door behind you."

Delray mumbled, "Thank you, sir," as he closed the door. As he made his way across to a desk that was about half the size of his office, Delray wondered again what the meeting was about. He had received a phone call from Underwood fifteen minutes earlier, but he hadn't given him any clues. Audiences with the commissioner were rare, especially without his boss, Assistant Commissioner Leo Cunningham, being present.

As Delray settled into a chair opposite the commissioner, Underwood said, "Thanks for coming on short notice, Felix."

"No problem, sir."

Underwood closed the file and sat for a moment not quite looking at Delray as he collected his thoughts. Although much shorter in stature than Delray, the fifty-something commissioner had a giant of a brain and preferred silence while he thought.

Delray waited patiently until Underwood said, "Detective Cash, she's now back in the precinct?"

"She started back on Monday, sir."

Underwood nodded. "That was one heck of an investigation she pulled off in Sanbury."

Delray allowed himself a slight smile as he thought about his star recruit who had been sent to a remote mountain township to investigate the disappearance of a fellow officer. "Yes, it was."

"I'd rather she'd found John Tyson alive but finding his body and his killer was very impressive. So, what's she working on now?"

"She's been assigned to investigate the two bodies that were found in the cave in Stone Bay this morning."

"And who's her new partner?"

Delray shifted in his seat a little. Bridgette's partner, Lance Hoffman, had been shot and killed three months earlier while they were working a serial killer case. He responded, "No one yet, sir. To be frank, I didn't think she'd wrap up the Sanbury case quite this quickly, and finding someone to replace Lance is proving difficult."

"That's what I wanted to talk to you about." Underwood got up from his desk and walked over to a panoramic window that gave him uninterrupted views of a city park and the river. Without turning back, he continued, "Detective Bridgette Cash is a remarkable young woman, Felix, but she's not bulletproof. The reason we sent her to Sanbury was to get her out of this precinct until we could guarantee her safety."

Delray sighed as he recalled what was now known as the basement shooting incident. With Delray's permission and on her own time, Bridgette had been reviewing microfilm records of her mother's cold case murder late one evening in the archives room when she'd been shot at. Bridgette had survived the attack, but the microfilm had been stolen. Delray answered, "I intend to work closely with her on this next case until we find a replacement partner."

Underwood turned around. "You don't have enough time, Felix. You lead a team of twelve detectives, and your unit has the biggest caseload in the precinct. It would be irresponsible to expect you to manage this situation as well."

Underwood returned to his desk and sat down before he added, "Internal Investigations have made little progress on the basement shooting. We've got one of our own detectives sitting in a jail cell facing charges of attempting to murder a fellow police officer and stealing police records, and he refuses to say anything. You've been on the force for over thirty years, so what does that tell you?"

Delray thought for a moment about Charlie Bates, one of his brightest junior detectives. It still pained him to think one of his own team had been involved in the incident, firing shots at a fellow officer, no less. "It tells me Bates was probably working for someone very powerful, and he's afraid. But you know that already."

Underwood pushed back in his chair. "Since the incident, I've had the records department open every box in the archives room, but we can't find the original paper file on that murder case."

Delray mused, "Perhaps it's somewhere else in the building? It wouldn't be the first file that's gone missing."

Underwood shook his head. "We'd have found it by now. The records manager is adamant the paper file hasn't been checked out in close to ten years. My guess is it was stolen a long time ago by someone who has a lot to lose if evidence from a twenty-year-old murder case ever became public."

Delray knew Underwood was probably referring to a cop or an ex-cop but wasn't about to verbally join the dots. Instead, he tactfully responded, "Sir, if there's anything I can do to help…"

"There is. I want you to explain to Detective Cash that I don't want her investigating her mother's murder any further, even on her own time. I'm fairly sure whoever hired Bates doesn't have access to our building, but I can't be certain. Until we get to the bottom of this, this matter is to be left with Internal Investigations—are we clear?"

"Perfectly, sir."

"Are we going to have a problem with Detective Cash following orders? The assistant commissioner believes she's a maverick despite her obvious talent."

"Sir, I've never agreed with that assessment, and I don't believe she'll have any issue following my orders. Frankly, she's still a little rattled by the whole incident."

Underwood scratched his chin. "Well, that's not surprising." He paused for a moment and then added, "I've been giving this matter a lot of thought, and I don't want Detective Cash working on her own until we have this basement issue resolved. I've talked to Assistant

Commissioner Cunningham, and we've come up with a plan."

Delray did his best to avoid rolling his eyes at the mention of his boss's name again. Cunningham was more a bureaucrat than a police officer and rarely agreed with Delray on anything. Delray did his best to avoid Cunningham and knew the feeling was mutual. As tactfully as he could muster, Delray replied, "And what is that, sir?"

"Cunningham is going to assign one of his detectives from Internal Investigations to be Bridgette's partner until this matter is resolved. Not only will it solve your immediate resourcing problem, but it will give someone from that team an opportunity to learn more about the case from Bridgette herself."

"Did he say who he had in mind?"

"Detective Aaron Sterling."

Delray couldn't hide his surprise. Delray found Sterling obnoxious and agreed with the sentiment of most cops that Sterling was looking for a quick path to the top and didn't care how many careers he burned in the process. "Sir, with all due respect, Aaron Sterling interviewed Bridgette on the night of the basement shooting and treated her like a common criminal."

"I'm aware there has been tension between Sterling and Cash, but this is an opportunity for them both to learn how to work with one another."

Out of respect for the commissioner, Delray did his best to hide his disappointment as he responded, "I'm not sure how this will work out, sir, but if that's your decision, we'll give it a try."

Underwood responded, "It was the assistant commissioner's decision, and I'm happy to run with it for now." Underwood paused a moment to study Delray and then continued, "I know you and Cunningham don't get along, but for the sake of Detective Cash, I'm asking you to give it a try."

Delray knew better than to argue with the commissioner and responded without enthusiasm, "If that's what you want, sir."

Underwood seemed satisfied. "I'm hoping we will have this matter resolved in days, not weeks. As soon as we have whoever is ultimately responsible for this behind bars, Sterling goes back to Internal Investigations."

"Yes, sir."

Underwood opened a file on his desk. "Well, that's all for now, Felix. My door is always open. If there are any developments, I'll let you know."

Delray went to rise from his chair but sat down again. "So how soon will the transfer take effect, sir?"

Without looking up from his paperwork, Underwood responded, "Tomorrow or Friday at the latest. I'm sure the assistant commissioner will be in contact with you tomorrow to make the final arrangements."

Delray thanked the commissioner for his time as he always did and left the office to head for the elevator. He had known Cunningham for long enough to know there was always an ulterior motive with any offer. Aaron Sterling was the last man in Vancouver Metro that should be paired with Bridgette, and Cunningham knew it. He would need to find out what Cunningham's agenda was before Sterling joined his team.

Thursday - 7:05 A.M.

Bridgette arrived at the Vancouver Metro Southern Precinct building a little after seven a.m.—her normal time for starting work. After taking the elevator to the second floor of the modern concrete and glass structure, she made her way past a row of cubicles with gray metal desks and filing cabinets to her desk in the rear corner of the Homicide room. She shared the room with eleven other detectives and six support staff, most of whom didn't start work until seven thirty or later. She enjoyed the peace and solitude at this time of day and began to make notes on a scratch pad as she thought back about the crime scene of the bodies in the cave.

Bridgette had barely written two points when she heard a familiar gravelly voice call out, "Hey, Bridgette, come and join me in my office when you're ready."

Bridgette looked up to see her burly boss walking back toward his office with a takeaway coffee in each hand. Chief Inspector Felix Delray had been the only boss she had ever known in her short career at Vancouver Metro. He was firm but fair, and he was teaching her as much about life as he was about being a good detective.

Bridgette knew better than to keep Delray waiting. She picked up her meager notes and followed him back to his office.

She knocked politely on the door before entering. "Good morning, chief."

Delray was just settling into his office chair. "C'mon in, Bridgette, and close the door behind you."

Bridgette's gut tightened slightly. Her boss operated with an open door policy and only ever closed it if he needed to chew out one of his detectives.

Delray read Bridgette's face and added with a slight grin, "Relax, you're not in trouble." He continued in a more serious tone, "But I do need to discuss something with you at the end of our meeting which we don't need the world knowing about—at least not yet."

Slightly relieved, Bridgette sat down.

Delray slid one of the two coffees across his desk between two piles of papers toward her. "White with no sugar—right?"

Bridgette said, "Thanks, chief," as she picked up the coffee. She took a sip. "Perfect." She'd spent most of the night going over in her mind what she had seen in the cave the day before and had found sleep difficult. The caffeine hit was just what she needed to get her day off to a good start.

Delray took a large sip of his coffee. "You're always the first one in, so I thought we'd share a coffee while you give me a rundown on what happened yesterday."

Before Bridgette could respond, Delray continued, "I got an email from the coroner's office about the bodies on

Rook Island. It sounds like I had more fun at the funeral than you did in that cave?"

Bridgette nodded. In her mind, she was back in the cold, damp cave with the smell of death surrounding her. As she recalled the image of the two bodies slumped against the wall, she said, "It wasn't a whole lot of fun."

"Ray gave me a quick rundown, but it was mostly medical jargon, so I'd appreciate your take on it before we go out there today."

Bridgette gave Delray a summary. She started by explaining how the cave could only be accessed by a narrow, hidden sea entrance and then gave Delray a description of each body and its location in the cave but spared him the worst of the gory detail.

"And they were both shot in the head?"

"Yes. Ray believes both bodies were moved to the cave shortly after they were murdered."

"And one body has been there a long time? At least ten years?"

"Yes. The first victim is not much more than a skeleton."

"And you think each victim was killed by the same person?"

Bridgette considered the question for a moment and then said, "I didn't get much sleep last night. This was one of the questions I was wrestling with. The cave is very well hidden. The diver who discovered it was a local who has lived in the area for thirty years. I interviewed him late yesterday afternoon. He knew nothing about the cave, and I think it's safe to assume no one else did either…except for the killer."

Delray leaned back in his chair and clasped his hands

behind his head. "So what is this—some sort of private tomb for a serial killer's murder victims?"

"Possibly."

Delray raised his eyebrows. "Possibly?"

Bridgette had studied serial killer profiling as part of her criminology degree. Delray didn't have a degree, but she respected his experience and didn't like to challenge him.

As if reading her mind, Delray said, "Spit it out, Bridgette. The only experience I've had with serial killers is the Selwood case that we solved three months ago—and if memory serves, it was actually you who solved it."

With a license to speak her mind, Bridgette responded, "Serial killers generally kill on a regular basis unless they're locked away in jail or are incapacitated in some other way. Typically, the gap between murders is anything from a few months to a few years at most. The gap between the murder of these two victims is at least ten years and maybe a lot longer. Unless he was only keeping victims with a special significance to him in the cave and discarding other victims elsewhere, this doesn't fit with the pattern of a normal serial killer."

Delray leaned forward again and picked up one of the crime scene photos he had printed out from the email. As he studied the image of the two victims propped up against the rear wall of the cave, he said, "I've seen some grisly murder scenes during my career, Bridgette, but this looks like one of the worst."

"Did Ray mention he only has an hour and a half of work time in the cave each day?"

Delray nodded as he continued to study the photograph. "The tide thing is really hampering the investigation. It's going to take him several more days to complete his examination on-site. The water police aren't happy about it.

They've got to leave a boat and an officer moored out there twenty-four seven until we finish with the crime scene."

"So it might be several more days before he gets the bodies out?"

Delray looked up from the photograph. "I think they're going to remove the bodies today. He's keen to get them back to his lab so he can start trying to figure out who they are. He's going to leave the rest of the forensic work at the cave to his team."

They were both silent for a moment while they sipped their coffee.

Delray broke the silence. "So what's your take on this, Bridgette?"

Bridgette thought for a moment and then said, "I'm not sure, chief. Like I said to Ray in the cave yesterday, I'm hoping we can identify the victims as soon as possible and then see if we can establish a link between the two men."

"A common link is always a useful kickstart to an investigation."

"I thought I would head over to Missing Persons this morning and go over their files of who's gone missing in the last few months. Ray believes the most recent victim is Caucasian and most likely in his early forties. It's not a lot to go on, but it's worth checking if anyone matching that general description has gone missing."

"I think that's a good use of your time, and until you get a new partner, you are lead detective on this."

Bridgette responded, "Thanks, chief, I know I've got a lot to learn, but I will give it my best shot."

She noticed Delray looked distracted as he responded, "You'll be fine…"

Bridgette frowned. "Something the matter, chief?"

Delray let out a breath. "As a matter of fact, there is." Delray paused for a minute to collect his thoughts.

Bridgette wasn't sure what was coming. In the three months she had worked with the chief inspector, she had rarely ever seen him at a loss for words. She waited patiently for him to continue.

"About the new partner thing for you... There's been a development."

"Okay."

"You're not going to like it, and I for one damn sure don't..."

Bridgette couldn't think of anything else to say and repeated as her gut tightened further, "Okay."

"Aaron Sterling from Internal Investigations is joining the Homicide Team—he's going to be your new partner."

Bridgette did her best to hide her surprise, and she repeated the name, "Aaron Sterling?"

Delray nodded. "I'm afraid so...."

Bridgette tugged on what was left of her left earlobe, a habit she was finding hard to break when she was thinking intensely. She recalled the evening when she had been shot at as she sat alone in a portable office in the archives section of the building's basement. While being fired upon as she sat studying the microfilm records of her mother's cold case had been traumatic, the harrowing interviews she'd had to endure with Internal Investigations afterward, at the hands of Aaron Sterling, had caused her sleepless nights. Rather than being a victim, she was portrayed as someone who was involved in stealing the microfilm even though she'd been wounded in the process.

Bridgette stammered, "I don't understand. Why would Aaron Sterling want to join Homicide?"

"I'll give you one answer—Assistant Commissioner Leo Cunningham."

Bridgette nodded. It now made sense to her. Too stunned to know how to reply, she waited for Delray to continue.

"I argued against the appointment with the commissioner himself, but I was overruled. Until we get a complete resolution to what happened when you were shot, his Internal Investigations team gets a lot of say about what happens around here."

"And that includes appointing their staff to work on your team?"

Delray nodded. "It's a tricky situation, and as you well know, Cunningham doesn't trust anyone down here on level two. I thought about it a lot last night, and the only angle I can come up with is that he's using this situation to get one of his trusted lieutenants into our ranks to dig up dirt on us. The frustrating thing is there's not a damn thing I can do about it."

Bridgette took a sip of her coffee as she tried to absorb the information. She had no idea how she would work with Sterling. "Is the appointment permanent?"

To her relief, Delray shook his head. "No. As soon as we figure out who is ultimately behind this, he'll go back to Internal Investigations."

Bridgette thought of her mother's murder case. She had been only seven when her mother was brutally murdered. In almost twenty years, the only suspect Vancouver Metro had ever pursued was her father, who had been exonerated after his death. She responded, "That might take a while?"

Delray grimaced. "We're confident Charlie wasn't working alone, but in all the interviews so far, he's not been prepared to admit anything."

Cold Hard Cash

Bridgette recalled the shot she had fired into the darkness as she fled from the basement. She was positive she'd hit her assailant high on the left shoulder, which was ultimately Bates's undoing when Delray and one of his own detectives discovered him concealing a wound that matched. "It would be nice to recover the microfilm he stole. I'm sure we'd get to the bottom of this very quickly."

"I don't think that's likely, Bridgette. It took us three days to figure out it was Charlie who was involved."

Bridgette sighed. "More than enough time to sell the microfilm to whoever really wanted it. So when will Sterling be joining our team?"

"I'm waiting to hear from Cunningham officially, but I suspect we've got two days to get used to the idea." Delray studied Bridgette for a moment before adding, "You constantly show maturity beyond your twenty-seven years, Bridgette, and this is no exception. I'm confident if we keep our heads down and do our jobs, we'll ride this out."

Bridgette went to respond, but Delray's desk phone rang. Delray glanced at the caller ID screen. "It's Ray Warner, I gotta take this."

Delray pressed answer. "It looks like I'm not the only one getting an early start, Ray." He listened intently for about twenty seconds before he replied, "Okay, we'll be there in twenty minutes." Delray hung up the phone. "Doc Warner has something he wants to show us from the Rook Island murders."

Bridgette frowned. "But they haven't recovered the bodies yet?"

"He said he's collected some trace evidence that might give us a head start on the investigation." Delray got up from his chair.

"Did he say what it was?"

Delray shook his head as he retrieved his coat from the back of his chair. "He said it would be best if we come and see for ourselves."

"Okay, I'll grab my coat."

Bridgette walked back to her cubicle. She was angry about the prospect of having Aaron Sterling as a temporary partner but pushed it to the back of her mind as she thought about Delray's phone call with Ray Warner. She was intrigued by what he'd discovered and hoped it would kick-start the investigation.

Delray pushed the button for the elevator as Bridgette approached. "We'll talk more about your situation with your new partner later."

"Thanks, chief. I'm kind of glad I've got the Rook Island case to focus on. Hopefully, Ray will give us our first real lead to work on."

Delray nodded as the elevator doors opened. "I've known Ray a long time, and if he says it's important, it generally is."

Thursday - 8:10 A.M.

Bridgette looked up at the City Morgue building as Delray eased the late-model gray Ford sedan into a parking space out front. The two-story brown and tan brick structure with its narrow windows and flat roof looked depressing—an almost perfect fit for its purpose, she thought. She'd visited the morgue before but had never looked forward to a visit until today. Keen to learn about Ray Warner's discovery, Bridgette followed Delray up the steps, through two heavy glass and timber doors, and into a tiled foyer area that looked like it hadn't been remodeled since the early sixties.

Delray pointed to a corridor on the right. "Ray said to go straight to his office." He set off at a brisk pace. Bridgette quickly caught up with him, realizing Delray was as keen as she was to learn more about Warner's discovery.

Pausing in front of the second door on the left which was signposted as the Coroner's Office, Delray knocked.

The heavy wooden door was opened almost immediately by a bleary-eyed Ray Warner, who said, "Good morning," as he ushered them in.

He was still wearing the same clothes he had on yesterday, and Bridgette wondered where he'd spent the night.

Delray paused for a moment in the open doorway. "You don't mind me saying so, Ray, you look awful!"

Warner confessed, "I slept here last night. It was after one this morning before I finished my work, and I decided it wasn't worth the drive home."

Warner showed Bridgette and Delray into his office. It was larger than Bridgette expected. To the left was a scarred wooden desk piled with papers and a computer, and to the right was a long, narrow bench that was built into the wall. In front of her, Bridgette could see about forty color photographs from the crime scene in the cave pinned to two large corkboards. One corkboard showed photographs of the entire cave, carefully pinned together side by side to provide a wide-angle view of the crime scene. The second corkboard was a more random collection of closeup images of each of the two victims.

She realized Warner had been busy last night as he said, "I've got a lot to show you, but nothing more important than this."

Stepping across to the bench, Warner pointed to a digital microscope that was connected to a computer screen and said, "This is what I want to show you first."

They waited while Warner switched on both the microscope and the screen. Within seconds, an image appeared on the screen that looked to Bridgette like a long black cylinder with brownish edges.

Warner pointed at the image. "While I couldn't bring back the bodies last night, I was determined to gather as much evidence as I could from the crime scene to examine. The most recent victim was wearing a suede jacket at the time of his murder. Suede is a good material for catching fibers, and although it was filthy, I took several samples with a lint roller along with other samples I picked up off the cave floor. I didn't have much luck with identifying any of the samples, with the exception of this sample here. It's a hair of some description, and I found three of them in my sample from the jacket. When I put them under the microscope, I knew they weren't human, and that's when the fun began... At first, I figured they might be a cat or a dog which is a natural place to start as many people have pets. I compared this sample to samples on file for both dog and cat hair, but they weren't a close match. I widened the search, and I knew I was getting close when I compared it to cow hair, but there were too many ovoid bodies, so I kept searching. Eventually, I tried horsehair and got an almost perfect match for the sample you're now looking at."

Delray stepped forward and bent down to get a closer look at the computer screen. "So you're saying that's definitely horsehair on the man's jacket?"

"I'm positive, Felix. I know it's not a lot to go on yet, but at least it's something."

Delray said, "This is good work, Ray. It may help us narrow down our search in missing persons. If we zero in on anyone missing who works with horses as a trainer, or a breeder, we might get lucky."

Bridgette wasn't so ready to jump to conclusions. "Is there any way you can detect how long the hair has been on the jacket?"

Warner frowned. "Not really. Why do you ask?"

"I agree with the chief that we should look at all possibilities of the victim working with horses, but I'm also wondering if he was perhaps transported just before or after his murder in, say, a horse trailer. Can you tell that from your forensics?"

Warner shook his head. "Not at this stage, Bridgette, but it's something to think about. I should find out more when I get the jacket itself back here in the lab."

They were all silent for a moment as they stared at the image of the horsehair. Bridgette broke the silence by asking, "Do you think you will be able to recover the bodies today?"

Warner replied, "I'm hoping to recover the most recent victim today." He paused to look at his watch and then added, "I plan on leaving the office in about twenty minutes to head across to Stone Bay. We've got about an hour and a half of work time today in the cave during low tide. You're welcome to join me."

Delray turned to Bridgette. "What do you think, Bridgette? You fancy another trip out to the cave?"

Bridgette grimaced at the thought of spending more time in the damp underground cave with two decomposing bodies. She didn't think she would learn a lot more from the crime scene but replied, "I'm scheduled to go to the firing range after this, but I'll do whatever you want me to do, chief."

With an amused look, Delray replied, "I'll take that as a no."

Bridgette replied firmly, "I'm happy to go if you want me to."

"You've already seen the crime scene, and you're a lot better with the computer research than I am, so I'll go with Ray. You can take the car to the range for your assessment and then head back to the office."

Bridgette did her best to hide her relief. "Thanks, chief."

Delray said to Warner, "We came in one car, Ray. You mind if I get a ride with you?"

"No problem. I'm just about to load up my equipment, so if you're up for it, I could use a hand?"

"Happy to help." Delray turned to look at Bridgette who seemed distracted by the photos on the pinboard. "You find something, Bridgette?"

"Not really. I was just thinking about something Ray said to me in the cave yesterday."

Warner looked puzzled. "What did I say, Bridgette?"

Without turning around, Bridgette said, "You asked me why the killer would go to the trouble of placing the bodies in a cave when it would be easier to feed them to the sharks."

"I remember. I also remember your answer—because you thought they were important to him."

Bridgette nodded as she continued to study the photographs. "I didn't get much sleep last night because I'm not so sure about my answer."

Delray frowned. "Your answer makes perfect sense. The killer has gone to a lot of trouble to get those bodies into that cave. And then setting them up carefully against the wall surely means they're important."

Bridgette moved forward and pointed at a closeup photo of the bullet hole in the forehead of the man who had been recently murdered. "What does this photo tell you?"

Delray studied the photograph for a moment. "The victim has been shot at close range. It looks like the bullet hit the victim exactly where the shooter intended. I'd say it's a professional hit."

"That's my take on it too. Whether a victim is stabbed, shot, bludgeoned to death, or even poisoned, there's usually some form of passion in a murder if it's the work of a serial killer. There's no passion in this."

They all stood for a moment silently staring at the photos.

It was Warner who broke the silence. "So if these are just two professional hits, why put them in that cave?"

Bridgette replied, "That's a really good question."

Thursday - 11:05 A.M.

Bridgette wasn't sure how old Senior Sergeant Ken Dennehy was. Early sixties was her guess, but his bandy legs and stiff walking gait made him appear older. She watched as he pulled down her paper target and then heard him mumble, "Damn, these are good..." as he studied her last group of shots.

She wasn't sure if she was meant to hear the observation but smiled to herself anyway. After Delray, Dennehy was probably the cop she liked the most in Vancouver Metro. She'd first met him when her intake class had gone to Vancouver Metro's gun range for their first official class on how to handle and fire police weapons. Bridgette had expected the lanky officer to be arrogant and dismissive as many of her other instructors had been. His gentle and patient nature surprised her. Although all the recruits eventually got to fire a pistol, their first lesson had focused on gun safety. She'd never forgotten his words, "Bad enough when a perp shoots you, but unforgivable if you shoot yourself or your partner."

They had been sobering words as he told the story of a former partner who'd shot himself while parked in his patrol car. At first, Internal Investigations suspected suicide, but the autopsy revealed a single bullet wound to the neck as an unlikely form of suicide. The wound had severed his carotid artery, causing him to bleed out. Dennehy had taken the loss hard and more so when he learned his partner's death was accidental. Now a passionate advocate for gun safety, he'd left active duty in favor of the instructor role he now had at the gun range, and Bridgette suspected he told the story to every group of new recruits. As he walked toward her, she was sure it had a far more profound effect on recruits than any firearm mortality statistics or gruesome photographs they'd been shown.

Dennehy held the paper target up and said with a grin, "Good shooting, Bridgette—damn good in fact."

Bridgette studied the hole pattern in a target that resembled the head and torso of a life-sized human. Her shots were all close together in the middle of the chest area and spanned a radius of less than two inches.

Dennehy added, "This is only what…your fourth or fifth trip to the firing range?"

Bridgette nodded. "My fourth."

"And you never shot before you joined the force?"

Bridgette laughed. "Only a flare gun when I was in the Navy, but I don't think that counts."

"Well, this is great shooting. Very consistent—which is what we want. Folks with less than a couple of years' experience usually struggle to even get half a magazine clip this accurate. But you've managed to get every shot exactly where we wanted."

Bridgette allowed herself a smile. "I've been practicing."

Dennehy nodded. "That you have." He looked at his

watch before adding, "We made a lot of progress today, and you're well ahead of everyone else in your intake."

"Thanks, Ken, I appreciate that."

"We still have half an hour. Normally there are two of you at these assessments, but seeing as you're on your own at present, we got through this a lot quicker than I expected. If you're up for it, I'd like to teach you your next competency?"

"And what's that?"

"Learning how to shoot with your left hand."

Bridgette frowned. "My left hand?"

"It's something every police officer needs to be able to do. Hopefully, you'll never need to use it, but what happens if your shooting hand gets cut or your arm gets broken and you need to defend yourself?"

Bridgette conceded, "I guess that would be difficult."

"Most of us aren't great at doing things with our non dominant hands. Think of trying to catch a ball or even writing your name. Firing a gun is no different, and if your life depends on it, you want to make damn sure you're as proficient at it as you can be."

Bridgette would have preferred to have ended the session there and then devoting the other half hour to her case, but she respected Dennehy. "Okay, if this is something I need to learn, then let's get started."

Dennehy looked down at the concrete floor of the building everyone affectionately knew as the bunker. About the size of a basketball court, the concrete structure was separated into ten laneways where police officers came to practice their shooting. Within each laneway, there were individual markings enabling the instructors to position shooters closer to or further away from the target. He said, "Let's start you off at thirty feet."

They walked forward before stopping just short of the marker. Dennehy said, "I'll put up a fresh target for you. While I'm doing that, just practice your stance. Sometimes what feels good for your right hand doesn't feel so natural for your left."

Bridgette had always been comfortable with the Weaver stance—her left leg a full step in front of her right, almost like she was starting a race in an upright position. As Dennehy turned and walked away, Bridgette placed her right foot forward and her left foot back in a mirror of her normal stance. She then extended her left arm as if she was holding a pistol and cupped the base of her left hand with her right hand for support. Bridgette moved her position slightly, but nothing felt comfortable. Reversing her stance, she put her left foot forward and her right foot back before raising her left arm again to mimic firing with her left hand again.

After fixing a new target, Dennehy said, "You wouldn't be the first officer I've had who finds it hard to get a comfortable position for their non dominant hand."

"I thought I would just mirror my stance for my right hand, but it feels awkward."

Dennehy nodded as he walked back. "It's not uncommon for people to adopt a different stance when shooting with their other hand. Like I always say, there's no better or worse stance. The main thing is to be comfortable."

Bridgette nodded. "So what do you suggest?"

"Did I hear right that you're something of an expert in martial arts—two state titles if I'm not mistaken?"

Bridgette grimaced. "I used to be, but these days, I'm more of a gym junkie."

"The Weaver stance you use for shooting right-handed

is not much different to the starting position for martial arts. If you've spent as much time as I think you have in that position, we might need to mix it up—try something totally different. Let's try a couple of other stances to see if we can get you comfortable."

Bridgette said, "Okay," and lowered her arms.

"Let's try the Isosceles position first."

Bridgette knew the Isosceles position got its name from the triangular position of the shooter's stance if someone was looking from above.

Now that Dennehy was alongside her, Bridgette pulled her Glock from her shoulder holster. As she held the base of the gun up for Dennehy to see, she said, "No clip," to show the gun wasn't loaded. She moved forward to just behind the thirty-foot marker and placed both her left and right feet on the edge of the strip just over a shoulder width apart.

Dennehy moved around and stood next to her. "Have you ever fired in this position before?"

"Maybe a couple of rounds, but that's all. It never felt comfortable when shooting with my right hand."

"Try it with your left hand, it could be totally different." Dennehy studied her position for a moment and then added, "Okay, raise the gun with your left hand and then brace it with your right."

Bridgette obliged, but it didn't feel comfortable either.

Dennehy rested his right hand lightly on the top of her back. "Now lean forward slightly so that your shoulders are just in front of your hips…"

Bridgette did as she was instructed.

Dennehy took two steps back. "How does that feel?"

Bridgette shook her head. "It still feels awkward."

"Are you familiar with the Fighting stance?"

"Kind of a cross between the Weaver and the Isosceles?"

"That's it."

Bridgette nodded. "I think some of the guys in Homicide use it."

"Let's give it a try. Your feet should still be a little more than a shoulder width apart but with your front foot about six to eight inches in front of your back foot."

Bridgette shifted her left foot back about six inches and then raised her gun with her left hand again. After bending her knees slightly, she clasped her right hand around her left hand and said, "That feels better."

"Okay, good. If that feels comfortable, let's put five rounds in the target and see how you go."

Bridgette lowered the gun and inserted a fresh clip of ammunition. As she went to put on her earmuffs, Dennehy stepped back. "If you're like most of my students, changing hands means going back to the basics all over again until your brain gets used to the muscle memory. There will be a tendency for your support hand to drag your shooting hand down in anticipation of the recoil. For you, that will mean you'll shoot low and to your right. That's perfectly normal and will correct itself with practice." Dennehy put on his earmuffs. "Good to go."

Bridgette put on her earmuffs and raised the Glock into a firing position. She moved the gun left and right and up and down in a fifteen-degree arc until she was comfortable she could consistently fill the rear notch with the front gun sight when she adjusted the position of her weapon. After relaxing her shoulder muscles, she gently squeezed the trigger to fire off her first round. The hole in the target was easy to see at this distance—low and to the right just as Dennehy had predicted.

Cold Hard Cash

Bridgette whispered to herself, "Relax," and then fired a second and third round. She noticed these two shots were closer to the target and fired two more before lowering the weapon and removing the magazine clip.

As she removed her earmuffs, Dennehy said, "Not bad for your first effort, let's keep working at it."

Bridgette put on her earmuffs again and fired another two bursts of five shots. She noticed a slight improvement, but she was still nowhere near as accurate with the left hand as she was with her right.

Dennehy, as patient as ever, worked with her for the next twenty minutes, adjusting her stance and her hand grip, until her action was smooth and consistent.

At the end of the session, Dennehy grinned. "You're a lot more accurate with your left hand than you were half an hour ago, Bridgette. This is a good start."

As Bridgette pulled off her earmuffs, she said, "Thanks, Ken, I really appreciate this. I knew it would be hard, but I didn't appreciate just how hard."

"It's just another thing to work on. While you should spend most of your practice time shooting with your right hand, always take a little time to shoot with your other hand as well—you just never know when that skill could save your life."

"Let's hope it never comes to that." Bridgette removed the clip from her weapon.

As they walked back toward Dennehy's office, he asked, "So when do you get your new partner?"

Bridgette explained her situation and how Aaron Sterling would be joining the Homicide team.

Dennehy made a face. "Well, let's hope that's not a permanent arrangement. I haven't heard much about him, but what I have heard hasn't been very complimentary."

"Can he shoot?"

Dennehy's face broke into a grimace. "Even on his best day, my money would be on you shooting with your left hand."

Bridgette replied flatly, "Well, that doesn't fill me with confidence."

"If you want my advice, try not to get stuck with him any longer than you have to. If you're in a crisis, he's not the guy I'd want to be relying on."

Thursday - 12:15 P.M.

Bridgette had a tendency to drive slower when she was thinking about a problem, and in a city of three million people with heavy traffic, that meant her trip back to headquarters took far longer than expected. After completing her practice session at the firing range, she was still puzzled by why someone would want to store bodies in a cave after a professional execution. She recalled Delray's parting words as she left the coroner's office: "It takes patience, Bridgette. Solving murders is a lot like solving a jigsaw puzzle, only with a thousand extra pieces you never use." This was a piece of the puzzle that made no sense to her right now, but she was determined to find the answer.

After pulling into the underground parking lot at the Vancouver Metro police complex, Bridgette decided to take the elevator directly to the Missing Persons unit on level three. She had phoned the unit's senior detective, Jim Mahoney, while on her journey back and explained the case to him. Mahoney was keen to help and told her to come up immediately. She exited the elevator on level three and headed down the corridor.

Bridgette was surprised to see the work area looked empty and turned around to see Mahoney sitting in his office with the door open. He was on the phone, so she waited at his door, studying some of the missing person posters on the wall outside his office. There were photos of men and women of all ages, but it was the photographs of children, some as young as two and three, that tugged at her heartstrings.

As she wondered what had become of these young lives, Mahoney hung up and said, "Come on in, Bridgette."

Bridgette sat down opposite the senior detective. She'd worked with Mahoney previously on a missing persons case that turned into a murder and found the forty-something detective blunt but completely honest. She couldn't recall the quietly spoken man with a thin face ever smiling and sometimes wondered whether the job had gotten the better of him.

After sitting down, she said, "It looks quiet out there. Where is everybody?"

"We're doing a missing persons awareness day down at the city mall. Most of my crew are there today manning our stands and answering questions. Hopefully, we'll get a few leads on people's whereabouts."

Bridgette nodded. "Let's hope the public comes through for you."

Mahoney nodded. "This Rook Island case sounds intriguing, but I've only got two of my team here today, and they're both downstairs interviewing at present. I've got a busy schedule, so if you don't mind, unless you run into problems, I'll leave you to get started on your own."

Bridgette was familiar with the national missing persons

database that Mahoney and his team used. "No problem. Just show me which computer to use, and I'll get to work."

Mahoney pointed through his glass office window to a cubicle of four desks directly opposite. "You can sit at Paul Carroll's desk. His wife just had a baby, and I don't expect to see him back in the office until next week."

Bridgette thanked Mahoney and went to get up, but Mahoney motioned her to sit back down again. "Before you go, do you mind if I ask you a question?"

"Sure."

"I hope you don't think I'm prying, but like everyone else, I've heard all about the basement incident. Is Charlie Bates really involved?"

Bridgette nodded. "I'm afraid so, Jim."

Mahoney shook his head. "There was a young detective who I thought was going places. What the hell happened to him?"

Bridgette was reluctant to talk about Charlie Bates. She had worked with Bates on her first murder case and was still coming to terms with what had happened. She tactfully replied, "I'm not sure, Jim."

"Rumor has it he's been siphoning information from our police databases for months and then selling it. I knew he was smart with computers, so that makes sense."

"I've heard that too."

"Who do you think he was working for?"

"I have no idea. It's with Internal Investigations, but I don't think they have any solid information yet."

Mahoney nodded. "And Bates isn't saying anything?"

"Not to my knowledge."

"It's a dangerous game to play when you're a cop. When you get caught, you're totally on your own."

Bridgette didn't want to pursue the conversation. She

didn't like talking about the basement incident or reliving the memory of being shot at by a fellow officer. "I better get started with my search." She stood up.

Not easily deterred, Mahoney said, "Has he made bail yet?"

"He's up on multiple charges including attempted murder, so bail may not be granted."

"What an asshole—attempting to shoot a fellow police officer is about as low as it gets."

Bridgette replied, "Thanks for your help, Jim," and headed for the door.

"No problem and like I said, call me if you need anything."

Bridgette settled into her assigned desk and logged onto the NatTrack police database. NatTrack was a recent acquisition for Vancouver Metro and allowed police forces across the county to share their criminal and missing person records with each other. She could have just as easily gone back to her own desk to run the same searches, but it was good to have access to someone with Mahoney's experience if she had questions.

Bridgette allowed her fingers to hover just above the keyboard as she thought about her search parameters. Her first degree had been in computer science, and she knew the key to finding the right information was asking the right questions. She thought about the most recent victim in the cave. Warner had said the victim was a Caucasian male, most likely in his early forties who'd been murdered sometime in the last four to six weeks. It wasn't a lot to go on, but it was a start. With a few keystrokes, she set the search to return missing person records for white males between the ages of thirty-five and fifty-five who had gone missing in the last three months and pressed enter. An hourglass appeared on the screen, showing the computer was processing her request. She waited a moment before the screen refreshed, listing over three thousand matches.

She knew about fifty thousand people were reported missing each year and wasn't surprised by the high number. Some people only went missing for a few days. Drug and alcohol benders, mental illness, and domestic violence were all common reasons why people disappeared for short periods before they resurfaced. Three thousand was an impractical number to search through line by line but provided her with a healthy pool to work with. Bridgette decided to focus on local missing persons first and with a few more keystrokes limited the search to only show missing persons who lived in Vancouver and a fifty-mile radius of the city. After pressing enter, she watched the hourglass spin again and nodded her approval, whispering, "Better," as the refined search reduced the list to just twenty-three names.

Bridgette wasn't done yet and allowed her fingers to lightly dance across the keyboard while she thought. She moved the cursor to a field for additional keywords, whispered, "You never know," and keyed in the word "horse." Biting down gently on her bottom lip, she pressed the enter key and watched the hourglass spin again as the computer attempted to refine the search results even further. The search took longer than she had expected—usually a sign that there were no matching results. She was happy enough to go back and work through the list of twenty-three names if it came up empty and waited patiently.

When the screen eventually refreshed, she felt a tingle down her spine as the search displayed one match. Bridgette clicked on the matching record to open the missing person file. She stared at the headshot photo of a man in his early forties. He was white with a strong jawline and slightly longer than average dark brown hair. Bridgette pictured the image of the corpse she had seen in the cave. The bloated features, blackened skin, and decay made it impossible for her to tell whether this was the man she was now staring at. She scanned the information listed in the report. The man's name was Owen Whitecross. His height was listed as five feet eleven and his weight as one hundred and fifty-six pounds. Bridgette recalled Ray Warner's assessment of the victim's physical features in the cave. They were a reasonable match for the information she was staring at. Bridgette read more of Whitecross's details. The report noted him as a lifelong resident of Vancouver who was aged forty-three. It was when she got to his occupation and read the words, "Horse Breeder," that she allowed herself to smile.

"Let's hope we have a match," she whispered, and she sat for a moment enjoying the buzz of being able to use technology to do police work. Her moment was interrupted by her smartphone as it vibrated in her pocket. She hoped it was Delray and checked the number. It wasn't a number she recognized, but she pressed answer anyway and said, "Detective Cash."

The caller was silent. Bridgette could hear faint background noises but nothing else.

Frowning, Bridgette said, "Hello," and waited.

More silence followed. Bridgette was about to disconnect when a man's voice broke the silence. "It's me, Bridgette. Please don't hang up."

Bridgette felt her blood run cold as she recognized the voice. Too stunned to speak, she sat completely still, wondering why Charlie Bates would be calling her.

Delray sat at his desk, staring down at his pastrami and onion sandwich. It was almost two forty-five p.m., and he still hadn't eaten his lunch—a first for him. Normally unmoved by crime scenes, the dank and putrid conditions of the cave and the proximity to the two bodies with no fresh air had left him nauseous and in need of a long shower. He had picked up the sandwich from the cafeteria after Ray Warner had dropped him back at the office. But that was over an hour ago, and he still couldn't face it.

He was wondering about putting it in his top drawer for a while and eating it later when his phone rang. Thankful for the distraction, he picked up the phone. "Delray."

"Hello, chief, this is Doctor Carol Sanders."

"How are you doing, doc?"

"I'm fine. And you?"

Delray looked at his sandwich. "Couldn't be better. What can I do for you?"

"I have an appointment scheduled with Bridgette for tomorrow evening. I thought I'd call and get an update from you before our session."

"Well, she's back at work and going hard on a new case."

"How is she?"

"All things considered, pretty well, I think."

"In our last session, we talked a lot about the death of her mother. I hadn't imagined we'd be talking about her father as well."

"Yes, it came as a shock."

"How is she coping?"

Delray thought for a moment. "Having the person who pulled the trigger behind bars is providing her with some comfort at least."

"The newspapers were hazy on the details. Apparently you tracked him down by a license plate?"

"He rented a van in Bolton and put stolen plates on it before he got to Tangmere Falls. Being a fugitive for twenty years, Peter Cash was paranoid about anyone hanging around his village he didn't know. Mackenzie and Parker found a notebook in his car with all sorts of registration numbers and car descriptions. All of them were scratched out except the last entry. McKenzie looked it up and realized the plates were stolen."

"So that gave you something to work with."

"They spent almost two weeks checking security camera footage and eventually got a match for a gas station on the highway about an hour's drive from the murder scene. The stolen plates were captured on a van pulling into the station less than two hours after the murder. The van drove around the back and came out fifteen minutes later with a different set of plates."

"The legal plates?"

"You got it."

"From there, it only took them a couple of days to find the guy who rented the van. His name is Carl Rutherford. He protested his innocence, saying he'd never rented the van, but the guy from the rental company picked him out from a lineup, so game over."

"How did Bridgette cope with the news?"

"I think it helped a little knowing Rutherford is now behind bars."

"But he's not the one ultimately responsible, is he?"

"No, he was just the hired gun. We're sure this is all tied back to her mother's murder twenty years earlier."

"Do you have any idea who that might be?"

"My guess is a corrupt cop. Someone who worked here twenty years ago but probably doesn't work here now."

"Well, this is all useful information." Sanders was quiet for a moment before she added, "I'll need to think about how best to approach this with her."

"I think she's enjoying the routine of doing police work again. Although, you and I both know this will never be over for her until whoever is ultimately responsible is behind bars."

"Yes, and that's my challenge. If it remains unsolved, she will have to learn to live with it."

"I'm not sure that's possible, Doc. When she's ready, she'll go back to investigating this on her own time."

"Do you think that's wise?"

"Probably not, but that's the way she's wired."

Thursday - 3:55 P.M.

Bridgette spent the next three hours in the Missing Persons unit researching the Owen Whitecross case and only stopped when Delray called her to tell her he was back in the office and wanted a meeting. After packing up her research notes and thanking Jim Mahoney for his time, she headed back down to level two.

Before she got to knock on his open door, Delray beckoned her in. "Come on in, Bridgette, we've got a lot to talk about." Delray gave her a wry smile as she settled into a chair. "I can understand now why you were a little reluctant to go back in that cave."

Bridgette did her best to keep a straight face. "So, how did you find it?"

Delray grimaced. "Let's just say I'm looking forward to a long, hot shower tonight. I've witnessed some pretty horrific crime scenes in my time, but that's up there with the worst of them. I don't think I will ever forget that smell..."

"The awful part about it is not being able to walk away to get some relief."

Delray nodded his agreement. "The good news is Ray has recovered both bodies and they are currently being moved to the morgue. He'll begin autopsies first thing in the morning." Pointing to the research notes Bridgette had brought to the meeting, Delray added, "It looks like you've been busy too."

"I'm trying not to get ahead of myself, chief, but I think we might have a match for our murder victim." Sliding the missing person's report across the desk toward Delray, she added, "He's a forty-three-year-old Caucasian male, a life-long resident of Vancouver, and he's been missing for nine weeks."

Delray picked up the report and scanned the first page. "His height and weight are a reasonable match for the victim, so that's a good start."

"That's not all. Look at his occupation…"

Bridgette watched Delray's eyes widen as he murmured, "Horse breeder."

Delray removed his glasses. "There can't be too many people that work with horses on that missing persons list."

"I've checked the database thoroughly. Owen White-cross is the only person who has gone missing anywhere in the country in the last three months who works with horses."

Delray leaned forward in his chair. "This is great work, Bridgette. We might actually have our first breakthrough."

"Whitecross was reported missing by his wife. I spoke to Jim Mahoney upstairs, and he was happy for us to interview her now that it looks like he's possibly one of the Rook Island victims. I've called her and gently informed her that we've recovered a body that might be her husband. She was understandably upset but also eager for me to go visit her tomorrow."

"Good. While you're there, we need to get some of Whitecross's DNA from a hairbrush or something to see if we can get a match with the body." Delray chewed on the tip of his glasses as he read more of the report. "So he was a racehorse breeder?"

"Yes. According to his wife, he left early on the sixteenth of February to attend the Mercury Cup race meeting and never returned home that evening."

Delray frowned. "I'm not up on horse racing, but that's one of Vancouver's biggest racing events if I'm not mistaken?"

Bridgette nodded. "This year's attendance was over seventy-two thousand."

Delray let out a low whistle and frowned. "Tracking down people who go missing in large crowds can be problematic. What else have you learned from the report?"

"Whitecross has become very wealthy from breeding professional racehorses and attends most of the major horse racing fixtures on the east coast. It was a business day for him, and according to several stable hands, he arrived at Vancouver's NewFarm Racecourse around ten a.m. He was due to meet up with two of his business clients for lunch in the executive dining room but never showed."

"Did he have any financial troubles?"

"No mention of it in the report. Apparently, he was happily married and well-liked within the horse racing community."

Delray chewed on his glasses again. "You'll need to recheck that. It wouldn't be the first time a wife has no clue about what her husband is really getting up to."

"I'm reading through the other statements in the report now. They're all saying pretty much the same thing—he disappeared without explanation, and it was out of character."

Delray stared at the man's photo. "It's impossible to tell from the photograph whether this is the most recent of the victims."

"When Ray gets the bodies back, it would be good to get a photograph of the jacket. If we can show that to his wife and get a positive ID, we'll know straight away if we're on the right track."

Delray put his glasses back on. "Good point. I'll call Ray as soon as we're done here and get him to email us some photographs as soon as he can."

"Thanks, chief."

"So what else have you got?"

"I've also contacted two of the stable hands at NewFarm Racecourse. They were the last reported eyewitnesses to see Whitecross alive before he disappeared. I've set up interviews with them for tomorrow as well."

"Tomorrow's going to be a busy day for you."

Bridgette frowned. "Am I working on my own tomorrow?"

Delray paused a moment. Bridgette could tell by his grim face that bad news was coming. "I got an email from Cunningham earlier today… Aaron Sterling starts with us tomorrow."

Bridgette nodded and said, "Okay," but not convincingly.

"Cunningham's bringing him down himself at nine a.m. If you're out interviewing all day, at least you'll be spared one of his mindless lectures."

"Thanks, chief."

"Once we get this investigation up and running, Bridgette, I'm going to devote a lot of my time to figuring out who is ultimately behind this basement shooting. I don't want Sterling on my team a day longer than necessary, and the quickest way to get him out of here is to give Cunningham a name he can pursue."

Bridgette took a deep breath. She had been debating whether to tell Delray about the phone call from Charlie Bates but decided it was the right thing to do. "Speaking of the basement incident, there's something I have to tell you."

"Okay."

Bridgette paused a moment and then said, "Charlie Bates called me today."

Delray scowled. "What?"

"I was upstairs in the Missing Persons unit when I got a call from a number I didn't recognize... It was Charlie."

"But he's still in prison."

Bridgette nodded. "He couldn't talk for long. The guards allowed him two minutes."

"So what did he want?"

"I'm not exactly sure. He started by trying to apologize to me for what happened and..."

"And then what?"

"He wants me to go and see him."

"What? In jail?"

"Yes."

Delray frowned in disbelief. "Why on earth would he be wanting to see you?"

"He said it was important. He wants to apologize properly but not over the phone."

Delray leaned back in his chair and thought for a moment. "I'm not buying it. Charlie Bates is trying to beat an attempted murder charge. If he's found guilty, as I suspect he will be, he'll spend the next ten years in prison.

Apologizing to you would be an admission of guilt, and he's way smarter than that."

"I agree, chief. However…"

Delray frowned. "However, what?"

Bridgette sighed. "I've never understood it."

"Never understood what?"

"That night in the basement. Why would he want to shoot me if all he wanted was the microfilm? I guess I'd like some answers."

Delray chewed on the end of his glasses again while he thought. Eventually, he said, "Ordinarily, I would say this is a bad idea, but it might also be an opportunity for us. I've interviewed him twice, and so far, he's refused to say anything without his lawyer."

"This would be just me talking to him behind glass at the city jail just like any regular visitor."

"When?"

"Tomorrow afternoon."

Delray thought for a moment. "Do it. It's unlikely he's going to say anything incriminating, but you never know."

Bridgette got to her feet and headed for the door. She paused in the doorway and looked back at Delray who was chewing on his glasses again. "Any specific questions you want me to ask, chief?"

"We need to find out who he's been working for. He's not going to give you a name, but see if he'll open up a little. If we can find out if it's a cop or an ex-cop, at least that's something to start with."

Bridgette nodded. "Okay, got it."

Delray held her gaze. "Be careful. He may be behind glass, but don't let that fool you. I'm sure he wants something, and I don't want you in harm's way anymore."

Friday - 10:25 A.M.

Bridgette pulled into the public parking lot at the NewFarm Racecourse and eased her car to a halt next to an immaculately trimmed Leylandii cypress hedge. After switching off the engine, she sat contemplating the interview she'd just completed with Owen Whitecross's wife. She was distracted by the sight of two majestic racehorses cantering back toward the holding pen after completing their morning workout. She watched the jockeys dismount and wondered if the stable hands who came to lead the sweat-laden animals back to their stables were the men she was here to interview.

Her thoughts were interrupted as her smartphone buzzed. She looked at the screen and read a two-word message from her boss, "Call me." Bridgette smiled to herself. Delray was all thumbs and fingers with modern technology, and his text messages were usually cryptic and often misspelled because of his large fingers. Bridgette knew she had time to call him back before the interview and pressed speed dial.

Delray answered after two rings. "That was quick."

"I've just pulled into the parking lot at the NewFarm Racecourse. I thought I'd call you back before I interview the stable hands."

"I appreciate it. What time were you planning on getting back here?"

Bridgette replied as she watched a large black racehorse gallop around the track, "I don't have any set plans. I thought I would see what comes from the interviews here and play it by ear. Why do you ask?"

"My meeting with Cunningham and Sterling has been delayed. It's now at one p.m. So my advice to you would be not to get back to the office until mid afternoon at the earliest, just to be sure you don't have to put up with any of Cunningham's nonsense as well."

"Thanks, chief, I appreciate the heads-up."

"How did the interview go with Mrs. Whitecross?"

Bridgette continued to stare through her windshield at the racetrack. The galloping thoroughbred reduced to a blur as she recalled her heartbreaking conversation with Owen Whitecross's wife. "I showed her the pictures of the victim's jacket, and she broke down. It's a close match to the one her husband was wearing on the day he disappeared. I'm almost certain Owen Whitecross is the most recent of the two victims."

"That must've been rough, Bridgette."

Bridgette grimaced. "Not as rough as it was for Jane Whitecross. The interview was over as soon as I showed her the photograph of the jacket. She said she was almost certain it was his and was inconsolable after that. She gave me her husband's hairbrush, and I promised I would call again as soon as we had completed a DNA match against the body."

"Well, at least it will bring her closure."

"I dropped the brush off at the coroner's office on my way over here. Ray is getting one of his lab technicians to run a DNA match on it today, so we should know officially sometime tomorrow."

"That's good work. So who are the interviews with at NewFarm?"

"The two stable hands who were the last people we know of to see Owen Whitecross alive. Even though I'm not going to say anything official to them, I think it's safe to assume one of the victims is Owen Whitecross, so I'll try to learn as much as I can about what happened on the day he disappeared."

"Good plan. Anything you can learn over and above what is in that report will be useful."

Bridgette looked at her watch. "I better be going. I'm due to meet them in a few minutes, and I don't know my way around here."

"I won't keep you. Call me when you're done and give me an update."

Bridgette disconnected and got out of her car. She scanned left and right to get a feeling for the layout of the racecourse. To her right were three modern multistory buildings made of concrete, steel, and glass that faced the main straight of the racecourse. Bridgette studied the buildings for a moment. They all had tiered open balcony seating and corporate boxes behind floor-to-ceiling glass windows. She had agreed to meet the two stable hands in an office in the horse stable area and knew it was unlikely to be in that direction. She turned to her left. Her view of the buildings on the opposite side of the parking lot was obscured by a neatly trimmed ten-foot-high cypress hedge. Bridgette made her way across to a painted wood panel gate set into the hedge and signposted "No Public Access." She heard a horse neigh somewhere beyond and smiled to herself as she lifted the latch.

The buildings on the opposite side of the hedge were all one- or two-story. She could see two men washing down horses in a pen next to a two-story sandstone building that reminded her of a barn. As she approached, the younger of the two men called out to her, "Are you the detective?"

"Yes. Detective Bridgette Cash."

"My name's Nick." The man pointed to his partner and added, "This here's Walter."

Walter nodded in her general direction but didn't respond.

Bridgette said, "Pleased to meet you both."

Nick pointed to the sandstone building. "Walter and I will be about another five minutes here, detective. Once we get these two horses into their stalls, we'll come and meet you in our lunchroom at the far end, if that's all right?"

Bridgette sensed Nick was eager to cooperate. "Sure. No problem. Will I have any trouble finding it?"

"Last room on the right." Nick grinned. "There's hot coffee in there if you're game, but I wouldn't vouch for it."

Bridgette politely responded, "Thanks, but I'm trying to cut down," and left the men to finish their task.

She walked into the sandstone building through open double doors and stood for a moment admiring the architecture. The building was over one hundred and fifty feet long and had horse stalls to the left and right of a wide center concrete aisle that ran the entire length of the building. The high gable roof had skylights at regular intervals, giving the structure a light and almost cathedral feel. Bridgette ambled down the thoroughfare, looking to her left and right. Each stall had a sliding gate; the bottom half of the gate was made of timber and the top half of steel bars, which allowed her to see inside. Most of the horses ignored her, but a chestnut mare came to the edge of its stall and whinnied softly at her.

Bridgette made her way across to the stall and said, "Hey there," as she reached in to stroke the horse's muzzle.

The horse whinnied again and moved its head up and down slightly to vary the point where Bridgette scratched. Bridgette laughed and whispered, "I think you would let me do this to you all day if you had your way." She moved back to the middle of the aisle.

She walked into the last room on the right as instructed and knew she was in the lunchroom. The room was bigger than she'd expected and included a small kitchen, complete with microwave and coffeepot. She was relieved to find no one else in the room and made her way past two couches to a scarred wooden dining table which she thought would be a better place to conduct her interview.

She sat and enjoyed the silence, looking around at the pictures of horse riders and jockeys that lined the walls as she thought about the questions she would ask the stable hands now that she was positive Owen Whitecross had been murdered.

Minutes later, Nick and Walter walked in. Bridgette decided to keep the interview low-key, hoping to get them to open up and share information they may not have shared with Jim Mahoney.

She smiled. "I thought we'd be more comfortable sitting around a table." She pulled out two chairs next to her.

Walter, who she guessed was in his late sixties, with gray hair in need of a haircut and a wrinkly complexion from spending too much time in the sun, thanked her as he sat down.

Nick, who she guessed was about twenty-five, seemed to be the leader. "We're officially on a break, detective, so if you could keep this short, we'd appreciate it."

Bridgette thanked them for their time and promised she would keep it as brief as possible. After handing them each a business card, she gave them a rundown of the discovery of the two bodies on Rook Island and her meeting with Owen Whitecross's wife. She watched their eyes widen as she told them Whitecross's wife had identified the jacket from a photo. She allowed the men a moment to contemplate what she had said before adding, "While we can't formally identify Owen Whitecross as a murder victim yet, I'm confident that will change tomorrow."

Nick was the first to speak. "How was he murdered?"

"He was shot."

Nick let out a long breath. "I had a bad feeling about this the moment they discovered his car in the parking lot. But it's still a shock."

Keen to get Walter involved in the conversation, Bridgette turned to him. "And how well did you know Owen Whitecross, Walter?"

The man shrugged. "He was one of the bosses. I just do what I'm told. He treated me okay…"

Bridgette nodded as she realized that conversation with Walter would be harder. She went to ask him a friendlier question to get him to open up, but Nick butted in and asked, "So, do you have any suspects yet?"

"That's why I'm here. We're trying to get as much information as possible on the victim's last movements."

Nick said, "We'll do whatever we can to help, detective."

"I've read through your statements. You both say you were working here when Owen Whitecross came to check on horses?"

Both men nodded.

"So, what happened in your own words?"

Both men looked at each other before Nick responded, "He'd recently sold two mares to a Hong Kong racing syndicate for close to half a million dollars. One of the horses was having its first professional race, and Whitecross came along to watch. I think he had a meeting with the new owners too, but I'm not entirely sure."

"Did you get a chance to meet the new owners?"

"No. I don't think they were horse people as such. They were more your investor types that like to hang out in the members' bar and drink cocktails. A lot of them never go anywhere near the stables."

"And where did the horse place in the race?"

"It finished middle of the field, but for a first race, the horse showed a lot of promise."

Bridgette made a mental note to check up on the Hong Kong investor angle. There had been no mention of it in the missing person's report, and it was worth investigating.

"So, according to your witness statements, you were both working in the same stable when Owen Whitecross came in?"

"That's right. It was about ten thirty in the morning. We'd just unloaded a mare from a trailer and were getting her settled in a stall when he arrived."

"Did he stay long?"

Nick shook his head. "Two or three minutes tops. He just wanted to make sure his horse was okay, and then he left."

"What was his demeanor?"

"He was polite but in a hurry like he always was. He said he'd be back again in an hour, but we never saw him again."

"Did he say where he was going?"

Both men shook their heads.

Bridgette sat thinking for a moment. "Is it possible that some other stable hands saw him?"

Nick shrugged. "I guess anything's possible, but no one mentioned anything. The last detective who was here just after Whitecross disappeared interviewed everyone who was here on the day. It looks like Walter and I were the only ones to actually see him here at the stables…"

They were all quiet for a moment before Walter joined the conversation. "You said there were two of them in the cave. Two bodies?"

"That's right."

"Do you know who the other victim is?"

Bridgette shook her head. "We believe the other victim was murdered at least ten years ago. Why do you ask?"

"Just curious, I guess. Sorry, I'll let you ask the questions."

Bridgette spent another ten minutes asking them more questions about Whitecross's character and possible enemies. Nick cheerfully answered all her questions, but the answers didn't provide her with any new information.

Conscious they were on a break and needed to get back to work, Bridgette thanked them for their time and encouraged them to contact her if they thought of anything new. She spent the next forty-five minutes looking around the NewFarm racing complex to get familiar with the environment where Whitecross had last been seen. She counted off seventeen buildings and eight exits to a complex that covered one hundred and fifty acres and began to understand how it would be possible to get away with murdering someone in such a public arena. Investigating the Hong Kong investor angle would be her focus, but she hadn't discounted the possibility that Whitecross had left NewFarm either by foot or in another car and had been murdered somewhere else.

As she made her way back to her car, she mulled over the interview with the stable hands. Nick had been helpful, but the older man, Walter, had been reserved. She wondered why he'd asked about the other murder victim and decided it would be worth re-interviewing him on his own at some point. Bridgette checked her smartphone for messages as she got into her car. She half expected a message from Delray telling her Cunningham was insisting she attend the afternoon meeting and was relieved to see she had no new messages. As she put the car into reverse, she was startled by a rap on her driver-side window. She looked up, surprised to see Walter standing there. He seemed agitated as he motioned for her to wind the window down.

She wound the window halfway down and said, "Can I help you, Walter?"

In a hushed tone, Walter replied, "I think I may be able to help you with your investigation, detective, but I can't talk here. Do you know the Rose and Thorn bar?"

"Sorry, I don't."

"It's four blocks from here—corner of Sullivan and Bright. I'll meet you there in half an hour."

Without waiting for a reply, he turned and strode out of the parking lot.

Bridgette watched him through the rearview mirror until he disappeared from sight and pondered what he what could he possibly want to tell her?

Friday - 11:55 A.M.

Bridgette parked opposite a rundown two-story brick building at the corner of Sullivan and Bright. A peeling black-and-white sign above two heavy wooden doors informed patrons they were entering the Rose and Thorn sports bar. She didn't need to check her watch to know she was early for the meeting but decided to wait inside rather than sit in her car. As she pushed through the heavy double doors, she hoped Walter hadn't changed his mind. Even though she was new on the force, she had been stood up more than once by witnesses who had a change of heart. She stood in the low-lit entrance to the bar area, conscious that the lunchtime conversation had dropped to a whisper and every eye was on her. She did a quick scan of a large timber-paneled room that smelled of stale beer and sweat and counted off eleven men, including the bartender. All of them were over forty, and none of them were Walter. As she scanned left and right for a quiet place to sit, the door opened behind her, and she breathed a sigh of relief as Walter walked in.

Keeping it relaxed, she said, "Hi, Walter, I was just looking for a quiet place to sit."

Walter still looked anxious as he pointed to a row of booths at the back. "I don't come in here much, but it's usually quiet down there."

"Can I get you something to eat or drink?"

"I'm not hungry. And I gave up drinking eight years ago, so no thanks." The stable hand set off toward the booths without waiting for her.

Bridgette decided it would be rude to use the premises without buying something. She walked over to the bar and ordered two soda waters with ice. After collecting her drinks, she made her way to the rear booth where Walter was now sitting. She noticed the men in the bar had lost interest in her and had returned to their quiet conversations as they watched reruns of football games on several large flat screens mounted high up on the wall behind her.

Sliding into the booth opposite Walter, Bridgette smiled and slid one drink across the table. "Soda water. I figure that's a fairly safe option for someone who doesn't drink anymore."

Walter mumbled, "Thanks," without looking at her. She had casually watched Walter while she'd ordered the drinks and noticed he hadn't taken his eyes off the front entrance the entire time he had been sitting.

It was obvious to Bridgette that Walter was nervous about being seen with her, and she wondered whether he would open up. In an effort to break the ice, she said, "Thanks for coming, Walter. I know many people find it hard talking to cops, so I'm going to let you take your time."

Walter switched his focus to Bridgette. "I didn't want to say anything back at NewFarm. I'm not sure who I can trust and who I can't."

Bridgette didn't want to make any promises about keeping their conversation confidential and tactfully replied, "I was curious when you asked me about the identity of the other body in the cave."

Walter took a sip of his soda water. "I'm not sure where to begin…"

"Take your time."

Walter folded his gnarly hands. "I started working at NewFarm about twenty years ago with a man called Roy Pepper. We'd both been working as stable hands up in Bolton and came down to Vancouver to try our luck in a bigger city. I guess we'd been here about two months when it happened…"

Bridgette wanted to jump in and ask Walter what he meant but didn't want to break the mood and simply responded, "Go on."

"It was the day after the major spring racing carnival race meet. Over fifty thousand people attended, and Roy and I had worked our butts off the entire day. The following day, I get to work and there's no sign of Roy and nobody knew where he was. I didn't think too much of it at first—I thought maybe he just overdid it on the previous day. When he didn't show up two days in a row, I started to get concerned. It was out of character for him and even more so for not letting anyone know. I went around to where he lived to check up on him, but the place was locked up tight. That's when I really started to worry. I get back to work, and there are two cop cars in the parking lot, and I'm thinking this must be about Roy, but I was wrong."

"The cops weren't there for Roy?"

Walter shook his head. "They were searching for a man I'd never heard of—some big shot horse breeder. I asked them about Roy, but they weren't much interested. They told me stable hands were drifters and he'd probably turn up in time." Walter sighed and continued, "But Roy never came back. He had no family that I know of, and nobody ever filed a missing person's report. I kept my eye on the newspapers for months—looking at reports of who'd been murdered or met with an accident and such, but I didn't see anything about him. I'd almost given up hope I would ever see or hear from him again… That's when I got the call."

"A phone call?"

Walter lowered his voice. "I don't have a phone at home, but one night I get home from work and my neighbor gives me a small piece of paper with a number on it. She said this man called asking if I could call him back. There was no name, just a number. So I walked down to the public phone box and called the number, hoping it was Roy."

"And you were right?"

Walter nodded. "He wouldn't tell me where he was but asked me a lot of questions about what was happening at NewFarm Racecourse. He seemed nervous, scared almost. So I asked him what was going on."

"And what did he tell you?"

"He told me he'd witnessed a murder."

Bridgette's eyes widened, but she decided not to break Walter's train of thought with any more questions and allowed him to continue.

"He said he'd been mucking out a stall in one of the older stables at the back of the racecourse on the morning of the race meet. He thought he was there alone, but then he heard two men arguing. According to him, it sounded like they were in one of the other stalls. Roy kept quiet on account of being new and just listened. You couldn't see from one stall into another, and he realized they didn't know he was there as they got into a shouting match. It only lasted a minute before he heard a noise that sounded like a gunshot. Everything went quiet after that, and Roy froze, not sure what to do. He waited a couple of minutes, and then he heard footsteps of someone quickly leaving the stable. He waited a few more minutes until he thought it was safe, and then he walked out of the stall."

"So then what happened?"

"He checked the stalls just in case someone was lying wounded in one of them. Two stalls from where he had been working, he found a man's body covered in straw. He panicked and ran out of the stable but didn't get very far before he was confronted by a man he didn't recognize. The man demanded to know if he'd been in the stable. Roy lied and told him he hadn't, but the man didn't believe him. He knew by the man's voice he was one of the two men who'd been involved in the argument. The man tried to drag Roy back toward the stable, but Roy yelled for help. The man released him but pulled out a gun and threatened if he ever told anyone anything about what had happened it would be the last thing he ever did."

Walter paused for a sip of soda water. "Roy laid low for the rest of the day unsure if he should tell anyone and then walked home. He got to within a block of where he lived when a car pulled up to the curb next to him. It was the same man who had threatened him at the stables. Roy froze, expecting to be shot, but the man said, 'I know where you live,' and then drove off."

Bridgette raised her eyebrows. "That would make you think long and hard about reporting anything."

"It was all too much for Roy, and he packed his bags and left Vancouver early the next morning, vowing never to return. He risked a detour back to the stable to see if the man's body was still there. He'd decided if it was, he would phone the police anonymously, but the stall was empty. I wanted to ask him so many questions, but he wasn't keen to stay on the phone for long. I never saw him again, but every six months or so, I get a phone call from him. Always from a different number and he never gives me any clue where he is living or what he's doing."

"So, he's been calling you every six months for the last twenty years?"

"Pretty much. He always asks the same few questions. Have there been any cops hanging around the stables? Has anyone else suspicious been hanging around? I can tell by the tone of his voice that even after twenty years, he's still scared."

"So let me get this straight, he didn't actually witness a murder, he only heard a murder?"

Walter nodded. "Over the years, I would ask him a question or two every time he called. Sometimes I'd get an answer, sometimes I wouldn't. He never told me who the murderer was—perhaps he didn't know."

"What did he tell you?"

Walter stole a look at the front door again before locking his eyes back on Bridgette. "Until now, I've never told anyone about this, partly because I promised Roy and partly because…"

Bridgette now understood Walter's nervousness and finished his sentence, "Because you didn't want something bad to happen to you?"

Walter took a deep breath. "Roy believes he knows the identity of the man who was murdered. It was the same man the cops came looking for."

"Don't keep me in suspense, Walter."

"The man's name was Reid Whitecross…"

Bridgette frowned. "Whitecross? That can't be a coincidence?"

Walter replied grimly, "Reid Whitecross was Owen Whitecross's father."

Bridgette shook her head, barely believing what she was hearing. "So let me get this straight, the father of the man lying in the morgue, who we believe is Owen Whitecross, was murdered twenty years ago?"

As a million questions ran through her mind, she added, "That's why you asked me if we knew the identity of the other body in the cave, wasn't it?"

"It seemed too much of a coincidence. Reid Whitecross's body was never recovered, and you've found two bodies in a cave."

Bridgette barely heard Walter's reply. She sat staring at nothing as she wondered what could possibly motivate someone to kill a father and son twenty years apart?

Friday - 3:00 P.M.

Bridgette had hoped to brief Delray about the breakthrough in the investigation as soon as she got back to Vancouver Metro headquarters, but a call from Delray on the drive back changed her plans. Assistant Commissioner Cunningham was insisting she attend the meeting with her boss and her new partner. She checked her watch as she exited the elevator on level four. It was just after three p.m. —late, but not too late. As she approached Cunningham's office, she could hear raised voices from behind the closed door. There was no love lost between Delray and Cunningham, and it didn't look as though anything would change today.

She took a deep breath and knocked on the door. She heard Cunningham's baritone voice answer, "Enter." Bridgette opened the door and took one step into the room before Cunningham added with a surly tone, "Close the door behind you, detective."

Bridgette did as instructed and made her way across to Cunningham's desk. At fifty-four, the tall, lean frame of

Cold Hard Cash

Assistant Commissioner Leo Cunningham normally cut a striking figure in his dark suit and immaculately trimmed silver hair. Today, he looked flustered as he sat in his two-thousand-dollar leather chair—not unusual whenever Delray was in his presence.

Delray and her soon-to-be new partner, Aaron Sterling, were sitting opposite Cunningham and turned as one as she walked in. Delray greeted her with an "Afternoon, Bridgette," while Sterling gave her a cold stare before returning to face Cunningham again.

Cunningham allowed her to settle into her chair before saying, "This meeting was at three p.m., detective. You're five minutes late, and I don't appreciate—"

Delray interrupted. "Sir, as I explained to you earlier, Detective Cash has been conducting important interviews for the Rook Island murder case. I hadn't planned on her attending this meeting."

Cunningham glared at Delray. "And as I explained to you, Chief Delray, I believe it is in all of our interests that she is here for this meeting today, which is why I deferred it to three p.m." Cunningham paused for a moment and studied Bridgette. She easily held his stare as he continued, "You're still here by the grace of our police commissioner, and him alone. This basement incident has turned into a major media fiasco and an embarrassment for Vancouver Metro. Until it's resolved, I want you kept on a tight leash, so you can't cause us any further embarrassment. If I had my way, you'd be restricted to desk duties, but the commissioner has seen fit to allow you to continue your work as normal. I'm prepared to tolerate that only on the proviso that you're closely supervised." Cunningham looked at Delray and added, "And I don't mean by your boss…"

Bridgette stole a quick sideways glance at her boss and

could see Delray's face turning red as she waited for the next volley.

"As of Monday, Senior Detective Aaron Sterling will be assigned as your partner until this basement incident is resolved. He will take the lead role in all investigative work you're involved with and will be your day-to-day supervisor. Are we clear?"

Bridgette responded, "Perfectly clear, sir."

"As for the basement matter, you are not to interfere with the internal investigation that is currently being conducted. Nor are you to continue with any form of investigation into your mother's murder, either in work time or on your own time. Are we clear?"

Bridgette nodded.

"I'll need a verbal response, detective."

Bridgette did her best to avoid rolling her eyes. "Yes, sir."

Turning to Delray, Cunningham said, "Sterling is a highly regarded member of the Internal Investigations team. I expect you to give him your full support. Are we clear?"

Delray did little to hide his frustration. "Sir, I have no doubt that senior detective Sterling is a competent investigator, but he has no experience with homicide cases. I fail to see—"

Cunningham roared, "This is not your decision," and then paused for a moment while he stared down Delray. In a more composed voice, he continued, "I will not be playing referee on this. Sterling is joining your team, and that's the way it is. You are to provide him with your full support and respect him like you would any other member of your team. Are we clear?"

Delray mumbled, "Yes, sir."

Cunningham turned to Sterling. "Do you have any questions, senior detective?"

Bridgette held her emotions in check as Sterling leaned slightly forward and studied her for a moment. She wasn't a fan of Sterling's oily auburn hair, the acne scarring on his face, or his over-sized Adam's apple, but she did her best never to judge anyone by their appearance. She hadn't trusted Sterling since the night he had grilled her for hours after the basement incident and didn't think that would change anytime soon.

Without taking his eyes off Bridgette, Sterling responded, "I have just one question for Detective Cash, assistant commissioner, and that is does she think she can work with me?"

Sterling did his best to suppress a patronizing smile as he settled back in his chair. Bridgette knew if she answered, "Yes," she would be expected to be his lapdog, something she wasn't prepared to do. She also knew if she answered, "No," it would be seen as insubordination. Instead, she answered, "I'm prepared to give it a try if the senior detective is."

The assistant commissioner studied Bridgette for a moment. Bridgette tried not to look confrontational as she maintained eye contact. Cunningham seemed satisfied as he looked at his watch and said, "Unless there is anything else, this meeting is over. I expect you to give the senior detective a full rundown of your caseload on Monday morning, Detective Cash."

Bridgette nodded her agreement.

Turning to Delray, Cunningham added, "I expect everyone's full cooperation. Anything less and I'll be going straight to the commissioner."

Bridgette gave Delray five minutes to cool off after the meeting with Cunningham and Sterling before knocking on his office door. He seemed to be back to his usual amiable self as he invited her in with a friendly, "Come on in, Bridgette."

She knew he would want to discuss what happened in the Cunningham meeting and closed the door to give them some privacy. After settling into a chair opposite Delray's desk, Bridgette waited for her boss to speak first.

Delray let out a huge sigh. "Well, that went about as well as I expected."

Bridgette knew better than to complain too hard about a senior officer, even if it was Cunningham, and tactfully replied, "I'm not sure how you work with him, chief?"

Delray grinned. "When you love the job, you learn to put up with the assholes. If it wasn't him, I'm sure it would be someone equally obnoxious sitting in his chair, so let's not worry about that. What I am concerned about is Sterling. He'll be down here on Monday, and I intend to give him a very short leash. If he gives you any grief, I want to know about it—okay?"

Bridgette nodded. "Like I said upstairs, I'll do my best to work with him, but I don't want this to slow down the investigation."

"Good attitude. Let's see how it pans out. If things get out of hand, I'll go straight to Cunningham. Now, tell me all about your interviews this morning."

Bridgette spent the next few minutes filling in Delray on the interview she'd had with both stable hands and then said, "I was in the car and just about to leave when Walter turned up and asked me to meet with me privately."

Delray frowned. "He had information?"

"He said he thought he may be able to help with the investigation but didn't want to talk at the track."

"So what happened?"

"I met up with him in a bar half an hour later."

"And what did he tell you?"

Bridgette gave Delray the background on how Walter had worked with Roy Pepper twenty years earlier until his disappearance.

Delray barely moved a muscle as he listened. "So what happened?"

"He witnessed a murder…or I should say heard a murder."

Delray raised his eyebrows. "A murder?"

Bridgette relayed Walter's account of what Roy had heard in the stable and the threats he had received from a man as he tried to leave. Delray chewed on one of the tips of his glasses while he listened intently until Bridgette described the man stopping Roy close to his home to threaten him again.

Delray asked, "So he knew where Roy lived?"

"Looks like it. Roy took the threat seriously and left town the following day. Walter gets a phone call from him about every six months but has no idea where he lives." Bridgette explained how the man's body had been removed from the stable and then stopped to let Delray ask questions.

Delray drummed his fingers on his desk for a moment. "How do we know Roy is not the killer?"

"I asked Walter that very question."

"And what did he say?"

"He told me he'd given that a lot of thought over the years but didn't think Roy had a motive. Also, he said it would be totally out of character. According to Walter, Roy didn't have a mean bone in his body. He loved working with horses and—"

Delray interrupted, "Plenty of gentle guys have turned out to be murderers?"

"I agree, chief, but there's something else you need to know…"

"Okay."

"Two days after Roy disappeared, police came to the track asking questions."

"About Roy?"

Bridgette shook her head. "They were trying to locate the man who'd been murdered. But back then, they thought he was just missing. To Walter's knowledge, Roy had never met the man."

"Does this man have a name?"

"Reid Whitecross."

Delray frowned. "Whitecross?"

"Reid Whitecross was Owen Whitecross's father."

Delray let out a long breath. "I'll be damned."

"I think we'll find that when Ray does a DNA comparison of the two bodies, it will show them as father and son."

Delray pushed back from his desk. "This makes no sense. Why would someone kill a father and son twenty years apart?"

"That's a good question."

They both sat in silence, each lost in their own thoughts. Finally, Delray said, "So, what's your plan?"

"I haven't really thought about it yet. Interviewing the extended Whitecross family seems to be a good place to start."

"I agree. Two dead members of the same family… You can't help but think this is personal." Delray gave her a moment and then asked, "What are you thinking, Bridgette?"

Bridgette pulled at her left earlobe while she thought. She knew Delray would give her some latitude but was also looking for results. "Sterling joins us on Monday, and he'll want to take the lead on the family interviews. I think I'd like to use the weekend to see if I can locate Roy Pepper."

Delray raised his eyebrows. "I agree, Roy could be very helpful even if he didn't actually *see* the murder. But if he's been off the grid for twenty years, he's not going to be easy to find."

Bridgette nodded. "Walter says he still sounds scared whenever he calls. Hopefully, that means he knows something."

Friday - 4:30 P.M.

Since the phone call, Bridgette had tried to push the prospect of meeting Charlie Bates to the furthermost recesses of her mind. Now, as she went through x-ray screening at the city jail, she felt her heart race as she realized she would soon be face-to-face with the man who had almost ended her life several months earlier. Still not sure what she would say, she followed a prison guard down a short corridor and into a rectangular room with a brown tiled floor. On the right-hand side were a row of over-sized windows built into a concrete wall and separated from each other by narrow Perspex partitions. The guard pointed in their general direction and mumbled, "Number six, you got ten minutes," before turning and walking out.

Normal visiting hours were over, and Bridgette was relieved she was the only one in the room as she sat on the steel stool bolted to the floor next to window six. After letting out a long breath, she thought about the last time she had worked with Bates, running down leads on a serial killer case. She felt herself breaking into a cold sweat as she wondered again what the man who had tried to kill her could possibly want to talk to her about. She whispered to herself, "You're about to find out," as the door to the cubicle on the other side of the glass opened.

It had been two months since she had last seen Charlie Bates. As the long, angular frame of her former colleague shuffled into the small enclosure, Bridgette was surprised by how much weight he had lost and how much he had aged. Although only in his early thirties, Bates's sullen, gray complexion made him look closer to forty. He gave her a nod but no smile as he sat down and lifted the telephone receiver off its hook. She knew Delray was keen for her to learn as much as she could from the meeting, but as she felt her stomach churn, she wondered whether accepting his invitation had been a good idea. Bates motioned to her to pick up the phone, but she ignored him as she did her best to compose herself. Finally, when she felt ready, she lifted the handset and rested it against her left ear as she continued to hold Bates's gaze.

Bates was the first to break the silence as he spoke into his handset. "Thanks for coming, Bridgette."

Bridgette didn't hide her resentment as she answered, "Why am I here, Charlie?"

Bates broke eye contact for a moment before responding, "There are a few things I wanted to tell you...and something I wanted to ask you."

"You've got ten minutes."

Bates nodded. "Fair enough. How are you?"

"Still alive."

"I...I understand this can't be easy for you. I wanted to say I'm sorry about what happened..."

"Really?"

Bates let out a long breath. "I'm not admitting it was me

in the basement, Bridgette, and I intend to fight to clear my name. You need to know I—"

Bridgette made no attempt to hide her anger. "Charlie, you're not fooling me or anyone else. I might not have seen your face in the dark, but you've got a bullet wound in your shoulder where I shot you."

"Like I said, I fell off a bike, and my injury is not unlike a bullet ricochet. I've instructed my lawyer—"

"Don't insult me, Charlie. It demeans us both. Tell me why I'm here, or I'm leaving."

Bates was silent for a moment and then looked away. "It's important to me that you know I've never wanted to see you get hurt."

Bridgette felt her anger rising but didn't respond.

Bates looked flustered as he continued, "I came third in the state police shooting championships last year. Hypothetically, if it was me down there, do you think you'd still be alive if I really wanted you dead?"

"I don't deal in hypotheticals, Charlie."

They stared at each other for close to a minute before Bates broke the silence. "I don't expect you to understand, and I'm not seeking your forgiveness…but I want you to know that I am sorry."

Bridgette couldn't hold Bates's gaze any longer and looked away as she gave a barely perceptible nod of her head. She knew Delray would be keen for her to learn as much as she could from the meeting and decided she was ready to start asking questions. "You said you wanted to ask me something?"

"Yes… I'd like you to go to my apartment and get a book for me."

Bridgette frowned. "Why on earth would you be asking me for help?"

"Because…you're the only one I trust, and you're the last person they will suspect of helping me."

"They? Who are they?"

"I can't tell you that, but I'm not asking you to do anything illegal."

"What kind of book are we talking about?"

"It's a physics book my father wrote some years back when he was still a university lecturer. He died three years ago, and it's important to me for sentimental reasons."

Bridgette thought about the request as Delray's warning echoed inside her head. "I'm not promising anything, Charlie, but what am I supposed to do? Bring it here?"

"No. I have a bail hearing tomorrow. If I make bail, I'm not planning on going back to my apartment, and if I don't, then I'm likely to be stuck inside for ten or more years, so I'll never see it again."

"Why aren't you going back to your apartment?"

Bates's brow furrowed. "That's not a question I'm prepared to answer."

Bridgette was reasonably confident she knew the answer but pressed Bates, anyway. "Are you afraid, Charlie?"

"You know as well as I do that unless I'm meeting with my lawyer, these conversations are recorded. As a cop, my chances of survival inside aren't great, and I'm not doing anything to make that worse."

"Who were you working for, Charlie?"

Bates gave half a smile and shook his head. "Nice try, Bridgette, but if you were in my position, you wouldn't be answering that question either."

Bridgette decided she was unlikely to get any more information out of Bates. "So, if I agree to get the book, and I'm not saying I am, what do I do with it?"

"I've got a storage locker. It's at my gym. I know you've

got a photographic memory so…" Bates produced a small piece of paper and held it up to the glass window with the palm of his hand for Bridgette to read.

Bridgette read and memorized the three lines of information written in a neat block script which gave her the gym's address, locker number, and pin number.

She nodded once, and Bates quickly removed the paper. "I've got a few things stored in there that I didn't want to leave in my apartment. If you could put the book in there, I would really appreciate it."

"Where did it all go wrong, Charlie?"

Bates's expression turned sullen. "Like I said, I'm innocent."

"You're very talented and had a promising career. Surely you knew you wouldn't get away with this forever and that you'd eventually be caught?"

Bates's eyes narrowed. "This isn't an interview. I wanted to apologize and ask you a favor—that's all."

"How do I get into your apartment?"

"There's a spare key taped inside the door of my locker. It will get you in the front door, and there's no alarm. I can't guarantee what state it will be in as I'm sure Vancouver Metro has searched it top to bottom already. But the book's in the main bookshelf in the living room."

Bates held up the same small slip of paper to the glass again, only in reverse. Bridgette read the words "Physics in Practice" and nodded once before Bates removed it.

They stared at one another again for a moment before Bridgette said, "I'll get the book on one condition."

"And what's that?"

"You answer one question for me. A yes or no answer."

"What if I don't want to answer it?"

"Then the deal's off."

"I could always lie to you…"

"You've lied to me twice already. If you make it three, you'll never see the book again."

Bates held her gaze for a moment. "What's the question?"

"Did you know who you were working for?"

Friday - 6 P.M.

Bridgette took a deep breath as the elevator opened on level one of the Vancouver South Professional Center. This was not her first visit to see Doctor Carol Sanders, and she was sure it wouldn't be her last. She liked Sanders and, more importantly, trusted Vancouver Metro's resident psychologist. Walking in through glass doors to the reception area a few minutes early, she had planned on using the time to sit and think about what she would say to Sanders. Sanders liked to grill her about every aspect of her life, both professional and personal. Even though she knew the doctor was only trying to help, Bridgette resented the intrusion into her personal life and liked to plan out her answers.

To her dismay, the receptionist waved her away from the two leather chairs in the waiting area. "The doctor is free, you can go in now."

Bridgette faked a smile as she thanked the receptionist and closed the door as she walked into Sanders's office. Sanders, a diminutive woman in her early fifties with stylishly cut short brown hair flecked with gray, looked up from a file she was reading and peered over her reading glasses to study Bridgette as she walked in.

Bridgette never had to second-guess what Sanders was thinking, and today was no exception as Sanders skipped a greeting and opened with, "Have you lost weight, Bridgette?"

Bridgette suppressed a knowing smile and replied, "Hello, doctor," as she settled into a chair on the opposite side of the desk.

Sanders ignored the greeting. "So, have you lost weight?"

"Maybe a pound or two during my recovery."

Sanders got up and motioned for Bridgette to do the same. "Let's check it."

Bridgette followed Sanders across to a set of electronic scales and, after removing her shoes, stood on them at her doctor's instruction.

Sanders turned her head slightly to read the weight and said, "Not bad for someone who's five feet ten, but I'd like to see you at least two pounds heavier next time we meet."

Bridgette responded tactfully, "I'm working on it."

As she settled into her chair at her desk again, Sanders said, "I've been reading your file. It looks like you've been busy since we last met?"

"You could say that."

"I see you picked up an injury to your leg?"

Bridgette nodded. "My last case got a bit out of hand. I was stabbed in the leg while trying to arrest a murder suspect."

"Yes, I read about it in the paper. You were lucky to get out of that alive."

Bridgette nodded.

Sanders continued, "So did you stop eating?"

"I spent a few days in the hospital. A combination of blood loss and hypothermia. I don't like hospital food, but I'm back on three squares a day. And I'm going to the gym every second day."

Sanders frowned a little. "Are you sleeping?"

This was a question Sanders always asked. Bridgette responded as she always did, "Mostly."

Sanders took off her glasses and glared at Bridgette. "I can't help you if you give me vague answers, Bridgette. 'Mostly' doesn't cut it as an answer."

Bridgette shrugged. "I sleep a lot better now than I used to. Most nights I'm getting five or six hours of sleep, which is a big improvement on when I first started visiting you."

"Are you still having the nightmares?"

Bridgette studied Sanders for a moment, knowing the doctor would not like her answer. "Sometimes."

"Sometimes?"

"Maybe once or twice a week…"

Sanders responded, "Lean forward and hold out your arm," as she opened a blood pressure kit that seemed to sit permanently on her desk.

While Sanders took Bridgette's blood pressure, she said, "Are you still taking the sleeping tablets?"

"No. I haven't taken them for close to a month."

"Well, that's a positive sign. Is it still the same nightmare?"

Bridgette breathed in and then said, "Yes," as she recalled the memory of hiding in a bedroom closet when she was seven years old.

"Describe it to me…"

Bridgette resisted the urge to roll her eyes. Every visit, Sanders wanted her to relive the nightmare, hoping to spot changes that would show progress. "It hasn't changed. I'm still hiding in the closet, and then I hear the shot…"

"And then what happens?"

"It's quiet for a while, and then the door opens."

"And…"

"Someone grabs me by the hand and leads me out into the bedroom. They tell me not to look at the bed, but I do…"

"I know this is difficult, Bridgette, but what do you see?"

Bridgette bit down on her lip as tears formed in her eyes. "I see my mother lying on the bed in a pool of blood…"

In a softer voice, Sanders asked, "Is there anything different about what you're seeing now from what you were seeing two months ago?"

Bridgette closed her eyes. "Not really."

The room went quiet until Bridgette opened her eyes. Sanders continued in a gentle tone, "You know, some people live with traumatic nightmares from their childhood all their lives. While time can be a great healer, professional counseling and confiding in people you trust is what's most effective. I know you're not fond of coming here, but I am seeing progress…"

"If you say so…"

"Let's talk about your father for a minute."

Bridgette thought, *Let's not*, but knew that wouldn't fly with Sanders and instead responded, "Okay."

"Is he appearing in your nightmares?"

"No. I occasionally dream about him, but never in a nightmare."

"Are you an adult or a child in your dreams?"

Bridgette thought for a moment. The dreams about her

father were pleasant but vague. "To be honest, I'm not sure. He's just there holding out his hand."

Sanders nodded. "You never experience anxiety in dreams involving your father?"

"Not now…"

"What do you mean, 'Not now'?"

Bridgette had only recently learned of her father's murder. Even though she hadn't seen him in twenty years, his death had still come as a shock to her. "I now know he didn't kill my mother, and that's a big relief." Keen to change the subject, Bridgette added, "How's my blood pressure, doctor?"

"One-twenty over eighty—perfectly normal."

Sanders seemed to sense that Bridgette was done talking about her mother and father and changed the subject as she packed away her blood pressure kit. "So how's work going?"

"It's going okay."

"You're normally a lot more enthusiastic about your work. What's going on?"

Bridgette explained the situation about Sterling joining their team. Sanders listened politely and then responded, "Have you got any strategies in place to manage this? The last thing we need for you right now is more stress."

"The chief will be monitoring it closely. If it looks like it's going to be unmanageable, he's promised he will step in. It's not so much the stress I'm worried about but the politics."

"Well, it's good you have a confidant inside the organization, Bridgette. The worst thing you can do is bottle things up and not talk to anyone."

Bridgette nodded once.

Sanders continued, "Speaking of confidants, are you still reaching out to Linda?"

Linda was Bridgette's father's partner. Bridgette never knew about her until after her father's death. After a rocky start, the two of them had formed a strong bond as they grieved his passing together. "After I got out of the hospital, I was forced to spend another week on medical leave before I got clearance to return to work. I stayed with Linda. It was good therapy for both of us."

"And Linda still lives in that cottage at the foot of the Catalin Mountains?"

"Yes. We'd walk every day to help strengthen my leg."

"Well, that's a great place to recover. And only an hour's drive from Vancouver means you can catch up with her regularly, right?"

"Yes."

Sanders stared at Bridgette for close to half a minute. "I know we've had this conversation before, Bridgette…but we're going to have it again."

Bridgette knew what was coming but said nothing.

Sanders continued, "I've seen too many cops, good people, not make it because they've isolated themselves and refused help. I don't want that happening to you."

The suicide talk had come up on most previous visits. Bridgette knew it needed to be discussed and replied, "I understand I was on the edge, but I've walked back…a long way back, and I don't plan on ever going there again…"

"I don't normally say this to my patients, Bridgette, but I'm going to say it to you. Is there anything else I can do for you?"

Bridgette thought about the question for a moment. "Not really. My gut is constantly in a knot, and I don't think that will change until I find out who murdered my parents…"

Sanders nodded thoughtfully. "You have to be careful, Bridgette. If this becomes all-consuming, it will kill you."

"I don't have a death wish anymore. I'm aware of the signs now, and I'm managing it."

Sanders didn't look convinced. "My door is always open. If you need anything, you know where to find me."

"I crave peace, more than anything. But until I find out who killed them, this will never be over."

Saturday - 4:05 P.M.

Bridgette looked up from her computer when she heard the elevator chime as it stopped on level two. Normally, the background noise of ringing phones and detectives engaged in conversation masked any background sound. But as she sat alone in the Homicide room at just after four p.m. on a Saturday afternoon, she could have heard a pin drop. A moment later, she watched Delray, dressed in a bright yellow polo shirt, brown checkered pants, and a pair of Adidas shoes, walk into the office. Bridgette rarely saw her boss in anything other than a business suit and said, "Golf?" as he walked toward her.

Delray nodded. "The clothes, right?"

Bridgette smiled. "Kind of."

Delray stopped at her desk. "Alice has gone to Bolton for the weekend, so I'm making the most of it." His mood turned serious as he looked at his watch. "I hope you plan on going home soon. I appreciate your dedication, but you need downtime as well."

It wasn't unusual for Bridgette to pull long hours when

she was working a case. "I plan on leaving around five. What about you?"

"I'm just here to pick up a couple of files for a report I have to write. It's due on Tuesday, and with Aaron Sterling starting on Monday and God knows whatever else happening around here, I thought I'd get a start on it this weekend." Delray paused and pointed at Bridgette's desk which was covered in files and notes. "So what are you working on?"

"I thought I'd spend the day trying to find out as much as I can about Roy Pepper. I still think he's the key to this case."

Delray nodded. "Before we get into that, how did your visit with Bates go?"

Bridgette filled in her boss about the visit and then informed him that Bates wanted her to go to his apartment to get a book. She added, "I haven't been to his apartment yet, I wanted to check with you first."

Delray frowned. "Why on earth would he be wanting a book from his apartment?"

Bridgette explained the sentimental value of the book to Bates and then told Delray about the locker.

"So he's not going back to his apartment?"

"Doesn't seem like it."

"Do you think he's on the level?"

"I don't know. He seemed genuine enough and even apologized for what happened in the basement in a roundabout way."

"This is bizarre. Why on earth would he be asking you of all people to get a book from his apartment?"

"I'm not sure, chief. He said he trusts me."

Delray pulled up a chair from a neighboring work cubicle and sat down next to Bridgette. He thought for a moment and then said, "We've searched his apartment from top to bottom and taken everything that could possibly be helpful in prosecuting the case against him. I don't see any harm in getting a book for him, but I want to see it first before you put it in his locker."

"I can pick it up on my way home tonight and bring it in on Monday if you like?"

"I'm not sure I like the idea of you going to his apartment on your own."

"If I get there and it looks suspicious, I'll leave immediately. I also have my Glock."

Delray still didn't look convinced. "I guess it's just a normal apartment block, so it should be safe enough."

"If you like, I'll text you before I go in and as soon as I come out?"

Delray nodded. "I'll enjoy my evening more if I know you've gotten out of there safe." He paused for a moment. "By the way, I got a progress email from Carol Sanders last night."

"Okay…"

"How did it go?"

"Okay…"

"She said you are making progress, but the good doctor is still worried about you. I promised her I would keep a close eye on you."

"She seemed concerned about Sterling joining our team. I told her I'd be okay if I can keep out of the politics."

Delray grimaced. "Wouldn't we all." He studied Bridgette for a moment and then said, "Let's keep this dialogue going. If anything gets too much for you, I want to be the first to know. Okay?"

Bridgette nodded. She knew Delray and Sanders had

her best interests at heart, but she preferred not to be the center of attention.

Delray changed the subject. "So tell me about the case. Have you made any progress trying to find Roy Pepper?"

"Not really. I've spent four hours in NatTrack trying to find anyone who is a close match for Roy. He is unusually short and, according to Walter, walks with a pronounced limp because of a horse racing accident that ended his career as a jockey when he was nineteen. I haven't found anyone about his age in the criminal system that's a reasonable match and worth pursuing."

"What about the driver's license database?"

"There is no one in the system by the name of Roy Pepper that comes close to matching either his height or age. I've tried broadening the search with various aliases for both the names Roy and Pepper but didn't have any luck with that either."

Delray looked downcast. "Well, if you can't find them in the system, nobody else will either."

"I'm trying a different tack now."

"And what's that?"

"Walter said Roy had a gift with horses almost like a horse whisperer. He's sure wherever Roy ended up, he'd be working with horses again, and most likely racehorses."

Delray looked skeptical. "Well, that doesn't narrow it down much. He could be working anywhere in the country."

"I agree, but I've tried to think like Roy. If he's still in hiding, it's unlikely he'll be working at any racecourse, equestrian center, or riding club that's open to the public."

"That makes sense. So what are you focusing on?"

"For now, private studs and horse breeding centers. There's a national database of registered studs and horse racing breeders. I know it's a long shot, but if he's as passionate as Walter says he is, it's a reasonable place to start."

"I agree, but there must be thousands of those across the country?"

"I've limited my current search to the east coast. I've also discounted any facilities in major cities or regional centers."

"So how many do you have on your list?"

"One hundred and eighty-seven."

Delray let out a low whistle. "That's a lot of telephone calls."

"I'm about halfway through the list already, although I'm leaving quite a few messages."

"Any luck so far?"

Bridgette smiled. "Kind of."

Delray raised his eyebrows. "Don't keep me in suspense, Bridgette."

"About half an hour ago, I called a horse stud near Tangmere Falls. When I gave the owner a description of Roy, he was positive someone matching that description had worked for him for a short period about six years ago. He remembered the pronounced limp."

"Did he get a forwarding address or phone number?"

Bridgette shook her head. "He hasn't heard or seen from the man since. But it gives me hope that I'm on the right track."

"Well, let's hope something comes from it." Delray looked at his watch. "I need to get going. Promise me you won't work too late tonight. I don't like the idea of having to answer to Carol Sanders if you get sick."

Bridgette half smiled. "I promise." She looked down at the list of names she had been working her way through.

"Nine more phone calls and I'll be halfway through the list. As soon as I've made those calls, I'll pack it in and head home."

"Sounds like a plan. Don't forget to text me when you have been to Bates's apartment."

Bridgette replied, "Will do," and picked up the handset for her desk phone as Delray headed to his office.

She sighed as she looked at the list and dialed the next phone number. After the third ring, her call was answered by an answering machine, informing her that her call was important before asking her to leave a message. Bridgette went through her normal spiel, explaining that she was a detective with Vancouver Metro police and then gave her phone number and asked for a return phone call as soon as possible.

Bridgette made a brief notation against the name and then dialed the next number on the list. It too went through to voicemail, and Bridgette left the same message. As she returned to the list, she noticed the farm also had a mobile number, which she dialed.

The phone was answered on the fourth ring by a man with a deep baritone voice who introduced himself as Blaine.

Bridgette went through her introductory spiel again and explained she was trying to track down a stable hand who went by the name of Roy Pepper. After giving a description of Roy, she asked the man if he'd ever come across anyone fitting that description.

The phone went quiet for a moment before the man responded, "Where did you say you were from again?"

Bridgette felt a tingle in the base of her spine. "Vancouver Metro, sir." The phone went quiet again.

Finally, the man responded, "Is this Roy in trouble?"

Bridgette decided not to be too specific. "Like I said, we think he may have witnessed something in relation to a cold case murder we are investigating. We'd just like to ask him a few questions."

Her heart raced as the man responded, "And he walks with a pronounced limp?"

"Yes, he used to be a jockey before he broke his pelvis in a horse racing accident."

"I have a man who works for me who matches your description, only he goes by the name of Ray, not Roy…"

Bridgette tried to hide her excitement. "Would it be possible for me to come and interview Ray?"

"We are a good three and a half hours' drive from Vancouver, detective."

"I'm happy to make the drive out there tomorrow morning if that's convenient?"

"I'll be here 'til around eleven a.m. Ray will be here all day, but I'd like to meet you before you talk to him."

Bridgette did the driving time math in her head and then said, "I can be there around ten?"

"You have our address?"

Bridgette read off the address that she had listed and then waited.

"That's it. If you've got Google Maps or something similar, you won't have any trouble finding us."

Bridgette thanked the man for his time and then said, "I'd appreciate you not mentioning my visit to Ray."

He responded, "You'll find me in the timber house at the top of the driveway," and then disconnected.

Bridgette let out a long breath. She'd spent over nine hours on the case today but was convinced she had the breakthrough she was looking for. She hoped the man would do as he promised and not mention her visit to Roy.

Driving three and a half hours to find the key witness had disappeared again would be frustrating, and she knew that he would be more cautious than ever after that, which could make him almost impossible to find again.

She whispered, "You'll know soon enough, Bridgette," as she replaced the handset.

Saturday - 6:05 P.M.

Charlie Bates's gymnasium was a block and a half from his apartment. Bridgette had found the key taped inside the door of the empty locker just like Charlie had explained. The two-minute walk to Bates's apartment gave Bridgette an opportunity to text Delray to let him know she was ready to enter. She had been standing in front of the inner-city apartment block for close to five minutes, trying to get a feel for the place Bates used to call home. Constructed of brown brick, with large inset colonial-style windows and white trim, every apartment appeared to have a small balcony. Bridgette guessed the monthly rent for apartments in the building was about double what she could afford on a detective's salary and wondered again what Bates was involved in to afford the rent. As she watched people come and go, she focused on level fourteen, two floors from the top. Most of the apartments on that level were in darkness, and she wondered which one of them belonged to Bates.

Keen to get a good night's sleep ahead of her road trip

the following day, Bridgette pushed through the double front door of the building into a spacious tiled foyer and headed for the elevator. Level fourteen was as well-lit as the foyer, and she had no trouble finding apartment nine. She inserted the key into the door and twisted the handle. The door opened silently, exposing a living area that in the shadows looked about twice the size of her entire apartment. Bridgette found the light switch and frowned when the apartment remained in darkness after she switched it on. She worked the switch up and down several times and wondered whether a lightbulb had blown or if the power had been cut to the apartment as the room remained in darkness. After switching on the flashlight on her smartphone, she made her way across to a table lamp on a wooden coffee table next to Bates's leather couch. She turned the lamp's switch off and on but nothing happened. Reasonably confident the electricity had been disconnected, Bridgette raised her smartphone to give her better light as she turned to face the bookcase. She frowned again as she stared at the bookshelves which were almost devoid of books. She lowered the beam of light and played it over the floor in front of her which was strewn with books, papers, framed photographs, and other items. Bridgette knew Vancouver Metro had searched his apartment but was surprised at the state they had left it in as she shone the light around the living area. Every drawer and cupboard had been opened and the contents left discarded on the floor. Had it not been for the police search, she would have sworn the apartment had been ransacked by thieves.

Bridgette let out a sigh and positioned her smartphone on the edge of one of the bookshelves so that its light shone downward toward the floor. Kneeling down, Bridgette began searching through the pile of books. She remem-

Cold Hard Cash

bered Bates saying his father's book had been a textbook, so she ignored the paperbacks and methodically worked her way through the hardcovers, piling them neatly in a stack to her left as she read the title of each work. After two minutes, she picked up a book with a green cover and whispered, "Bingo," as she read the title, *Physics in Practice*. Bridgette stood up and held the book close to her smartphone while she flipped through the opening pages. There was a picture of the author, a man in his early fifties, on the inside front cover. Bridgette could see facial similarities between the man and Charlie Bates and had little reason to doubt Bates's claim that the author was indeed his father. She slowly flipped through the pages of the book. Not entirely sure what she was looking for, she stopped when she got about halfway through as she sensed a presence behind her. As she went to turn, she felt an explosion of pain in her kidneys. Bridgette dropped the book and staggered forward as a thick arm reached over her shoulder. Before she had a chance to recover, a hand squeezed her mouth closed with a vice-like grip to prevent her from screaming. Instinctively, she propped forward on her right foot as the person behind her tried to push her into the bookcase.

Startled by the attack, she resisted the urge to panic as the man tightened his grip. Bridgette spent at least three nights a week in a gym and was a ninth dan in martial arts, but she knew even with her training she was no physical match for a strong male attacker at such close range. She feigned twisting to her left and then twisted right and with a clenched fist swung it back as hard as she could into the man's groin. The man loosened his grip slightly, allowing Bridgette to pivot and swing her left elbow into the man's ribcage. The man groaned as he let go but pushed Bridgette forward and sent her sprawling into the bookcase.

Momentarily stunned as her head hit the bookcase, Bridgette collapsed to the floor. She willed herself to turn around to face her attacker as she got to her knees but as she looked up into the darkness her attacker was nowhere to be seen. She pulled her Glock from her coat pocket as she heard the frantic footsteps of someone in the hallway outside the apartment. Bridgette grabbed at the bookcase to steady herself as she struggled to her feet. Slightly dizzy from the knock to her head and nauseated by the blow to her kidneys, she drew a couple of deep breaths and then hobbled out into the hallway. She couldn't see the man but heard rapid footsteps in the stairwell and knew the man had opted for the stairs rather than the elevator. With no time to lose, Bridgette sprinted as best as she could to the stairwell. She could hear the footsteps of her attacker as they echoed through the stairwell and figured he was about three floors below.

Keeping a firm grip on her Glock and ignoring her pain, Bridgette descended the fourteen flights, three stairs at a time, until she pushed her way through the fire escape door on the first floor. She found herself standing in a poorly lit alleyway at the rear of the building. After scanning left and right and seeing no one, she sprinted out of the alleyway and onto the side street. She stood for several seconds, scanning left and right, but saw no one. Knowing every second counted, Bridgette willed herself to sprint again to the front of the building. She scanned the street to her left and her right. There were a few people out walking, mostly in pairs, some on their own, either smoking or talking on phones. All of them moved at a leisurely pace, seemingly unaware of what had just happened. As a car drove by at low speed, Bridgette swore under her breath. It had been too dark in the apartment for her to make out any of her attacker's facial features. As she stood heaving and trying to catch her breath, she realized he could casually walk by her now without being recognized. She pocketed her Glock and swore again as she realized any hope of finding the man was gone.

Sunday - 9:55 A.M.

After a restless night trying to make sense of the attack at Charlie Bates's apartment, Bridgette gave up on sleep shortly after four a.m. She made herself pancakes for breakfast and then set out at first light for the three-and-a-half-hour drive to visit Roy Pepper.

The drive had been uneventful and had given her a lot of thinking time as she enjoyed the scenic countryside which was still green from recent heavy rain. She had turned off her GPS at Riverby, a small township she had driven through five minutes earlier, confident she would soon find her destination on South Road. As she came over a small crest in the road, she saw on her right an elaborate set of white gates supported by two large brick columns that marked the entrance to a property. After reading the freshly painted sign above the gates that marked it as Kenmore Stud, Bridgette knew she had reached her destination and pulled off the road. She checked her watch. Five minutes until her appointment with Blaine Kenmore—time enough to call Delray. She pressed speed dial on her smartphone and looked back across the road at the entrance to his property. The long gravel driveway that wound its way up to a large white house at the top of the hill was framed by a backdrop of red maple trees, suggesting Blaine Kenmore's horse stud was very profitable. Bridgette studied the expansive house at the top of the hill for a moment until Delray answered her call.

After what had happened the previous evening, she wasn't surprised by his concern as he said, "How are you feeling, Bridgette?"

Bridgette was less perturbed by the incident in Bates's unit than Delray was. She thought her attacker was simply motivated to get out of the apartment without being recognized. The early night she had hoped for hadn't eventuated. After calling in the incident, she had stayed back at the apartment for almost two hours to provide a statement and assist with searching the apartment for clues to her attacker's identity. It had been almost midnight before she crawled into bed, and sleep had not come easy as she wondered who had been in Bates's apartment and why?

Playing down how tired she was, Bridgette answered, "I'm fine, chief. Nothing a good night's sleep won't fix."

"Have you arrived at the farm yet?"

"Just pulled up out front. I'm a few minutes early, so I thought I would call you and let you know I've arrived safely."

Delray laughed. "You seem to have a knack for finding trouble, so I'm glad you have arrived there without incident. Let's see if you can make it all the way home as well…"

Bridgette allowed herself a smile. "No guarantees on that one."

"So, what's the plan?"

"I'm going to meet with the owner, Blaine Kenmore,

first. I think he's worried that he's been harboring a fugitive and wants more information."

"That's understandable. Has he told this Roy guy you're coming?"

"I hope not. I asked him to keep this confidential so the witness couldn't do a runner. I guess I'll know soon enough." Bridgette paused for a moment and then asked, "Any updates on the break-in at Bates's apartment?"

"Not so far. We've got forensics dusting for fingerprints this morning, but I'm not holding my breath they will find anything useful."

"Has Bates been told?"

"Not yet. I'm planning on interviewing him tomorrow before he goes back to court. I'm going to rattle his cage and see if we can find out what the guy was looking for."

"You can't help but think whoever he was working for is nervous."

"One thing for sure, Bates won't be getting his damn book back anytime soon."

Bridgette thought about the book for a moment. She'd spent close to an hour checking each page for clues while she waited for Delray and his team to arrive after the attack. She found nothing remotely suspicious and wondered whether it was just the sentimental value like Bates had said.

Delray added, "I didn't get much sleep last night either. I kept wondering whether the man in the apartment was waiting for you. Like you had been set up deliberately."

"I don't think so. He would have had to be holed up in that apartment for a long time if he was waiting for me."

"Unless of course, he followed you?"

"I'm sure he was in the apartment before me—probably the bedroom. Besides, I don't see the motive. If Bates wanted to have me roughed up, he wouldn't have needed such an elaborate plan which also implicates him."

Delray was quiet for a moment before he responded, "You're probably right."

"I think you were on the money when you said he was probably looking for something. That I ended up being in the apartment at the same time is most likely a coincidence."

"I hope you're right, Bridgette. I've had one of my detectives followed in the past, and it's not a pleasant experience."

Bridgette checked her watch and decided she needed to get going. Tactfully, she replied, "I'll call you after I've finished the interview, before I drive home."

"Sounds like a plan. What are you driving?"

Bridgette allowed herself a smile as she looked around the cabin of her car. "The Mustang." The car, a fully restored steel blue '67 Mustang Fastback, had been a recent acquisition. She didn't get to drive it much and added, "It's made for the open road, and I thought if I'm going to spend seven hours behind the wheel today, I may as well be enjoying myself."

Delray laughed. "Make sure you put in a requisition for your mileage. If you're not going to take a pool car, the least we can do is pay for your gas."

Bridgette replied, "I'll take you up on that," as she started the engine.

"Call me when you finish. If this Roy knows anything and is willing to cooperate, get a full statement from him. Also, like I said last night, we'll keep his location confidential, but we can also discuss witness protection if he thinks he needs it."

Bridgette thanked Delray for the offer, disconnected,

and then headed up the gravel driveway in low gear. As she approached the top of the hill, she marveled at the manicured gardens and hedges that surrounded the large white brick and timber house. She estimated the house had six or seven bedrooms and wondered if they employed a gardener as she parked in a circular gravel drive out front. Bridgette walked up a paved walkway to the double front doors and knocked.

Someone called out from inside, "Coming."

A moment later, the door was opened by a man about her height with salt-and-pepper hair in his early sixties. He had a relaxed manner as he extended his hand. "You must be Detective Cash."

Bridgette recognized the man's voice from their phone conversation yesterday. "Pleased to meet you, Mister Kenmore."

Kenmore responded, "Call me Blaine," and pointed to a wrought-iron table with two matching chairs on the patio as he added, "I know you're keen to interview Ray, but why don't we sit here for a moment and talk?"

After they settled, Bridgette said, "I can understand you must have questions, Blaine."

Kenmore nodded. "But probably not as many as you."

"Where did you first meet Ray?"

"Well, that's a story all of its own." When Bridgette said nothing in response, he continued, "I guess it was near enough to four years ago now. He was hitchhiking, and I normally don't pick up hitchhikers, but I made an exception in his case."

"Why?"

"He had a dog with him, a black-and-white cocker spaniel. They both were walking with limps, and I kind of felt sorry for them."

"So you picked them up?"

"Yeah. I was in one of my horse trucks. I'd had a five-hour drive that day delivering a young mare to its new owner, and I was on my way home. Ray was pleasant enough, and we got to talking. I asked him about his dog and why it was limping. He said he didn't know exactly. He'd found it on the side of a road two days earlier and thought it might have been hit by a car.

"I asked him a few more questions, and he confided in me he had nowhere to go. I figured a man who helps a wounded animal like he did couldn't be all bad, so I told him he could bunk down here for a day or two in my stable until he figured out where he was headed. He didn't want charity and said he knew a lot about horses and wanted to help. I put him to work the following day and discovered he had a real gift with horses. To cut a long story short, after a few days of watching him work with some of my best breeding stock, I offered him a job, and he's been here ever since. He lives in a small cottage on the other side of my property. He even acts as a caretaker when I'm away."

Bridgette observed Kenmore's defensive posture and replied reassuringly, "Like I said yesterday, Blaine, he's not in trouble with Vancouver Metro. We just want to interview him."

Kenmore nodded. "I'm not sure how much you know about Ray, but walking is painful for him and always has been since his accident. He doesn't own a car and doesn't drive much. He prefers to stay here, and perhaps after our conversation yesterday, I can understand why."

"It sounds like you trust him?"

Blaine nodded. "Ray has become more like a friend than an employee. I hope this doesn't change anything for him. He's had a hard life and deserves better."

"I can't make any promises, Blaine, but I respect your concern."

Kenmore nodded again and looked at his watch before saying, "I need to get going soon. Ray's cottage is on the northwest boundary of my property. It's close to a ten-minute drive by road, so if you don't mind, we'll take a shortcut through my farm. I'll get you to follow me—he's expecting you."

Bridgette tried to suppress her frustration. "I thought we agreed you wouldn't tell Ray about my visit?"

Kenmore held her gaze for a moment and then responded firmly, "If I was worried about Ray running, I wouldn't have said anything, but I've told him out of respect. I'm confident he'll be there."

Bridgette responded curtly, "Well, I hope you're right."

As he got up from the table, Kenmore responded, "I'd appreciate a call from you later today or tomorrow to let me know how things went, detective."

Bridgette promised she would call as she got up from the table. She wondered whether the trip had been a waste of time as she followed Kenmore out through the gate. Roy Pepper had been told about her visit last night, and that would have given him plenty of time to pack and disappear again. She tried to push the thought to the back of her mind as Kenmore pointed to a gravel driveway that continued around the side of his house. "My truck's out back, near the stables. Follow the driveway around and wait for me. Once I get my truck started, you can follow me."

Bridgette followed Kenmore's truck along a dirt track through several fields toward the rear of the property. After coming over a rise, Kenmore stopped his truck in front of a footbridge made of thick rough-sawn timber. The bridge spanned a small running stream and led into a tree-lined ridge on the other side.

Bridgette pulled up alongside Kenmore and wound down her driver's window.

Kenmore pointed at the bridge. "If you go over that footbridge and follow the path up that ridge, Ray's house is a two-minute walk down the other side once you get to the top." Kenmore stopped for a moment and stared at Bridgette before he added, "Go easy on him, detective. He's a good man and deserves your respect."

Bridgette promised she would as she got out of her car. She watched Kenmore's truck until it disappeared back over the rise and then sighed as she thought, *Let's hope this isn't a waste of time.*

After she crossed the bridge, the walk up a path through the trees to the ridgeline took her about three minutes. Normally, she would have enjoyed the walk, but the knot in her stomach knowing Roy had probably disappeared was all-consuming. Bridgette wondered what her next move would be as she crested the ridge. She stopped for a moment to take in the stunning view of the valley below. Scanning from left to right, she followed a graded road that wound its way across the middle of the valley until she fixed her eyes on a rustic brown cottage about four hundred yards below. While she couldn't see all the house through the trees, she had a reasonable view of the rear porch. She felt a tingle in her spine as she could see a small gray-haired man sitting on a chair on the rear porch. He appeared to be looking in her direction, but it was hard to tell from her position. Bridgette whispered, "It's time you and I met, Roy," and then headed down the path.

Sunday - 10:20 A.M.

Bridgette made her way down through the tree line toward the cottage. She kept a close watch on the man who sat in his rocking chair on the porch for fear he would turn and run when he noticed her approach. To her surprise, the man just sat there, watching and waiting. When she closed to within about eighty feet off the back porch, she could see the man's face clearly. It was hard to tell his age, but she guessed he was in his early to mid-fifties and had wavy gray hair and a pleasant face. She could see by the way he sat in the chair, almost like a child, with his feet barely touching the ground, that he was considerably shorter than she was—five one or two at most.

The man watched her every move as she walked down the hill and through a rusting gate into the rear garden. The man got up as she walked toward a porch that was barely big enough to accommodate his rocking chair. She could tell by the way he struggled to get to his feet and the way he stood with his left foot barely touching the ground that he would find walking difficult.

Cold Hard Cash

Bridgette stopped two feet short of the man and gazed into hazel eyes that radiated a mix of kindness, pain, and perhaps even fear. "I'm Detective Bridgette Cash, from Vancouver Metro. You must be Ray."

The man extended his hand and shook Bridgette's with a gentle grip. He replied in a high tenor voice, "Actually, my name is Roy."

"Your boss told you I was coming?"

Roy nodded. "He said a lady detective from Vancouver was coming to interview me today."

"And you didn't run?"

Roy sighed and looked down at the porch. "I'm too old to run anymore…"

Bridgette responded softly, "Is there somewhere we can talk, Roy?"

Roy motioned toward the back door. "I have a living room inside. We can talk in there if you like?"

"That will be fine."

Roy walked with a heavy limp to the back door and paused with his hand on the door handle. "You okay with dogs?"

Bridgette half smiled. "I hear you have a cocker spaniel?"

Roy opened the door. "His name is Spike." He waited as a mid-sized black-and-white dog emerged cautiously from the house. The dog came and stood by his master's side, looking up at him with moist charcoal eyes.

Roy added, "Spike is cautious around strangers."

Bridgette bent down on one knee and held her hand out, palm down, toward the dog. "I think it's good for all of us to be cautious around strangers, Roy."

Spike padded over to Bridgette and cautiously sniffed at

her fingers. Bridgette gave the dog a moment to get used to her scent before scratching him under the chin.

As Spike closed his eyes to make the most of the attention, Roy said, "I think you've made a friend."

Bridgette gave the dog a final pat and said, "I think so too."

Bridgette followed Roy into his house and surveyed the tiny spartan kitchen as she stood just inside the back door. No oven, just a microwave and a freestanding two-burner stove. The kitchen was separated from the living room by a teak bench with two overhead cupboards that Bridgette guessed dated back to the mid-sixties. The cottage was neat and clean and had a homely feel to it.

Roy pointed at two chairs in the living room. "Please have a seat, detective. I'm going to make a cup of tea. Would you like one?"

Bridgette was about to respond, "No," but realized she hadn't had anything to eat or drink since before six a.m. "That would be nice. Thanks, Roy."

"I mainly drink green tea, on account of my arthritis, but I've also got peppermint and black?"

"I'm a big fan of peppermint, so that would be great."

While Roy busied himself in the kitchen, Bridgette looked around the living room. After seeing the man's disability, she decided there was no chance that he would run and turned her back to him. There were two non-matching easy chairs facing a small TV that sat on a low-set rectangular bookshelf that leaned slightly to the right. Next to one of the chairs was a shallow wicker cane basket, lined with a navy-blue blanket. She smiled again as she watched Spike settle into his bed. She lifted her gaze and noticed there were no pictures or photographs on any of the walls and just a few magazines and paperbacks in the bookshelf.

Cold Hard Cash

She concluded Roy lived a frugal life and probably had few, if any, visitors.

Bridgette walked to the front window and gazed out at a picturesque view of the valley below. The cottage was set amongst trees about a hundred yards up from the graded road below. She noticed a single-cab Toyota utility truck with a sign on the driver's side door that read "Kenmore Stud" parked next to the cottage.

She said over her shoulder, "Your boss provides you with a truck?"

"Yes, Mister Kenmore is very generous. On account of my injury, it's painful to walk too far, so I'd be lost without it."

As she watched a late-model Ford sedan drive slowly along the graded road below, she asked, "How did you get injured?"

"I was an apprentice jockey. I had a fall in a race when I was nineteen and broke my pelvis and left leg in three places. I had a lot of operations and was lucky I didn't lose it."

"That must have been tough."

As he began pouring hot water into the cups, Roy replied, "It finished my career as a jockey, but I try not to dwell on it."

"So you've been a stable hand ever since?"

"I love all animals, but horses in particular. I figured if I couldn't race them anymore, I still wanted to be around them and involved somehow." Roy was silent for a moment and then added, "Is that how you found me?"

Bridgette turned to face Roy. "I found out quite a lot about you from your friend Walter. When he told me about your passion for horses, it made me wonder."

As Roy hobbled across to the easy chairs with two mugs

of tea, he said, "I always knew this day was coming. I'm just surprised it took so long..."

Roy handed Bridgette her tea and then settled down into his easy chair.

Bridgette sat in the chair beside him and said, "I guess your boss has told you I'm investigating a double murder?"

Roy nodded.

Bridgette added, "Why don't we start at the beginning and you tell me what happened twenty years ago?"

Roy sighed and set down his mug on a side table. He thought for a moment and then said, "Walter and I had only been in Vancouver a short time. We were working as stable hands at the NewFarm racetrack. One day, I was working on my own in one of the older stables that were rarely used. It was mid-morning, and I was mucking out one of the stalls when I heard two men talking as they came in through the far entrance. I thought nothing of it at first and just kept working. Pretty soon, it became an argument, and then they started shouting at one another. They moved into a stall just down from where I was working, but I don't think they knew I was there."

"What were they arguing about?"

"I couldn't hear very well, but I remember it had nothing to do with horses. It sounded like they were arguing over money, almost like they were family."

"Why do you say that?"

"I could tell by the sound of their voices that one man was a lot older than the other. The young man was asking when he would get his money, but the old man laughed. That's when the young man got angry and started shouting. The older man started shouting back, and then I heard what sounded like a muffled bang, and then everything went quiet..."

"So what did you do?"

"I froze. I was pretty sure I'd heard a gunshot, but I wasn't one hundred percent certain. I kept looking at the entrance to the stall, figuring someone was going to walk in and shoot me next."

"But that didn't happen?"

"No. There was some scuffling noises, and the next thing I heard was footsteps as someone walked back out the far entrance."

"So what did you do then?"

"I was terrified. I don't think I moved a muscle for a good five minutes. In the end, I went to the edge of the stall and peered out into the walkway. I look both ways and couldn't see anyone, so I decided to go and check…"

"And what did you find?"

"I couldn't see anything at first, just a bunch of straw in an empty stall. But when I looked closer, I saw two legs underneath the straw."

"And then what did you do?"

"I moved away the straw to see if I could help and uncovered a man's face. He was one of the owners, and I'd seen him around the stables."

"Reid Whitecross?"

Roy nodded. "He had a bullet hole just above his eyes. His eyes were still open, like he was staring at something. I'll never forget it."

"So what happened next?"

"I covered his face back over. I'm not sure why, but I just did. I waited for another couple of minutes, debating what to do. I knew I had to get out of there, but I was afraid someone might be waiting outside. Eventually, I left and walked as casually as I could to the manager's office to report what had happened. I got about halfway when a man walked up behind me and grabbed me by the shoulder and demanded to know if I'd been in the stable."

"Had you ever seen him before?"

Roy shook his head. Bridgette could see beads of sweat forming on his forehead as he relived the moment. She thought he was telling the truth and waited patiently until he was ready to continue.

"I tried lying to him. I told him I hadn't been in the stable, but he didn't believe me. He pulled open his jacket and showed me a gun and said if I ever said anything to anyone I was as good as dead."

Bridgette could see Roy's chest heaving and hoped he wasn't having a heart attack. "Are you okay, Roy?"

"It's a nightmare that I've never gotten over. I thought he was going to shoot me there on the spot, but he turned and walked away. I wasn't sure what to do, so I just walked around for about half an hour. In the end, I went to the manager and told him I wasn't feeling well and left for the day."

"You didn't mention what you had seen?"

Roy shook his head again. "I was too scared. I didn't know what to do, so I thought I would go home and think about it first."

"Walter told me about the man coming after you again in his car."

"I was almost home. I'm not sure if he'd been following me all the way or not, but when he told me he knew where I lived, I decided there and then it wasn't worth hanging around. I figured I was a loose end that he'd eventually take care of. So I packed my bags that night and got out before he got a chance…"

Bridgette wanted to ask Roy if she thought he could still recognize the man twenty years later but noticed his face was turning red. Instead, she said, "I know this is hard for you, Roy. Let's take a break for a moment."

Roy mumbled a thank you in response and closed his eyes. Bridgette took a sip of her peppermint tea and decided to give Roy a couple of minutes to compose himself. In no hurry to return to Vancouver, she felt confident Roy would tell her everything he knew if she gave him time. She got up from the easy chair and walked over to the front window to admire the view again. She frowned as she looked down through the tree line to her right and noticed the green Ford she had seen earlier now parked in a cluster of trees just off the graded road.

Without taking her eyes off the road, she said, "The road below us, Roy, where does it lead to?"

She received a weary reply, "Nowhere. It's a dead end about two miles further down the valley. Why do you ask?"

"Who else lives on this road?"

"Just the Smiths and old Bill Mason."

"Do any of them drive a green Ford?"

"Not that I recall. What's going on?"

"Do you get many people visiting the area?"

"Hardly ever."

As Roy got out of his chair, Bridgette responded, "There's a car parked down there…" She paused as she spotted a man making his way cautiously up through the tree line toward the cottage.

Bridgette controlled her breathing as she continued, "Roy, I want you to go into the kitchen and pretend like you're making another cup of tea."

"What's going on?"

Bridgette moved back from the window but maintained a position that enabled her to watch the man's progress. She felt her gut tighten as she replied, "There's someone moving through the tree line below your house. If he were a visitor or a salesman, I would have expected him to walk up your driveway."

Bridgette paused as she watched the man's slow but steady progress. She could tell by his movements that he was trying to remain hidden from view as much as possible and swore under her breath as she caught sight of a pistol in the man's right hand.

Without taking her eyes off the man's progress, Bridgette pulled out her Glock. "How far can you walk, Roy?"

With alarm in his voice, Roy replied, "I can walk for hours if I have to, only every step is painful."

Bridgette had seen enough. The man was less than one hundred yards from the house and closing fast. She knew every second counted. "We need to get out of the house now. Whoever it is, they've got a gun, and they'll be here within a minute."

Sunday - 10:45 A.M.

Bridgette gripped Roy's shoulder when they got to the back door. She whispered, "Let me go first." Holding her Glock in a double-handed grip, she eased out the door and scanned to her left and right. She gambled the man was on his own but knew there was every chance they were walking into an ambush.

She saw no one, and as Roy appeared beside her, she said, "Is there anywhere close by we can hide?"

"Not really. You got a gun, why don't we shoot him?"

"There may be more than one of them. And the odds aren't good if that's the case."

Bridgette stepped off the porch. In a low voice, she said, "We'll go out through the back gate and then head up to the tree line. At least we'll have cover there."

As Roy hobbled after Bridgette at a speed that surprised her, he said, "And then what do we do?"

"We worry about that if we get that far."

Bridgette opened the gate and looked at two paths that

led up to the ridge. The first path she had used earlier and knew it would lead her straight back to her car. It was steeper than the second path that headed off on a diagonal to the left.

Bridgette desperately wanted to take the first path but didn't want to endanger Roy by asking him to do something he wasn't capable of. Instead, she said, "We need a place to hide, Roy. You know the area better than I do."

Roy pointed up to his left. "If we go up this way, I think there's a place we can hide further up."

Bridgette looked back toward the house. She guessed the man would be almost at the front of the house by now. Knowing every second was crucial, she pointed to the left-hand trail. "Hurry, Roy, let's go."

Roy took off with a lumbering gait that was only slightly quicker than a brisk walking pace. To her relief, Spike appeared beside them, oblivious to what was happening as he wagged his tail.

As she quickened her pace, Bridgette said, "Does Spike bark, because now would be a bad time to start."

Without looking back, Roy responded, "Only when he's spooked or frightened. If he stays close to me, I can generally keep him quiet."

Bridgette wasn't totally reassured by the response but decided there wasn't much she could do. They pushed on up a steep rocky path for close to two minutes until they closed in on a densely populated section of trees. Bridgette could hear Roy wheezing and wasn't confident he could go much further without a break.

After looking back over her shoulder to check they hadn't been spotted, she said, "How much further?"

Through labored breath, Roy replied, "About another two minutes."

They climbed another fifty feet, and Bridgette relaxed slightly as they moved into the tree line and out of open country. She was confident they could hide among the trees without being seen for a moment to allow Roy to catch his breath.

Roy sat on a fallen tree just back from the edge of the tree line with Spike sitting at his feet. Bridgette moved forward, hid behind one of the thickest trees she could find, and stared down at the cottage. She watched for close to a minute, relieved that Roy's raspy breathing had subsided. Bridgette was about to inform him it was time to move on when she saw the back door of Roy's cottage door fling open. Bridgette did her best to control her breathing as a man walked out onto the back porch and stood for a moment scanning to his left and right. She could see the gun in his right hand, held upwards and slightly away from his body. Without taking her eyes off the man, she whispered, "Are you ready to go?"

Roy responded in a low voice, "I'm good. You see anything?"

Bridgette watched the man move toward the rear garden gate, and whispered, "He's in your back garden." She watched for a moment as the man paused after opening the gate. She could see him scanning the tree line from right to left. Bridgette felt her gut tighten again as the man appeared to look straight at her. She had been confident she couldn't be seen, but now she wasn't so sure.

After watching the man take off at a sprint, she said, "Let's go, he's coming this way."

Bridgette followed Roy as he continued to hobble up the trail at a pace close to a slow jog. She felt sorry for having to push him hard but knew if they slowed down it could be fatal. Every five or six steps, she looked back over her shoulder, but so far, the man remained out of sight. As Roy shuffled over a small rise in the trail, Bridgette asked, "How much further now, Roy?"

Without stopping, Roy pointed up the trail. "You see that large rock about ninety yards ahead at the top of the rise?"

Looking up through the trees, Bridgette spotted a large flat sandstone boulder to the left of the trail where the ground plateaued. "I see it."

Roy's breathing was starting to labor again, but he continued moving. "That's where we hide." After taking a couple of breaths of air, he added, "The ground drops away beneath the boulder. Underneath is almost like a cave. You can't see it from the track, so unless he stops and starts looking, we should be safe there."

Bridgette looked back but still couldn't see the man. She wasn't sure how far back he was but knew it couldn't be far now. They hurried on until they reached the plateau. Close to exhaustion, Roy limped off the trail and over to the boulder that formed part of the plateau's edge. The boulder was about fifteen feet wide and close to flat. On any other day, Bridgette would have stopped and used it as an observation point to view the valley below. With no time to lose, she followed Roy around the right-hand side of the rock and peered over the edge. The ground dropped away steeply and was covered with a mix of loose rock and weeds.

Roy pointed at the base of the boulder about ten feet below. "It's kind of hollow underneath. I think we can squeeze in there."

Bridgette glanced back and still saw no sign of the man. Doing her best to remain calm, she said, "Do you want me to go first?"

Roy shook his head. "I'll be okay." He eased his way down the slope one step at a time. Bridgette was impressed with how nimble Roy was despite his injury. She waited until he and Spike had taken several steps and took one final look back along the trail. She couldn't see the man yet but could now hear the footfalls of someone moving quickly over rocky ground. Pocketing her Glock, she made her way down the slope using the side of the boulder for balance. When she reached the base, Bridgette pulled out her Glock and looked back up. Still seeing no one, she breathed a small sigh of relief and followed Roy as he squeezed in underneath the overhang.

The overhang was about twelve feet square. Bridgette and Roy huddled in the middle in a squat position with their backs pressed up against the rock face. Bridgette looked out from underneath the overhang to her left and her right. She was reasonably confident the man couldn't see them if he stayed on the path. Spike put a paw up on his master's knee and started a soft whine. Bridgette tensed as she thought he might bark but relaxed a little as Roy motioned for the dog to jump up onto his lap. Spike obeyed and gave Roy a lick on the chin as he settled. Roy whispered, "He won't bark now," and they were silent again.

Bridgette took several deep breaths to compose herself and closed her eyes for a moment to get her breathing under control. Her heart was racing, not through the physical effort of climbing to the ridge but because of what might be coming. She hoped it was only one man and that their hiding place would keep them safe. Bridgette was impressed by Roy's stoic resolve and opened her eyes again to look at the tiny man who sat quietly beside her. She managed half a smile as she watched him calmly pat and soothe his dog while they waited.

Bridgette began to wonder if he'd ever been in such a situation before, but her thoughts were interrupted by the sound of footsteps. She felt Roy's body tense up beside her as they both heard someone moving about above them. Roy looked at Bridgette and pointed upwards with his right finger, and Bridgette nodded. They both knew the man was now standing on the rock-face directly above them. They heard footsteps, two or three at a time before silence and then the pattern repeating itself. Bridgette pictured the man scanning the valley below for any sign of his quarry. She prayed he would move on quickly and not spend any time examining the rock itself. They both heard footsteps again before everything returned to silence. Bridgette looked at Roy who shrugged as if to say, "What's happening?"

Neither of them moved for close to a minute. Bridgette could hear her heartbeat and the sound of a bird calling but nothing else. She wondered if the man had moved on and motioned to Roy that she was going to check. Moving toward the edge of the overhang, she stopped just short, careful not to expose her position to anyone standing above, and looked up to scan the ridgeline as best she could. She tensed again as she saw the man following the trail at a steady pace about sixty feet ahead. Realizing he would be able to spot them if he turned back to look in their direction, she moved back from the edge and whispered, "He's moving further around on the ridgeline."

"He's following the trail again."

"Where does it lead to?"

"Nowhere. It ends in a sheer drop about four hundred yards further around."

Bridgette estimated they had just five or six minutes of breathing space if the man walked the whole distance before turning back. She wasn't sure how closely he would check everything on the way back and decided they wouldn't wait to find out. Moving to the opposite side of the overhang, she said, "Let's go, Roy. Hopefully, we can make it to my car without being spotted."

Sunday - 11:10 A.M.

After climbing out of their hiding place, Bridgette, Roy, and Spike set off at a hurried pace down the trail toward the cottage. They had only gone about two hundred yards before Roy pointed to his left and whispered, "We'll go this way and cut through the trees. There's no path to follow, but we'll get to your car a lot quicker."

Bridgette figured if she didn't know about the shortcut their pursuer wouldn't either. Hoping it may give them the edge and enough time to escape, she replied, "I'm right behind you, Roy."

They made their way up through trees toward the top of the ridge. Bridgette thought moving through long grass and over an occasional fallen tree was much harder for Roy than staying on a trail, but he didn't complain and managed to keep up a steady pace. Although she kept looking back, she couldn't see any sign of the man.

When they reached the top, Roy turned back. "Any sign of him?"

"No, but that makes me nervous. He could be anywhere."

Roy looked down to the footbridge that led to Bridgette's car. "Just a couple more minutes and we'll be out of here."

Bridgette frowned as she surveyed the landscape below. "The trees don't provide us much cover. If he's hiding somewhere, he could easily pick us off..." She thought for a moment and decided they had little option but to keep moving. After taking a deep breath, she added, "We'll have to risk it."

They set off down through the trees toward the bridge, this time with Bridgette leading. The two-minute walk seemed to take twenty as Bridgette kept looking back over her shoulder, expecting to be ripped apart by a bullet at any moment. After crossing the footbridge, Bridgette breathed a sigh of relief as she settled Roy and Spike in the passenger seat of her Mustang.

After getting into the car, she said, "The Mustang is loud, so if he's up there somewhere, he's going to hear it."

Roy nodded. "So I take it we're not hanging around?"

Bridgette shook her head as she started the engine. Shifting the gear shift into reverse, she yelled, "Hang on," as she looked out the rear window and dropped the clutch.

The rear wheels of the Mustang gripped on a mix of dirt and gravel and propelled the car backward. Bridgette backed up for about thirty feet until she felt the car gaining speed. Turning the steering wheel slightly left, she waited a moment until she felt the front of the car start to drift right and then pulled up hard on the handbrake to make the car spin through an almost perfect one-hundred-and-eighty-degree turn.

Roy allowed himself a smile as Bridgette accelerated up the track. "Where did you learn to drive like that?"

Bridgette mumbled, "Police school," in response as she looked in the rearview mirror. She could see no sign of the man and let out an audible sigh. After coming over a rise in the track, she got her first glimpse of Kenmore's house. "Your boss will have left by now, so we're not stopping."

Roy looked slightly bewildered as he nursed Spike on his lap. He nodded in compliance and asked, "So where are we going?"

Bridgette glanced at the rearview mirror again as she shifted into third gear. "Vancouver. No sense stopping until I can guarantee you're safe."

They drove on for close to ten minutes without speaking. Bridgette kept a keen eye on the rearview mirror. So far, she could see no sign of the green Ford that had been parked on the road below Roy's cottage, but she wasn't about to breathe easy. After passing through Riverby, Bridgette turned left onto a road that would lead her back to the main highway.

Roy broke the silence by asking, "Any sign of him?"

Bridgette checked her mirror again. "No, but that doesn't mean anything."

Roy nodded. "Thanks for getting me out of there. I'm pretty sure he'd have eventually found me if I'd been on my own."

Bridgette replied ruefully, "You've got nothing to thank me for, Roy. I'm the one that got you into this mess."

Roy frowned. "I'm not following?"

"This wasn't a coincidence."

Cold Hard Cash

They were silent for a moment before Bridgette added, "I don't understand it. I only discovered your location yesterday afternoon and called your boss on a secure phone from inside police headquarters. Only my chief knew I was coming, and I know he wouldn't have told anyone."

"Perhaps someone else overheard you?"

"I doubt it. Nobody else was in the office."

"Could you have been followed?"

As she glanced in the rearview mirror again, Bridgette replied, "I'm sure I was. Call me paranoid, but I saw no one suspicious in my rearview mirror, and I checked regularly."

"Did you tell anyone my address?"

Bridgette shook her head. "Like I said, only my boss."

Roy let out a sigh as he patted Spike. "So what happens now?"

"When I get a few more miles under our belt, I'll call my boss. You'll have to be placed in witness protection until we figure out who's behind this."

Roy let out another sigh. "I'm going to miss Kenmore Stud. I really liked it there…"

"I'm sorry, Roy. Had I known I was putting you in so much danger, I would have done things differently…"

Bridgette left Roy to his thoughts. She was furious with herself for what had happened and wondered again how someone had managed to track her every move. When she couldn't come up with any answers, she decided to come back to it later with a clearer mind. Bridgette knew she should call Delray but wanted to ask Roy a couple of questions first.

Without taking her eyes off the road, she said, "We never finished our interview. Do you mind if I ask you a few more questions?"

"Okay."

Bridgette admired Roy's positive attitude. He had every right to be bitter with her for exposing him, but he seemed to be accepting of his fate.

"The man who threatened to kill you twenty years ago. Would you recognize him if you saw him again now?"

"Maybe. People can change a lot, so I'm not sure. If I saw a photo of him from twenty years ago, I'd definitely recognize him."

Bridgette nodded once but kept her eyes focused on the road. "And you'd never seen him before? He wasn't a regular at the racetrack?"

"No. I described him to Walter later on, but he didn't seem to know who he was either. That was the reason I kept calling Walter every six months. I just wanted to know if he'd come back looking for me."

Bridgette pondered the answer for a moment. Roy's confidence in being able to identify the man made him valuable to her case, but after their narrow escape, it was clear he had every right to still fear for his life.

Bridgette went to ask another question but let out an audible gasp instead and exclaimed, "Son of a bitch!"

Roy looked at her with alarm as she changed down gears and pulled a hard left onto a side road. "What's wrong?"

Bridgette bit down on her bottom lip for a moment to calm her nerves. Through gritted teeth, she said, "Maybe nothing, maybe everything…"

Bridgette drove about a hundred yards down the road before she braked hard and stopped the car. After switching off the engine, she said, "Sit tight, Roy. This won't take long."

Reaching under the dashboard, Bridgette pulled a lever

that popped the Mustang's hood. She got out of the car, walked around to the front of the vehicle, and stood for a moment studying the grill. Moving forward, she undid the safety latch and raised the hood. She studied the engine bay for close to two minutes but couldn't find what she was looking for. Frowning, she lowered the hood and checked underneath her car.

With curiosity getting the better of Roy, he got out of the car and asked, "What are you looking for?" as he watched her feel inside the Mustang's left rear wheel arch with her hand.

Bridgette mumbled, "Got it," as she removed a small magnetized box about the size of a cigarette packet. She had no doubt what it was even before she held it up for Roy to see.

After studying it for a moment, Roy said, "Is that what I think it is?"

Bridgette nodded. "It's a GPS tracker. This is why I never saw him following me. With one of these, he could follow me on a laptop or even on his phone from a safe distance, probably miles back."

Roy asked, "What are you going to do with it?" as he watched Bridgette place it on the hood.

As she pulled out her smartphone, Bridgette responded, "I'm going to photograph it and leave it here."

Roy frowned. "I don't want to tell you your job or nothing, but shouldn't we be taking it with us? Maybe you can get fingerprints off it or something?"

"Possibly, but I don't have the equipment, and right now, we need to get out of here."

After taking two photographs, Bridgette picked up the device and hurled it into long grass about twenty feet off the road.

Roy watched it land. "You're not going to destroy it first?"

Bridgette shook her head. "Right now, he's almost certainly still following us. If I destroy it, he'll know we've found it. Better to leave it here and keep going. I'll let my boss know it's location and we'll get a local cop to come find it later."

As they climbed back into the Mustang, Bridgette said, "I'm sorry, Roy. This wouldn't have happened if I'd gone into work and gotten a pool car."

"So how did he know you'd be driving your Mustang?"

Bridgette looked at Roy as she started the engine. "That's a great question. When I figure it out, you'll be the first to know."

Bridgette put the car into gear and pulled a U-turn to head back to the main road. She would have given anything for some thinking time to ponder Roy's question, but right now, she needed to call Delray. After turning left onto the main road again, she pressed speed dial on her phone before glancing in her rearview mirror as the car accelerated. She saw no one following her and hoped it would stay that way as she shifted into top gear.

Sunday - 2:05 P.M.

After finishing her call with Delray, Bridgette needed time to think. She had been surprised at how calm he remained as she relayed the story of being followed to Roy's cottage and their subsequent escape. Delray had promised to organize witness protection for Roy, and they both agreed that now she was back on the main highway, a police escort was probably unnecessary. She was still troubled by the knowledge that someone had placed a GPS tracker on her Mustang and had spoken to Delray about it. He was also perplexed and adamant he hadn't spoken to anyone. They both doubted a phone tap had been set up inside police headquarters, but Delray promised to have it checked out, anyway. She did the math and realized whoever had placed the tracker on her car had less than ten hours to do so before her road trip. It seemed improbable that someone would know so much about her investigation and be able to respond so rapidly. Bridgette wasn't easily deterred from any problem and was confident in time she could find the answer.

She glanced across at Roy, who sat impassively on the passenger seat stroking Spike as he stared out through the windshield. She realized the road trip might be her last opportunity to interview Roy properly before he went into witness protection, and she still had a few more questions to ask him. After glancing in the rearview mirror, she said, "How are you feeling, Roy?"

"Okay, I guess. This has all been a big shock…"

"We're not going to be taking any risks. When we get back, you'll be placed in witness protection. I'm hoping tomorrow or Tuesday, they'll allow me to interview you again to see if we can identify the man who came after you with a gun."

"Like I said before, if you've got a photo of the man, I'm sure I could identify him."

"I don't have any firm suspects yet, so we'll start by using a software program to help build a likeness for the man you saw. We'll get one of our police graphic artists to sit with you, and you can describe the man's features as best you can."

Roy nodded. "Can I ask you a question, detective?"

"Sure, but call me Bridgette."

"You said you were investigating a double murder?"

Bridgette realized that she hadn't given Roy the full background of the case before they had to escape. "We found two bodies in a cave on an island in Stone Bay. One body had been there a long time which we believe is a horse breeder by the name of Reid Whitecross."

"And the other body?"

"The other body has only been there several months. The victim was also shot in the head. We're running DNA matches against the two victims now, but we believe the other victim is Owen Whitecross, Reid's son." Out of the corner of her eye, Bridgette noticed Roy's chest heave. "You knew Owen?"

"Not well, but I'd met him a few times at NewFarm. He was a nice young man. Treated all us stable hands well." Roy paused for a moment and then added, "There's something else you should know…"

Bridgette tried to hide her eagerness. "Okay."

"I never told Walter that I recognized the man who'd been murdered in the stable. I figured the less he knew the better, for his own safety. When I called him about a year ago, he mentioned Owen Whitecross had started asking a lot of questions about what had happened to his father. He even asked Walter if he knew where I was."

This was new information to Bridgette. She made a mental note to interview Walter again. "Did Walter know why Owen was suddenly interested in his father?"

"According to Walter, Owen never stopped trying to find out what happened. Walter isn't sure, but he thinks Owen must have found out something. But he didn't say what."

Before she could ask her next question, Roy added, "When I called Walter six months ago, I asked about Owen again, and he said he was still looking for answers. According to Walter, he was spending more time than ever trying to figure out what happened."

"I interviewed Owen's wife briefly on Friday. We weren't sure at that stage if the body in the cave was her husband. But now that we know for sure, I'm going to need to visit her again."

"She may not be able to help you."

"Why do you say that?"

"After my last call to Walter, I got Owen's phone number and decided to call him."

"After all these years, why contact him now?"

"I was afraid for him. I guess I didn't want him to end up like me or worse, so I called to warn him."

"So what did you say to him?"

"I told him everything I just told you. I told him about the argument and even described the man who had threatened me with the gun."

"And what did he say?"

"He said, 'It all fits.'"

Bridgette frowned and checked in her rearview mirror again. "That's all he said?"

"That's the funny thing—not for one moment did I get the impression he thought I was involved. It's almost as if he knew who killed his father but couldn't prove it. I kind of got the feeling he knew he was on dangerous ground and was being very careful."

"So what happened then?"

"He begged me to turn myself in to the police and tell them everything I knew. But after everything I'd been through, I couldn't… We spoke for a couple more minutes, and he kept pleading with me. I felt sorry for him, but there was no way I was coming back."

Roy let out a sigh. "I told him I didn't think it was a good idea to be pursuing this and after what you just told me, I guess I was right…"

They were quiet again, before Roy added, "It just doesn't make sense. A father and his son murdered twenty years apart. Who the hell does that?"

"We don't know yet, Roy, but you've given us a lot to work with."

Bridgette kept checking the rearview mirror as the Mustang cruised down the highway at just above the legal speed limit, but she saw no sign of the green Ford. After another twenty minutes of driving, she was alone with her thoughts as Roy and Spike both drifted off to sleep.

She continued to puzzle over how someone had managed to find out about her road trip and follow her. While she didn't have the whole answer yet, she had a theory that was worth exploring. She had a lot to talk about with Delray when she got back to Vancouver and mentally added another item to the list.

Sunday - 10:00 P.M.

Felix Delray answered his desk phone on the third ring. It was late on a Sunday night, and he was keen to leave the office and head home to sleep. He answered with his usual trademark, "Delray," and absentmindedly drummed his fingers on his desk as he listened intently. After about thirty seconds, he responded, "So we'll schedule the interview for Tuesday then?"

Delray listened for a moment longer before the caller disconnected. He looked at his wall clock and sighed as he thought about the busy week ahead of him. After mumbling, "One more call," he pressed speed dial and was relieved when his call was answered.

"Hi, chief."

"Hi, Bridgette. I just got the call from Maystone. Roy and his dog have arrived at the safe house, and they're settling in."

There was silence for a moment before she responded, "Well...that's a relief."

"Like I said, Bridgette, don't beat yourself up over this. You weren't to know you were being followed."

"I can't help but feel responsible."

"He's still alive, Bridgette. You got him out of there safe and sound. That wouldn't have happened if you hadn't been thinking on your feet."

"How is he feeling?"

"According to Maystone, he's in good spirits, but they won't let us re-interview him until Tuesday. They want him to settle in first, and they need to do their own debriefing."

"Are we allowed to bring a graphic artist with us? Roy is confident he can give us a good likeness of what the man looked like twenty years ago."

"I'll organize that tomorrow after we hear back from Maystone."

"So I guess we won't be meeting Roy at the safe house?"

"Not a chance. The interview will probably happen in the back of a van, but that's their call. We won't know the location until about twenty minutes beforehand." Delray stifled a yawn and then continued, "Our witness protection program has a perfect record, and they're keen to keep it that way. After what happened today, they won't be taking any chances."

There was a pause before Bridgette responded, "I know you're tired, chief, but can I discuss one more thing with you?"

Delray smiled to himself. He had deliberately sent Bridgette home to get some sleep but realized that wouldn't happen if she was still churning things over in her mind. As he looked up at his wall clock again, he answered, "Go for it."

"I've been thinking through how someone managed to place a tracking device on my car to follow me."

"Okay."

"I think they just got lucky."

Delray frowned. "I'm not following?"

"I didn't leave the office until well after six last night. The only person who knew I was going on a road trip less than twelve hours later was you. I've been working this case since Thursday, and I've interviewed a number of people…"

"So what are you saying? Somebody was already tracking you?"

"I have no proof of that, it's just a theory."

Delray scratched his chin. "It makes sense. It wouldn't be the first time someone from Vancouver Metro's been followed while on an investigation."

"They may have had no idea where I was headed but followed me anyway."

Delray drummed his fingers on his desk again. He knew it would have been harder for someone to track her if she had come in and gotten a pool car, but hindsight was a wonderful thing. Instead, he responded, "I've got to say, Bridgette, after your close call, the thought of someone following you like this concerns me."

"I'm more worried about Roy. The more I think about it, the more positive I am he did the right thing running twenty years ago."

"Well, whoever is after him is out of luck. Nobody knows where he is now, not even you or me."

"Hopefully our graphic artist can get a good likeness of the man."

Delray nodded as he pictured the two murder victims slumped against the wall in the cave. "We've come a long way since last Wednesday, Bridgette, mostly thanks to you.

Finding Roy alive and well puts us in a good position to close this case sooner rather than later."

"Let's hope so."

"What are your plans for tomorrow?"

"I thought after I meet my new partner, we'd interview Jane Whitecross. Now that Roy has confirmed the identity of the older of the two victims as her husband's father, I don't think we need to wait for the DNA test. Also, I want to go and re-interview Walter. I don't think he tipped off whoever has been following me, but I want to make certain."

Delray thought Bridgette was being overly generous referring to Aaron Sterling as her new partner but let it slide. "I like your thinking. Now that we've got a clear pathway forward, I'm going to lay down some ground rules for Aaron Sterling. You're doing a great job, and I don't want this derailed by someone who, frankly, I don't trust."

"Thanks, chief. I appreciate your support."

"I'll see you tomorrow morning. Try to get some sleep."

Bridgette promised she would and disconnected. Delray hit another speed dial button on his desk phone and waited to be connected. After the call was answered, he said gently, "I'm on my way," and then replaced the handset. He stretched for a moment before rising from his desk. As he put on his coat, he managed a weary smile as he thought about his wife of thirty years. He marveled at how patient she was with his long hours and made a mental note to buy her flowers before the week was out.

After switching off the light to his office, Delray headed for the elevator. He was pleased with the progress of their investigation but was still troubled by the thought Bridgette had been followed. She had survived today, but he knew whoever came after her was still out there.

He sighed as he pushed the elevator button to head to the basement parking lot. He hoped now that Roy Pepper was in protective custody that would be the end of it, but his gut told him otherwise.

Monday - 9:25 A.M.

Bridgette pulled up in front of the two-story white colonial house in Stone Bay and sat with the motor running while she thought about what was ahead of her. She had last visited the stone and timber house in the upmarket suburb three days earlier with photos of the jacket worn by the most recent of the two murder victims. The interview had been cut short as Jane Whitecross had broken down as soon as she saw the photos. Bridgette hoped the interview would go better today but wasn't convinced. She had called earlier to set up the time and found it difficult to answer Whitecross's question if she knew for sure the murder victim was her husband. Her response, "I'd like to discuss this when I meet you," had left Whitecross in tears and Bridgette fully expecting this interview would also be short.

Bridgette sighed and switched off the engine. There were parts of her job she really loved and parts she despised. Being stuck in an underground cavern with two decomposing bodies seemed pleasant in comparison to what she was about to do. As a detective with less than three months' experience, she couldn't imagine ever getting used to this part of the job.

Her phone rang as she stepped out of the car. She pressed answer, and Delray's voice cut in before she had time to say hello.

"You at the Whitecrosses' yet?"

Bridgette glanced at her watch. "I've just arrived, although I feel guilty that I'm not going to be in that meeting with you."

"I'm sure Cunningham will chew me out a little, but after what happened yesterday with Roy Pepper, I don't want this investigation slowed down while Sterling settles in. I won't keep you, but I wanted you to know the coroner's office has confirmed the DNA match for Owen Whitecross."

Bridgette sighed. "Well…it's good to have final confirmation of the victim's identity."

"I know this won't be easy for you, Bridgette, but I'm sure you can handle it."

Bridgette grimaced. "It's not me you have to worry about," she said as she looked up at the colonial house again.

"I have to go. Call me when you've finished the interview." He disconnected.

Bridgette walked up the cobblestone footpath and braced herself before pressing the doorbell. She took one step back as she heard the bell chime somewhere inside the house. After waiting close to thirty seconds, the door was opened by a woman in her early forties with a slender figure and shoulder-length brown hair. Bridgette could tell by the redness in her eyes that Jane Whitecross had been crying.

"Hello, Jane, thanks for seeing me on such short notice."

Whitecross responded wearily, "Come in, Bridgette."

Bridgette was led into a large formal living room that contained three chestnut-colored leather couches set up in a U shape around a stone fireplace.

Whitecross said, "Please sit down, Bridgette, I won't be long," and then disappeared through a door on the far side of the room.

Bridgette had no idea where Jane Whitecross had gone but was thankful for the extra time she had to rehearse what she was about to say.

Whitecross returned a moment later followed by a man with a medium build in his early forties. Dressed in chinos and a blue shirt, the man had a somber look on his face as he walked into the room.

As the two sat down next to each other, Jane Whitecross made the introductions. "Ethan, this is Detective Cash. Detective Cash, this is Owen's brother, Ethan. He doesn't live far away, and I decided I couldn't hear this on my own…"

They both sat stony-faced, staring at Bridgette and waiting for her to speak. Bridgette decided there was no point delaying the bad news any further. "We got a call from the coroner's office this morning." She paused a moment. "They confirmed a DNA match for one of the victims with Owen's hair sample."

As Jane Whitecross burst into tears, Bridgette added, "I'm so sorry, Jane…"

All three sat without speaking for close to a minute. Bridgette felt like an intruder as she watched Jane Whitecross weep while Ethan Whitecross did his best to comfort his sister-in-law.

Knowing she had no words of comfort, she waited until Jane Whitecross was ready to speak.

After wiping her eyes, Whitecross looked up. "So what happens now? Do I need to identify Owen's body?"

"That won't be necessary. Your husband's body will remain at the coroner's office for the time being. I'm not sure how long that will be, but the priority is finding out who murdered him."

Ethan Whitecross spoke for the first time. "So what about the other body? Do you know the identity yet?"

"Not yet."

Ethan held Bridgette's gaze. "But you think it's my father, don't you?"

"We don't have a final DNA report on the second victim yet, but the coroner thinks it's likely."

Ethan closed his eyes. "When will you know for sure?"

"Probably tomorrow."

Ethan Whitecross tried to compose himself. Bridgette could see the muscles in his neck twitch as he demanded, "Who does this? Why would someone do this to my family?"

Bridgette studied Whitecross's body language, which was a mixture of grief and anger but mostly anger. So far, his grief seemed genuine, but even in her short career, she had been exposed to people who were masters of deception.

She let the question hang for a moment and then responded, "That's what we're going to find out, Ethan."

Whitecross let out a long breath. "So what happens now, detective?"

"We have a full-scale murder investigation underway." Bridgette explained the breakthrough they had made in finding Roy Pepper but was careful to avoid mentioning his name.

Jane Whitecross frowned. "So this man saw Reid's murder?"

"Not exactly. He was working in a nearby stall and heard what sounded like a gunshot. He was threatened outside the stall some minutes later by a man with a gun who we believe is the killer." Bridgette explained how they were going to re-interview Roy tomorrow and hoped to have an artist's impression drawn up of what the man looked like. "Once we have this impression, I'd like to come back and show it to you and other family members. It's possible the man who murdered Reid Whitecross, and probably Owen as well, is known to you."

Bridgette watched the body language between Jane and Ethan Whitecross. She saw pain and grief in their eyes. Neither of them seemed to fear the prospect of the artist's impression being developed as Jane Whitecross responded, "So this could be the breakthrough?"

"We're hoping so, yes."

Jane Whitecross stared at Bridgette for a moment. She could see the pain giving way to anger as Whitecross responded, "It's a pity this man didn't come forward earlier. My husband might still be alive if that were the case."

Bridgette decided there was nothing to be gained by getting into an argument trying to defend Roy. She steered the conversation by asking, "I know this is a very hard time for you both, but now that we know for sure Owen is one of the victims, I'd like to ask you some questions."

Ethan Whitecross's eyes widened. "Surely you don't suspect either of us of being involved in these murders?"

"This is just routine. I'd like to begin by compiling a list of Owen's relatives, friends, and business associates. Also, if you know of anyone who had a grudge against Owen, even if it was a long time ago, I'll need that information as well."

Jane Whitecross looked drained. "I'm not sure I'm up to this right now."

Bridgette was relieved when Ethan Whitecross said, "Well, I am, so where do you want to start, detective?"

Two hours later, Bridgette emerged from the house armed with a mass of new information about Owen Whitecross. She considered the interview had been productive and had received cooperation from both Jane and Ethan Whitecross. As she headed for her car, she checked her phone messages. There were two from Delray, both asking her to call him as soon as possible.

After getting into her car, she pressed speed dial and waited to be connected.

Delray answered on the fourth ring. "I was wondering when I'd hear from you. How did the interview go?"

"Better than I expected." Bridgette explained how Ethan Whitecross had been present at the interview and how she had gained a lot of useful background information about Owen, his father, and their wider family.

"Do you think either of them is involved in the murders?"

"It's too soon to tell, but I don't think so. Ethan Whitecross was only seventeen when his father was murdered, and Jane Whitecross was Jane Pierce back then and didn't meet her future husband until three years after Reid Whitecross disappeared. That makes them unlikely suspects based on what we found in the cave."

"I agree. I think we're looking for someone who murdered both of them. So what's next for you?"

"I was planning on re-interviewing Walter unless you need me back at the office?"

"No, don't come back here. I'll be forced to saddle you

with Aaron Sterling, and I'd like to avoid that for as long as possible."

"How did the meeting go this morning?"

"Predictable. Cunningham went off his head when you weren't here. I waited 'til he'd finished and then explained the developments with Roy Pepper. He seemed to calm down then but was insistent you bring Sterling into the investigation today."

"I'm happy to swing by the office and pick him up on my way out to see Walter."

"No. He'll only slow you down. Come and see me when you get back, and we'll work out a plan."

"Okay. I'll head to NewFarm."

"There's something else you need to know…"

"And what's that?"

"Charlie Bates made bail this morning."

Bridgette reeled a little. "How did that happen?"

"I asked the same question. I talked to a prosecutor who was in court this morning. He seemed to think Charlie's old lawyer was more interested in keeping him in the jail than getting him out on bail."

"Old lawyer? I'm not sure I'm following?"

"Derek Sirocca was his lawyer until Friday, but Bates fired him. With no prior record and no witness to identify him as the man who shot at you in the basement, Bates *should* have made bail. My prosecutor friend believes Sirocca was doing his best to keep Bates inside. We know he can't afford someone of Sirocca's caliber, so my bet is whoever hired Sirocca gave him instructions to keep Bates in jail."

"Maybe he thinks Charlie is a threat? It would be much easier to control someone if they're in jail rather than out on the streets."

"Or have them killed, which I think is where this was heading…"

Bridgette thought for a moment about her jail visit with Bates. "Do you think he'll hang around?"

"My guess is no. If he thinks whoever he was working for has got it in for him, he's got more than an attempted murder charge to worry about."

Bridgette couldn't help but agree as she said goodbye to Delray and disconnected. She thought back to her last conversation with Bates and his apology, which seemed heartfelt and genuine. Part of her still despised the man for betraying her, but part of her also felt sorry for him. She whispered, "You've dug yourself a deep hole, Charlie," as she started the engine. As she pulled out from the curb, she wondered what he was doing now that he was out on bail.

Monday - 3:15 P.M.

Bridgette pulled up against the curb a full block short of Charlie Bates's apartment block. She looked down the street through the gathering crowd of onlookers and counted off six police cars and one ambulance in front of the building. Amidst the chaos of flashing lights and a traffic jam, she watched as uniformed police officers instructed bystanders to keep back from the police tape that sectioned off the main entrance and driveway. Knowing this was as close as she would get with her car, she switched the engine off and sat for a moment surveying the scene in front of her.

The call had come through from Delray fifteen minutes earlier just as she was returning to the South Metro building after interviewing Walter Denphy. Delray had been brief, informing her that Charlie Bates had been murdered outside his apartment block. He'd given her a few sketchy details about the crime scene, but the shock of learning about Bates's demise had shaken her, and she heard little of the remaining conversation. She thought Delray mentioned Bates had been found in his car, but she wasn't sure. Bridgette took a deep breath as she got out of the car. A thousand thoughts raced through her mind as she walked toward the crime scene. A small voice inside her told her this was all connected to her mother's murder—something Bridgette found hard to challenge.

As she weaved her way through the crowd of onlookers and approached the police tape, she spotted Delray to her left in deep conversation with a uniformed officer. She was about to change direction but stopped dead in her tracks as the crowd parted and she saw Charlie Bates's white Honda resting up against a retaining wall just a few feet short of the street. She could see scrape marks on the wall behind the vehicle. Telltale signs that the Honda had careened into the wall at the side of the building and plowed forward for several feet before finally coming to a halt. Bridgette felt her stomach churn as she caught sight of Charlie Bates's body slumped in the driver seat. Her view was partially obscured by a police photographer who was busy taking photographs of her former colleague. She moved to her right to get a better view and stopped again as she saw the single small spiderweb bullet hole in the Honda's windshield. Bridgette flashed her badge at a young uniformed officer who was doing his best to keep the crowd at bay and moved in under the police tape. She found herself moving toward the Honda as if being drawn by a magnetic force. She closed to within about fifteen feet before she felt a firm hand grab her by the shoulder. As she was spun around, she expected to see Delray and was slightly startled as she stared into the face of Aaron Sterling.

Sterling wasted no time with pleasantries. "You're not authorized to be inside the police tape, detective. This is an Internal Investigations matter now and has nothing to do with you."

"I thought you became my partner today?"

"The assistant commissioner has made me lead investigator for this." Sterling couldn't suppress a condescending smile as he added, "I'm not sure who's going to babysit you now, but it won't be me."

Bridgette ignored the put-down. "So what happened?"

Sterling took a quick glance back toward the Honda. "Bates got himself shot in the head is what happened. And like I said, this is a crime scene, and we don't need a crowd, so move back behind the tape."

Undeterred, Bridgette responded, "Surely as a detective and a former colleague of Charlie's, I have a right—"

Sterling raised his voice. "Are you deaf? Move back now!"

Before she had a chance to respond, she heard Delray's voice behind her. "Sterling, stop making an ass of yourself and keep your voice down."

Sterling responded, "I'll remind you, chief inspector, neither you or the detective here have any right to be behind this police tape."

Delray shot back in a low voice, "And I'll remind you, detective, we all work for the same police force, and right now, you're drawing attention to yourself in a public place where there are news crews with cameras operating."

Sterling held Delray's gaze and lowered his voice. "I'm still going to have to ask you to move back behind the police tape. I have my orders from Assistant Commissioner Cunningham."

Delray turned to Bridgette. "Detective, please move back behind the tape. I'll be with you in a minute."

Bridgette nodded once. She was in no mood for an argument and was happy to leave that to Delray and Sterling. After moving back behind the tape, she made her way through the crowd and around to the apartment block's driveway to get a closer look at the Honda. Bridgette studied the bullet hole in the windshield. It was impossible to tell the angle of the shot, but she wondered if the shooter had fired from directly across the street or higher up. She had no sooner turned to study the building opposite when Delray joined her.

Delray shook his head. "Sorry you had to put up with that nonsense. Sterling needs to learn some manners."

Without taking her eyes off the building opposite, Bridgette asked, "Did you get it sorted out?"

"Let's just say, I'll be having words with Cunningham. I'm not a fan of making official complaints, but the guy needs to take his head out of his ass."

Delray followed Bridgette's gaze and looked up at the building as he added, "I've spoken with two uniformed cops. Only one witness has come forward so far. He was waiting for an Uber across the street and saw Bates walk down the driveway into the underground parking lot. The Honda appeared less than a minute later. He heard a bang and thought it was the car backfiring at first until the Honda hit the wall."

"So Charlie wouldn't have had time to go back to his apartment?"

"Doesn't look like it. I guess he knew how much trouble he was in and just wanted to get his car and get out of here."

Delray sighed and turned back to face the Honda. "Death was instant. He took a bullet to his left temple as he came up from the parking lot."

"A professional hit?"

Delray nodded. "Almost certain. One shot. The guy who did this knew what he was doing."

"Charlie was a free man for less than four hours. Whoever did this was well organized."

"It makes you wonder what they're trying to hide when they act so quickly." Turning to Bridgette, Delray said in a softer voice, "I can't help but think this is all connected to the basement incident and to your mother's murder."

"The same thought crossed my mind."

"I want you to continue to focus on the Rook Island murders, Bridgette. Cunningham's made it clear we're to stay out of this."

Bridgette let out a long breath. "It's hard when you know this is probably connected to your family…"

Delray held Bridgette's gaze. "I made a promise to you that we would get to the bottom of this, and we will. I might not be investigating Charlie's murder, but the commissioner still wants my help with resolving the basement incident, so this doesn't change anything."

Bridgette nodded.

Delray added, "Do you trust me?"

"Yes."

"When something breaks, you will be the first to know."

"Thanks, chief."

Delray and Bridgette turned as one to face the Honda as a stretcher was placed next to the car in preparation for the removal of Charlie Bates's body.

Delray choked a little as he said, "What he did was very wrong, but I can't believe he's gone…"

Bridgette thought back to her last conversation with Bates at the city jail. The image of him saying "I'm sorry" through the thick glass that separated them would be forever etched in her memory. While she still found it hard to forgive him, she hoped he had found some comfort in his remorse. Suddenly keen to get away from the crime scene, she said to Delray, "I've got a lot to tell you about my interviews today, but this isn't the time or place."

"I'm going to hang around until Cunningham arrives, but I'll see you as soon as I get back to the office."

As Bridgette turned to leave, Delray said, "I find it hard to believe whoever did this could organize a professional hit so quickly."

Bridgette's eyes were drawn back to the Honda as two ambulance officers lifted Bates's body out of the car and carefully laid it on the stretcher. As she watched a sheet be placed over his body, she replied, "I asked Charlie if he knew who he was working for when I visited him in prison."

"And what did he say?"

"He wouldn't give me a direct answer. He hinted he was fairly sure he knew who it was, but I got the impression he had no hard proof."

"Well, if Charlie can find out, so can we. We've just got to make sure no one else gets killed in the process."

Part II

Tuesday - 3:15 P.M.

After getting the call from witness protection that her interview with Roy Pepper was going ahead, Bridgette drove as instructed to a shopping mall in the affluent suburb of Beaumont Park. She then waited in the mall's street-level parking lot for close to twenty minutes, with her companion Raylene Griffin, Vancouver Metro's resident forensic and courtroom sketch artist.

Griffin, a slim African-American woman with a penchant for beads in her hair, leather jackets, and sunglasses, took the opportunity for a quick nap. Other than her initial meeting with the witness protection unit on Sunday, this was Bridgette's first time meeting someone in the program. She had studied this part of policing as part of her criminology degree but had learned the practice of managing people in a program depended very much on each individual's circumstances.

Without opening her eyes, Griffin said, "Relax, detective, they'll call soon."

Bridgette looked across at Griffin. "You can tell I'm not relaxed?"

Griffin smiled a little. "Tapping your fingers on the steering wheel. A sure sign you're a little tense."

She stopped tapping. "I'll try to remember that."

As Griffin opened her eyes and straightened up, Bridgette asked, "So how long do you think until the next call?"

"Hard to say," said Griffin as she put on her sunglasses. "The guys that run witness protection are understandably neurotic."

"So what normally happens from here?"

"One of three things. One, we get told to go somewhere else and wait for further instructions. Two, we get told to drive to a location for the meet. Or three, if they don't like the setup or think someone has followed us, they'll cancel."

Bridgette was about to respond when her phone rang. Griffin smiled and said, "There's your answer."

After picking up the phone and pressing answer, she said, "Detective Cash."

The voice on the line said, "We're clearing you to proceed to the meet location. It's one-forty-one Maxwell Street in Beaumont Park. You should be in position in less than five minutes."

"So we're meeting at a safe house?"

"No. Pull up out front and wait. It's a quiet leafy street with good exits at both ends. We'll do the interview in the back of the van if everything checks out."

The line went dead. Bridgette relayed the message to Griffin as she looked up Maxwell Street on her smartphone.

Griffin replied, "Meeting in a van is quite normal if it's just one person in the program, particularly in winter when it's not so hot. There's less risk than with moving the witness in and out of a house, and if something looks off, the van can disappear quickly."

Bridgette started the engine and checked her rearview mirror as she exited the parking lot. Roy had been on her mind all morning, and she hoped he was settling into his new life.

As they drove toward the meeting point, Griffin said, "This Roy Pepper, how old is he?"

"Mid-fifties would be my guess."

Griffin nodded. "And this guy who I'm sketching—Pepper hasn't seen him in twenty years, right?"

Bridgette glanced sideways at Griffin as she continued driving. "No. Is it going to be hard to get a likeness?"

"Yeah. People's memories of faces they don't see regularly fade after just a few months unless there was something memorable about the meeting."

She hoped this would be the case with Roy. "So what's the plan?"

"I've brought a laptop with the software, but I think we'll go old school?"

Bridgette indicated right and said, "As in draw by hand?" as she turned into a suburban street.

"You got it. When it's hand sketched, we're leaving it more open to interpretation. It's just a likeness, and people you show it to are more inclined to think, 'Maybe I've seen this guy.'"

"That's not the case with a computer image?"

"No. People tend to be definitive and sometimes get it wrong."

"This is going to take a while?"

Griffin nodded. "I've got a book of face shots of people I'll give him to pick eyes, chins, and so on from. That will help speed up the process, but it might still be a couple of hours before we get a solid image we're happy with."

They drove on until Bridgette turned left into Maxwell Street. She could see why witness protection had picked the street. It was long and straight and provided an uninterrupted view of both adjoining crossroads. As she cruised down the tree-lined street looking for number one-forty-one, Griffin admired the row of houses, mostly two stories with double garages and all with manicured gardens. "Man, this is some neighborhood."

There were only a handful of cars parked on the street, and Bridgette had no trouble parking in front of a two-story Tudor-style house with a matching brick mailbox that read one-forty-one.

Griffin added, "So what do you think houses go for here?"

Without taking her eyes off the rearview mirror, she responded, "I'm not up on real estate, Raylene, but well over a million would be my guess."

Bridgette's focus switched to the street in front of them as Griffin said, "They'll come in a large van. Usually white, and usually a Mercedes."

They waited another two minutes before Bridgette saw a large white van turn into Maxwell Street. It was a late-model Mercedes, just as Griffin had predicted. Bridgette thought the magnetic signs stuck on the side panels that read "Edward's Carpet" were a nice touch.

The vehicle cruised up the street at a slow speed before pulling up to a stop directly behind them.

Griffin said, "We wait here. They'll come and get us when they're ready."

Thirty seconds later, a marshal from the witness protection program got out of the van and made his way around to Bridgette's door. After she wound down her window, the man leaned in close and ignored Bridgette for a moment as he greeted Griffin. The two had obviously worked together before, and Bridgette waited patiently until he turned his attention to her and said, "I'll get you to follow me to the side door of the van, detective. Roy is waiting in the back for you."

The marshal went on to explain that because of space issues Bridgette and Griffin would be on their own in the back with Roy. As they walked toward the van, he added, "My partner and I will remain up front with the engine running. If we see anything we don't like, we'll pull out and go mobile."

Before she could respond, the marshal opened the door and motioned for her to climb in.

Bridgette's face broke into a brief smile as she saw Roy sitting on a bench seat behind a small table on the opposite side of the van. As she climbed into the van, she said, "Hello, Roy. It's good to see you."

Roy smiled back. "It's good to see you too, Bridgette."

Bridgette sat next to Roy and introduced Griffin as she settled in on the opposite side of the table. After the two exchanged greetings, Bridgette filled the gap in conversation while Griffin set up her sketchpad and pencils on the table.

"How's Spike?"

Roy nodded. "Spike's good, but they wouldn't let me bring him. One marshal stayed back at the safe house to mind him."

"How are you settling in?"

"Okay, I guess. I'm not sleeping very well. I think it's going to take me a while to adjust."

"I'm sure that's normal."

Griffin finished setting up her drawing equipment. "Okay, Roy, are you ready to start?"

A bead of sweat formed on Roy's brow. "I guess."

Bridgette said, "We know it's been a long time, Roy, and nobody is expecting perfection."

Griffin added, "What we're really after is just a likeness—an image that may prompt someone to say, 'Maybe I know this guy.'"

Griffin flipped a large wire-bound folder around to face Roy. As she opened it up to the first page, she said, "This is a photo album of people with all different faces, skin colors, and hairstyles. None of them are criminals—they're just faces we'll use to help us put together a composite of the man who attacked you."

Roy looked at Bridgette. "I'll do my best, but I've never done anything like this before."

Bridgette said reassuringly, "Almost everyone who does this is doing it for the first time. You'll be fine."

Griffin said, "I'm assuming your attacker was white?"

Roy nodded.

"The front section is all Caucasian males. Just relax and take your time. See if you can see anyone that has a face shape like your attacker's."

Roy frowned. "Face shape?"

Bridgette said, "See if you can pick out anyone with a similar jawline. We can use that as a starting point."

Griffin added, "Don't worry if the nose, ears, or mouth are different. Just concentrate on the shape of the face itself."

Roy answered, "Okay," and then began to flip through the pages. Bridgette relaxed a little when Roy settled into a pattern of studying each face for a few seconds before moving on to the next one. After he had studied about six pages of photographs, he pointed to a photo. "That's pretty close to the face shape."

Griffin said, "That's great, Roy," as she turned the folder around to face her. Bridgette and Roy watched as Griffin drew a large faint cross with a ruler and pencil on the center of the drawing pad. As she switched pencils, she added, "I always start with a background cross to give balance. The T section of the cross is where I'll draw the eyes in later." In under two minutes, she had the outline of a face rendered on the page. She swung the pad around to face Roy. "Does this look about right?"

Roy studied the drawing for a moment. "Maybe the chin could be a little squarer?"

Griffin flipped the pad around again and made a few neat strokes with a pencil. Bridgette marveled at how rapidly the jawline changed. Satisfied with her work, Griffin swung the pad around to show Roy again.

Roy studied the drawing for a moment. "That's pretty close."

Griffin nodded. "Good work, Roy. I have a couple more questions before we move on. First, did your attacker have facial hair? You know, a mustache or beard?"

Roy shook his head. "No, he looked like a regular businessman."

"So his hair, it was short too?"

"Short and brown."

"Okay, that's good to know. Hairstyles change over time as people age, so we'll add that last. For now, I'd like us to work on his eyes…"

Two hours later, Roy looked exhausted. The van had been quiet for almost ten minutes while Griffin made the finishing touches to the sketch. After studying her work for a moment, Griffin spun the sketch around for Roy to look at again.

They were all quiet while Roy studied the drawing. After a few anxious moments, Roy said, "I think that's pretty close."

Bridgette and Griffin exchanged a knowing look before Bridgette returned her gaze to the drawing. While there was no doubt Griffin was a talented artist, the sketch was just that—a sketch. Bridgette stared at the image and wondered how much the man had changed in the past twenty years. If he had gone bald, grown a beard, or put on weight, she knew the sketch could be next to useless.

She hid her skepticism as she thanked Roy for his time. She promised to keep him updated on the investigation through the marshals but warned him it may take time.

Roy looked apologetic. "I hope I haven't wasted your time."

Bridgette responded, "Not at all, Roy," as the van's side door slid open. After thanking Roy for his time and reassuring him he'd done a good job, Griffin got out of the van. Bridgette lingered a moment. "Thanks again for today, Roy. I know this wasn't easy for you."

Roy looked glum. "I'm not sure how much use it's going to be. That face could be a rough match for half the men under thirty in this country…"

Bridgette placed a hand on Roy's shoulder. "These sketches can be invaluable. They only have to trigger a memory in one person to make all the difference in solving a crime."

"I suppose…"

Bridgette glanced at the marshal who was patiently holding the door open before returning her gaze to Roy. "I'd better be going. This might be the last time I see you for a while."

Roy half smiled. "Thanks again for Sunday. I know you blame yourself, but I've been living on borrowed time for years. I knew they would eventually find me, and I'm just glad I'm still alive."

Bridgette gave Roy a warm smile. "Good luck with your new life, Roy." She moved to the door. After getting out of the van, she turned back to look at Roy. She pretended not to notice the lost look on his face as she said, "Make sure you give Spike a pat for me."

After the marshal closed the door, she asked, "So what happens now?"

"For now, he goes back to the safe house. If the program decides he needs long-term protection, he'll be given a new identity and relocated."

"And we'll never see him again?"

As the marshal got into the front of the van, he replied, "Not unless you can come up with a suspect he might be able to identify."

Standing in the middle of the street, she watched the van pull away from the curb and slowly speed up. She thought about Roy and wondered how safe he really was. Bridgette doubted whoever wanted him dead would stop searching just because he was now in witness protection. She sighed and headed back to her car. Her first stop with a copy of the sketch would be the NewFarm Racecourse to show it to Walter Denphy and anyone else who had worked at the track twenty years ago. She figured she would know before the day was over if the sketch would help them find the killer or not.

Tuesday - 6:10 P.M.

Felix Delray paused in the open doorway of Chief Commissioner Underwood's office and gently knocked.

Underwood looked up from a laptop on his desk. "Come in, Felix, and close the door behind you."

Delray walked across the palatial office space and settled into one of three leather office chairs in front of Underwood's desk. Twenty-four hours on from Bates's murder, he knew the commissioner had a lot on his mind and decided now wasn't the time for pleasantries or small talk. He waited for Underwood to speak first.

"Bates's murder is turning into a circus. Normally I would have asked the assistant commissioner to join us, but he's busy fending off the media right now." Underwood shook his head. "There's something I want to show you." He turned his laptop around so that Delray could also see the screen. As Delray moved in closer, Underwood continued, "We've got a suspect for Bates's murder."

Delray raised his eyebrows. "That was quick."

"Cunningham's got Internal Investigations working

around the clock. They've collected video from all the security cameras surrounding Bates's apartment block. While there's still a lot to work through, they've already got some footage to kick-start the investigation. When you're ready, press play."

Delray pressed the spacebar on the laptop, and a grainy color video of a driveway at the front of a building came to life on the screen.

Underwood said, "This is the security video in front of Bates's apartment block. The time is just after midday..."

Delray watched as a man crossed the road and walked toward the camera. A lump rose in his throat as he realized he was looking at Charlie Bates.

Underwood continued, "What you're witnessing now is the last ninety seconds of Bates's life."

Delray watched as Bates moved forward at a hurried pace with his head down and his hands in his coat pockets. He continued to move forward until he disappeared from view under the camera.

Underwood added, "In a moment, you'll see his Honda as it comes up from the underground parking lot."

The two men sat in silence for over a minute until Bates's Honda appeared at the bottom of the screen driving toward the street. Delray held his breath as he watched the car suddenly veer to its left and collide with the concrete retaining wall at the side of the apartment block.

"The video doesn't really show it, but Bates has already been shot."

Delray was speechless as he watched the Honda continue to roll forward, scraping against the concrete retaining wall for about ten feet before coming to a halt.

"That camera has a good view not only of the driveway but also of the front of the building on the opposite side of the street. There was no sign of anyone close by at the time of the shooting, so the current theory is the shot wasn't taken from street level. This view is supported by the ballistics done on Bates's Honda."

Delray let out a long breath. "I've been on the force for thirty years, and I gotta say this is some of the hardest footage I've ever had to watch, sir."

Underwood nodded. "When it's one of your own, even if they've gone astray, we all take it personally, Felix."

Underwood flipped the laptop around to face him again. While he deftly made a few more keystrokes, he said, "Now I'm going to show you another security video. This is from the building opposite Bates's apartment block. The time stamp is four minutes after Bates was shot..." Underwood turned the laptop back toward Delray. "When you're ready..."

Delray pressed the spacebar again and studied the grainy image of what appeared to be the back of a multistory building.

"This footage is taken from a camera at the back entrance to the apartment block on the opposite side of the street."

They were quiet for a moment while they watched a man wearing a baseball cap and carrying a duffel bag walk out of the building. The man kept his head down and turned left into the rear alleyway before he quickly disappeared from view.

Delray said, "He's got a distinctive walk."

"We noticed that too. His toes touch the ground before his heels. Not too many people walk like that, so maybe it will help us find him."

"Apart from the fact he left the building shortly after the shooting, is there any reason you're honing in on this guy?"

Underwood nodded. "Internal Investigations have scanned all the available tape of people entering and exiting that building over the previous two weeks. The only time anyone who walked like that entered the building was ninety minutes before the shooting. Of course, it could be just a coincidence, but we're running it to ground before we make that call."

"So where do they think the shot came from?"

"We think from the roof. There's no lock on the access door, and there are two air-conditioning units up there. If he wedged in between them, he would have almost perfect cover. We're interviewing everyone who lives in the apartment block, but so far, everyone checks out."

Both men sat in silence for a moment before Underwood said, "I'm hoping whoever is behind this has overplayed their hand. When something like this is put together in such a hurry, mistakes are normally made. Hopefully, this will give us the edge we need."

"Is there anything I can do to help?"

"Right now, I'm happy with the progress Cunningham and his team are making. I just want you available to answer any questions about Bates that may come up. You were his supervisor and probably knew him better than anyone else on the force."

Delray nodded. "I can't argue with that."

Underwood frowned slightly. "We have notified Bates's family of his passing. None of his close family live in Vancouver, but they're expected to fly in tonight. A police liaison is taking care of that, but it would be good if you could make yourself available to talk to them as well if they want."

"Of course, sir." Delray paused a moment and then

added, "How do you want me to handle the corruption allegations if they come up?"

Underwood pulled at his beard again as he pondered the question. Finally, he responded, "All we say for now is it's an open investigation."

Underwood leaned back in his chair and let out a long breath. Delray rarely saw Underwood in any form other than a consummate professional leader. He took it as a positive to see him drop his guard, even if only for a moment.

Underwood looked at his watch. "I don't really have any more information for you right now, but I thought you should know we are making progress. Perhaps you could inform the team who worked with Bates that we are doing all we can?"

"I will, sir. Right away."

"Well, if there's nothing else, I'll let you get back to work."

Delray felt his gut tighten slightly. "As a matter of fact there is...if you have a couple of minutes?"

Underwood replied evenly, "What's on your mind?"

Delray took a deep breath and withdrew a folded piece of paper from his internal jacket pocket. As he flattened it out on the desk, he said, "Shortly after the basement shooting, I had a meeting with Bridgette. She was still pretty shaken up by the incident, but she gave me this for safekeeping..." Delray paused and slid the sheet of paper across the desk toward Underwood.

As Underwood picked it up, Delray continued, "What you're looking at is a printout of a photograph Bridgette took on her smartphone just before she was shot at in the basement. It's a page from the microfilm she was viewing on the reader."

Underwood studied the grainy photographic image. "A witness list?"

Delray nodded. "The original witness list from her mother's murder file."

"So this is from the microfilm that was stolen?"

"Yes."

"So why would she want a picture of it? Surely this is all in the computer records now?"

"She noticed a discrepancy."

"A discrepancy?"

"There were twenty-six names on the original list in the paper file. In the computer record, there are only twenty-four. Two names are missing, and she wanted to know who they were. So she took a photo of the display to check against the computer records, to see who hadn't made it across."

Delray could tell Underwood wasn't happy as he chewed on his bottom lip while he studied the piece of paper. Finally, he said, "Physical and microfilm copies of this case have been stolen, one officer has been shot at, and another is dead." Underwood looked up at Delray. "Did Detective Cash follow up on the two missing witnesses?"

"Not yet. She was doing that on her own time, but after what happened in the basement and the death of her father, she said she needed a break." Delray paused a moment and then added, "In light of Bates's murder, I realize I should have brought this to your attention earlier, sir. I accept full responsibility…"

"We all make mistakes, Felix, and hindsight's a wonderful thing." Underwood held Delray's gaze. "Is there anything else you need to tell me?"

"No, sir. That's it."

Underwood slid the paper back across the desk. "Ordinarily, this would be a matter for Internal Investigations. But given their workload, I want you to investigate this and report back to me. Don't involve Detective Cash or anyone else from your team. We've got one dead cop on our hands, and I don't want the body count rising any further."

"Yes, sir."

"We'll figure out where we go from here if anything comes of it."

After promising Underwood that running down the two missing witnesses would be his number one priority, Delray left Underwood's office and headed for the elevator. Even though Underwood had chosen to overlook his mistake, he was embarrassed he had been sitting on evidence. After pressing the button, he looked down at the list again. It would be a simple task to figure out which two names were missing from the computer file but a much harder task to find them. Delray scanned the names, knowing that after twenty years the odds were high that some of them would now be dead. As the elevator door opened, he hoped the two he needed to interview were still alive and wondered what they knew about the murder.

Wednesday - 7:15 A.M.

Bridgette knocked on the open door that led into Delray's office. "You wanted to see me, chief?"

Delray pressed the spacebar on his keyboard to freeze a video he was watching. "Good morning, Bridgette, come on in." As she settled into a chair, Delray added, "I didn't have a chance to catch up with you yesterday. How did it go with Roy?"

Bridgette gave Delray a rundown of the second interview with Roy and explained how Raylene Griffin had produced an artist's impression of the man who had attacked Roy.

After hearing the background, Delray asked, "So how good a likeness do we have?"

Bridgette opened a file she had brought with her, withdrew a copy of the sketch, and slid it across the desk. "It's a good sketch, but that's all it is."

After putting his glasses on, Delray picked up the drawing and studied it for a moment. "It's a pity he doesn't have any distinguishing features. I'm no demographer, but I guess this could be a rough match for more than a million white men in this country."

"That and it's twenty years out of date."

Delray frowned. "So have you circulated it?"

"I had copies made up yesterday. I visited Jane Whitecross and showed her the image, but she didn't immediately recognize the face. After that, I went out to NewFarm Racecourse and showed the image to Walter Denphy and a few other stable hands who worked there twenty years ago. No one recognized the man, but I'll keep trying. Today I plan on visiting more of Whitecross's family and business associates. Hopefully, the sketch will trigger a memory with at least one of them."

As he put the sketch down, Delray said, "It only has to trigger a memory in one person, and we can bust this case wide open. Keep at it and let me know if you need any help."

"I'm good for today unless you have a new partner for me?"

Delray rolled his eyes. "Not yet. Cunningham and Sterling are consumed with the Bates investigation. I think you can plan on working solo for a while."

"Have they made any progress?"

"As a matter of fact, they have." Delray paused while he swung his computer monitor around for Bridgette to see and started the video again. She watched intently as a man emerged from a building carrying a duffel bag.

Delray added, "Internal Investigations have been collecting video from all the security cameras in the surrounding area. This video comes from a camera at the back of the apartment block opposite Bates's building. They think this is the guy who shot Bates. They have video of him entering the apartment building about ninety minutes before the shooting. This video is taken four minutes after Bates was murdered…"

Bridgette felt sick to her stomach. Even though she hadn't been close to Charlie Bates, stark reminders of his murder were difficult to handle. After composing herself, she said, "Do they know where he took the shot from?"

Delray shook his head. "They're still working on that, but they believe it was from the roof."

Bridgette frowned for a second. "Do you mind if I borrow your computer mouse?"

Delray looked slightly perplexed. "Go for it."

Using the mouse, Bridgette restarted the video again and watched a second time as the man exited the apartment building. As he walked away from the camera toward the rear alleyway, she said, "Did you notice his walk?"

"Yes. He places the ball of his foot on the ground before his heel. It's unusual—almost like he's got very mild cerebral palsy or some other physical condition."

"That must make him easier to find."

"Internal Investigations are scanning NatTrack right now to see if we can match him with anyone on file who has a similar walk."

They were quiet for a moment while Bridgette played the video again. As she bit down hard on her bottom lip, Delray asked, "What's the problem?"

Bridgette took a deep breath. "I think I've seen this man before." She paused the video just before the man turned into the alleyway.

Delray's eyes widened. "Really? When?"

As she recalled the image of the gunman walking toward Roy's cottage, Bridgette answered, "On Sunday." She closed her eyes for a moment and replayed the memory in her mind. "I think this is the same gunman who was after Roy."

"What? At the farm?"

"When I saw the gunman heading toward the house, Roy and I got out as quick as we could through the back door. We headed up to the ridgeline and hid among the trees and waited to see what would happen. The man came out through the back door and stood on the porch holding a gun looking for us. I remember thinking we weren't safe where we were, so we kept moving... I never thought about his walk until now, but even though I was at least two hundred yards away, I distinctly remember it." Bridgette pressed play on the video again. "He walked toe to heel, just like this guy..."

"Do you think this could be just a coincidence?"

Bridgette shook her head. "There can't be too many hit men out there with that kind of walk."

Delray looked skeptical. "You don't mind me saying, Bridgette, it sounds like a long shot. I can't imagine how one man could be involved in both a cop killing and trying to silence a witness of an unrelated twenty-year-old murder case...particularly all in the same week."

Bridgette nodded but said nothing in response. She wasn't a big believer in coincidences and pondered how the two cases might be connected.

Bridgette sat down at her desk but didn't switch on her computer as she normally did. Instead, she stared at the darkened screen as she replayed in her mind the video Delray had just shown her of the man walking out of the building. Delray had been skeptical, but she was positive this was the man she had seen at Roy's cottage. The walk was identical, almost like a fingerprint.

Bridgette pulled a scratch pad and a pen out of her desk and contemplated the possible linkages between the gunman and the two cases. She drew a small circle at the top of the page and wrote the word "*Gunman*" inside it in a neat cursive script. A third of the way down the page, she drew two more circles, side by side but spaced apart. In the circle on the left, she wrote the word "Bates," and in the circle on the right, she wrote "Roy." She chewed on the end of her pen for a moment before drawing two lines in the shape of an upside down V to link the new circles to the top circle. Next to the Bates circle, she wrote the word "*murder,*" and next to the Roy circle, she wrote "attempted murder."

As she chewed on her pen again, she thought about the motive for Bates's murder. Whoever had hired him to steal the microfilm copy of her mother's murder file was going to great lengths to protect their identity. Convinced they had the most to gain from his murder, she drew a circle below the Bates circle and wrote her mother's initials in it. Bridgette stared at the circle with Roy's name in it and then drew a circle directly below it and wrote RW inside it as code for Reid Whitecross.

As she focused on the gunman's circle again, she wondered if it was all just a coincidence? From the little she knew about Bates's murder, she was sure it was a professional hit. Whoever would ultimately benefit from Bates's death probably hadn't pulled the trigger.

She thought back to a conversation she had with Roy in her car as they drove back to Vancouver. Even though he didn't get a close look at the man who had come after them, he was adamant it wasn't the same man who had threatened him at NewFarm twenty years earlier. She was sure he was a hired professional and wrote the words "one client or multiple clients?" next to the gunman's circle at the top of the page. As she underlined the words, she knew this was a question she needed to answer. Multiple clients would mean the two cases weren't connected, but a common client gave her a thread that could lead to his identity.

Bridgette decided it was time for research. Both the murder of her mother and Reid Whitecross happened twenty years ago. She was confident if she could find a point where their lives crossed, she would have something tangible to work with as a motive for both their murders.

As she switched on her computer, she whispered, "If I can find a connection, I can find the killer…"

Wednesday - 4:05 P.M.

Bridgette studied the photo board of the two bodies in the cave as she waited in Ray Warner's office. As she looked at each image, she was drawn back to that afternoon less than a week ago when she was ferried out to the island by boat. She felt a shiver run down her spine as she recalled the dank, claustrophobic conditions of the watery tomb. Bridgette repressed the feelings as best as she could. She knew the images would haunt her for months if not years and longed for a breakthrough in the case. She sighed as she thought about her progress. Bates's murder had been much more than an unwanted distraction, something she worried would drain her of the emotional and physical energy she needed for this case.

She whispered, "You've made very little progress," as she focused on close-up images of the bloated body of Owen Whitecross and the withered skeletal remains of his father.

Her thoughts were interrupted as Warner walked into his office and said, "Thanks for coming, Bridgette."

Bridgette turned around. "Good afternoon, Ray, no problem."

To Bridgette's surprise, Warner remained standing rather than sitting at his desk. "Are you okay?"

Bridgette nodded but was aware she sounded less than convincing as she responded, "I think so."

Warner sucked in a deep breath. "I'm still trying to get my head around Bates's murder. I can't believe it…"

"Nobody can, Ray."

"Felix called me, but I'd already heard. It was all over the news…"

"Internal Investigations have a strong lead, so we're hoping they'll find the shooter shortly."

"Felix told me this guy has a strange walk and maybe is the same guy who came after you on Sunday?"

"It's possible."

Warner shook his head. "Well, I hope they find the scumbag sooner rather than later."

"Me too."

Warner nodded toward the photo board. "Are you making any progress with the investigation?"

"I was just thinking about that when you came in. It's going slower than I would like, but it was good finding Roy Pepper."

"That's the guy who's been in hiding, right?"

Bridgette responded, "Yes," and then gave Warner a brief recap of her interview with Roy on Sunday. She added, "We're hopeful the artist's impression of the man who threatened him after the murder of Reid Whitecross will trigger a memory for someone."

"Any luck yet?"

"Not so far."

"Well, keep at it. Sometimes these things just take time."

"I will. I'm continuing to interview people to find out more about the background for both Reid and Owen Whitecross. So far, they come across as law-abiding citizens, who both got wealthy out of the horse racing industry. The only dirt I've found so far is that it appears Reid Whitecross was cheating on his wife."

"That's always a good motive for murder. Have you spoken to his wife?"

"No. She died a few months before Reid disappeared."

"Suspicious circumstances."

Bridgette shook her head. "Leukemia."

"Well, maybe what I've found will help you. I want to show you something interesting." Without waiting for a reply, Warner headed for the door.

Bridgette took a deep breath before following Ray Warner into one of the morgue's examination rooms. Being near dead bodies was something she was not sure she would ever get used to as she stared at the blackened and withered skeletal remains of Reed Whitecross who, now devoid of his clothes, was laid out on the stainless-steel examination table.

Warner was seemingly impervious to the smell that permeated the room. Bridgette was thankful for his sensitivity when he asked, "Do you want a mask?"

Bridgette mumbled, "Yes, please," and was thankful Warner didn't engage her in any further conversation until she had the mask fitted firmly over her nose and mouth.

As Warner beckoned her to join him at the examination table, he said, "You'll get everything I'm about to tell you in the report, but there are a few things I want to show you first."

The mask wasn't helping as much with the smell as Bridgette hoped, but she managed, "No problem," without gagging and waited for Warner to continue.

"I'll start with some basics for you. As I confirmed with Felix yesterday, this is almost certainly Reid Whitecross. You can read the full details for yourself, but we have a better than ninety-eight percent DNA match between the two victims. I'm prepared to stake my reputation on the fact they are father and son, but you knew that anyway."

Warner picked up a steel pointer that reminded Bridgette of a slender chopstick and pointed at Reid Whitecross's skull. As he moved the pointer toward the bullet hole, he said, "The bullet entered Whitecross's skull just above the bridge of his nose. It's in an almost identical position to the bullet hole we found in his son. I've only been able to recover fragments of the bullet, so it's going to be hard for ballistics to determine if the same weapon was used to kill both men." As Warner waved the pointer around in a circle about an inch away from the bullet hole, he added, "The diameter of the bullet holes in each skull is almost identical."

"So it's the same caliber weapon at least?"

"More than likely."

"Do you have any idea what kind of weapon it was?"

"Not yet. What I can tell you is the diameter of the bullet holes is smaller than most. Much smaller than a thirty-eight for example. We're letting ballistics figure it out for certain, but my guess is it was probably fired from a twenty-two caliber weapon."

"A pistol?"

Warner nodded. "Almost certainly. We know the shot that killed Owen was fired from extremely close range because of the gunpowder residue we found on his skin.

Cold Hard Cash

This bullet that killed his father was likely fired from very close range as well, probably almost touching the skull. But that's more theory than anything else. After twenty years, a lot of the forensic evidence to support the theory is no longer evident. There is, however, one anomaly that I wanted to show you."

Warner walked across to a stainless-steel bench that ran along the far wall. He pointed to a stainless-steel tray lined with a white paper towel next to a large electron microscope. "Come and have a look at this."

Bridgette moved across to the bench and stared down at seven small circular disks on the tray. Despite their blackened appearance, they were easily identifiable as coins. She looked up at Warner. "These came from the victim?"

"Yes. They were retrieved, along with his wallet, from what was left of his trousers." Warner moved across to the microscope. "I want you to look at this."

Bridgette peered into the eyepiece at another blackened coin under low magnification. Warner waited a moment and then asked, "What do you see?"

"I see another coin."

"Correct. This also came from the victim's pocket." As he adjusted settings on the side of the microscope, he added, "I'm increasing the magnification. What do you see now?"

Bridgette studied the coin for a moment and could see two semicircular rings at odd angles on the surface of the coin. "I see what look like circles on the face of the coin."

Warner responded, "Correct," and increased the magnification again. "Do you notice anything different between the two rings?"

Bridgette was about to respond, "No," but studied the

rings in more detail. Finally, she said, "One ring looks slightly wider than the other?"

"You're right. I also found similar markings on some of the other coins."

Bridgette frowned as she looked up from the microscope. "So, what does that mean?"

As Warner removed the glass slides that contained the coin from the microscope, he said, "I have another coin sample from the victim I want to show you." After fitting a second slide to the microscope, he said, "Look at this and tell me what you see."

Bridgette peered into the eyepiece again to study the new coin. She took her time and then responded, "This coin appears more green than black?"

"That's what I thought too."

"Is that significant?"

"I'm still running tests, but I don't think that coin has been in the man's pocket for anything like twenty years."

Bridgette frowned. "I'm not following."

"All the other coins are very black, consistent with them being there since whenever the body was dumped. The oxidization on this coin isn't as thick, nor is the discoloring as profound. At first, I thought it was just a different type of coin or perhaps it hadn't been in circulation for as long."

"But that's not the case?"

"I don't think so. The two rings on some of the other coins are the giveaway. If they hadn't been disturbed in the man's pocket, you would expect them to only have one ring where they had been resting on one another."

"So something has disturbed them?"

"That's what I'm thinking. Even in Whitecross's trouser pocket, air gets in and causes some oxidization. Of course, it's possible that some small animal or large beetle got in there and disturbed the coins, but I don't think that's likely."

"So what are you saying? Someone deliberately placed another coin in the man's pocket?"

"I know it seems unlikely, but I have no other explanation…"

Bridgette stared at the bones of Reid Whitecross on the examination table. She wondered how Warner's theory could possibly be correct. "Why would someone go to the trouble of placing a coin of no real value on a dead body?"

Thursday - 9:20 A.M.

Delray pressed the spacebar on his computer keyboard and froze the video he was watching. After letting out a long sigh, he mumbled, "She's got to see this," and picked up his coffee cup. He thought about what he would say as he drained the last of his coffee. He knew the video would be challenging to watch and decided the conversation would be best had in his office as he picked up his phone and dialed Bridgette's extension.

His call was answered on the third ring. Delray said, "You got a second, Bridgette? Can you come see me in my office?"

After putting the phone down, he used the time while he waited to reset the video to the right location.

A moment later, his rookie detective appeared in the doorway. "You wanted to see me, chief?"

"Come on in and close the door behind you, Bridgette. There's something I want to show you."

After Bridgette had settled into a chair opposite his desk, Delray said softly, "There's been a breakthrough in the

Cold Hard Cash

Bates case." He pressed the spacebar on his computer. As the screen came to life, he swung it around to give Bridgette a better viewing angle. "This came in from Bolton police about an hour ago."

They both watched as the tiny orange image of a man against a dark purple backdrop came to life. Bridgette frowned as she watched the man walk across the screen. "A thermal imaging camera."

"Yes. This was taken from a stealth drone high above the Bolton State Forest."

As they watched the man walk between trees, Delray added, "The man's name is John Hanway. Bolton Police have had him under investigation for over four years as a person of interest in six murders. They've long suspected him of being a professional hitman, but they've never been able to prove anything. We circulated the video of the man leaving the building after Bates's murder to other jurisdictions and got a hit from Bolton almost immediately. One of their guys recognized the man's distinctive walk as being almost identical to Hanway's."

Bridgette kept her eyes focused on the computer screen. Even from a small camera several hundred feet up, Bridgette could still discern the man's distinctive walk.

Delray continued, "They took the video to a judge who authorized an around-the-clock surveillance and a phone tap. Last night, they followed him at a safe distance out of the city to the Bolton State Forest. They put a drone up with an infrared camera, and this is what they observed."

Bridgette watched as the man walked on. Without taking her eyes off the screen, she said, "He appears to be carrying something."

"Yes. In a few more seconds, you'll see what he's up to."

She watched as the man began pacing steps in a small

open area of the forest before he bent down and appeared to start scraping at the ground. Bridgette cocked her head slightly to one side and watched for another minute until the man straightened up again. The orange figure seemed to grab something in both hands that didn't emit a thermal image. She watched as he hunched over and thrust his arms forward. "Is he digging?"

Delray nodded as he maneuvered his mouse. "I'm going to move the video forward now. He digs for another five minutes, which isn't important, but what comes after that is…"

After Delray pressed play again, Bridgette watched as the figure appeared to drop what she presumed was a shovel and get down on his hands and knees.

Delray said, "What you're looking at now is Hanway removing a steel box he'd buried earlier."

Bridgette watched as the man appeared to lift something out of the ground, but the image was too grainy for her to see what it was. All of a sudden, the image of the man seemed to be growing larger. She frowned. "It looks like the drone is descending?"

"You got it. This is where it gets interesting."

Together they watched as the man stopped what he was doing, spun around, and looked up, seemingly toward the camera.

Bridgette asked, "He's heard the drone?"

"Yes, but it doesn't matter now."

They continued to watch as the grainy orange images of six figures rushed in toward the man from different angles.

Delray commented, "What you're seeing now is six Bolton police officers moving in to make the arrest."

Bridgette watched Hanway drop whatever he was holding and sprint to the left of the screen. She watched for another thirty seconds as three officers closed in on him and tackled him to the ground. Within seconds, the whole area was illuminated. The purple backdrop was gone, replaced by a visual of other officers swiftly moving through the trees to join their colleagues who held the man firmly on the ground. The whole image turned into a chaotic blur of police officers standing over the man as the drone descended even further.

Delray pressed the spacebar on his computer to freeze the video again. "There's a lot more video I can show you, but for now, you have an idea of what happened at the take down."

"Okay."

Delray's expression grew somber. "After parking his car at the edge of the forest, Hanway took a rifle and a shovel from his car and walked for about twenty minutes into the forest. The police found the rifle next to the steel box he'd dug up. He was obviously there to bury it, and we believe it was the weapon used to kill Bates, but we won't know for sure until they've completed their ballistic tests. They found another three rifles and two pistols in the box he had buried."

"So this was where he stored his arsenal?"

Delray nodded. "So far, he's not saying anything. But we're hoping that will change in time as he realizes his situation is hopeless."

"There's a good chance he has no idea who actually hired him." Bridgette stared at the frozen image of the hitman lying on the ground surrounded by six police officers.

"You're right, but they all make a mistake eventually, Bridgette. We've just got to make sure we're smart enough to pick up on it…"

Friday - 11:00 A.M.

Bridgette pulled up in front of Jane Whitecross's two-story colonial house for the second time in three days. She had missed a call on the drive from the South Metro precinct building and sighed when she glanced down at her phone and saw the number for Doctor Carol Sanders. She didn't want to speak to Sanders but knew not responding would only lead to more questions. Bridgette checked her watch. She knew the sought-after clinical psychologist had her appointments scheduled on the hour and decided this was a safe time to call back and leave a message. To her dismay, Sanders answered on the third ring.

"Sanders."

Bridgette grimaced. "Hi, doctor, this is Bridgette returning your call."

"Thanks for calling back. I just called to check in and see how you're doing?"

Bridgette thought about her response. While not comfortable lying, she wasn't about to give Sanders any more information than necessary. "I'm okay."

"Did you sleep last night?"

Bridgette had slept very little. Her meeting with Delray had gone well into the evening. They had talked a lot about Bates's murder, and then Delray had asked her pointedly about how she was coping with her father's death. After heading home for a shower and a frozen meal, she had lain awake for most of the night thinking about the last conversation she'd had with her father. She'd not seen him in twenty years and wasn't even sure he was still alive when he'd made the surprise phone call late one evening. After getting over the shock, her father had apologized for abandoning her and explained she could also be in danger if she continued investigating her mother's murder. The call had been brief but long enough for her to realize he had been framed. She replayed the conversation over in her mind as she thought about Carl Rutherford, the man who had pulled the trigger less than forty-eight hours later to end his life.

"Bridgette, are you there?"

She shook her head as Sanders's voice brought her back to reality. "Sorry, yes."

"Did you sleep last night?"

"Kind of. There's a lot going on at present."

The phone was silent for a moment before Sanders responded gently, "Talking about it can only help, Bridgette."

"I had a long talk with the chief yesterday."

"And what did you talk about?"

"Everything really. All the way back to my mother's murder, which seems to be the trigger for everything that's happened since."

"Your boss gave me some background. It doesn't sound like this is close to being solved."

Bridgette sighed. "The men who killed my father and Charlie were hired professionals carrying out orders on behalf of someone else. The chief is personally working the case at the request of the commissioner."

"Are you assisting?"

Bridgette stared up at the white colonial house. "I'm full-time on the Rook Island murders."

"What about your own time?"

"It's the chief's investigation now." Bridgette shifted her gaze from the house to the tree-lined street in the upmarket residential neighborhood where Jane Whitecross lived. "I know I'll have no peace until this is solved, but I'm not about to interfere."

"I think that's wise."

Bridgette didn't want to prolong the conversation and waited for Sanders to continue. "It's important that you sleep, Bridgette. I know you don't like taking the tablets I've prescribed, but they will help."

In an effort to cut the conversation short, she said, "I promise I'll take one tonight if I can't get to sleep."

"And if they don't work, I want you to come in and see me. Fair enough?"

"Fair enough."

Sanders said goodbye and then disconnected, leaving Bridgette alone with her thoughts. She reflected on the closing part of the previous evening's meeting with her boss. Delray indicated he had a lead on her mother's murder case he would pursue today. He hadn't told her what it was, and she hadn't asked, but she was sure he wouldn't have mentioned it if it wasn't solid.

Pushing the conversation with Sanders to the back of her mind, Bridgette picked up a copy of the sketch of the man who had attacked Roy and got out of the car. As she walked toward Jane Whitecross's front door, she made a mental plan of how she would conduct the interview. While she didn't think Whitecross or her brother-in-law were serious suspects, she was keen to observe their reaction when she showed them the drawing.

The door opened shortly after Bridgette knocked. Jane Whitecross was again immaculately dressed, this time in dark blue designer jeans and a hand-knitted white cable sweater. Still not able to manage anything close to a smile as she greeted Bridgette, Whitecross invited Bridgette in and led her to the living room.

Bridgette could see no sign of Ethan Whitecross as she sat down. "Is Ethan joining us?"

Jane Whitecross shook her head. "No, he called to say he couldn't come over."

Bridgette frowned. She had wanted both of them in the same room when she showed them the sketch. Not trying to hide her anger, Bridgette responded, "When I set up this interview, it was for the two of you. I could have rescheduled if Ethan wasn't available."

Whitecross nodded once and responded coolly, "I'm not in charge of my brother-in-law. I think in the future you should make arrangements to speak to him separately."

"I'm happy to make those arrangements, Jane, but as I recall, it was you who initially suggested I interview you both together."

Whitecross's shoulders sagged a little. "None of us are handling this very well, detective, particularly Ethan…"

Bridgette sensed Whitecross wanted to say more and simply nodded in response.

After a few moments, Whitecross added, "Ethan and

Owen were very close. He's dealing with several challenges apart from his brother's death."

"What kind of challenges?"

"Financial, mainly. He broke away from the family's horse breeding business some years ago to do his own thing in real estate. It hasn't worked out so well. Owen was helping him get back on his feet financially with several loans and even gave Ethan a job a few months back helping with our business."

Bridgette had a photographic memory and rarely used a notebook. She made a mental note to investigate Ethan Whitecross's background more thoroughly. "Did that strain their relationship?"

Whitecross hesitated for a moment. "Owen hasn't really been himself for the last six months, but I don't think that has anything to do with Ethan."

"In what way hasn't he been himself?"

Whitecross looked downcast. "Restless. We've been married for almost twenty years and have always been open with each other…until about six months ago. If it had been connected to Ethan, I'm sure he would have told me. At first, I thought he was having an affair, but then he began having bouts of moodiness, almost depression. He saw a doctor to get sleeping pills…"

"And you have no idea why?"

"No. I tried to get him to open up, but he wouldn't. He assured me it wasn't anything to do with our relationship or his business. But that's as much as he would say."

Bridgette made another mental note to look further into Owen Whitecross's background. "Perhaps he had business problems he didn't want to share with you? That's not uncommon."

Jane Whitecross shook her head. "No. I saw our accountant shortly after Owen disappeared. Financially, we were doing as well as ever when he disappeared. Unless there's something else going on with his business that I don't know about, I don't think that's it."

"Could it be connected with his father's disappearance?"

"Possibly. Owen never really got over that. When I first met him, he believed his father had simply abandoned what was left of his family after his wife died and disappeared somewhere to start a new life. Over time, he began to change his view and finally believed someone had murdered him."

"Did he say why?"

"He hired a private investigator about ten years back to try to find him without success. I remember him coming to talk to Owen about three months after he started his investigation. He was adamant Owen's father had been murdered."

"And how did Owen react?"

"At first, he was quite emotional. He'd always thought his father had been a lowlife who had abandoned his family. After he got over the shock, he went to the police and pleaded with them to treat his father's disappearance as murder. They promised to investigate, but nothing ever came of it. Owen even hired the same private investigator again who continued to look into it for another six months, but in the end, he admitted that unless some new evidence came to light, it was highly unlikely they would ever find out what happened."

"So you say that happened ten years ago. Did Owen give up his quest?"

"No. It was something he kept working on in the background. He wouldn't say much about it, but now and then I'd see notes in his office or overhear phone calls, and I knew they were about his father."

"Could his recent change in behavior be connected to his father's murder? Perhaps he learned something that troubled him?"

"Possibly, but like I said, he never told me."

"I know Owen's home and work offices have already been searched by our Missing Persons unit, but would you mind if I took another look? It may amount to nothing, but if we can find out what caused Owen's recent change of behavior, we may be a step closer to understanding why he was murdered."

Jane Whitecross replied, "Be my guest, detective." As she rose from her chair, she added, "Come this way, and I'll take you to his office."

Bridgette motioned for her to sit down again. "Before we do that, I've got something I want to show you." As she withdrew the artist's sketch from her folder, Bridgette added, "Last Sunday, we located a man who we believe was a witness to Reid Whitecross's murder." Bridgette gave her a brief background of what Roy Pepper had seen and heard on the day of the murder and then concluded by adding, "As he was on his way to report the murder, this man confronted him with a gun and threatened him."

Bridgette handed the sketch over to Whitecross and watched her body language as she studied the image. Whitecross frowned, and Bridgette could tell immediately she either didn't recognize the man or was feigning having never seen him before.

Bridgette added, "This is what the man looked like

twenty years ago. Of course, you have to imagine him now being twenty years older..."

Whitecross studied the image for close to thirty seconds before she finally looked up. "I'm sorry, detective, but it doesn't look overly like anyone I ever recall seeing or meeting."

Bridgette nodded. "Please keep the sketch. It may trigger a memory you can't recall right now."

She studied Whitecross for a moment. The woman looked racked with grief at the loss of her husband. There were more questions she wanted to ask her about her husband, but she decided they were better left until she had checked the office. "Perhaps we could see the office now?"

Whitecross responded, "Of course," as she got to her feet. She led Bridgette out of the living room and down a well-lit Spanish-tiled hallway. She stopped at the second door on the left. "This is Owen's office."

Whitecross led her into a spacious room with a mahogany desk, matching file cabinet, and bookcase. There was one empty in tray on the desk and no sign of a computer or laptop. The walls were lined with pictures of horses. Most of them included a man she recognized as Owen Whitecross who was proudly posing with each animal as he held its bridle.

Whitecross said, "I don't come in here much, it's too painful. If you don't mind, I'll leave you to look around by yourself."

Bridgette nodded as she surveyed the photos on the wall. "These are Owen's horses?"

As Whitecross moved back toward the door, she responded, "Yes. Most of these horses he raised from foals. Many have gone on to be champion racehorses."

Bridgette stopped in front of a black-and-white photo

that looked out of place. The image was grainier and showed a man and three small boys standing together with a racehorse.

Whitecross added, "That's Owen's father. That picture must have been taken forty years ago."

Bridgette leaned forward to study the image. "Who are the three boys?"

"Owen and Ethan when they were young. I'm not sure who the third boy is."

Bridgette often found photos were a good way to learn about someone's past. "Did he have a happy childhood?"

"I met him when he was twenty-six. His mother had passed about eighteen months earlier and his father was already missing. Family wasn't something he wanted to talk about. He's told me snippets over the years, but he's never really wanted to talk much about his childhood."

"Didn't you find that odd?"

Whitecross tilted her head to one side as she thought about the question. Finally, she said, "Owen was never one for looking back, he was always looking forward. It was one of the reasons he was so successful in business."

Bridgette studied several more photographs as she thought about Jane Whitecross's answer. She paused in front of a smaller black-and-white photograph on the wall to study the image of a man and a woman standing beside a thoroughbred horse at the front of a stable.

Whitecross added, "That's another photo from Owen's childhood."

"His mother and father?"

"Yes. Owen was about six at the time as I recall. You can see him playing in the background if you look hard enough."

Bridgette moved in even closer and studied the photograph. In the background, she could just make out the tiny image of three boys sitting cross-legged with their backs up against a stable door. The image quality was poor, and it was impossible to make out their faces, but it appeared to Bridgette they were talking to each other and ignoring the camera.

"Three boys again. Owen, Ethan, and someone else."

"Yes, I'm not sure who the third boy is, I assume it was a family friend."

Bridgette returned her focus to the first black-and-white photograph and studied the image of Reid Whitecross and the three boys. "Do you think it's possible that this is the same boy?"

Jane Whitecross moved alongside Bridgette and studied the two photographs. "I'm not sure. You can't make out the faces in the second photograph."

"Did Owen and Ethan have any cousins?"

"Yes, two, but they were both girls."

"Did Owen ever speak of a close childhood friend?"

"No one specific. Do you think his childhood friends are important?"

"Probably not."

The two women were silent for a moment before Whitecross said, "Well, if there's nothing else, detective, I'll leave you to your search. The cabinet and desk drawers are unlocked, so you have access to all the records Owen kept here."

Bridgette thanked Whitecross and waited for her to leave the room before turning her attention back to the photograph of Reid Whitecross and the three boys.

She studied the image of the third boy in the photograph. He looked nothing like Owen or Ethan, and she wondered again if he was a relative or a family friend. She hated loose ends, and right now, this was a loose end. After taking a step back, she pulled out her smartphone and took pictures of each of the two black-and-white photographs. She focused her attention on the second boy in the larger photograph, a boy with short sandy hair, and whispered, "I have a lot of questions for you, Ethan."

Friday - 12:55 P.M.

Felix Delray stood across the street from the townhouse complex at the corner of Makerstone and Fairfax. He'd been studying the two-story townhouse block for close to two minutes but barely noticed the Spanish-style architecture with its stucco finish, arched windows, and tiled roof as he focused on house number nine. It looked no different from the other eleven houses on the block, but he knew its history made it tragically unique. He thought about the seven-year-old girl who had lived there twenty years earlier. By all reports, she had been a happy child: attending the local school, getting straight As, and living quietly with her parents without a care in the world. That had all changed one Saturday afternoon when police found her hiding in a bedroom closet, her mother lying dead on a bed not twelve feet from her with a bullet wound to the head.

He wondered how the events of that day had shaped his young detective's life. Losing her mother in such violent circumstances and never seeing her father again had to have had a profound effect. He shook his head as he thought about how remarkable it was that she had moved on, developing into a capable young woman who was making the most of her life.

Delray turned his focus to house number four as he crossed the street. After walking up three steps and past a potted geranium, he knocked on the door and waited. A few moments later, Delray heard the unmistakable sound of several security latches being undone before a diminutive white-haired woman dressed in a blue cardigan opened the door. He guessed her height at a touch over five feet, and while her body was showing signs of the aging process, her piercing blue eyes told Delray her mind was as sharp as ever. As often as not, Delray would pull out a business card rather than his police badge when interviewing people, but something told him Connie Swayne would prefer official protocol.

Holding up his badge, he said in a pleasant tone, "Good morning, you must be Mrs. Swayne?"

The woman responded, "That I am," as she examined Delray's badge. Seemingly satisfied, she added, "And you must be Chief Inspector Delray."

"Thank you for seeing me on such short notice, I really appreciate it."

The elderly lady responded, "Call me Connie," as she motioned for Delray to come inside.

Delray followed Connie into a spotlessly clean small living room. After sitting down on a floral-covered easy chair, he studied some family photos on the wall for a moment before saying, "You have a very nice home, Connie."

"Thank you. I'm eighty-four, and the stairs are starting

to get a bit much for me, but I'm not ready to leave yet. Would you like a cup of tea or coffee before we start?"

"No, ma'am, but thank you for asking."

Connie nodded but said nothing else. Delray took that as a cue she wasn't interested in small talk. "Thanks again for seeing me on such short notice. I didn't give you very much information on the phone, so I guess you're wondering why I'm here?"

Connie raised her eyebrows a fraction. "Well, I'm too old to be getting into mischief, so I'm hoping it might have something to do with what happened here twenty years ago."

"I'm sure you're aware we never solved the murder of Annie Casseldhorf in house number nine."

"Yes, it was a terrible business. I read recently that Peter Casseldhorf has died. It's such a shame that poor little girl has lost both her parents."

"I'm not sure if you are aware, but that little girl is now twenty-seven."

Connie thought for a moment. "Yes, that would be right. It seems like only yesterday I watched little Bridgette being taken away in a police car. I wonder whatever happened to her?"

"Would you believe me if I told you she joined the police force?"

Connie half smiled. "I'm sure that would have made her father proud. I never believed for a moment he had anything to do with Annie's murder."

"Neither do I, Connie, and that's why I'm here. Vancouver Metro has recently discovered some anomalies with the evidence in Annie's murder case, and I'm trying to clear them up."

"How can I help?"

"I won't bore you with all the details, but we have two witness lists. The first is the original list that came with the paper file, and the second was a copy on the computer. We're not exactly sure what happened, but two names from the original list never made it onto the computer—your name and Mary Keaton's name."

"Mary lived in number three until about seven years ago when she got sick. She died about three years ago, inspector."

"Yes, I found that out yesterday."

The elderly woman removed her glasses. "If you don't mind me saying so, this is all rather strange. Why has this taken so long?"

Delray grimaced. "There's a strong possibility there has been a cover-up. The paper records for the case disappeared many years ago, and we now believe the computer records are incomplete. I'm now trying to get to the bottom of it."

"Well, I'll do my best to help. Annie and Peter were my friends."

"Did anyone ever take your statement?"

"No, which really surprised me."

Delray removed a notepad and pen from his pocket. "What do you remember about that day?"

Connie sat with her hands clasped together as she pondered the question. Finally, she said, "I remember it was a Saturday, same as any other day. Mary had come over, and we were eating lunch when we heard a bang. I thought it was a car backfiring, but Mary swore it was a gunshot. We were too scared to go outside, so I peered through my front window. We saw three men running across the street. The first man was definitely Peter."

"And the other two men?"

"They were some distance back. There was lots of shouting, and one of them had a gun out—he looked like the man who I'd seen here an hour before, but I couldn't be sure."

"What man?"

"He'd been walking up and down out front. Even though he was wearing a suit, he looked suspicious. I approached him and asked him what he was doing, and he flashed his badge at me and said it was routine police business. I thought no more of it and went inside to wait for Mary."

Delray wrote on his pad. "So then what happened?"

"Mary and I weren't sure what to do. It looked like the other two men were chasing Peter, but we couldn't be sure. They could have all been running together and Peter was just faster. When they disappeared out of sight, we thought about calling the police, but this man said he was a police officer, and we knew Peter was a police officer, so…"

Connie clasped her hands together again and stared at the floor as she concentrated. After a few moments, she continued, "I'm not sure how long it was after that, but we heard another gunshot."

"Did it sound distant or close?"

"It was close, just like the first shot."

"So what did you do?"

"We peered out the window again but couldn't see anything. By now, we were scared. I went and checked my front door to make sure it was locked. Then we just sat quietly and waited. A few minutes later, we heard sirens, and we looked outside again. We counted two ambulances and three police cars all blocking off the street out front. There were police everywhere. We stood just outside my front door and watched. We saw little Bridgette being led away, and later they loaded a body covered in a sheet into the ambulance... We later found out it was Annie."

Delray noticed Connie's chest heaving a little. "I know this must be very traumatic for you, Connie, even this many years later, so take your time."

"We weren't sure what to do. We'd heard gunshots and thought that was important information, so we spoke to a uniformed police officer who said he'd organize for a detective to come and speak to us."

"And did that happen?"

"Kind of. The detective who I'd seen out front an hour before the shooting started came back and took our names and spoke to us for about two minutes. But we never saw him again, or anyone else, for that matter."

Delray frowned. "This is the same man who you saw chasing Peter Casseldhorf?"

Connie nodded.

"Did he give you his name?"

"No."

Delray paused for a moment. "How old do you think this man was?"

"Around thirty. Maybe a little younger."

"White?"

"Yes."

"How tall would you say he was?"

"Not as tall as you, but not short either."

Delray was six feet two. He jotted down the man's height as around six feet. "And what about the color of his hair?"

"Dark brown."

"What kind of build would you say he had? Was he thin?"

"No, but he wasn't fat either."

Delray made several more notes. "Do you think you would recognize him if you saw him again?"

Connie Swayne held Delray's gaze as she responded, "My eyesight may not be what it used to be, inspector, but that day is seared into my memory. Unless he's had plastic surgery, I'm sure I'd recognize him."

Friday - 2:35 P.M.

Bridgette paused at the top of the third flight of stairs to get her bearings as she searched for apartment number fourteen. After completing her interview with Jane Whitecross, she had contacted Ethan Whitecross requesting an urgent meeting. Whitecross had sounded hungover as he answered the phone and did his best to stave off the interview with excuses about being unwell. Undeterred, Bridgette had insisted on a meeting and had taken the freeway to the inner-city suburb of Morton, a twenty-minute drive from Stone Bay.

The three-story apartment block that Ethan Whitecross called home was a far cry from the residence his sister-in-law lived in. As she walked across fraying carpet and down a dark hallway badly in need of painting, Bridgette guessed the building was close to forty years old. Pushing her surprise at Whitecross's squalid living conditions to the back of her mind, she knocked on the door to apartment fourteen and waited.

She heard a muffled voice inside the apartment

respond, "Hang on a minute," before everything went quiet. After waiting for over a minute, Ethan Whitecross opened the door. Bridgette ignored his unshaven face, unkempt hair, and dirty linen shirt as she focused on his eyes. Whitecross's pupils were dilated, and she immediately suspected he was high on drugs. Police officers on the Narcotics team often used the term "cocaine eyes," and she wondered if this was what she was witnessing as she said, "Good afternoon, Ethan. Thanks for seeing me on such short notice."

Whitecross nodded in her general direction. "I hope this isn't going to take long. I've got a bad case of the flu, and I want to go back to bed."

Whitecross turned and walked back into a combined living room and kitchen. Bridgette followed him inside and noticed the curtains were drawn, giving the room a dark, depressing feel. Doing her best to ignore the smell of cigarettes and body odor as it wafted up from a pile of dirty laundry on the floor next to a worn leather couch, Bridgette knew the visit would be memorable, perhaps for all the wrong reasons.

Whitecross sat in an easy chair and pointed toward the leather couch. "Have a seat."

After sitting down, Bridgette said, "I visited your sister-in-law this afternoon and was hoping to interview you at the same time. I—"

"Like I said, I have the flu and should be in bed. Besides, Jane is a pain in the ass. I'm not keen on spending any more time with her than absolutely necessary."

"For someone who has just found out their brother and father have been murdered, you don't seem overly concerned?"

Whitecross dropped his head and shook it slightly.

"Don't be laying that guilt trip on me. I get enough of that from my sister-in-law."

"Ethan, look at me."

Whitecross looked up. Bridgette noticed Whitecross's eyes darting about the room as if he was having trouble focusing on her. "I don't know what you're on, but you need to focus."

"I've been taking medication for the flu, that's all."

"I'm not stupid, Ethan."

Whitecross finally focused on her with a silent stare.

Bridgette pulled out a piece of paper in a clear plastic sleeve from her folder. "This is a sketch of the man we believe killed your father…" She briefly explained how they had found Roy Pepper and then added, "We're almost certain this man was involved in the murder of your father."

Bridgette focused on Whitecross's body language as she asked, "Have you ever seen this man before?"

Without looking up from the sketch, Whitecross said, "This could be anybody."

"That's not answering the question."

Whitecross looked up and snapped, "What do you want me to say? My father's murder was twenty years ago. I wasn't much more than a kid, and I know lots of guys that look similar to this picture, but I couldn't say for certain it was any one of them."

Before she could respond, Whitecross handed the sketch back and added, "I can't help you, detective."

Bridgette pulled out her smartphone and opened it up to the first of the two pictures she had taken in Owen Whitecross's study. She held the device up for Whitecross to see. "Does this look familiar?"

Whitecross leaned forward slightly to study the image. After a few seconds, he responded, "Kind of."

"You know where this comes from, don't you?"

Whitecross nodded. "My brother's study."

"You, your father, your brother...and a third boy."

Bridgette paused to study Whitecross's facial expression, which remained sullen. "Who was the third boy?"

"How should I know, detective? That photo must have been taken thirty-five years ago."

Bridgette swiped right on her smartphone and showed Whitecross the second photo. "This is another photo. Your mother and father if I'm not mistaken?"

Whitecross nodded.

"If you look closely, you can see three small boys in the background sitting cross-legged with their backs against the stable door."

Whitecross leaned in again to look at the photograph. "Okay."

"Don't you find it interesting that your brother has only two photos from his childhood in his office and both feature three boys, not two?"

Whitecross stared off into space and said nothing.

Bridgette added, "I'm good at my job, Ethan. If you don't tell me, I'll find out eventually. Let's make this easy on both of us."

Whitecross said nothing for almost thirty seconds and then mumbled, "His name was Simon. He lived with my family from the time he was a baby. His father and my father were business partners."

"Why did he come to live with your family?"

"I don't know the whole story, but there was a car accident—his mother and father were killed. My parents adopted him."

"Okay, so where is he now?"

"I have no idea."

"You have no idea?"

"Simon had a big falling out with my father just after he turned eighteen. They had a huge fight."

"What was the fight about?"

"I don't know. I was only fourteen. My father told Owen and I it was none of our concern."

"So then what happened?"

"I came home from school the following day, and he was gone. His room was empty, and I never saw him again."

"So he never tried to contact you?"

"No."

"And you never tried to find him?"

"I was a screwed-up fourteen-year-old, detective. My mother lost a battle with leukemia and my father rarely spoke to me."

"Did Owen ever speak about Simon?"

"We used to talk about it a lot after it first happened. But after a while…"

Bridgette frowned. "I find it hard to believe you never wanted to find out what happened to him?"

"Like I said, I was pretty screwed up, and it wasn't exactly happy families after my mother died."

"So you have no idea where he lives now or what he's doing?"

Whitecross shook his head. "He could be dead for all I know."

"Did Owen ever try to find him?"

"If he did, he never mentioned it to me."

"You didn't think this worthwhile information to pass on to me in our first interview?"

"This happened thirty years ago. I don't see how it's relevant to my brother's murder, or my father's, for that matter."

Bridgette studied Ethan Whitecross for a moment. There were more questions she wanted to ask him, but she decided to wait until she knew more about his stepbrother. As she got up from her chair, she said, "I have one last question for you. Simon's surname, was it changed to Whitecross when he was adopted?"

"As far as I'm aware, yes."

"So that should make him easy to find?"

"I don't know… You're the detective, not me."

Friday - 2:45 P.M.

Felix Delray let out a long breath before knocking on the open door to Commissioner Underwood's office. Even though this wasn't the first time Underwood had called him up for a meeting on short notice, he felt uneasy knowing what he was about to say could permanently damage his career. Underwood was engrossed in a phone call, listening intently and throwing in the occasional "okay" as his contribution. Without looking up, Underwood pointed at a chair on the opposite side of his desk, which Delray took as his cue to enter.

As Delray sat down, Underwood said to the caller, "I'm just about to start another meeting, can we talk about this later?" Underwood listened intently for a moment before replacing the telephone handset.

After looking up at Delray, he said flatly, "My nineteen-year-old daughter is currently on vacation in Europe and wants to extend her stay. The only problem is she is running short of money…"

Delray nodded and said diplomatically, "I'm sure she appreciates your support, sir."

Underwood's face broke into a rare smile. "I'm sure she does."

The smile quickly vanished as Underwood continued, "I have another meeting in fifteen minutes, but when you called to say you'd made some progress on the basement shooting, I thought it prudent to get an update from you as soon as possible."

Delray nodded. "I think we may be close to a breakthrough, sir." He explained his interview with Connie Swayne earlier that day. He concluded by adding, "We know Peter Casseldhorf was working undercover at the time his wife was murdered. It wouldn't be the first time an undercover cop has discovered corruption in his own police force."

Underwood scratched at his chin for a moment. "How old did you say this witness was?"

"She's eighty-four, sir."

Underwood grimaced. "We all want this solved quickly, Felix, but how reliable do you think she is? Eighty-four is not exactly young."

"Sir, I take your point, but her mind seems to be very sharp."

"How can you be so sure?"

"When Bridgette first joined Vancouver Metro, she asked me if she could investigate her mother's murder on her own time. I remember her telling me what she remembered as a seven-year-old girl on the day her mother was murdered."

"And what did she say?"

"She told me it happened on a Saturday. She remembers

her mother leading her upstairs and saying she needed to be quiet while her father had an important meeting. They heard male voices, and the conversation quickly became a shouting match. All of a sudden, they heard a gunshot. Her mother pushed her into a closet and made her promise not to come out until it was safe. She was scared but eventually fell asleep and was woken by another loud noise sometime later."

"Another gunshot?"

"Yes, we believe that was the shot that killed her mother. The timing of what she heard is consistent with Connie Swayne's testimony."

Underwood nodded. "So you said after the first shot your witness saw two men chasing Peter Casseldhorf away from the building. Why would they come back and kill Annie Casseldhorf?"

"We believe they would have killed Peter Casseldhorf if they'd caught him, but he got away. My guess is they came back and killed his wife as a warning."

"A warning?"

"Bridgette also said that straight after she woke up, the door to the closet opened, and she briefly saw the silhouette of a man looking in before the door closed again."

"The murderer?"

"Peter Casseldhorf stayed a fugitive for twenty years and never came in to testify. I've often wondered why?"

"They killed his wife and threatened to murder his daughter as well?"

Delray nodded.

Underwood reflected, "While I might be a little flippant about my daughter's spending habits, there's nothing I wouldn't do for her. I'm not sure what I would have done in Peter Casseldhorf's position. It must have been a nightmare."

Cold Hard Cash

Both men were silent for a moment before Underwood added, "Your theory would certainly explain why the murder file went missing."

"It also explains why Peter Casseldhorf let two armed men into his home. If they were cops, he probably had no idea what was about to happen."

Underwood pushed back from his desk and stared off into space as he thought for a moment. Finally, he said, "So what's your next step, Felix?"

Delray's gut tightened as he pulled out a scrappy piece of paper from his jacket pocket. After smoothing it out, he placed it on Underwood's desk. "I made a list of all the detectives who worked here twenty years ago when Peter Casseldhorf was on the force. I have refined the list based on who is still alive and who has the most to lose if something about their past became public. There are nine names in total…"

Delray swallowed as he slid the list across the desk toward the commissioner. "With your approval, sir, I'd like to take copies of the photographs of each detective on the list to show to Connie Swayne."

"And where do you plan to get photos that are twenty years old?"

"We still produced yearbooks back then, sir. Every detective on the force had his photo taken for the yearbook."

"Having spent most of my policing career in Rochford, I'm not sure I will recognize most of these names, Felix."

"I'm happy to fill you in, sir."

Underwood picked up the list. "Top of your list is John Cotton. If I'm not mistaken, John Cotton is now a senator?"

"That's correct, sir. John Cotton left the force in his early thirties to enter politics. He's done well for himself and is now in a very powerful position and has a lot to lose."

Underwood nodded. "Number two is Paul Ferringa."

"Paul Ferringa was Peter Casseldhorf's partner for a short time. He spent much of his time in Narcotics before joining the Fraud squad. Like Cotton, he left early and has made a name for himself in real estate and construction. He is rumored to be worth about forty million dollars."

Underwood let out a low whistle. "Plenty of motive there." He glanced at the list again. "Number three is Nathan Alexander?"

"Alexander used to be a homicide detective. He studied law part-time and left the force about seventeen years ago after graduating. While he's nowhere near as wealthy as either Cotton or Ferringa, he has developed a solid profile as a defense attorney and has made a lot of money."

Underwood held Delray's gaze and said flatly, "I note the fourth person on your list is still an active member of the Vancouver Metropolitan police force?"

Delray shifted in his chair. "Sir, you may think I'm biased because Assistant Commissioner Cunningham and I don't get on, but I am trying to remain objective. Twenty years ago, he was in charge of Internal Investigations and dismissed corruption allegations made by Peter Casseldhorf and some other officers." Delray wanted to say more, but Underwood's body language suggested he had said enough.

"We can't be investigating a senior officer based on hearsay, Felix, and that's all you've got. While I may not be particularly fond of the approach Cunningham takes in performing some of his duties, I have no reason to doubt his professional standing." Underwood studied the list for a moment longer. "I don't see any other active officers on the list?"

Cold Hard Cash

"No, sir."

Underwood held Delray's gaze. "If this ever gets to a point where we think we need to investigate an active senior officer, I'll need to take legal advice. My job is as much political as it is anything else, and if the media ever got wind of what we were doing, all hell would break loose."

"Let's hope it doesn't come to that, sir."

The conversation was interrupted by Underwood's phone as it rang again. Underwood picked up the handset and listened for a moment before saying to the caller, "Give me a minute." After hanging up, he said, "My next appointment is here, so I need to keep moving. I'm happy for you to produce photographs of the top three names on your list to show the witness. Please be discreet and then report back to me. If we get a match, well and good, if not, we'll need to figure out what we do next."

"Yes, sir."

"Before you go, I have a question. Detective Cash's parents' name is Casseldhorf? Have I missed something?"

"While Peter Casseldhorf was a fugitive, he used the name Cash, an abbreviation of his real name."

"Okay."

"Bridgette lived most of her life believing her father was responsible for her mother's murder. It was only after his death we all realized that assumption was incorrect. This is her way of saying she isn't ashamed of him or who he had become."

Underwood responded, "Good to know," as he slid Delray's suspect list back across the desk toward him. He held Delray's gaze for a moment. "I wouldn't be showing this list to anyone else, Felix. Careers have been irreparably damaged for far less."

"Yes, sir."

Delray said a brief goodbye and breathed a sigh of relief as he walked out of the office and headed for the elevator. Leaving Cunningham's name on the list had been a risk, but he wasn't about to compromise a murder investigation because of police politics. After pressing the elevator button, he looked down at the list again. Delray knew Underwood was expecting answers quickly and decided to set up the second interview with Connie Swayne as soon as he got back to his office. As he stepped into the elevator, he wondered what Underwood would do if she didn't recognize anyone from the photos. He mumbled, "Let's hope your memory is as good as you say it is, Connie," as he pressed the button for level two.

Friday - 6:25 P.M.

Delray looked up when he heard the knock on his office door. He said, "Come on in, Bridgette," and then added as an afterthought, "Probably best if you close the door as well."

Delray noticed Bridgette tense a little and added, "You're not in trouble, but we don't need the entire world listening in either…"

Delray closed an open file on his desk as Bridgette sat down. "I've been investigating the witness list from your mother's murder. I followed up on the two names on the microfilm copy that never made it onto the computer record."

"Okay."

"Connie Swayne and Mary Keaton."

"They were neighbors of my mother and father."

Delray clasped his hands together. "Mary Keaton died three years ago, but Connie Swayne is still alive. In fact, she still lives in the same townhouse complex. I've been to see her twice today…"

"And how is she?"

"Old, but apart from that, she's doing well."

Bridgette nodded.

Delray continued, "She's now eighty-four but still remembers a lot about that day." Delray continued in a softer voice, "She told me about the first gunshot and your father being chased by two men...and the second gunshot about twenty minutes later."

Bridgette closed her eyes.

Delray went on to explain how Connie had seen a man claiming to be a plainclothes detective conducting surveillance an hour before the first gunshot. He paused and then said, "I know this is hard for you, Bridgette."

"I'm okay, chief. I need to hear this."

Delray explained how the man had come back later as part of the police contingent and how he had briefly spoken to Connie but never took a formal statement.

"Did she remember his name?"

"He never gave her his name, but she gave me a good description. I used it to make a shortlist of detectives who worked for Vancouver Metro back then who might be a match. I took photocopies from the yearbook of the three detectives that were the closest to her description and went back and visited her late this afternoon." Delray opened the file on his desk again and withdrew a black-and-white photocopied image. As he passed it across to Bridgette, he added, "She recognized this man as soon as she saw the photograph..."

Delray watched as Bridgette stared at the image of a serious-looking man in his late twenties and dressed in a business suit.

Bridgette responded, "This is a cop?"

"Was a cop. He left Vancouver Metro a long time ago. I

can't tell you any more until I've met with the commissioner."

"You said there were two of them chasing my father?"

"If this is the guy, it was probably his partner. But he died about eighteen months after your mother's murder."

"How convenient."

"Not for him. He got hit by a cement truck three days before he was due to testify in an Internal Investigations hearing. The word at the time was he was dirty and trying to save his skin by testifying against other cops. But he never got the chance…"

Bridgette mumbled, "Karma," more to herself than to Delray.

Delray said, "I know we shouldn't get ahead of ourselves, but I think we're closing in on who did this."

Bridgette looked up from the photocopy. "So what happens now?"

"I'm waiting for the commissioner to call me. I need to give him a briefing before we do anything else. The testimony of an eighty-four-year-old woman about a twenty-year-old murder won't stand up in court, particularly as she didn't actually witness a murder. This is a good start, but we need a lot more evidence."

As Bridgette handed back the image, she said, "Thanks for keeping me in the loop, chief. I really appreciate it."

"Please keep this to yourself. I'm not supposed to be telling you or anyone else about this, but I thought you'd like to know we're making some progress at least."

Delray studied Bridgette for a moment. She seemed to be accepting of the news which he took as a good sign. "As soon as I can tell you more, I will. Okay?"

"Thanks."

"There's something else I need to talk to you about."

"Okay."

Delray grimaced. "Cunningham's been in my ear. After the arrest of John Hanway for Charlie Bates's murder, they've decided to scale back the team working on the case."

"Even though we know Hanway is just a hired gun?"

Delray nodded. "Cunningham looks after the budgets. Charlie Bates's murder is now old news because they've arrested someone. A case that is getting heavy media attention gets priority. As soon as that changes, resources get reassigned. Unfortunately, it's all about perception with Cunningham—that's how he works. It's still a high priority for the commissioner, but just a smaller team... Sterling starts with us on Monday."

"Okay."

"Like I said before, I don't want him here a moment longer than absolutely necessary. Once this basement incident is solved, and I believe we're well on the way, he's out of here."

"It's fine, chief, I'll find a way to work with him."

"I appreciate your attitude, Bridgette." Delray looked at his watch. "The commissioner hasn't called yet, so why don't you fill me in on your progress with the Rook Island murders?"

Bridgette placed a copy of the sketch of the man who had attacked Roy Pepper on Delray's desk and explained how she had shown it to both Jane and Ethan Whitecross.

"Did they recognize him?"

"Jane Whitecross claims she has never seen the man before. Ethan did too, but I'm not so sure he was telling the truth." Bridgette went on to explain how she thought Ethan Whitecross was on drugs and how that made it difficult to gauge his reaction.

"So you think maybe he recognized him?"

"I'm not certain, but my gut tells me yes."

"Let's get him in here for an interview, and we'll play some tag team on him."

Bridgette replied, "I'd like to leave it for a day or two, chief," before explaining how she had learned that Owen and Ethan Whitecross had an adopted brother called Simon.

Delray frowned. "An adopted brother could have all kinds of motives, particularly when a father and son are both murdered."

"That's what I was thinking. But finding anyone by the name of Simon Whitecross with links to Reid Whitecross is proving more challenging than I expected. I spent two hours trawling our databases and got nowhere, so I called Walter Denphy, the stable hand from NewFarm Racecourse. He didn't really know Reid Whitecross but put me in touch with a retired racing official who did."

"Have you interviewed him yet?"

"The man's name is David Monaghan. I interviewed him this afternoon. He's retired now but has fond memories of working with Reid Whitecross."

"And what did he have to say?"

"According to Monaghan, Reid Whitecross had a business partner, and they were close, almost like brothers. This partner and his wife were killed in a car accident. They had a child, a baby called Simon, who survived the accident. Whitecross and his wife were godparents and adopted Simon and raised him as their own."

"So if he's no longer on the scene, what happened?"

"Monaghan recalled Reid Whitecross going through a rough period when Simon was seventeen. His wife had died of leukemia, and he and Simon weren't getting along. Apparently, Simon's birth parents were wealthy, and they left their estate in trust for him to inherit on or after his eighteenth birthday."

Delray frowned. "On or after his eighteenth birthday? What does that mean?"

"According to Monaghan, it was discretionary. The will stated the inheritance was only to be passed on when the Whitecross's were satisfied Simon was mature enough to handle the money properly. Apparently, the inheritance was over a million dollars."

Delray let out a low whistle. "So then what happened?"

"When Simon turned eighteen, he approached Whitecross requesting he be given the inheritance, but Whitecross said no. They had a massive argument, and Simon stormed out, never to return."

"Plenty of motive there."

"Kind of, but Reid Whitecross lived for another ten years before he was murdered. Monaghan thinks Simon had already received his inheritance by then."

"Nonetheless, this all needs investigating."

"I agree."

"So where is this Simon guy now?"

"According to Monaghan, he owns a construction and investment company here in Vancouver called the Minos Group—"

"Did you say Minos?"

"Yes. He's also reverted to using his birth name and is reportedly worth about forty million dollars. I'm trying to set up an interview with him, but contacting him is proving difficult. I've gotten as far as leaving a message with his personal assistant, but..."

Bridgette paused for a moment to study Delray, who no longer seemed to be listening. She tilted her head to one side. "Something wrong?"

Delray frowned. "This name change...was it just his last name?"

"No, his first name as well."

"What's his first name?"

"Paul."

Delray stared in disbelief for several seconds. "His last name's Ferringa, isn't it?"

Bridgette nodded. "How did you know?"

Delray let out a long breath and then slid the yearbook photo Connie Swayne had identified across his desk. He twisted it around until it was side by side with Roy Pepper's sketch and facing Bridgette. "Do you see any similarities?"

Bridgette's eyes widened as she studied the images. "It can't be..."

Delray held Bridgette's gaze. "Paul Ferringa used to be a police officer. He left the force just before he turned thirty to start a company called the Minos Group. He's now a multi-millionaire." As he stared down at the two images again, Delray added, "It's the same guy..."

Friday - 8:05 P.M.

Bridgette changed down gears as she pulled into her gymnasium's parking lot in the light industrial suburb of West Raton. As it was only two minutes off the freeway, she usually tried to make a six-thirty class with her gym pals on the way home from work. Tonight was different—her meeting with Delray hadn't finished until well after seven. As she walked into a building that was once a fruit canning factory, she could only see a handful of people who were still working out. She scanned the main gym area which was about the size of two basketball courts but didn't see anyone she recognized. Normally, she enjoyed the company of others for a CrossFit workout, but tonight she was happy to exercise on her own—there was a lot to think about.

After changing, Bridgette walked into the main workout area and found herself a spot in the far right-hand corner. She started with a few stretching exercises to warm up while she thought back to her last conversation with Delray. It had come as a complete shock to both of them that Paul

Ferringa, a.k.a. Simon Whitecross, was the prime suspect in both murder cases. The thought of finally knowing who was responsible for her parents' murders had been hard to take in, and she had spent close to an hour talking it through with Delray. They had only just begun piecing the links together when Delray had been called up for his meeting with the commissioner. Having no idea how long the meeting would go for, Delray told her to go home, adding they would meet again first thing in the morning.

Now warm, she decided to start with some jump squats as she thought about the man they now knew as Paul Ferringa. Standing with her feet apart and her toes pointed slightly, Bridgette bent at the knees and extended her arms. She recalled Delray saying Ferringa had been a smart and savvy cop—but not someone you would ever trust. Pressing down through her heels, Bridgette jumped high off the ground and clapped her hands above her head before landing in a standing position with her legs slightly bent.

As she repeated the exercise, she planned to learn all she could about Ferringa. A number of questions played on her mind, going as far back as the car accident that had killed his birth parents. She would need to spend time reviewing the newspaper archives to learn what she could. She was suspicious of a business partner obtaining control of a large sum of money for a child until they became an adult. Now working up a sweat, she knew it would be challenging uncovering the real truth of what happened twenty years ago.

Bridgette thought about the relationship between Reid Whitecross and his adoptive son as she neared the end of the exercise. She wondered what caused the problems in their relationship. Ethan Whitecross was the obvious person to ask, but he wasn't proving to be a reliable witness. She decided she would re-interview David Monaghan to learn as much as she could about the family.

After completing her fourth set of fifteen squat repetitions, Bridgette stood for a moment to catch her breath. She wondered what had prompted Simon Whitecross to change his surname back to Ferringa. It was reasonable to assume it was because of the fallout with his adoptive father, but was that the answer? Switching to the use of his middle name had also seemed odd. Delray was emphatic he had always been known as Paul Ferringa during his time in Vancouver Metro. As her breathing returned to normal, Bridgette lay down faceup on the workout mat and slid a folded towel under her lower back. Ferringa's name change continued to bother her. People who changed their name normally had a good reason, and she was determined to find out why.

Bridgette brought the soles of her feet together to form a diamond pattern with her legs. As she started the first of sixty butterfly sit-ups, she thought back to the gruesome find of Reid and Owen Whitecross in the water cave on Rook Island. Being murdered by a family member now began to make sense, but hiding their bodies in a cave still puzzled her. She whispered, "There has to be a reason," as she felt her abdominal muscles begin to burn as she continued the routine.

After completing her sixtieth sit-up, Bridgette stood and wiped sweat from her face with her towel. She thought back to the timeline of events while she rested. Whitecross had changed his name back to Ferringa shortly after leaving home, just after his eighteenth birthday. According to Delray, Ferringa had joined the police force as a cadet just before his nineteenth birthday and made it all the way to the rank of senior detective during his nine years of service.

He had received his inheritance at age twenty-five, eighteen months before Reid Whitecross disappeared. With no murder weapon, witness, or real motive beyond being an adopted member of the family, she knew the evidence against Ferringa was thin.

After setting up in a squat position, Bridgette dropped into a push-up and then, in one slick motion, jumped up and clapped her hands above her head before landing on her feet again. As she repeated the exercise routine known as a burpee, Bridgette knew she barely had enough evidence to question Ferringa, let alone make an arrest. A lot more investigation was required. Bridgette felt a twinge in her gut as she wondered again whether she would be allowed to continue on the Rook Island case now that Ferringa was the prime suspect.

This was the last question she had posed to Delray before he'd left for his meeting with the commissioner. She believed Delray had been straight with her when he said he didn't know. The commissioner had been adamant he didn't want her involved in her mother's murder investigation, and now that it all looked connected, there was every chance she would be pulled from this case as well. Bridgette pushed on with her routine. The decision was out of her control, and she would work as hard as she could while she had the opportunity.

At the end of her burpee routine, she stood with her hands on her hips for a moment while she caught her breath. She hadn't wanted to think about the day her mother had been murdered again, but in light of Connie Swayne's testimony, she was now certain it had been Ferringa and his partner her father had let into their home. Bridgette closed her eyes as she heard the sound of the first gunshot as a frightened seven-year-old again. She visualized awaking to the sound of the second noise and her heart almost beating through her chest as the closet door opened. The thought sent a shiver through her spine as she wondered if it had been Ferringa's silhouette staring down at her before the door closed again.

Bridgette shook her head to clear her mind of the image and walked over to a wooden exercise box. It all began to make sense, and she was now convinced Ferringa had come back to murder her mother and frame her father. With her back to the box, she placed her palms face down and gripped the box's top edge as she visualized the image of the twenty-seven-year-old cop posing for a yearbook photo. She had never been this close to knowing who had killed her parents before, and it made her stomach churn. A small part of her wanted to know why, but mostly, she just wanted revenge. Uncomfortable with the feelings of hatred that began to stir within her, Bridgette tried to focus on the exercise. She stretched out her legs and bent her arms at the elbows to lower her body. She held her body weight in the lower position for a moment before straightening her arms to raise her body again. She continued the exercise, which to onlookers looked like a reverse push-up, until the lactic acid became unbearable.

After taking several deep breaths, Bridgette stood up again and walked across to the exercise mat. She wondered why Ferringa had come after her family. She reasoned he must have been one of the targets in her father's undercover investigation. Delray would no doubt have more information, and she intended to learn as much as she could about the ex-cop's service record in the coming days. Even though her body wanted a break, Bridgette pushed on and started a series of lunge hops. She completed sixty repetitions before dropping down into a standard push-up position. As she began a series of push-ups, she saw heavy beads of sweat fall from her face to the mat below. Bridgette ignored the sweat and pain as she mused why Ferringa had left the police force. Delray believed it was because he was corrupt and afraid of being caught. While it seemed an obvious answer, it needed to be tested. She wondered what he did with the inheritance. A million dollars could bring big changes to a person's life; was that a factor?

After completing her push-ups, Bridgette whispered, "So many questions," as she rolled onto her back. Not caring that she was lying in her own sweat, she stared up at the steel rafters that supported the building's roof as she planned what she would do next. Tomorrow was Saturday, a day she normally wouldn't work, but that had all changed. Now that an ex-cop was the main suspect in two separate cases, she was sure the commissioner would insist on a team investigation. Her gut tightened again as she faced the prospect she would be shut out because of her family connection. Bridgette sighed at the possible injustice. She'd been the one who made the breakthroughs in the Rook Island murders, but she knew none of her achievements would matter.

Bridgette rarely got into a bad mood, but as her frustration grew, she knew a workout with weights would help. She walked over to the barbells and stood for a moment looking at the discs, contemplating how much she wanted to lift. Normally she lifted over a hundred pounds, but that weight required all her concentration. Tonight, she would settle for ninety-eight. While fitting the weights, she thought about how soon a team could be assembled. The job would likely fall to Cunningham who was a nine-to-five cop who liked his weekends. She thought it unlikely a team would be operational before Monday, which would give her at least two more days on the case. After moving the barbells out into the center of the lifting mat, Bridgette lowered herself into a squat position. As she gently gripped the bar, she thought about what she should focus her time on. Her best source of fresh information would be an interview with Paul Ferringa himself. While she doubted he would give much away, seeing him up close and observing his body language and how he operated would be invaluable in learning if he was the one.

Bridgette gripped the bar firmly with both hands and let out a gasp as she lifted the barbell. Rolling her wrists in a fluid motion as she lifted, she brought the barbell to a rest on her chest just below her collarbone. Bridgette let out three long breaths as she prepared for the final part of the lift. She wondered how she would react when she saw Ferringa up close. Bridgette pushed the barbell high above her head until she felt her elbows lock. With her arms wavering slightly as she held the weight, she knew she would need all her mental resolve to get through any meeting without reacting emotionally. She counted to three in her mind and then dropped the barbell to the floor. As she let out a long breath, she realized getting an interview with Ferringa before Monday would be almost impossible. She stood for a moment and played back in her mind the phone conversation she'd had with his personal assistant earlier that day. She whispered, "There might be a way," as a plan began to unfold in her mind.

Dropping back into a squat position, she concluded there was no way she could pull it off without Delray's help. As she gripped the bar again, Bridgette decided she needed to call him tonight. After a deep breath, she lifted the bar again and held it for a count of three before dropping it to the floor. She picked up her towel to wipe her face and then looked up at the gymnasium's clock. It was closing in on nine p.m. Ordinarily, she would have pushed on for another twenty minutes, but not tonight. She would call Delray on the way home and pitch him her idea. If he liked what she had to say, there was going to be a lot for her to do between now and tomorrow morning.

Friday - 9:10 P.M.

Bridgette wasted little time showering and changing after her workout. She called Delray shortly after getting back on the freeway for her final fifteen-minute drive home.

Delray picked up on the fourth ring and said a garbled, "Hello."

"Sorry, chief, have I caught you in the middle of dinner?"

"No problem. I can talk if you don't mind me eating. Are you in the Mustang?"

Bridgette had installed a hands-free phone kit in her fully restored '67 Mustang Fastback as one of the few concessions to modern motoring. The technology worked fine, but her car wasn't quiet, even at moderate speeds. "Yeah, are you getting background noise?"

"A little."

Bridgette spotted a suburban turnoff ahead. "I'll be off the freeway in under a minute. Will that work for you?"

"Sure. What's up?"

"I've been thinking about Paul Ferringa. I think I may

have figured out a way we can interview him tomorrow without making an appointment. We'll probably learn more if we can catch him off guard."

"It's a good strategy, but I thought you only got as far as leaving a message with his assistant?"

"I did, but it was something she said that makes me think we might be able to interview him tomorrow."

"I'm all ears."

As she turned off the freeway, Bridgette said, "When I asked his assistant about setting up an interview, she told me he was busy until mid-next week."

"Okay."

"I told her it was urgent, but as she started making excuses, I learned quite a lot about his schedule. He's flying out early on Sunday for a two-day conference in Bolton, but tomorrow he's going to the football match to watch the Dragons play the Chargers."

"That's a home game here at Power Stadium if I'm not mistaken?"

Bridgette responded, "Yes," as she parked her car. "I've done some quick research on my smartphone. It was his company that built Power Stadium. Apparently, he's a huge fan, and they've made him the number-one ticket holder. So you know what that means…"

"He's got a private box."

"Exactly."

The line was silent for a moment before Delray said, "I'm liking the element of surprise. We can turn up unannounced to ask him a few questions. It's ballsy, and he'll probably complain, but it we'll catch him unprepared."

"I was thinking we could use the angle that we have come to inform him of the death of his adoptive father and brother. My guess is if he's so disconnected from the Whitecross family, he won't have been told by anybody."

"The irony is, if he's the killer, he'd have known before anyone else."

Bridgette smiled to herself at Delray's deadpan humor. "Yes, I see your point."

"We have to plan the questions carefully. We'll start by informing him of the discovery of the bodies as you suggest and then build it from there. He'll probably lawyer up at some point and refuse to answer any more questions, but if we structure this correctly, we might learn a lot before that happens."

"I'll be home shortly. I thought I would spend time tonight doing some research on him. The more we know about him, the more—"

Delray cut her off. "Don't go at this too hard tonight, Bridgette. Like I said earlier, we're running a marathon here, not a sprint. You need your downtime too." He paused for a moment and then added, "What time is kickoff tomorrow?"

"Two thirty p.m."

"The stadium is about forty-five minutes from our precinct. We don't want to get there too early, and we don't want to get there too late, just in case he leaves early."

The two discussed the timings and agreed they would start work at eight in the morning with the aim of leaving for the stadium around one p.m.

Delray added, "We'll have plenty of time tomorrow morning for research. Now that we know who we're dealing with, we can use our time wisely developing the right questions to ask him."

"Sounds good, chief."

"Well, if there's nothing else, I'll see you in the morning."

Bridgette felt her gut tighten. "There is just one other thing…"

"Shoot."

"Did you discuss my future on the case with the commissioner?"

"We did touch on it."

"And?"

There was a slight pause before Delray responded, "I'm not going to sugarcoat this, Bridgette—the commissioner has a policy that nobody works on cases that are connected to family members…"

Bridgette tried to hide her feelings of disappointment. "Okay, I understand."

"But he values your considerable investigative skills and is happy for you to stay working in a supervised capacity on the Rook Island murders, at least until we get a team up and running. He might chew me out for taking you tomorrow, but technically, I'm not disobeying an order."

Bridgette let out a sigh of relief. At least she wasn't being kicked off the case straight away. She was fairly sure Delray had been advocating for her to stay on and this was the commissioner's concession for now. "Thanks, chief, I really appreciate it."

"No problem. Is there anything else?"

"Not for now and thanks for taking my call."

Delray responded, "I'll see you in the morning," before disconnecting.

Bridgette sat still for a moment trying to imagine how the interview with Paul Ferringa might play out tomorrow. Delray would take the lead which she was happy about. She wondered again if Ferringa really was the killer. Everything pointed to him directly or indirectly. She thought about the last time she had seen her mother and father alive and whispered, "Hold it together, girl," as tears welled in her eyes. Bridgette shook her head to clear her mind of the melancholy and then started her car.

After waiting for the traffic to clear, she pulled a U-turn and headed back to the freeway. She wondered how Ferringa would respond to their questions and whether they would really learn anything new. Suddenly, she was impatient for answers as she headed up the concrete ramp that led back onto the freeway. Bridgette consoled herself as she whispered, "Tomorrow will come soon enough," and then shifted into top gear.

Saturday - 7:25 A.M.

Bridgette couldn't sleep and gave up trying shortly after five a.m. After a long shower, a bowl of muesli, and a peppermint tea, she headed to work to get an early start. She arrived well before seven a.m. and enjoyed the early morning solitude and having the whole floor to herself. Bridgette spent close to an hour searching NatTrack for any information she could find about either Simon Whitecross or Paul Ferringa. Unsurprisingly, there were no references to Simon Whitecross in connection with any cases, but Paul Ferringa was a different story altogether. She had only just begun to collate the information when she heard the chime of the elevator as it stopped on level two. Bridgette looked up and saw Delray walking toward her cubicle holding two coffee cups.

"Good morning, chief."

"Morning, Bridgette. I hope you haven't had your coffee yet?"

Bridgette smiled. "No, only a peppermint tea."

"I know you only drink one cup a day, but being this early, I thought there was a chance you hadn't had it yet."

Delray handed her one of the cardboard cups and went to retrieve a chair from the neighboring cubicle as Bridgette thanked him. As they sat and sipped their coffee, Delray asked, "Did you get any sleep last night?"

"Not as much as I would have liked."

"Paul Ferringa?"

Bridgette nodded.

"For what it's worth, I didn't sleep much either…" Delray studied Bridgette for a moment before adding, "If you don't want to do this interview, Bridgette, I understand. I'm more than happy to call in one of the other guys to come with me. I can't begin to imagine how hard it must be facing—"

"I've thought about it a lot, chief—I want to do it. I've come too far to walk away."

Delray responded, "Fair enough," before taking a long sip of his coffee.

They were quiet for a moment before Bridgette said, "I've been searching NatTrack this morning for the names Simon Whitecross and Paul Ferringa."

"And what have you found?"

"Nothing on Simon Whitecross, but quite a lot on Paul Ferringa, indirectly."

"Indirectly?"

"His company is connected to a number of cases."

Delray stopped drinking his coffee. "What cases?"

"They stretch back ten years. They have interviewed Minos Group employees in connection with two murders, one missing person case, and three cases of bribing a public official. No convictions have ever been recorded, but it makes you wonder. I know it's a big company, but…"

"Well, if he's as dirty as we think he is, nothing surprises me."

"I'm still working through NatTrack. This is all I've found so far, but I wouldn't be surprised if I find more when I dig deeper."

"The more background we get on him, the better." After pausing a moment to pull a paper list out of his coat pocket, Delray continued, "I worked up a few questions last night to ask Ferringa today. They're in no particular order, and I'm sure you've got a few you want to add, but at least it's a starting point. We need to get the sequencing right so we get as much out of him as we can before he clams—"

Delray turned toward the elevator as it chimed again. He mumbled, "Someone else is getting an early start on Saturday," as they both looked up to see who it was.

A moment later, Aaron Sterling stepped out of the elevator and headed toward them. To Bridgette, he looked every bit as pompous as he did Monday through Friday when he wore a suit, even though today he was dressed in jeans, sneakers, and a leather jacket.

Bridgette did her best to keep her surprise to herself as Sterling stopped a few feet short of them and said with a sarcastic smile, "It looks like I'm too late for the coffee."

Delray replied deadpan, "And good morning to you too, detective. I thought you weren't starting with us until Monday?"

Sterling helped himself to a chair. "I got a call from Assistant Commissioner Cunningham last night. It appears you've made a breakthrough connecting a former police officer with two cases. Cunningham suggested I should move my start date forward from Monday to today…so here I am."

His condescending smile was not lost on Bridgette, nor

Delray, as he shot back, "Well, I appreciate your offer of assistance, detective. I'm sure we can find something for you to do today."

Sterling raised his eyebrows. "You might want to check with the assistant commissioner, chief. He told me he wanted me as lead detective on the case."

Bridgette stole a sideways look at her boss. Delray could suppress his feelings when he needed to, and this was quickly developing into one of those situations.

Delray sipped his coffee. "Well, for starters, detective, this is *still* two cases. We have a common suspect in both, but that's as far as it goes. I met with the commissioner last night to give him a briefing, and my orders haven't changed. So until I hear otherwise, my team is still running the Rook Island case, and we're assisting the commissioner and Internal Investigations as required with the basement incident."

There was an awkward pause before Sterling responded, "Well, I'm sure they can sort it out on Monday."

Delray responded, "I'm sure they can," and then gave Sterling some background on the two cases. Bridgette admired Delray's professional and inclusive manner, despite his well-known personal dislike for Sterling. Bridgette watched Sterling as he listened and took notes throughout the briefing. She realized she had a lot to learn about politics, particularly working with people you didn't like or trust. For now, all she saw when she looked at Sterling was a man in his early thirties with acne scars, oily hair, and an arrogant disposition, especially toward women. She was glad she was working with Delray. Barely a day went by when she didn't learn something from him, and today was no exception. She admired his ability to hold his dignity when those around him sought to challenge and undermine his authority.

At the end of the briefing, Delray added, "Do you have any questions?"

"What time are you planning to head to the stadium today?"

Delray answered, "Around one p.m. We plan to interview Ferringa before the half-time break."

"Good. That will give me time to get home and change back into a suit."

Delray shook his head. "No need, you won't be required for the interview."

Sterling demanded, "I outrank Detective Cash. Surely I should be your number two?"

"Not today. Detective Cash has conducted all the interviews for the Rook Island case. I need her there to ask questions relevant to that case."

Sterling's face flushed slightly. "I'm not sure the assistant commissioner will be happy with this?"

Delray responded flatly, "It's not his call, it's mine. He might outrank me, but this is still my case. If you want to argue, I suggest you and Cunningham take it up with the commissioner directly as he's taking a personal interest in this case." Delray paused for a moment while he held Sterling's stare before asking, "Any more questions?"

When Sterling shook his head, Delray stood up. "That's all for now. We'll reconvene at ten a.m. to shortlist the questions we want to ask Ferringa and talk tactics. Detective Sterling, you can assist Detective Cash with her research. Right now, this is your number one and only priority."

Before Sterling could respond, Delray walked off toward his office.

Bridgette took a sip of her coffee and then picked up a

thick file marked "Rook Island Murders." She didn't want Sterling interfering with her research or asking too many questions until they'd met with Delray again. She handed him the file. "This is the Rook Island case. Once you've read this, we can talk about the next steps in the investigation."

Sterling let out a small laugh as he took the file.

Bridgette frowned. "What's so funny?"

"I was just thinking…"

Bridgette did her best not to roll her eyes. "What were you thinking?"

"How does a rookie detective get to be heading up a murder case?"

"I don't have a partner right now…"

"We know how it ended for your last partner, don't we?"

Bridgette felt her face flush at the reference to her former partner who'd been killed three months earlier while solving their first case together. She knew Sterling was trying to get a rise out of her. *What would Delray do?*

She wanted to say, "I'll work with anyone—the fact I'm sitting next to you is a testament to that," but settled for, "There's close to two hours of reading in that folder. You get through it quick enough, we might have time for a few questions before we meet with the chief at ten…"

Bridgette didn't wait for a response and turned to face her computer. She pushed Sterling to the back of her mind as she opened the NatTrack database again. As she continued her search, the only name she was focused on right now was Paul Ferringa. With just a few hours until their first meeting, she still had a lot to do to prepare.

Saturday - 2:25 P.M.

Bridgette followed Delray up a third flight of stairs and out onto a concrete terrace. She looked down through a sea of people at the playing field below. The emerald green surface of Power Stadium was emblazoned with advertising logos and white line markings, making for a colorful backdrop. Bridgette watched both teams form into separate huddles to get their final instructions as two enormous replay screens at each end of the field started a final ninety-second countdown.

Above the roar of the crowd, Delray yelled, "This way," as he pointed to his right. They made their way up another four steps between rows of fans eager for the game to begin to an entrance marked "Corporate Boxes—No Public Access."

Delray walked up to two security guards who were blocking the entrance. "Good afternoon, gentlemen." After flashing his badge, he explained they had come to break the news of a murder to one of the VIP guests. One guard studied his badge for a moment before opening the heavy glass door to allow them to enter. Delray thanked the guards as they entered a long carpeted hallway.

Unsure where they would find Ferringa, Delray stopped a slim young man dressed in a waiter's outfit. "Excuse me, I'm looking for the VIP box for Paul Ferringa. Can you help me?"

"Sure, Mr. Ferringa is in suite one. I've just delivered them champagne." He turned and pointed down the corridor before adding, "The last door on the right. You can't miss it."

Delray thanked the waiter, and they continued on. A moment later, they heard a roar from the crowd that was close to deafening.

Bridgette said, "I guess that means the game has started?"

"You got it. They spent about one-point-five billion on this place, but apparently that doesn't buy you sound-proofing back here."

"I'm surprised at how many people are here today."

"About eighty thousand. Apparently, it's a sellout."

Delray glanced at Bridgette as they walked on. "How are you feeling about all this, Bridgette?"

"Tense. And maybe a little nervous…"

"I'd say that's fairly understandable, given who we're about to meet."

"I guess."

Delray stopped walking. "I'd understand if you don't think you can go through with this. There's no shame in knowing your limits…"

Bridgette shook her head. "No. I want to do this."

Delray responded, "Well, we'll play it like we planned," and started walking again.

"Okay."

Delray lowered his voice as they passed another waiter. "I'm not sure how long we'll get with Ferringa, but I'd like to document the entire conversation as best we can once we get back to the office. You never know what we might learn when we do a review."

Bridgette could normally remember a conversation, even as long as twenty minutes, almost word for word. Today she wasn't feeling as confident and pulled out her smartphone. "If you don't mind, chief, I'd prefer to record today. I might be okay, but if I get out of my comfort zone, there's a chance I won't take everything in."

"Will that record from your pocket?"

"Yes."

"Turn it on and keep it out of sight. We're not after anything that's admissible in court today, so we don't need to tell him about it..."

They stopped in front of a door painted a mushroom color to match the hallway. Bridgette took a deep breath to calm her nerves as she stared at the door's solid brass plaque that bore the number "One." Normally cool under pressure, she felt her heart race as she realized she might be only seconds away from confronting the man responsible for the murder of her parents.

Delray held her gaze. "Ready?"

Bridgette let out a long breath and then nodded.

Delray knocked on the door three times. Their wait was less than ten seconds, but to Bridgette, it seemed much longer. She felt her mouth go dry when the door was opened by a man in his early thirties—not Ferringa.

The man had a goatee beard and was dressed in chinos, a cotton shirt, and a sports jacket. He was about Bridgette's height and had a confident manner as he stood in the doorway and said, "Can I help you?"

Delray said, "Yes, you can," and then held up his badge. "My name is Chief Inspector Delray, and this is Detective Cash. We're here from Vancouver Metro to see Paul Ferringa."

The man glanced at Bridgette before returning his focus to Delray. "This is highly irregular. I'm sure you realize the game has just started and—"

Delray interrupted, "We won't keep him long."

The man didn't budge from the doorway. "Do you have an appointment?"

Delray replied flatly, "We have some news for Mr. Ferringa. It's a family matter and not the kind of thing we felt comfortable discussing over the phone..."

Slightly irritated, the man responded, "Wait here. I'll see if he's willing to see you."

The man turned and walked back into the room. Bridgette tilted her head just slightly to take in as much of the room as she could. She had imagined the corporate box to be not much more than a small viewing room with a few comfortable chairs. The room was much larger than she had expected. Beyond the doorway was a large dining table capable of seating twelve laid out with a series of seafood and meat platters. She counted off nine bottles of champagne plus an assortment of red and white wines. Beyond the dining room table was a vacant area about twice the size of Delray's office, where she imagined people would mingle during breaks in the game. On the opposite side of the room, there were two rows of chairs to watch the game behind a floor-to-ceiling glass window that provided an uninterrupted panoramic view of the playing field. Eleven of the seats were occupied, and everyone seemed oblivious to their presence as they watched the game. With their backs to the doorway, it was impossible for Bridgette to tell which guest was Ferringa.

She kept her eyes focused on the man with the goatee as he moved to the left-hand side of the front row and spoke softly to a man sitting on the end seat.

She was too far away to hear the conversation, but from his body language, the man with the goatee seemed apologetic. Bridgette couldn't see the face of the seated man, but Delray seemed in no doubt as he whispered to her, "That's him." They watched as the conversation went on for close to half a minute before the man with the goatee returned to speak with Delray.

"Mr. Ferringa has asked me to convey to you that he is entertaining clients and has requested you make an appointment."

Delray responded, "It's very important that we speak to him now. We wouldn't be here otherwise."

The man retorted, "This is very inconvenient."

Delray shot back, "Murders normally are."

The man scowled. "Follow me."

Delray and Bridgette followed the man inside. They only made it as far as the vacant area beyond the catering table before he pointed to a door on the left marked "Private" and said, "Wait in there. Mr. Ferringa will be with you shortly."

Delray opened the door and motioned for Bridgette to step in first. The room was a lot smaller than the main room, had no windows, and was furnished with one table and two chairs. Bridgette noticed three jackets and two shoulder bags lying on the table and figured they only used the room for storage.

Delray closed the door and said in a low voice, "Ferringa is playing games. My bet is he'll keep us waiting for at least ten minutes..."

Delray had the timing almost perfect. After nine agonizing minutes, the door finally opened.

Bridgette felt breathless as she stared at Paul Ferringa for the first time. He was taller than she expected and dressed in expensive dark gray slacks, an open-collared shirt, and a designer black leather jacket. His short, slightly wavy, brown hair was receding and had an unnatural evenness in color—probably dyed. He was broad across the shoulders without carrying any weight. To Bridgette, he didn't quite fit the picture she had in her mind of a sophisticated business executive as he stood in the doorway staring at Delray through thick black-rimmed glasses.

Delray broke the silence by saying, "It's been a long time, Paul."

In a baritone voice, Ferringa responded, "Why are you here, Felix?"

Delray replied flatly, "We're investigating a double murder."

Ferringa moved inside the room and closed the door. With a slightly amused look, he asked, "So, how can I help?"

"The murder victims were Reid and Owen Whitecross..." Delray let the sentence hang in the air.

Bridgette noticed Ferringa's eyes widen just a fraction before he responded, "Why are you telling me this?"

"I thought you'd want to know. They are your stepfather and brother, aren't they?"

"I haven't seen either of them in close to thirty years."

"I'm curious. Why did we never know about your family when you were on the force?"

"I never got along with my adoptive father and left home when I turned eighteen. I haven't seen him since."

"Their bodies were discovered almost a week ago. Reid has been dead for twenty years. Owen maybe just a few months…"

"Their deaths mean about as much to me as someone stepping on an ant."

"I didn't know you had a fallout with Owen as well?"

"You haven't changed, Felix." The hint of a wry smile formed on his face. He studied Bridgette for a moment before asking, "And who are you?"

"My name is Detective Cash. I'm leading the investigation into the murder of Reid and Owen Whitecross." Despite her mouth being dry, she was relieved her words came out clearly and calmly.

Ferringa held her gaze. "I've heard about you."

"What have you heard?"

Ferringa let out a short laugh and then turned back to face Delray. "If there's nothing else Felix, I need to be getting back to my guests."

"There is one more thing, Paul…" Delray let his words hang again before adding, "We're investigating another murder case at present."

Ferringa's voice was almost mocking as he replied, "Just one?"

"Do you remember the Annie Casseldhorf murder case?"

"Is there anyone who doesn't?"

"We believe the computer records were tampered with for the case. We found two witnesses from the original case file that never made it onto the computer."

"Why are you telling me this?"

"You might remember them. Their names were Connie Swayne and Mary Keaton…"

Ferringa held Delray's stare for a moment before he reached into his pocket and withdrew a card. As he passed it to Delray, he said, "This is my lawyer's number. If you need anything further, you'll need to speak to him."

As Ferringa turned to leave, Bridgette said, "I have one question for you…"

Ferringa paused mid-turn. With an amused look, he said to Bridgette, "And what might your question be, young lady?"

"Did you know Charlie Bates kept records?"

Saturday - 2:50 P.M.

After refusing to answer her question about Charlie Bates, Ferringa threatened to call the commissioner if they didn't leave immediately. Although not frightened by the threat, Delray promised he'd stay in touch as they left the VIP box.

They were about halfway down the corridor toward the exit before Delray said, "We're out of earshot now. How are you feeling, Bridgette?"

"Better than I expected."

"You did great in there. I thought Ferringa would hyperventilate when you asked him that last question."

"He maintained his composure, but only just."

"The fact he threatened to call the commissioner is very telling."

"He definitely knew Charlie."

Delray nodded. "What made you think of it?"

"It just popped into my head. He was very evasive. He answered most of your questions with questions to maintain control. I thought, poke the bear and see what happens."

Delray grinned and said, "Well, the bear certainly reacted," as he opened the glass door at the exit.

They found it hard to talk over the noise of the crowd when they got outside and said very little until they were out of the stadium.

As they headed toward the parking lot, Delray asked, "Did your recording work?"

"Yes."

"Good. He didn't say much, but I'd like to hear it over again."

"He likes to be in control."

"Ferringa has always been like that. I'd almost forgotten how arrogant he was until he started giving me those smart-ass answers."

"I'm surprised he didn't at least try to feign grief when you told him about the murders?"

"If he's confident we can't prove anything, he won't pretend. Hopefully, his confidence is something we can exploit."

"I wasn't sure what I was expecting, but I thought he'd be more…sophisticated or engaging."

"Ferringa was always a detached son of a bitch. That line about their deaths meaning as much to him as someone stepping on an ant was fairly typical of him as I recall."

"He didn't give up much about his relationship with Reid Whitecross."

"No. We're going to have to do a lot more digging on that front."

"I wonder what he's thinking right now?"

"I doubt it's football."

"Your mention of Connie Swayne and Mary Keaton seemed to rattle him."

"Yeah. He's not the first guy I've interviewed who's

pulled out a lawyer's business card when he doesn't want to answer."

"Do you think he's the one?"

Delray stopped walking. His face grew grim. "It pains me to say this, Bridgette, but yeah, I do. Any tiny doubt I still had when we compared the sketch to the photo disappeared in that meeting."

"Murderers don't look any different to other people, do they?"

"Not on the outside at least."

"He's been involved in the murder of five people we know about. I wonder if there's anyone else?"

"We have to stop him."

"That won't be easy."

Delray let out a long sigh. "No. Being as wealthy as he is, he's got the money and resources he needs to make sure nothing sticks."

As they walked on, Delray added, "That question you asked about Charlie Bates keeping records."

"What about it?"

"Did you throw it in just to get a reaction?"

"I was hoping it would throw him off guard, but it's also something I've been thinking about."

"The night in his apartment when you went to get the book?"

"Nobody trashes a place like that unless they're looking for something. The fact they turned the whole place upside down makes me think they didn't find what they were looking for."

"Charlie didn't strike me as the kind to keep a diary?"

"Maybe not a paper diary, but Charlie dealt in information. That's what he was supplying Ferringa, and I'm sure that's what got him killed."

"So what kind of records are we talking about?"

"I remember when I worked with him on cases, he was meticulous with the records he kept—bordering on fanatical. Information was king. I can imagine him keeping a record of every piece of information he stole and who he stole it for. He wouldn't be the first digital thief to do that."

Delray frowned. "If that's the case, those records could be anywhere. Charlie was such a whiz with computers—it could be on a server in Romania for all we know, and we'd never find it."

"If he's like a lot of IT geeks I know, he'll have a local backup. There's something comforting about having a local copy as well."

Delray pressed the remote to unlock his car as they approached. "So if there is this backup copy and it's not in his apartment, then where is it?"

Bridgette pondered the question as she got into the car. When nothing came to mind, she said, "I have no idea, chief."

After starting the car's engine, Delray said, "If it exists, we need to find it. I don't fancy going back to the office to entertain Sterling for the rest of the day, so let's make a start on it right now."

"Where are we headed?"

"Back to Charlie's apartment. We need to learn as much as we can about him, and that's as good a place as any to start."

Paul Ferringa sat down on one of the two chairs in the side room of his private box. His appetite for football had evaporated after his encounter with Delray and Cash. Ferringa needed time to think and had instructed his assistant that he wasn't to be disturbed. He occasionally practiced yoga and went through several minutes of breathing exercises to clear his mind. He had initially been angry when Cash had asked him the question. But anger was an emotion he had little use for. As he felt his heart rate drop and his mind focus, he opened his eyes again.

Satisfied he could now think clearly, Ferringa thought back to the interview. Delray had been crass, but that had always been his way. Apart from putting on a few pounds, his former colleague hadn't changed much, and he was confident he knew how to deal with him. Cash, on the other hand, was an entirely different matter. He had followed her career closely, and she was now proving as tiresome as her father had been, making her unpredictable and dangerous. The most effective solution would be to have her removed permanently, but the witness testimony linking him to her mother's murder complicated things. He wondered how Delray got her name. Possibly the microfilm? Bates had been too slow in following his instructions, but none of that mattered now. Ferringa pulled a small Nokia phone from his coat pocket as a plan began to form in his mind. The Nokia was a phone he carried everywhere but rarely used. He pressed speed dial for the only number in the device's memory and waited for the call to be answered.

A cultured male voice said, "Good afternoon, Paul."

"Are you free for dinner tonight?"

"I can rearrange my schedule. The usual time and place?"

"Yes. Something's come up that I need to talk with you about."

"I can meet earlier if you like?"

"No, I'm at the football game, entertaining clients. I've spent too long away from them as it is."

"It's always amazed me that you spend so much time attending a game you're not overly interested in."

"My clients like football. What can you do?"

"Is there anything I need to do to prepare for our meeting?"

"No. You remember Felix Delray from Vancouver Metro?"

"Homicide?"

"Yes—he just paid me a visit."

"What about?"

"He came to inform me of the deaths of Reid and Owen Whitecross."

"Hardly surprising. That connection was always going to be made."

"I'm not concerned about that. He was also fishing for information on the Annie Casseldhorf murder case. He claims they've found the two witnesses."

The line was silent for a moment before the caller responded, "Well, that is a setback. Did he say what they claim to have witnessed?"

"I didn't give him a chance—I gave him your card, so you may get a call."

The caller was silent for a moment before he added, "As long as they didn't see you actually enter or leave the house, it will be hard for them to make a case."

"Only one of them is alive now."

"Even better."

"My main concern is the detective he brought with him."

"Bridgette Cash?"

"Yes. She hinted strongly that Bates kept records."

Both men were lost in their thoughts before Ferringa added, "We need an effective solution…"

"What do you have in mind?"

Ferringa answered, "I'll discuss that with you tonight," and then disconnected. He closed his eyes again to repeat his breathing exercises, but he couldn't get the image of the young female detective out of his mind. He would sound out his plan with Derek Sirocca. One way or another, a final decision about Cash's future would be made tonight.

Saturday - 3:10 P.M.

Twenty minutes later, Bridgette and Delray were standing in what was left of Charlie Bates's apartment. As they stood surveying the mess, Bridgette said, "I'm not sure what I was expecting, but it looks like it hasn't been touched since we were here last."

"Internal Investigations were back here after you were attacked, but it's not their job to clean this up. Technically, it's still a crime scene, so it might be some time before that happens."

"So how do we approach this, chief?"

"I'm not sure. Internal Investigations have cataloged everything in the apartment. I've read what they've put together, but nothing stands out. I'm hoping that being here might give us a perspective that we won't get from reading a file on a computer."

"So where should I start?"

"Why don't you start here in the living area and I'll start in the kitchen."

As Bridgette walked to the bookcase, Delray surveyed

the kitchen floor. The surface was covered in flour, cooking utensils, half-empty boxes, and other cooking products he found hard to identify. He mumbled, "This is going to attract rats," as he stepped into the mess and headed for the refrigerator.

Bridgette called out to him, "His laptop computer, was that recovered?"

"Yeah, it's currently in the computer lab being examined. They haven't found much on it other than some kind of encryption program and a few other pieces of software he's written. I don't pretend to understand it, but the lab guys are impressed with his coding skills."

Bridgette thought about this as she worked her way through the pile of books. Finally, she said, "On the day he was arrested, he went to work like any other day. The only difference was he never came home…"

"That's right."

"So, if they didn't find anything incriminating on his laptop, what about his phone?"

Delray shook his head. "The only phone we found on him was his police-issue smartphone. We've been through all the contact numbers and its data, and nothing suspicious showed up. We also searched his desk and locker at work but found nothing suspicious."

"That doesn't sound right."

"The lab guys think he stores everything somewhere on the Internet."

"Don't you think it's odd he doesn't have a personal phone?"

"I don't have a personal phone. I just use the one supplied by Vancouver Metro. Maybe he's like me and doesn't like carrying two around?"

"He has to be leaving a footprint somewhere."

"A footprint?"

"A digital footprint. If he's been working for someone like Paul Ferringa, he has to have some way of contacting him and getting the information out. There will be phone records, files, or some other evidence. Even if he's thorough and wipes the information, it's not easy to completely erase the data. The lab team is good at data recovery. If they haven't found anything on his phone or his laptop, there has to be another device."

Delray straightened up and closed the fridge door. He looked around the apartment. "So where was he hiding it? Internal Investigations are very good at finding things. If it was here, they would have found it."

Bridgette had to agree as she surveyed the living area of the apartment. The couches had all been slashed and searched internally. The light fittings and vents had all been removed and searched. Even the carpet on the floor had been lifted in places. As she surveyed the mess, she tried to think like Charlie Bates. Finally, she said, "If it was me, I'd be keeping it somewhere safe but accessible. If it's not here, we just have to figure out where."

Bridgette and Delray spent a further two hours searching Bates's apartment. They learned he liked sushi, space opera sci-fi novels, and European vacations, but nothing more. It was close to five p.m. when they left the apartment.

Feeling slightly disappointed that their search had yielded nothing positive, Delray said, "I'll drop you back at work so you can pick up your car, and then I'm heading home."

As they approached his car, Bridgette noticed her boss looked a little pale. "Are you okay?"

Delray appeared to stumble as he went to open his car

door. He said, "I just feel a little lightheaded," as he held onto the car door for support.

Bridgette rushed around to his side of the vehicle. By the time she got to him, he was waving her away, saying, "I'm okay." Delray held onto the door for a second before lowering himself into the driver's seat. He gave her a weak smile. "Probably something I ate."

"Should you be driving?"

Delray replied, "I'll be fine in a couple of minutes," as he dabbed his forehead with a handkerchief.

"Perhaps I should drive?"

"I'm starting to feel better. Hop in and I'll drop you back at the precinct."

Bridgette felt a little relieved as she noticed the color returning to Delray's face. "Why don't you just head home? Going across the Iron Bridge to drop me off and then coming all the way back is going to cost you at least twenty minutes. If you're not feeling well, you should be heading home now."

"How will you get back to the precinct?"

"I think I'll walk. There's a lot to think about."

Delray frowned. "That will take you a good half hour, Bridgette."

"The walk will do me good."

Delray needed no more convincing. Bridgette watched him start the car and pull a U-turn to head home. She was still concerned about the turn he'd had and hoped it was nothing worse than food poisoning. When his car had disappeared, her mind returned to the search they'd just conducted. She replayed her own words in her mind, "I'd be keeping it somewhere safe but accessible," as she thought about a hiding place.

She frowned for a moment as she thought about the

myriad of possibilities and then whispered, "There is one place…"

Bridgette checked her watch as she set off at a brisk pace. She figured she would know in under ten minutes if her hunch was right.

The walk to Charlie Bates's gymnasium took Bridgette just under three minutes. Located two blocks from his apartment and on the ground floor of a twelve-story steel commercial building, the facility catered mainly for bodybuilders, most of whom were men. Bridgette pushed through the heavy glass doors and walked into the reception area which doubled as a shop front for selling gym equipment and protein powders. She thought about Charlie Bates as she stood surveying the room. Charlie had been tall, thin, and gangly, and in the time she'd known him, he'd never mentioned a word about fitness or working out. It occurred to her when she had come here to get his apartment key that this was an unusual place for someone like Charlie to be hanging out at.

She glanced at a sign on the counter which offered lockers for hire on a monthly basis and wondered again about Charlie's locker.

Bridgette walked into the main workout area and ignored the stares of the men who were busy lifting weights and running on treadmills.

As she headed to the back of the gym, Bridgette focused her attention on the locker she knew Charlie had rented. Located in the second row, locker number forty-two had a push button mechanical combination lock and looked no different from any of the other eighty-three lockers on the back wall.

Bridgette keyed in the four-digit combination from memory and opened the steel door. Apart from Charlie's apartment key, the locker was empty. She hadn't expected it to be any different, now that Charlie was dead. After quietly closing the door, she glanced over her right shoulder at the men who were working out. They all seemed to have lost interest in her and were focused on their workouts again, which suited her fine.

Bridgette stood staring at the lockers as she pondered the possibility that Charlie had rented more than one. It would be easy enough to ask the receptionist, but if he'd used a different name, that would make the job of finding it much harder. The easiest way would be to get a search warrant to search them all, but that would mean waiting until Monday at the earliest. Patience had never been a strong point for her. She tried to put herself in Charlie's position. If she were renting more than one locker, she'd want them close together if not side by side.

Stepping forward, she stared at the locker to the right of Charlie's locker—number forty-six. After taking another look over her shoulder, Bridgette took a deep breath and keyed in the code she'd used to open forty-two. Even though she didn't hear the click of the door unlocking, she tried turning the handle. The door remained locked. Undeterred, Bridgette used the same combination on the locker to the left. Her heart sank as the door to this locker didn't open either.

Bridgette checked over her shoulder again. The room was filled with the smell of sweat and the noisy sounds of men working out. Seemingly not attracting any attention, Bridgette repeated the process, trying to unlock the lockers diagonally and directly above forty-two. To her dismay, the code didn't work with any of them either. She wondered if Charlie had used a different code for a second locker. Possible, she thought, but most people were creatures of habit and avoided having more codes than they needed.

Bridgette decided to try the code on the lockers below locker forty-two. She whispered, "If this doesn't work, it's a search warrant..."

Bridgette focused on locker forty-three, which was directly below forty-two. She keyed in the code and swore under her breath when the door didn't unlock. Two to go, she thought, as she tried opening locker number forty-seven which was on the right. After pressing the four-digit combination, her heart skipped a beat as she heard the unmistakable click of the door unlocking. She glanced over her shoulder again. Satisfied she still wasn't being watched, she opened the door. The locker was empty except for one item. It was slightly larger than a cigarette pack and black in color.

No longer caring who heard, Bridgette said, "Bingo," as she stared down at a portable computer hard drive.

Saturday - 5:50 P.M.

Bridgette wasted no time in retrieving the hard drive and called Delray on her way back to the office. She felt guilty, knowing he wasn't feeling well, but she knew he'd want the update.

Delray answered on the fifth ring. She could hear background noise and realized he was still driving home. She went to apologize, but Delray got in first and said, "Hang on a minute…"

Bridgette waited for almost a minute before Delray came back and said, "I've just parked in my driveway. What's up?"

"Sorry to bother you, chief, I know you're not well, but we may have a breakthrough."

"Let me have it. By the way, where are you?"

"I'm in an Uber, heading back to the office."

"I thought you were going to walk?"

"I only got as far as Charlie's gym. The search of his apartment wasn't as futile as we first thought."

"You will need to explain that to me…"

"In all the time I worked with Charlie, I never heard him mention anything about going to a gym."

"Me neither."

"We found nothing in his apartment that said he was into fitness or working out. No magazines, no workout routines, nothing at all really."

"But we know he had a locker at a gym."

"Yes. After you left, I got to thinking about how Charlie wanted me to get that book his father wrote and put it in his gym locker. It made me think maybe he was using the locker to store things that he didn't want left in his apartment. It's only a five-minute—"

Delray interrupted. "Okay, but I thought you said the locker was empty, apart from the key?"

"I wondered if maybe he had another locker. One he didn't tell anyone about."

"Okay."

"There are eighty-four lockers in Charlie's gym. Too many to search without a warrant, but I decided to try his passcode on the lockers immediately around his. I figured if you're going to have more than one locker, maybe you'd want them together."

"Okay, now I'm interested."

"Charlie's code worked on a second locker."

"What was in it?"

"A portable hard drive."

Delray let out a low whistle. "That would explain why we found nothing on his computer."

"Yes."

"I don't suppose you've been able to check what's on the drive yet?"

"No. I plan on plugging it in when we get back to the

office, but I'm not hopeful we'll be able to see anything. I'm fairly sure it will be encrypted."

"It just occurred to me, if you found this in a different locker, how can we be sure it belongs to Bates? Maybe you just got lucky with the code?"

"I showed my badge to the receptionist on the way out and explained what I was doing. She pulled up the owner of locker forty-seven from her database. It's registered to a Chris Batalee."

"Never heard of him."

"Chris Batalee is an anagram of Charlie Bates…"

"Well, that covers that. Good work, Bridgette."

"Thanks."

"Give me a call when you get back to the office. I'd be very interested to know what you find."

"Will do, chief, but I'm not holding my breath."

"I'll arrange for one of the lab guys to come in tomorrow if you have no luck. If it's encrypted like you say, it might take some time to find out what's on it."

Delray disconnected, leaving Bridgette with her thoughts. As the Uber made its way across the Iron Bridge, she stared down at the evidence bag that contained the hard drive. She didn't share Delray's optimism. After graduating with a computer science degree, Charlie Bates had spent most of his career as part of the Cyber Crime team before his transfer to Homicide. She knew if he'd written his own encryption program, getting access to the data could be next to impossible.

It was close to six p.m. when Bridgette arrived back at the precinct. She was surprised to see the lights still on in the

Homicide room at this hour on a Saturday night. As she approached her desk, she saw Aaron Sterling working in the cubicle next to hers.

He looked up as he heard her approach. "Well, you've certainly taken your time."

As much as it pained Bridgette to apologize, she said, "Sorry, we got delayed."

"So what happened?"

Bridgette gave Sterling a rundown of their meeting with Paul Ferringa and how they had gone from the stadium to Charlie Bates's apartment to conduct another search.

"So where's Delray?"

"He went home, he wasn't feeling well."

Sterling nodded, but his body language suggested he didn't believe her. Bridgette sat down at her desk and placed Charlie Bates's portable hard drive carefully on the desk.

She did her best to ignore Sterling, but he was persistent and asked, "What have you got there?"

"A portable hard drive." As much as it annoyed her, Bridgette knew she shouldn't be withholding information from a fellow police officer and explained to Sterling how she had found the hard drive in Charlie Bates's gym locker.

Sterling nodded. "I'm impressed. That's good detective work."

For the first time since she'd met Sterling, she felt the words coming out of his mouth were genuine.

Unsure what to say, she mumbled, "Thanks," as she plugged the portable drive into her laptop computer.

"What are you doing now?"

"I'm checking to see if we can read any files on the drive, but I'm not confident. We found an encryption program on Charlie's laptop that he'd written himself. I expect this drive will be encrypted, but I need to check before I call the chief."

Sterling wheeled his chair over to Bridgette's cubicle and sat beside her. His aftershave and body odor made for an unpleasant aromatic cocktail. She would have preferred him to stay in his cubicle and did her best to ignore his presence as she watched the portable drive power up.

Bridgette dialed Delray's home number from memory on her desk phone and placed the call on loudspeaker.

The phone was answered on the fourth ring by her boss who simply said, "Delray."

"Hi, chief, it's Bridgette here. I'm back in the office with Detective Sterling and just powering up the portable drive now."

"Okay, I'll wait on the line."

Bridgette opened up the file explorer program on her laptop. "I've connected the portable drive to my laptop, and it's coming up as the E drive."

"So far, so good."

Bridgette clicked on the E drive icon on her laptop, hoping it would show a listing of files from the portable drive. She watched as a tiny green light on the portable drive began to flash on and off as the laptop attempted to read the files. After almost ten seconds, the green light stopped flashing. Bridgette grimaced as she looked at her laptop screen and read the error message: *The disk you inserted was not readable by this computer.*

"No go, chief. I'm getting an error message."

"Is there a problem with the drive?"

"I think it's most likely not reading the disk because it's encrypted."

"So we need the lab guys?"

Bridgette thought for a moment. "Yes, but I think we'll also need Charlie's laptop."

"Why do we need his laptop?"

"If he's written his own encryption program, there's a good chance we'll need his software as well as the passcode to unlock it."

"I'll need to make some phone calls, but I doubt I'll be able to get you any access before tomorrow morning."

Bridgette stared at the blank screen. "That's fine, chief. I think this may take a while to crack."

"We'll take it one step at a time. If Bates got himself killed over this, we'll leave no stone unturned trying to find out what's on it."

Bridgette glanced at her watch. "There's not much more we can do now, so I think I'll lock it in the safe and head home."

"Sounds like a good plan for both of you. I'll make some phone calls now and text you a time when the lab guys will be in tomorrow."

"Thanks, chief."

Bridgette and Sterling heard Delray disconnect and the line go dead.

Bridgette looked at her watch and decided there was little more she could accomplish today. She glanced at Sterling. "I'm going to put this drive in the safe and then call it a day."

"Okay."

Bridgette went to get up from her chair, but Sterling grabbed at her sleeve. "Why don't we talk for a moment?"

Bridgette wasn't in the mood to be manhandled and said bluntly, "What about?"

Sterling let go of her sleeve and settled back into his chair. He studied her for a moment and then said, "It's been a long day for both of us. Why don't we go grab a meal together?"

Bridgette was horrified by the thought but managed to say, "I'm tired, I just want to go home."

Sterling persisted, "It doesn't have to be a late night. Now that we're going to be working together, we should get to know each other a little better, don't you think?"

Bridgette looked at the floor while she tried to compose herself. Finally, she looked up. "I'm prepared to work with you because, as a professional police officer, that's what I have to do. But the way you treated me after the basement shooting incident... I don't want to spend any more time with you than necessary."

Sterling retorted, "You have to understand, as an internal investigator, I was just doing my job."

Bridgette made no attempt to hide her anger as she responded, "You treated me like a common criminal."

"I was using tried and tested interviewing techniques, that's all."

"You accused me of—"

Sterling cut her off. "I was just doing my job." The edges of Sterling's mouth turned upwards in something approaching a smile as he added, "This will give us an opportunity to bury the hatchet, so to speak. It doesn't need to be a late night, we can—"

It was Bridgette's turn to cut Sterling off. "Thank you for the invitation, but I'm going to pass. I'm tired, it's been a long day, and I want to go home."

Sterling smiled again. "Perhaps another time?"

Bridgette stood up. "I don't think so, Aaron. I've made it a policy of mine not to socialize with anyone from Vancouver Metro unless there's a group of us."

Bridgette didn't wait for a response. She picked up the

portable drive and headed for the office safe. She hoped she'd been blunt enough.

Saturday - 7:45 P.M.

Paul Ferringa ignored the maître d' as he walked into the expansive reception area of the Caronne restaurant. He also ignored the guests waiting to be seated and barely noticed the glass chandelier and opulent surroundings as he headed for a set of highly polished blackwood stairs that led to the mezzanine level. Although he frequently dined in public, tonight's meeting with Derek Sirocca would be a private affair, and he had no desire for small talk or having his presence photographed by someone with a smartphone.

The mezzanine level was split into two private rooms reserved for special guests who wanted privacy. Ferringa was very careful about where he conducted business and was comfortable with the setting. Sirocca had defended the restaurant owner, Vince Caronne, eight years earlier when he'd been charged with attempted murder. Despite the testimony of six patrons who saw Caronne stab a former organized crime figure in front of his restaurant when an argument turned ugly, he had walked free and was forever grateful to Sirocca for his legal skill.

The Caronne restaurant specialized in Italian food. Ferringa preferred French cuisine, but this was a business meeting, and the food was inconsequential. He checked his watch as he ascended the stairs. It was close to seven forty-five p.m. He normally gave Sirocca time to settle in before he arrived. After pushing through a heavy wooden door on the left at the top of the stairs, Ferringa said, "Good evening," to his lawyer as he entered a room that contained several dining tables covered with starched white tablecloths. Sirocca was the only guest and seated at the closest table which was laid out with ornate silverware and stemmed glasses.

Sirocca got up from his chair and greeted Ferringa as the sound of smooth jazz played softly somewhere in the background. Even though the lawyer earned well over half a million dollars a year, he was still the hired help and knew his place with his most valued client. As they sat down, Sirocca said, "I've ordered a McLaren Vale Shiraz and a grilled portobello and pear salad to start with, Paul."

Ferringa replied, "Excellent choice," as he sat down.

Sirocca waited until Ferringa settled before saying, "I gather we have a lot to talk about?"

Ferringa nodded once and said, "We do," before pausing as the restaurant owner entered the room with a tray containing their salads and wine. Vince Caronne was a shade under six feet tall and almost as wide. After a stint in jail in his twenties, Caronne had been largely straight ever since but still hated cops.

They made polite conversation with their host, who still had a full head of jet-black hair even though he was in his early sixties. After serving their entrees and pouring their wine, he took their orders for the main meals and then added, "There are no cops in here tonight, and we had the place swept for bugs on Monday as usual."

Sirocca smiled. "Your attention to detail is appreciated, Vince."

Caronne nodded. "Enjoy your meals, gentlemen."

Ferringa waited until Caronne had left the room and then said, "This witness Delray found. Should I be concerned?"

"Like I said on the phone, unless she's prepared to say she saw you entering or leaving the Casseldhorf residence, you have nothing to worry about. You were a police officer at the time, and surveillance was a regular part of your work."

As Ferringa held the glass of wine up to his nose to smell its bouquet, he said, "It was a sloppy affair. Something I've regretted ever since."

"Without a gun, a fingerprint, or a witness who saw you pull the trigger, Delray doesn't have a case."

Ferringa took a sip of wine. "I didn't pull the trigger, but that doesn't matter. This could still get very ugly."

Sirocca grimaced. "I might be your lawyer, Paul, but you don't have to tell me everything."

With an amused look, Ferringa responded, "We've been working together for eighteen years, Derek. You know as well as I do, there are no secrets." He studied his lawyer as he dabbed his mouth with a napkin. Sirocca's fondness for fast cars had almost been his undoing when he was still an up-and-coming young lawyer. He had already started doing legal work for Ferringa and had shown he was not only a savvy legal practitioner but someone who was prepared to break the law if he could get away with it. Ferringa had liked this, and they had formed a good working relationship. Late one evening, Ferringa had received a call from Sirocca from a payphone. Sirocca told him how he had lost control of his Porsche on a wet strip of coastal road and crashed through a barrier, badly injuring his girlfriend. Ferringa had been the only person Sirocca had called to ask for help. Ferringa arrived an hour later to find his lawyer hiding in long grass, covered in blood, and smelling of bourbon.

Ferringa had been blunt in his assessment of the situation when he asked, "Who do you want to save?" He knew the answer before it came out of Sirocca's mouth, and together they pushed the car over an embankment and watched it crash into the ocean. Ferringa offered Sirocca an alibi, knowing it would buy his lawyer's complete silence and loyalty for life. Sirocca readily accepted the offer and reported his car and girlfriend missing. Her body washed up on a beach two days later, and he was never formally investigated.

Ferringa was understandably relaxed as he elaborated on the problem. "My partner at the time was Rudy Blaxland. We were making more than double from our side deals than what we were from the good city of Vancouver as police officers. We got word Peter Casseldhorf was working undercover and was maybe going to turn us in, so we paid him a visit. The plan was simply to threaten him to start with, but Rudy panicked. A shot was fired, and suddenly we're chasing Peter Casseldhorf through the back streets of his neighborhood. We searched for half an hour but couldn't find him, so we returned to his house to wait. Rudy wanted to check he hadn't doubled back on us and went inside. He didn't expect Casseldhorf's wife and daughter to still be there and panicked when he found them in an upstairs bedroom."

Sirocca nodded.

Ferringa continued, "Rudy became a liability and eventually decided he would testify against some of his fellow officers to save his skin."

"I hear he got hit by a cement truck just before the hearing?"

With an amused look, Ferringa responded, "That was rather unfortunate for poor Rudy." Ferringa took another sip of wine. "I've made it a point ever since never to partner with anyone, and I'm very careful about who I work with."

"So I've noticed…"

"It's a pity Hanway got himself arrested."

"He won't be a problem."

Ferringa frowned. "We still have unfinished business."

"Roy Pepper?"

"He's the only one that can connect me to Reid Whitecross. I've been searching for him for twenty years, and it's extremely disappointing Hanway got so close but couldn't finish the job." Ferringa pulled out a single folded sheet of paper from his jacket pocket. "I need someone else with Hanway's skillset that we can trust." He passed it across to Sirocca.

"I assume money is no object?"

"No."

"I thought this might come up." Sirocca slid a large white envelope across the table to Ferringa. "His name is Ryan Visontay. I'm already negotiating with him. He's got no record and lives right here in Vancouver."

Ferringa opened the envelope and pulled out a photograph of a man in his early thirties. He had short brown hair, and apart from a small scar through his upper lip, he looked no different than tens of thousands of men walking the streets of Vancouver.

Sirocca added, "He comes highly recommended. What do you have in mind?"

"Two jobs to start with." Ferringa pointed at the piece of paper he'd given Sirocca. "Open it…"

Sirocca unfolded the sheet of paper and frowned as he scanned the contents. Looking up, he said, "What's this?"

"It's an address list of all the safe houses in Vancouver."

Sirocca's eyes widened. "Where did you get this?"

"It was a gift from Charlie Bates. Kind of his way of showing what he was capable of when he was first recruited. I don't expect Pepper will be held in one of these locations for long, so we need to act quickly."

"What do you have in mind?"

Ferringa filled him in on his plan. Sirocca knew better than to challenge his boss but said, "It sounds risky."

"Not as risky as Pepper testifying." Ferringa held Sirocca's gaze and then added, "This could be bad for all of us."

Sirocca understood the subtle threat and sighed. "I'll make it happen, but it might take a couple of days."

"We don't have that long. You need to start making calls as soon as we've finished dinner." Before Sirocca could respond, Ferringa added, "There's something else…"

"And what's that?"

"In the interview today, Cash asked me if I knew Charlie Bates kept records."

"That was a ballsy thing to say."

"She was just after a reaction."

"And what did you say?"

"Nothing. I ignored the question and asked them to see themselves out."

"Do you think Charlie kept records?"

Ferringa put his glass down. "I'm sure he did."

"Charlie never met you, nor did he know your true identity, so it will be hard to prove any association with you."

"You're making an assumption. I need to see those records before I can be sure."

"If they're on the Internet somewhere, they'll be next to impossible to find."

"I got the feeling from Cash she was talking about a physical copy."

"Hanway searched his apartment twice and found nothing."

Ferringa scratched his chin as he thought. Finally, he said, "If anyone knows for sure, it will be Cash…"

"What do you have in mind?"

"I think it's about time we had one final conversation with the young detective."

"I'm not sure that's a good idea, Paul. Right now, you need to—"

Ferringa interjected, "This is something I should have taken care of a long time ago…" He paused to spear a slice of pear in his salad with his fork. "She won't stop until she discovers the truth or dies trying." Ferringa forked the pear into his mouth. "I prefer option two."

Sunday - 8:50 A.M.

Bridgette was normally an early starter, but after getting an early morning call from Delray informing her he wouldn't be coming in unless needed, she decided she needed a workout at the gym before facing the day—and Aaron Sterling.

After parking in the basement, she stopped by the evidence safe on level one to retrieve Bates's hard drive before heading up to level two. She noticed Sterling was already at his desk as she got out of the elevator. Without looking up from his computer, he said, "You're a little late, aren't you?" as she walked past his desk.

Bridgette rolled her eyes. "And good morning to you too, Aaron."

"Have you heard from Delray?"

"He called me earlier to say he wasn't coming in, but he's organized one of the tech analysts to be here around nine."

"Delray's not coming in? What's that about?"

Bridgette thought back to the phone call with her boss

as she placed Bates's hard drive on her desk. Their conversation had been brief, and Delray had made no mention of the dizzy spell he'd suffered the day before. She wasn't about to share any of this with Sterling. "He tries to take a day off each week, but he said he'd come in if we found anything." She added as Sterling gave her a disapproving look, "I'm not confident we'll make much progress today…"

Sterling swiveled his chair around to face her. "And why is that?"

"Charlie was in a league of his own with computer security. If he's written his own encryption algorithm to protect the drive, it could be almost impossible to break."

Sterling answered, "Well, we're about to find out," as he pointed to the elevator.

Bridgette turned to see Louis Solomon heading in their direction. Solomon was one of the team of technical analysts who worked for Vancouver Metro. He was short in stature and still had acne even though he was now in his early thirties. Bridgette had never seen him dressed in any color other than black, but despite his geeky appearance, Bridgette liked Solomon and respected his abilities.

She said, "Hi, Louis," as he approached.

Solomon returned her greeting and nodded in Sterling's general direction as he placed a laptop he'd been carrying on her desk. "I got a call from my boss last night. Apparently you guys want to take a look at Charlie Bates's laptop?"

Before Bridgette could respond, Sterling jumped in. "That's right. We've recovered a portable hard drive from a locker Bates was using at a gym. We think there's vital evidence on it, but it's encrypted, and we think we'll need his computer to unlock it."

Solomon raised an eyebrow as he glanced at Bridgette as if to say, *"Does this guy know what he's talking about?"*

Bridgette tactfully added, "The drive won't power up when it's connected to a normal computer. We're hoping we'll have more success if we connect it directly to Charlie's laptop."

As Solomon picked up the drive off Bridgette's desk, he asked, "Is this it?"

Bridgette nodded. "We think he's written a special interface program for it."

Solomon opened up Bates's laptop and said, "Of course, the drive could be just faulty, but if I know Charlie, breaking into Fort Knox might be easier," as he pressed the laptop's power button.

Bridgette responded, "We'll know soon enough," as she watched Solomon press and hold down several keys on the laptop as it went through its start-up routine.

Sterling demanded, "What are you doing?"

Solomon answered, "I'm bypassing the laptop's operating system password to get in. It's kind of like entering a house through the back door."

"How long is that going to take?"

Solomon let go of the keys and then made several keystroke combinations before announcing, "Not long at all if you know what you're doing." He turned the laptop around to face Sterling.

Sterling raised his eyebrows slightly. "You're in already?"

Solomon nodded. "That was the easy part. There was nothing on the laptop's drive that Charlie thought was worth securing." Solomon paused while he connected the portable hard drive and then said, "Getting into this baby, if it powers up, will be a completely different story."

Bridgette watched as the tiny green light on the portable

drive flashed as the laptop tried to read the files. "This is as far as we got when I connected the drive to my laptop."

Solomon watched the screen on Bates's laptop for a few more seconds before a small program window popped up. The window was about a quarter of the size of the screen, with blue edges and a teal and white background. At the top of the window was a banner which read "CB *Safe*." Inside the window and next to a small picture of an old-style padlock was a white box for entering a password. Below the box were the words "*0* of 10 attempts."

Solomon studied the screen for a moment and then looked at Bridgette. "Well, it powers up, so your theory was correct. You ever heard of CB Safe?"

Bridgette shook her head. "There are no screen instructions, so I don't think this is a commercial program. I'm thinking 'CB' probably just stands for 'Charlie Bates'?"

Solomon nodded. "That makes sense."

Sterling seemed annoyed that he was being excluded from the conversation as he exclaimed, "What do you mean there are no screen instructions?"

Solomon explained, "If it was a commercial software program, it would say something lame like 'enter your password here.' But if he's written the software, and it's only for himself, instructions are unnecessary."

Sterling got up and stood next to Bridgette as Solomon studied the laptop screen. Finally, Solomon started repeatedly pressing the Q key on the laptop.

Sterling frowned. "What are you doing?"

Solomon ignored the question, mumbled, "Interesting..." and then pressed the backspace key.

Bridgette pointed at a small counter in the bottom right-hand corner of the window. "It's counting down from thirty-two with every key you press."

"My guess is he's using one-twenty-eight-bit encryption, and he's got a thirty-two character password."

Bridgette frowned. "That will be impossible to break."

Sterling said, "Slow down, guys. What's all this about thirty-two characters and encryption?"

Solomon stopped pressing keys. "The drive's encrypted, meaning the data is scrambled so you can't read it without a key. The—"

Sterling shot back, "I know what encryption is, but what's with the thirty-two characters?"

"He's using a thirty-two character password. In reality, the password is a key that unlocks the encrypted data on the drive, but I won't bore you with the technical details."

Solomon kept pressing the Q key until the counter showed zero and then hit enter. The screen displayed the error message *Incorrect password. 9 attempts remaining.*

Sterling looked from Solomon to Bridgette. "What happens when we get through nine more attempts?"

Solomon looked at Bridgette as if to say, "You should answer this…"

Bridgette took the cue. "My guess is it will self-destruct."

Sterling said, "Self-destruct? What does that mean?"

Solomon said, "Bates's program will erase all the data on the drive is my guess. And he'll do it in such a way that it will never be recoverable."

Sterling shook his head. "And you just wasted one of our access attempts with your little experiment. Are you out of your mind?"

Bridgette responded, "This is not a password you can guess. It's probably not even a password Charlie carried around in his head. Even if there were no restrictions on how many times you could enter password combinations, the odds of stumbling on the correct one are in the billions."

They all stared at the screen for a moment before Sterling asked, "So what do we do now?"

Bridgette responded, "We have to find the password. Without it, this drive is useless."

Sterling frowned. "This is a waste of time."

As Bridgette went to respond, her smartphone buzzed. She looked down at her desk and picked it up when she recognized the number. After pressing answer, she said, "Hi, chief, I was going to call you shortly with an update."

"I have an update of my own."

Bridgette could tell by the tone of his voice that something was wrong. "What's up?"

"It's Roy Pepper. He's disappeared."

Bridgette frowned. "What do you mean disappeared?"

"There were two detectives guarding him at the safe house. One was sleeping in the same room as him. He took his dog out for a bathroom break at around five a.m. and never came back in. They assembled a team and have spent the last three hours searching the neighborhood."

"And?"

"There's no sign of either him or his dog."

Part III

Sunday - 9:15 A.M.

Bridgette disconnected from her call with Delray and stared off into space as the shock of Delray's news began to sink in. She let out a long breath as she confronted the reality that Roy Pepper might be dead.

Solomon stared at her. "What's the problem, Bridgette? You look like you've seen a ghost."

Bridgette relayed the brief conversation she'd had with Delray to Solomon and Sterling.

Sterling said, "So who knew about the safe house?"

Bridgette shrugged. "It was all managed by witness protection. I believe it was just the marshals and one or two of their managers."

Sterling said, "You realize he's dead, don't you?" with no trace of compassion.

Bridgette thought back to her first meeting with Roy, their escape from the horse ranch, and the car trip back to Vancouver. She wasn't ready to concede that the gentle and soft-spoken man might no longer be alive. "All I know is he's missing and there's a team out looking for him."

Sterling got up from his chair. As he put his coat on, he responded, "I'm sure they'll find what's left of him sooner or later."

"Where are you going?"

"I need some air and thinking time. Paul Ferringa is the prime suspect in two murder investigations, and witnesses for both cases are either dead or missing. That strikes me as something of a pattern, don't you think?"

Bridgette calmly replied, "We established that fact two days ago."

"Yeah, well, right now you've got jack, and unless that changes, Ferringa will continue to do as he pleases."

Sterling didn't wait for a response and stormed off toward the lift.

Solomon shook his head as he watched Sterling's exit. "Sorry you have to work with that."

"Hopefully it's only temporary."

"What do you want me to do with the laptop and drive?"

Bridgette stared down at the laptop for a moment. "Until we figure out what the password is, this is next to useless."

Solomon said, "I agree," and picked up the laptop and drive. "Seeing as how I've been called in for the day, I'll take this all back to the lab and do some more investigation, although I'm not hopeful. From what I can tell, he stored nothing on the laptop itself—it looks like it was all on the drive."

"Thanks, Louis. You never know, there might be a clue on the laptop we've overlooked."

Bridgette watched Solomon walk off toward the elevator. Now alone and with the whole office to herself, Bridgette walked to the window and stood with her arms folded across her chest. She normally found the view of the Catalin River a welcome distraction that helped her focus.

She watched a ferry make its way under the Iron Bridge but found no solace in the view as her thoughts were consumed by Roy Pepper. It had been one week since she had tracked him down. He had survived for twenty years on his own running from a man they now knew to be Paul Ferringa. But her intervention had most likely cost him his life. Bridgette wouldn't give up hope until she knew for sure, but she wondered how this would change her. She'd heard of people who felt responsible for someone's death never getting over it. She wondered if that was her destiny. Would Roy be the first thing she thought of in the morning when she woke up? Would he haunt her in her dreams?

Her police training had given her techniques to manage stressful situations in police work, but reality was different. This was no longer theory, and her actions had almost certainly led to the death of someone who was an innocent victim.

Bridgette let out a sigh as she watched a small boat with a family of five cruise down the river. They didn't seem to have a care in the world, which was how she thought life should be most of the time.

Peace seemed further away than ever. She tried to push Roy out of her mind and focus on what she could do to help with her case. Sterling's storming out allowed her to work on whatever she wanted which was something she hadn't planned for.

She thought about calling Ray Warner to see if he'd made any further progress with the evidence from the bodies and the crime scene, but he rarely worked on Sundays. She also contemplated going back through NatTrack looking for any possible links between Paul

Ferringa and any other cases. But after the news of Roy's disappearance, she didn't think she could focus sitting at a computer all day.

She wondered what Ferringa was doing right now. She was sure if Roy had been taken, Ferringa would be ultimately behind it. She whispered, "You wreak misery and chaos wherever you go," as she thought about the murder of her mother and father again.

Bridgette hugged herself as if she was shivering from cold. Alone in the office, she made no move to hide her emotions as a single tear rolled down her cheek. She stood perfectly still, staring out the window but not seeing the view, while she contemplated her dilemma. As much as she hated to admit it, Sterling was right. Without evidence directly linking Ferringa to his crimes, they had no hope of making an arrest. She had learned enough about the man to know he liked to get others to do his dirty work—the hiring of Carl Rutherford to murder her father had been a case in point. Being one or two steps removed from the crime itself and being able to hire the best legal defense money could buy made him close to untouchable. But the Whitecross murders were different—they were personal, and it was far more likely he had committed the crimes himself. There were two witnesses she could re-interview to hopefully learn more: Ferringa's stepbrother, Ethan Whitecross, and Reid Whitecross's former business associate, David Monaghan.

Bridgette turned and looked back toward the elevator. She knew Sterling could be gone for the whole day, but equally, he could walk back into the Homicide room at any moment after cooling off. Bridgette didn't need any more time to think and returned to her desk to make some calls.

She started by calling David Monaghan. Monaghan

knew something of Paul Ferringa's childhood, and it was time to find out more. She called his number, but the call wasn't answered. She left a message asking him to call her back as soon as possible and then called Ethan Whitecross. She expected to have to leave a message for him as well and was surprised when he answered the call.

"Whitecross."

"Hi, Ethan, it's Detective Bridgette Cash here."

"Why are you calling me on a Sunday?"

"There's been a development in the murder investigation."

"What kind of development?"

"We've located your stepbrother."

"Why is that a development?"

Bridgette thought about Roy Pepper. He had been their strongest and only real lead tying Ferringa to the murders of Reid and Owen Whitecross. Now that he was missing, she didn't want to go into specifics. "We think he killed your father and brother."

Her answer was greeted with silence. Bridgette decided to wait it out. After a pause of about ten seconds, Whitecross responded, "Have you arrested him?"

"No."

"Then why are you calling me?"

"We know more about the murders and a lot more about your stepbrother since we last talked. We also think he's involved in another murder case."

"Well, if you want to talk, it has to be today."

That suited Bridgette fine, but she couldn't resist asking, "Why?"

"My sister-in-law fired me yesterday. She's assumed control of Owen's business, and apparently I'm no longer required."

"I'm sorry to hear that."

"Not as sorry as I am. I'm leaving town tomorrow. I'll be back for the funerals, but other than that, I'm not planning on returning any time soon."

"Can I come and interview you this morning?"

"If you think it will help."

"Will you be at your apartment?"

"No, I'm out at the NewFarm Racecourse. Owen has his main office here, and I'm cleaning out my stuff."

"NewFarm is a big place. Where will I find you?"

Whitecross gave her directions and then disconnected.

Bridgette sat for a moment thinking about the conversation. She wondered why Jane Whitecross had fired her brother-in-law. If he took drugs as regularly as she thought he did, that would be reason enough. She thought it would be worthwhile interviewing her again as well and picked up her phone to make the call. As she dialed the number, the chime to the elevator sounded again. Bridgette held her breath as the door opened and was relieved when it was only one of the cleaners and not Sterling. Bridgette decided to make a hasty retreat just in case Sterling returned. She could call Jane Whitecross from her car, so she gathered what she needed for the interviews. Not wanting to tempt fate any further, she decided taking the back stairs would give her the best opportunity of getting out of the building without running into her new partner. She heard the elevator chime again as she opened the door to the stairwell but didn't look back. As she descended the stairs, she was determined to make the most of the day, and that would only be possible if she didn't have Aaron Sterling in tow.

Sunday - 9:20 A.M

Derek Sirocca loved most things about his job. He liked getting the better of judges and prosecution lawyers. He loved the huge payday he got from winning a case. And finding a legal loophole that allowed him to get a client off on a technicality gave him a high that could last for weeks. There was little about his profession he didn't like, but what he was doing today he detested. He called it blood work although he'd never expressed the sentiment out loud.

Not one to risk being photographed intentionally or otherwise, he stood in the shadows with his head down and waited until Paul Ferringa had driven into the warehouse and the steel door had begun to close before he stepped forward. Ferringa normally drove a black Maserati when he wasn't being chauffeured, but today he'd opted for a run-of-the-mill silver BMW sedan. Sirocca hadn't seen the car before and assumed Ferringa had chosen it because it was less conspicuous.

He waited for his boss to alight from the vehicle before he approached. "Good morning, Paul."

Ferringa ignored the pleasantries. "Where's Visontay?"

"He'll be here shortly. I got a call from him ten minutes ago, just after I arrived. He didn't want to wait out front just in case a random cop car showed up."

Ferringa looked around a warehouse that was about the size of two basketball courts. There was a row of racks packed with boxes that ran along the rear wall, but apart from that, the facility was empty. "Who owns this?"

"One of my other clients. He doesn't use it very often and assured me we would have total privacy today."

Ferringa looked up at one of the security cameras. "You brought me to a place that has cameras?"

"They're not connected to anything. My client conducts a range of…let's call them business transactions here with people he doesn't necessarily trust. The threat of being recorded seems to help everyone behave." Sirocca sensed the answer hadn't put Ferringa fully at ease and added, "This is the right place to meet, Paul. You don't want to be doing this in any of your facilities just in case they're under surveillance."

Ferringa seemed satisfied with the answer and moved on to his next question. "So the operation went according to plan this morning?"

"That's what I've been told."

"So, Visontay, what's his background?"

Sirocca leaned up against the BMW and pulled a pack of cigarettes and a lighter from his pocket. "Ryan Visontay spent nine years in the military. He started out as a combat medic before going into special ops."

Ferringa frowned. "So he goes from a job where he saves people to a job where he kills people? Doesn't that strike you as a little odd?"

Sirocca shrugged as he lit his cigarette. "Life is full of paradoxes."

"So what next?"

Sirocca blew a smoke ring. "He got an honorable discharge from the military and found there was a demand on the outside for his rather unique skill set."

"How long has he been out?"

"Three years. He only has a small circle of well-paying clients. I think he could be a good fit for us long-term now that Hanway is no longer available."

"Let's see how today goes."

"I told him today was a trial. He said that—" Sirocca paused mid-sentence as his phone rang. He looked at the screen and said, "That's him," as he pressed the answer button.

Sirocca listened for about ten seconds and then responded, "I'm opening the door now."

Sirocca produced a remote control from his coat pocket and pressed a button. As the electric motor of the large warehouse roller door whirred to life, Sirocca added, "Visontay just turned onto the street. He should be here any moment now."

Both men watched as a late-model white Ford Transit van cruised up the street before turning left into the warehouse. Ferringa and Sirocca took a couple of steps back to allow the van enough room to park alongside Ferringa's BMW. Ryan Visontay got out of the vehicle and nodded once in the general direction of Ferringa and Sirocca. Visontay was lean and around six feet one. His curly dark brown hair was longer than in the photograph, but there was no mistaking the small scar on his upper lip.

Sirocca said, "Is he in the van?"

Visontay nodded. "Yes."

"Let's take a look."

They walked around to the back of the van and waited while Visontay opened the rear door. Sirocca and Ferringa stepped forward and stared into the cargo area. Lying on a black plastic tarp was the body of a small man in his mid-fifties. Next to the man was the body of a small black-and-white dog.

Ferringa studied the body of the man for a moment before he remarked, "Pepper hasn't aged too well." He frowned and moved a further step forward. "Is he still breathing?"

Visontay responded calmly, "He's sedated. I didn't want him bleeding all over the back of the van. Sedation is easier than trying to wrap a body up tight enough so that blood and other bodily fluids don't escape. When it comes time to dispose of the body, I'll put a bullet in his head or break his neck or whatever you want."

"I'm not comfortable with this. What happens if he wakes up?"

Visontay shook his head. "He won't. I'm giving him regular shots of Propofol."

"I'm surprised you brought the dog along?"

"If I left the dog behind, there'd be no doubt someone had taken Pepper. This way, the cops are also dealing with the possibility the old man just wandered off. Besides, I don't kill dogs."

Ferringa gave Sirocca a look which said, "I'm not happy."

Visontay picked up on the look. "Gentlemen, it's entirely your call if I continue or not. If you're not comfortable with me doing the second part of the job, tell me and I'll dispose of this and be on my way."

Sirocca stubbed his cigarette out on the concrete floor. "Give us a moment."

He then motioned Ferringa toward the stairs on the left-hand side of the facility that led to a mezzanine-level prefab office. Ferringa and Sirocca made their way up to a room that was ten feet wide and barely any longer. It was furnished with an old wooden desk, three non matching chairs, and a metal cabinet. Everything was coated with a layer of dust, prompting Sirocca to suggest they stand as he closed the door behind them. Sirocca let Ferringa speak first.

Ferringa said, "I was expecting to see a dead body," as he lit a cigarette with his Zippo lighter.

"He comes highly recommended, Paul. I know of five jobs he's carried out for two separate clients. There have been no issues with any of them. If I thought he was a risk, I wouldn't have hired him."

Ferringa frowned. "And what's with the dog? He'll happily break a man's neck but won't kill a dog?"

"I'm not sure, but he's not the first professional I've come across who won't kill animals. We all have moral boundaries somewhere."

They both stared out the glass window at the warehouse floor below. Visontay had closed the van doors and was now leaning up against the side of his van checking something on his smartphone as if he didn't have a care in the world.

Ferringa said, "It's too late to change plans now. I want this finished tonight. Pepper is the only witness tying me to my stepfather's disappearance, and if we can clean up the other mess as well, I'll be untouchable."

Sirocca wasn't about to argue. "We shouldn't leave him down there too long. What do you want to do about Pepper?"

Ferringa thought for a moment. "Provided he doesn't leave Pepper unattended, and he keeps him knocked out, I can live with it."

"The plan is for him to wait here in the warehouse until he's required this evening."

"I've got business I need to take care of. I won't be back here until around six tonight."

"I'm happy to wait here with him, Paul—even help tonight if that's required?"

"No, the fewer people involved tonight, the better." Ferringa looked at his watch. "This will be all over in twelve hours, and frankly, it can't come soon enough."

Sunday - 10:40 A.M.

Bridgette got out of her car and headed across a gravel parking lot toward a sign which read "NewFarm Offices." She had been unsuccessful in two attempts to reach David Monaghan and Jane Whitecross and had left messages for them to call her as soon as possible. She was thankful she could at least re-interview Ethan Whitecross this morning. Located on the southwest corner of the NewFarm racing complex, the office block comprised three narrow two-story brick buildings. The offices looked well maintained, but the timber windows and external air conditioning units reminded Bridgette of a sixties-style motel complex. The complex was surrounded by another of NewFarm's impressive cypress hedges which masked a six-foot-high security fence, and Bridgette could see no other entrance other than a driveway for delivery vans. She walked in through the open gate. Whitecross had told Bridgette he was on the upper level of Building 1 when she called to set up the interview. Turning left, she walked across the brick pavement toward the building on the left which had a large brass number "1" affixed to its brickwork. She continued up an external staircase that led onto a breezeway on the upper level.

The building looked deserted except for one door about halfway down that was open. Bridgette stopped at the open doorway and looked inside. She could see Ethan Whitecross sorting through a pile of documents on a desk on the opposite side of the room. She gave a polite knock on the door and waited. Dressed in a pair of faded blue jeans and a white polo shirt, Whitecross looked up and mumbled, "Come in," as he dropped a large pile of documents into a large open box, which she assumed he was using as a trash bin.

Bridgette walked into an open-plan office area. There was room enough for four desks with computers and a bank of filing cabinets. A large year planner and whiteboard occupied much of the space on the office's left-hand wall, while the rear wall was wall-to-wall photographs of horses, many of which included Owen Whitecross posing for the camera.

"Good morning, Ethan." Bridgette noticed he was clean-shaven and was relieved to see his pupils weren't dilated.

Without looking up, Whitecross asked, "What can I do for you, detective?"

"First, I'm sorry to hear you've lost your job. That must be tough on top of all the other bad news you've received this last week."

Whitecross shrugged. "Yeah, well, what can you do?" As he dropped another pile of documents in the open box, Whitecross added, "In truth, I'm glad it's over. I never really wanted to work for that bitch anyway. This just sped up the decision I was always going to make."

"Can I ask why she fired you?"

Whitecross finally looked up. "She wants to take the company in a new direction was her official line. The truth is, we never got along, and she only tolerated me because I was Owen's brother. She knows nothing about breeding horses, so I'm not sure how this is all going to work out for her."

"She could be in for a tough time in more ways than one."

Whitecross said, "I don't care," as he opened a drawer in his desk and began sorting through the contents.

Bridgette responded firmly, "Ethan, I need you to stop what you're doing and focus."

Whitecross kept sorting through his desk drawer. "I'm on a tight schedule here, detective. I'm leaving town first thing in the morning, and I'm making sure I don't leave anything behind that my sister-in-law can use against me."

"Do the murders of your father and brother mean anything to you, Ethan?"

Whitecross stopped what he was doing and grimaced. He let out a long sigh and said, "You've got ten minutes," as he slumped down into his desk chair.

Bridgette wheeled a chair from one of the other desks across to Whitecross's work area. "There's been some developments in the murder case." She withdrew a folder from her shoulder bag and added, "Do you remember that sketch of the man I showed you?"

"Kind of…"

"Let me refresh your memory." She withdrew a copy from the folder and placed it in front of Whitecross. She added as he stared at the image, "Remember now?"

Whitecross nodded.

"The witness who provided this sketch was in witness protection until early this morning…"

"Okay."

"He's missing. He may have wandered off, but I doubt it."

Bridgette pulled the yearbook photo of Paul Ferringa from the folder and placed it alongside the sketch. "Do you recognize the man in this photo?"

Whitecross looked at the photo but wouldn't respond.

"That's your stepbrother, Ethan. He now goes by the name of Paul Ferringa and was a Vancouver Metro cop for almost ten years."

"Why are you telling me this?"

"Do you see the resemblance between the sketch and the photo?"

Whitecross shrugged but said nothing.

"He's now wanted in connection with another two murders."

"I don't know anything about any other murders."

Bridgette held Whitecross's gaze. "We have a lot in common, Ethan."

"What do you mean?"

"Simon or Paul, or whatever you choose to call him, is the prime suspect in the murder of my parents. I'm not sure whether he actually pulled the trigger or not, but he's the reason they're dead."

Whitecross's eyes widened slightly as he mumbled, "My god…"

They stared at one another for close to a minute before Bridgette broke the silence. "I want to play something for you…"

She pulled a small Dictaphone out of her coat pocket and placed it on the desk. As she pressed play on the device, she said, "I recorded this when we interviewed your stepbrother yesterday. The first voice you'll hear is my boss, Chief Inspector Felix Delray. The second voice I'm sure will be familiar…"

The room was silent for a moment before the Dictaphone came to life.

"We're investigating a double murder."

"So, how can I help?"

"The murder victims were Reid and Owen Whitecross…"

"Why are you telling me this?"

"I thought you'd want to know. They are your stepfather and brother, aren't they?"

"I haven't seen either of them in close to thirty years."

"I'm curious. Why did we never know about your family when you were on the force?"

"I never got along with my adoptive father and left home when I turned eighteen. I haven't seen him since."

"Their bodies were discovered almost a week ago. Reid has been dead for twenty years. Owen maybe just a few months."

"Their deaths mean about as much to me as someone stepping on an ant."

Bridgette pressed the pause button on the device and then stared at Whitecross. "I thought you'd want to know how much Simon thought of your family…"

Whitecross shrugged. "What do you want me to say, detective? I don't know Simon anymore."

Bridgette felt herself losing control. "Don't you care?"

Whitecross became sullen. "My family died when my mother died. Simon wasn't the only one who didn't get on with my father."

Bridgette slammed her palm down on the desk. "This is your father and brother! If nothing else, they are the people you grew up with. You may not think too much of your father, but your brother? From what I can see, he had your back…"

With his jaw set firmly, Whitecross responded, "Detective, nothing you say or do will bring my brother back."

Bridgette shook her head as her frustration grew. After observing Whitecross's obstinance, she began to understand why Jane Whitecross had fired him. She took a moment to compose herself and then said, "Paul Ferringa is an evil man. He was responsible for the deaths of my parents, and I'm certain he murdered your father and your brother as well. The fact their bodies were hidden in a secret cave, where he could visit them for whatever macabre reason, makes me certain of that."

Bridgette paused again as she fought her anger. In a more controlled voice, she added, "He's very rich and very powerful and has a team of minions that do his dirty work. Right now, we know he's responsible, but we can't prove anything. If there's anything you can think of that can help us…"

Whitecross pushed the Dictaphone across the desk toward Bridgette. "I can't help you."

Sunday - 7:25 P.M.

Bridgette sat at her dining room table staring at nothing. She'd barely moved in the last forty minutes as she continued to think about Roy Pepper. Her daily gym routine normally made her a voracious eater, but tonight she had barely touched her chicken salad. After putting her fork down, she sighed as she pushed her plate away.

She checked her phone again for messages as she now feared the worst after contacting the witness protection team at five p.m. They had confirmed he was still missing but wouldn't say anything more. She knew the odds of finding Roy alive now were very slim. The gnawing sensation she'd felt in her gut ever since Delray had phoned her to break the news began to intensify. Feeling helpless and frustrated, she got up from the table and walked out onto the tiny balcony of her apartment. She stared down at the traffic below. The evening traffic was thinning out, and none of the cars seemed to be in a hurry, almost as if they were trying to delay the onset of Monday morning.

She tried to focus on her case and thought back to the

meeting earlier in the day with Ethan Whitecross. It was the first time since joining the force she could recall losing her temper during an interview. She prided herself on being able to maintain control, no matter what the circumstances, and wondered what Delray would have thought of her actions.

She was still trying to work Whitecross out. His sullen and apathetic demeanor was frustrating, but she wasn't sure it was totally genuine. She hadn't been able to get a read on him at their first one-on-one interview because he'd been high on drugs. But she'd learned a lot more about him during today's meeting. His reluctance to make eye contact and the charade of not being interested in catching his brother's killer made her suspect there was more to him than he was letting on.

She looked up at the view back to the city. Nightfall had come, transforming the landscape into a sea of lights. From her vantage point, the vista took on a picturesque purple and blue hue, but it was lost on her. Bridgette stood still, almost transfixed, as she fought down the urge to scream. She hated not being in control and whispered, "There is nothing you can do," as her mind refused to stop thinking about Roy.

The sound of her smartphone interrupted her as it vibrated. Thinking it might be Delray with news about Roy, she walked back inside to take the call. She balked when she saw the number on the screen—Aaron Sterling. Bridgette debated letting it go through to voicemail but didn't want to miss an update on Roy, just in case he had one. After pressing answer, Bridgette put on as pleasant a tone as she could muster and said, "Hi, Aaron."

"I got back to the office late, so I thought I'd check in to see if you'd made any progress today?"

"Not really. I re-interviewed Ethan Whitecross this morning and then spent most of the afternoon with Louis Solomon trying to figure out the encryption code for the hard drive."

"I'm guessing that was a bust?"

The sarcasm in Sterling's question wasn't lost on Bridgette. Grudgingly, she responded, "Yes, but we learned quite a lot about the encryption program itself. Charlie's been very thorough. It's unlikely anyone will be able to break it without the passcode." Keen to change the subject, Bridgette added, "Have you heard anything more about Roy's disappearance?"

"No. I called Cunningham and let him know what happened. Needless to say, he wasn't happy about losing a witness."

Bridgette replied flatly, "I was more concerned about the man's life."

There was a slight pause before Sterling asked, "So where are you now?"

Bridgette responded, "I'm home," and then added, "just finishing dinner," just in case Sterling had any ideas of inviting her out again.

Sterling seemed to take the hint. "Okay, I guess I'll see you tomorrow then…"

Keen to keep the conversation as short as possible, Bridgette said, "Good night, Aaron. I'll be in around seven tomorrow," and disconnected.

After slipping her smartphone into her jeans pocket, Bridgette walked back out onto her balcony again. She stood there taking in the view of the city but not really enjoying it. Her phone buzzed again. She hadn't heard from Delray all day and wondered if he was calling to check in for an update.

Bridgette frowned as the number displayed on her screen wasn't one she recognized. She pressed answer. "This is Detective Cash."

"Detective, it's Ethan Whitecross."

Bridgette was taken aback but recovered quickly. "I didn't expect to be hearing from you again so soon, Ethan. What can I do for you?"

There was silence for a moment before Whitecross responded, "I've been thinking about what you said earlier today…"

"Which part?"

"You said Simon was an evil man. I've been doing my own digging, and I think you're right."

Bridgette dared to hope Whitecross was finally beginning to understand what a monster his stepbrother was. "And what have you found out?"

"Enough to know that I could be the next target."

"Ethan, I get the feeling that Paul Ferringa only kills people that get in his way or are a threat to him."

"But there are no guarantees."

Bridgette conceded, "No, but Owen had hired a private investigator to look into his father's murder. I can't prove that yet, but I think that's ultimately why your stepbrother came after him."

More silence followed before Whitecross replied, "This all makes me very nervous."

"I don't think you're in any imminent danger. If you've been honest with me and haven't had contact with him, there's no reason he would come after you now."

"I'm not taking any chances."

"Ethan, if you have any information on your stepbrother—"

"That's why I was calling. I found an old laptop of mine

while I was packing up my stuff. I remember I loaned it to Owen last year for about two months after his got stolen. I haven't touched it since I got it back. I know the cops came and collected his new one shortly after he disappeared, but nobody's seen this one. There might be nothing on it, but if you want it, it's yours. Otherwise, I'm throwing it off the Iron Bridge on my way out of town tonight."

"You're leaving town tonight?"

"After learning what my stepbrother is really like, I'm not hanging around a second longer than I have to."

Bridgette didn't like the idea of Whitecross leaving town but knew there was very little she could do about it. "Where are you headed?"

"I'm not sure yet, but you can reach me at this number if you need to contact me. So do you want the laptop or not?"

"Yes, of course."

"I plan on leaving in about thirty minutes. Can you be here to collect it before then?"

Bridgette thought for a moment. "From where I live to your apartment is going to take me at least forty minutes, even on a Sunday night."

"I'm not at my apartment. I'm back at the NewFarm Racecourse finishing my clean out. After you played me that recording this morning, I decided to go home and pack straight away. The guy's a psychopath, and I don't plan on being his next victim."

Bridgette looked at her watch. "If I leave now, I can be there in twenty minutes."

"They lock the gate at six o'clock, so just call me when you get to the parking lot, and I'll bring it out to you."

Bridgette frowned. "Ethan, if you found the laptop earlier today, why are you only telling me about it now?"

"Up until about five minutes ago, I was throwing it off the bridge to make sure Simon had no reason to come after me…but then I thought about Owen. If it might help, then you should have it."

"I'm leaving now. I'll see you in twenty minutes."

"Call me when you get to the parking lot."

Bridgette disconnected and walked into her bedroom to retrieve her car keys and coat. She looked at her watch—it would be well after eight when she arrived at the NewFarm Racecourse. She didn't think there was any serious risk to her safety meeting Ethan Whitecross in a well-lit parking lot, but she decided to take her Glock anyway.

Sunday - 8:05 P.M.

After getting a good run with Sunday night traffic, Bridgette pulled her Mustang off the street into the parking lot at the NewFarm Racecourse right on schedule. The only other car in the parking lot was an older-model blue Toyota parked next to the security gate in front of the office block. Bridgette brought her car to a halt next to the Toyota and switched the engine off.

The dim lighting emitted by the parking lot security lights gave Bridgette just enough light to see inside the Toyota. The rear seat was packed almost to the roof with a myriad of boxes, shirts and trousers still on coat hangers, and other bags that all seemed to have been hastily thrown in. Bridgette figured this had to be Whitecross's car and went to call him to announce her arrival but paused to look around the parking lot. She figured she was a good fifty yards from the main road and at least another hundred and fifty from any houses in the adjoining residential area. The parking lot, no matter how well lit, was isolated.

Bridgette knew enough about Vancouver Metro standard operating procedure to know she shouldn't be here on her own without someone knowing her whereabouts. She dialed Delray's number from memory and crossed her fingers as she waited for him to answer. She cursed under her breath as the call went through to voicemail. "Hi, chief, this is Bridgette. It's just after eight p.m., and I've just pulled into the western parking lot at the NewFarm Racecourse to pick up a laptop from Ethan Whitecross. It's a long story, I'll tell you all about it tomorrow. Just calling to check in. Call me back if you want, otherwise, I'll see you tomorrow."

Bridgette bit her bottom lip as she stared down at her phone. She knew leaving a message wasn't good enough and debated who she should contact next. Police operations were on duty twenty-four hours a day, but she thought that was overkill. They had to go by the book and log it into the computer, which sometimes took ten minutes or more if you had to wait for an operator. Bridgette decided to text Aaron Sterling instead in the hope she would get a response.

Bridgette thought about what she would say. She didn't want to alarm Sterling or encourage him to call her back. After a moment's thought, she composed a message.

"Just arrived back at NewFarm (west parking lot) to pick up a laptop from Ethan Whitecross (I'll explain tomorrow). Just checking in so someone from HM knows where I am. Will text shortly when I'm on my way home. Regards Bridgette"

Bridgette read the message back to herself and then pressed send.

She keyed in Ethan Whitecross's phone number to call him but was interrupted by the reply from Sterling.

"Rather late to be working on your own? I can be there in fifteen minutes?"

Bridgette let out a long breath—at least someone now

knew where she was. The last thing she wanted was for Sterling to be getting in a car and coming over to interfere. She composed a reply and pressed send.

"No need. I'll only be here for five minutes. Thanks anyway."

Bridgette immediately dialed Ethan Whitecross's number, just in case Sterling tried to call her. The call was answered on the second ring.

"You out front, detective?"

"Yes. I'm parked next to your car. Do you want me to come in?"

"No need. I'll bring the laptop out to you and pass it through the gate, and you can be on your way."

"Okay, I'll go and wait."

Whitecross disconnected. Bridgette looked across at her Glock service pistol in its holster on the passenger seat. She debated whether she should take it or not before she slipped the weapon into her coat pocket.

Bridgette got out of her car and scanned the parking lot. Not seeing or hearing anything untoward, she closed the car door and walked toward the gate. A cool breeze swept across the parking lot, reminding her that spring was still a month away. She was glad for her coat as she placed her hands in the pockets and thankful for the Glock as she felt the cold steel of the weapon in her right hand. Bridgette stopped just short of the gate and looked up at the office complex. It was dark, except for one light burning on the first floor. She watched as the door opened and Ethan Whitecross emerged carrying a box. After turning off the light and pulling the door closed, Whitecross walked along the breezeway with only the feeble light from a cigarette he was smoking to guide his path.

She frowned as she watched him carry the box down the

stairs—Whitecross had made no mention of the box, and it was far too big to contain a laptop. As he approached the gate, Bridgette said, "That's a big box for a laptop?"

"I finished my clean out, this is the final bit of trash." Whitecross sidled up to the gate, still holding the box in both hands. "The laptop is on top. Just reach through and grab it. I'm not sure it will help, but you never know."

Bridgette's gut told her to be careful. She took a moment to grasp her Glock inside her coat pocket with her right hand before moving forward. She could see an old laptop in the semidarkness on top of the box and reached through the gate with her left hand. Before she could grasp the laptop, Whitecross dropped the box. At first, she thought he had just been clumsy, but then she realized she'd made a terrible mistake in trusting him. There were only a few pivotal decisions in Bridgette's twenty-seven-year life that she profoundly regretted, and this was one of them. Time seemed to slow down for her as Whitecross grabbed her left wrist with both hands.

Instinct took over as she felt an adrenaline rush through her body. She tried to withdraw her hand, but Whitecross's grip was too strong. He leaned back and used his weight to pull her forward. Bridgette was momentarily dazed as her body crashed into the gate, leaving the left side of her face numb as it struck the gate's vertical bars.

As her instincts took over, Bridgette tried to withdraw her Glock, but the gun snagged on the coat pocket. Whitecross sensed what she was doing and grabbed at her right arm as he screamed, "She's got a gun."

With both arms now pinned, Bridgette's heart sank as she realized Whitecross wasn't alone. A moment later, cold steel pressed hard into the back of her neck. A presence moved close behind her.

A calm male voice said, "This will end badly for you if you struggle. Take your hand off the gun now."

Bridgette guessed the age of the other attacker at somewhere between thirty and thirty-five. It was a voice she'd never heard before—calm and direct. She got the impression he'd done this before as he pressed the gun deep into her neck muscles at the base of her skull. She could feel his warm breath on the side of her face as he whispered, "It makes no difference to me whether you die now or later, I still get paid."

Bridgette found it difficult to breathe as the man leaned his body weight against her back, pushing her even harder up against the gate. With Whitecross still holding both of her wrists, she realized the situation was hopeless and there was nothing to be gained by struggling and giving her attacker an excuse to pull the trigger.

Bridgette silently cursed herself as she relaxed her grip on the Glock. She felt the man reach into her right coat pocket and grab the weapon before he said to Whitecross, "I've got the Glock."

Whitecross responded, "So what do we do now?"

The man remained calm as he answered the question. "You're going to let go of the detective's right hand. She is then going to withdraw it slowly from her pocket, put it above her head, and grip the gate. If she fails to follow these instructions, you're going to wind up with her brains all over your face."

The man leaned in even closer and whispered, "And that's not a threat, detective. I've done this before."

Bridgette managed, "I understand."

The man said to Whitecross, "Let go of her wrist."

Bridgette felt Whitecross's grip loosen. She said, "I'm

withdrawing my hand and placing it over my head on the gate."

The man shoved the gun even harder into her neck. "Slowly."

Bridgette slowly withdrew her hand from her pocket and reached it up to grab the railing of the gate high above her head.

The man then instructed Whitecross to let go of Bridgette's other arm. With her heart almost beating out of her mouth, Bridgette raised her other arm and grabbed the gate.

Gripping her coat collar and keeping the gun wedged firmly against her neck, the man pulled her away from the gate and made her fold both arms behind her back before instructing Whitecross to join him. Whitecross reached behind one of the gate's brick supporting columns and pressed a button. The gate slid silently open. Whitecross waited until it was open about three feet before he pressed the button again and slipped through the opening as it closed.

The man kept his grip firm on her jacket as he twisted Bridgette around ninety degrees. "You see that opening in the hedge on the other side of the parking lot?"

Bridgette looked up, read a sign on a large wooden gate which said "Garner Stables," and nodded once. The man added, "That's where we're headed," and pushed her forward.

The walk was less than fifty yards. With the gun still planted firmly in the back of her neck and her arms folded behind her back, she knew struggling or trying to escape would only hasten the inevitable.

As they approached the gate, Whitecross went ahead to open it. He had double-crossed her, but she wasn't sure why.

Cold Hard Cash

He refused to make eye contact with her as she was marched through the gate and down a path that led to an old stable block. The one-story stable was a wood and brick structure about a hundred feet long. There was a row of small wooden windows just above head height that ran down the length of the structure. Bridgette noticed none of this detail as she focused on a single window toward the far end of the structure that had a dim light coming from it.

The man pushed Bridgette through an open doorway and into the main aisle of the stable. In the semidarkness, Bridgette counted eight horse stalls on either side of the aisle as she walked forward. The place was quiet, and all the stalls appeared to be empty.

The dim light that flooded out of the stall near the end of the stable gave Bridgette a sense of foreboding, and she felt her heart rate rise even further. As they neared the entrance, she felt a huge push on her back as she was shoved forward and off her feet. The concrete floor of the stall was covered in straw, but it did little to break her fall as she fell heavily. Winded and with blood dripping from her nose, Bridgette got up onto her knees and stared up into the face of Paul Ferringa.

Sunday - 8:40 P.M.

Ignoring the blood that poured from her nose, Bridgette locked eyes with Ferringa and stared back defiantly.

Ferringa's lips spread into something approaching a grin as he stepped forward. "I've been looking forward to this."

After grabbing her roughly by the collar, he yelled, "On your feet," and dragged her across to a squat wooden table he'd set up in the middle of the stall. She got her first good look at the man as Ferringa pushed her down onto one of two stools. The small deep scar through his upper lip suggested he was used to violence and knew how to survive. She ignored the gun he had trained on her chest and turned her gaze to Ethan Whitecross who was hovering in the doorway. "Why, Ethan?"

Ferringa pulled a gun from his coat pocket, placed the barrel next to her left temple, and bellowed, "You don't get to ask the questions."

Bridgette did her best not to flinch as she sat and stared straight ahead.

Ferringa laughed and said, "You're one determined little bitch," before asking Visontay, "Have you patted her down?"

"In the parking lot. She was carrying a Glock and a phone."

"Was she driving her car or a police issue?"

"Her car, no radio."

Ferringa held out his left hand and said to Bridgette, "Give me your phone."

With one gun trained on her chest and another trained on her head, Bridgette knew it was pointless to argue. She reached inside her coat, withdrew the phone, and laid it down on the table.

Ferringa glanced at the screen and then demanded, "Unlock it."

Bridgette keyed in her four-digit pin number. Ferringa picked up the device and lobbed it across the stable to Visontay who caught it in his left hand.

Ferringa said to Bridgette, "We're just going to check who you've called in the last two hours."

There was silence for about a minute before Visontay said, "Since the call to set up the meeting, she's only made one phone call—nine seconds in duration."

Ferringa replied, "Probably a message. Do we have caller ID?"

"Yeah, a Felix Delray."

Ferringa smiled. "That's her boss. What about text messages?"

"Two. Both to a guy called Sterling."

"Sterling is her new partner. Read them to me."

Visontay read the messages. Ferringa nodded. "We need to keep an eye on her phone. If he texts again, we have to respond straight away and say everything is okay, otherwise he'll get suspicious."

"Got it."

Ferringa turned to Whitecross, who seemed preoccupied with his smartphone. "It's time to earn your money, Ethan. What's it look like out there?"

"The parking lot is all clear."

Bridgette guessed they had some sort of camera set up outside and trained on the parking lot which was feeding a signal through to Whitecross's phone. It was simple technology but effective enough to alert them to any car entering the parking lot. Bridgette felt the muscles in her neck and shoulders locking up under the stress and tried to block out of her mind what she imagined was coming. So far away from the main road, and hidden behind a high hedge, she knew no one would hear her scream. Although not overly religious, she knew she would need a miracle to survive now and silently prayed as Paul Ferringa reached down and searched around in the straw. A moment later, he straightened up and laid a hammer on the table in front of her. The hammer was about fifteen inches long but slender, not the kind used in construction.

Bridgette tried not to show any fear as Ferringa said, "It's amazing what you can find lying around a stable if you look hard enough, don't you think?"

Ferringa motioned Visontay to move closer. "Keep the gun pointed at her head."

Visontay nodded as Ferringa stowed his gun back in his jacket. After sitting down on the other stool, Ferringa picked up the hammer and slowly turned it in front of her eyes. He said in a conversational tone, "I'm told this is a farrier's hammer. One they use to shoe horses with." He paused and, after shifting his focus to Bridgette, added, "But I'm sure you could use it for other things as well…"

Bridgette's only response was to glare back defiantly at Ferringa. He laughed and said, "You're as stubborn as your father," before nodding once toward Visontay. Immediately, she felt Visontay's presence behind her as he asked Ferringa, "Right or left?"

After studying Bridgette for a moment, Ferringa answered, "Let's start with the right…"

Ferringa moved his stool closer to Bridgette. "I brought you here tonight because I have some questions I need you to answer. Now we can do this the easy way or the hard way. You can just tell me, or I can…encourage you." Ferringa grinned. "It's really up to you."

Bridgette kept her eyes locked on Ferringa. "I've got nothing to say."

Ferringa responded, "We'll see about that," and grabbed her right hand. As he flattened it out on the table, Visontay reached around and grabbed her right arm to pin it to her body.

Ferringa added, "Let's start with an example," and brought the hammer down hard on her little finger. The sound of the hammer striking her finger barely registered with Bridgette as she rocked her head back and groaned in pain. She tried to recoil her hand, but Ferringa was strong and held her firm. Gasping for breath as she felt a throbbing pain shoot up her right arm and into her body, she looked down and saw her little finger splayed out at an odd angle. She knew it was broken as it swelled and turned purple before her eyes. Bridgette closed her eyes and breathed in short gasps of air as she tried to cope with the excruciating pain.

Ferringa ignored her condition. "Charlie Bates used to

work for me. I'm sure you're aware of that. I know you found a hard drive he kept hidden. A drive I've been looking for ever since he got caught. I need to know what's on it."

Bridgette opened her eyes and stared up into Ferringa's face. Some of her defiance was gone, but not all. In as strong a voice as she could muster, she replied, "It's encrypted. Nobody knows what's on it except Charlie."

Ferringa shouted, "Wrong answer!" and brought the hammer down hard on her ring finger. Bridgette screamed and writhed in pain as she went into shock. With her eyes closed tight, she felt her skin turn clammy as she rocked her head back and forth. She felt herself drifting in and out of consciousness as Ferringa leaned in even further. "Did you know this is the stable where I killed my stepfather?"

Ferringa looked up at Visontay again and said, "Hold her firm," as he raised the hammer again. Bridgette refused to open her eyes, which prompted Ferringa to lean in again and say, "I may be cold and hard, but I'm not a sadist. We can do this the easy way or the hard way. You tell me what I need to know, and I'll put a bullet in your head, quick and clean. But if you don't cooperate, we've got another eight fingers and ten toes to work with. After I get through all of them, I'll know for sure if you're lying or not."

Bridgette opened her eyes and said weakly, "I told you the truth. I don't know what's on the disk, and neither does anyone else."

With a sadistic grin, Ferringa said, "It looks like it's going to be a long night."

Whitecross interrupted. "We've just had a car enter the parking lot."

Ferringa looked up. "A cop car?"

"No, a small car—a Ford, I think. It's making its way over to my car and the Mustang."

Ferringa pushed Bridgette off the stool and onto the floor and said to Visontay, "Keep the gun on her," as he walked across to Whitecross. He grabbed the smartphone off Whitecross and studied the screen for a moment.

Visontay said, "A text message has just come in on her phone. It's from Sterling."

"What does it say?"

"'Where are you?'"

"That's him in the parking lot. Throw the phone to me."

Visontay lobbed the phone to Ferringa who immediately passed it to Whitecross. "Text him back and say, 'There was a mix-up, and I'm at the Garner Stables on the other side of the parking lot.'"

Visontay asked, "So what's our next move?"

Ferringa responded, "There are cable ties in my bag. Tie her up, and we'll go wait for Sterling."

Bridgette knew it was pointless to resist as Visontay slipped cable ties over both of her ankles before joining them together with a third cable tie and tightening them. While he was repeating the process with her hands, Ferringa placed a large piece of adhesive tape over her mouth which muffled her groans of pain. As they left her and headed for the door, Whitecross asked, "What do you want me to do?"

Ferringa answered, "You stay in here and babysit her."

Whitecross said, "Okay," and moved into the stall.

As he sat down on a stool, Ferringa looked at Visontay and nodded once.

Visontay raised his silenced pistol and calmly said, "Ethan."

Ethan Whitecross's eyes widened slightly as he turned

his head to face Visontay; his confusion was short-lived as Visontay pulled the trigger. Bridgette watched with horror as a bullet tore through Whitecross's forehead, leaving only a small dark hole to show the projectile had hit its target. Whitecross hovered on the stool for close to a second before he toppled backward, his lifeless body landing next to her. Ferringa and Visontay slid the stall gate closed and latched it from the outside before moving off into the darkness.

Sunday - 8:45 P.M.

Aaron Sterling put on his left indicator as he approached the parking lot. He wasn't sure why Cash needed to pick up the laptop on a Sunday evening and mumbled, "This better be good," as he drove into the parking lot. He sighed as he changed down into low gear. A week ago, he'd been following Assistant Commissioner Cunningham's directions to the letter—looking for any opportunity to make her look bad. This was another one of those opportunities, but the more time he spent with her, the less inclined he was to do Cunningham's dirty work.

As he veered right and headed across the parking lot toward her Mustang, he thought back to their first meeting. It was a pity it had been under such difficult circumstances. Despite her being shot at and almost killed, Cunningham had insisted he go hard on her in the interview. He had dutifully obliged and had been a real hard-ass. He'd yelled at her, threatened her, and accused her of being involved in a conspiracy. He knew shortly after starting the interview that she was innocent, but defying Cunningham wasn't something he'd been prepared to do.

As he pulled his car to a halt beside her Mustang, he wasn't exactly sure why he'd come after getting the text message. At first, he thought it was simply another opportunity to ask her out. He'd never been backward in pursuing single women with hot bodies before, but on the drive over from his apartment, he sensed his motives were no longer purely physical. He grudgingly admitted the more time he spent with her, the more he liked her. Her intellect, humor, and integrity made her different from every other woman he'd ever dated. She treated people well too—even guys like the geeky Solomon, who was ugly and overweight. He liked that. She had time for everyone...everyone, it seemed, except for him. He couldn't blame her, but somehow he had to explain to her he was only following Cunningham's orders.

He decided he would apologize—maybe that would break the ice? She didn't appear to be the kind of person who held grudges, so maybe an apology would get him a date? Sterling glanced across at her silver-blue Mustang. In the shadows, it looked more gray than blue—but it was still an impressive car. He didn't know a lot about cars and had looked it up on the Internet after he'd seen her driving it into work one day. It was a '67 Fastback—fully restored and a real head-turner. He'd heard it was a gift from a grateful town she'd recently solved a cold case for, but he wasn't sure. Maybe he'd compliment her on her car and then ask her out?

Sterling shifted his gaze to the parking lot and twisted his neck as he looked around. The place was quiet. There were no other cars apart from hers and the other car which he assumed was Whitecross's.

How long does it take to pick up a laptop? He looked up at the office block through the security gate. While he didn't have a great view, the place appeared to be in total darkness.

Now slightly concerned, he picked up his phone, keyed in a cryptic, "Where are you?" text message, and pressed send.

He was relieved when a response came back almost immediately: "There was a mix-up. At Garner Stables (opposite side of parking lot)."

Sterling twisted in his seat and looked across to the other side of the parking lot. The stables were signposted but hidden behind another high hedge. He thought about sending her another text message to say he was coming but decided that was overkill as he got out of his car. He reached under his coat and felt reassured by the cold steel of his Glock as it rested securely in his shoulder holster. He didn't expect trouble, but you couldn't be too careful. After closing his car door, he took a moment to study the car parked next to Cash's Mustang. He was positive it belonged to Ethan Whitecross, and it was packed to the brim with clothes and personal items. It reminded him of his first road trip when he'd left home with almost everything he owned to move interstate to attend college. He wondered if Whitecross was getting ready to leave town. He figured he'd find out soon enough as he set out across the parking lot.

As he walked toward the gate that led to Garner Stables, he wondered why Cash would pick up a laptop from there rather than the office block. Maybe Whitecross was working there with a sick horse or something? Sterling stopped when he got to the gate and peered through. He could only see one dim light coming from the back of the stable and could barely make out the pathway in the darkness.

He frowned as he thought he saw movement in the

shadows and stepped back away from the gate. Something didn't feel right. He debated calling the Control Center to advise them of the situation but knew that might get Bridgette into more trouble with Cunningham if she hadn't followed proper police protocol.

He decided to call her first to check and dialed her number. As the call connected, he thought he heard a phone ring. At first, he thought it was coming from the parking lot and spun around to check behind him, but there was no one there. He was confused as the ringing stopped and someone softly called out his name. He was sure it was coming from behind the gate and turned around as he reached inside his jacket. He stared into the darkness beyond the gate as he pulled out his Glock. He thought he could make out the figure of someone standing in the shadows but couldn't be sure. The tiny orange flash that erupted from the barrel of the silenced pistol was lost on him. At a speed of two thousand five hundred feet per second, the bullet ripped through his cerebral cortex before his brain registered the flash from the fatal shot.

Sterling's world faded to black as he fell backward, his body landing heavily on the parking lot pavement. The lone figure of Ryan Visontay slipped out of the shadows and calmly walked through the gate. At first, it appeared he was heading toward the corpse, but at the last moment, he veered right and headed toward a glowing object that lay on the ground about nine feet from the body.

He picked it up and studied it for a moment before he called out softly, "The screen's broken, but it still seems to be working…" He pressed several buttons before adding, "He hasn't made any calls."

Ferringa stepped out from the shadows. "Drag him back

in behind the gate for now. We need to get back inside and finish what we started."

Visontay stared past him, appearing to ignore his instructions.

Ferringa wasn't used to anyone ignoring his commands. "Are you deaf or just—"

Visontay pointed back toward the stable as he interrupted, "The stable light just went out."

Ferringa swung around and swore as he stared back into the darkness.

Visontay added, "Are there any other exits?"

As Ferringa moved back toward the gate, he said, "There's a gate around the back that they bring trucks through. It's locked, but I'm sure she'll be able to scale it."

Visontay responded, "Let's hope her broken fingers slow her down," as he broke into a sprint.

Sunday - 8:55 P.M.

Bridgette rolled onto her back as soon as Ferringa and his accomplice disappeared into the darkness. Doing her best to suppress the pain from her broken fingers, she rocked backward and then forward until she got up into a sitting position. She found it hard to keep her balance as waves of nausea flooded her body. She did her best to ignore the body of Ethan Whitecross, whose sightless eyes seemed to stare straight up at her as she sat in the straw, and tried to think of what to do next. She figured it would only be a few minutes before they returned and hoped Sterling was calling for backup. Bridgette looked down at the cable ties wrapped around her ankles. Being shackled at both the wrists and ankles would make it impossible for her to escape even if she did manage to get the stall door open. She knew she needed to somehow cut the ties and looked around for anything she could use to help her. She spotted the wooden end of the hammer Ferringa had used to break her fingers sticking out of the straw and shuffled forward to pick it up.

With the nausea easing, Bridgette gripped the hammer

with her good hand and tried wedging it between the cable ties wrapped around her ankles. She tried various angles, but the ties had been pulled tight, almost to the point of cutting off her circulation, leaving her no gap to work with. Bridgette glanced at the stall door again and suppressed the urge to panic. Shifting her feet backward and forward, she cleared the concrete floor of most of the straw beneath her. She dropped the hammer and pushed down on the cable ties around her ankles, hoping to force them down low enough so that she could hit them with the hammer against the concrete. Bridgette maneuvered her feet as best as she could but couldn't get into a suitable position.

Growing frustrated, she whispered, "Think!" as she glanced up at the stall door again. Bridgette closed her eyes for a second and drew in a deep breath as she willed herself not to panic. *There has to be a way out of this.* She opened her eyes again. Glancing down at the corpse of Ethan Whitecross, she ignored his dead stare as she realized she hadn't searched his body yet. Twisting her hands apart as much as the cable ties would allow, Bridgette ignored the pain from her broken fingers as she frantically searched each of Ethan Whitecross's jacket pockets with her good hand. She cursed softly when she found nothing and then repeated the process with the pockets of his jeans. After extracting a packet of cigarettes from the right pocket, she reached in again and felt a tiny glimmer of hope as she withdrew a disposable cigarette lighter.

Bridgette refused to celebrate even a small victory as she flicked the lighter on and stared at the small blue flame it emitted. After glancing up at the door again, she twisted the lighter around and held the flame up against the cable tie on her left wrist. Bridgette broke into a sweat as she felt her skin burn. The pungent smell of her burning flesh mixed with plastic made her nauseous all over again, but she refused to stop. With gritted teeth, she held the lighter firm against her wrist for close to ten seconds. She breathed in and out rapidly as the pain became close to unbearable and then let out a long breath as the flame finally did its job and burned through the cable.

After stealing a glance at the stall gate again, Bridgette moved the lighter down to the cable ties around her ankles. Now better able to direct the flame with her good hand, she held the flame firm for just a few seconds before the cable ties melted and separated.

Bridgette liked to plan everything she did, but knowing a delay of just a few seconds could be the difference between living and dying, she rushed to the stable door and reached through the metal bars with her good hand to unlatch the door. She was thankful the latch was designed to keep horses in and not humans as she felt the mechanism release under her fingers as she lifted it. Bridgette slid the door open just enough to slip through. She peered out into the stable walkway and was relieved to see it was all clear. With her heart racing, she went to step forward but paused to look back at the hammer that lay on the straw next to Ethan Whitecross's body. It wasn't much of a weapon, but it was better than nothing, and she stepped back in to retrieve it. After checking the walkway was clear again, Bridgette moved out of the stall and looked left toward the building's entrance, expecting someone to appear at any moment. She fought down the pain from her broken fingers and burnt wrist and focused on what she should do next.

Bridgette decided it was too risky heading out through the front stable doors. Ferringa and his accomplice could be just outside, and she would have no chance against two guns with only a hammer for protection. She turned and tiptoed to the back of the stable. There were a few horse bridles hanging up on hooks and an old bench that made her think the area had once been a workshop. Bridgette's heart sank when she realized there were no doors that led outside. She focused on a small double hung wooden window in the left rear corner. Covered in dust and cobwebs, it didn't look like it had been opened in a long time. Bridgette moved in closer and tried the rusty latch. To her relief, the latch turned. Bridgette winced as the window made a small squeaking sound as she opened it. She hoped it hadn't attracted any attention as she surveyed the area outside.

There was a four-foot drop to a paved driveway below that led down to another gate about sixty feet in front of her. The gate was wide enough to allow a small truck to fit through and just as high. Beyond the gate, she could see a white van parked and presumed this belonged to Ferringa or his accomplice. The stable seemed to be fully enclosed by the hedge, and she couldn't see any other avenue for escape. The light coming from the stable bothered her. If the gate was locked and she was forced to scale it, she would be exposed and an easy target if she was discovered. Bridgette turned her focus back inside and stared at a gray metal box attached to the wall just above the workbench she had seen earlier. Like everything else, it was covered in dust and cobwebs, but there was no mistaking its function.

Her decision made, Bridgette stepped across and prized the door open. The electrical system for the stable was primitive and only had three porcelain fuses and a single mechanical safety switch. She pulled down on the lever and immediately plunged the stable into darkness. With her adrenaline pumping, she turned and sprinted to the window, knowing the small advantage of darkness might come at the cost of alerting Ferringa and his accomplice that she had escaped. Bridgette placed the hammer in her coat pocket before she climbed out the window. After silently dropping to the paved surface, she held her ground for a moment to allow her eyes to adjust to the darkness. She listened for any telltale signs she had been discovered—footsteps, whispers—but heard nothing. She was thankful she had worn boots with low heels as she lightly stepped across the open area. She glanced back into the darkness, expecting a bullet to be fired at her, but everything remained quiet.

Bridgette swore under her breath as she approached the gate. Even in the gloom and shadows, there was no mistaking the heavy link chain that had been threaded through the gate's vertical steel bars and secured to the steel frame with a heavy padlock. Bridgette looked up at the top of the gate. She guessed it was about seven feet tall—almost as high as the hedge. She knew she could get over it, but with two broken fingers, it was going to take time. Bridgette moved in for a closer look, gripping the gate to see if it would rattle when she climbed. She frowned as she thought she heard a noise—almost like a dog whimpering. She listened again for the whimper, but the stillness of the night was broken by the distant sound of a man's voice: "The stable light just went out."

Bridgette moved back away from the gate as she realized they now knew she had escaped. The sound of running footsteps from the opposite end of the stable forced her to make a decision on the run. With only a hammer to protect her and no place to hide, she sprinted back toward the stable. After taking cover at the back of the stable, Bridgette peered down the left-hand side and saw the silhouette of a tall, slim man emerge from the shadows. Bridgette quickly moved to the right-hand side, hoping she might be able to squeeze down the blind side to make her escape. In the darkness, the gap between the stable and the hedge was narrow, and she was afraid she would get stuck and become an easy target.

With no time to spare, she climbed back into the stable through the window. Bridgette kept her head down as she watched the man stop at the gate before he spun around, searching for her in the darkness.

Bridgette stole a look back through the stable to the open doorway at the other end. She couldn't see any sign of Ferringa, which bothered her. If he wasn't with the other man, where was he? She desperately wanted to sprint through the doorway and back to the parking lot to escape but knew she might run headlong into a trap. With her head still down, Bridgette looked out the window again, willing the man to jump the fence and continue his search beyond the stable. To her dismay, the man turned on a flashlight and began searching the interior perimeter of the stable compound. Bridgette debated what to do as the man moved around the right side of the building. Now that she knew the back gate was locked, there was little chance of her getting over it and away before being cut down in a hail of bullets, but staying here was just as futile. She decided to keep moving and crept forward along the center aisle, inching forward toward the doorway at the other end.

With her heart beating almost out of control and registering as a rhythmic thump inside her head, she almost missed Ferringa's voice as he called out softly, "You find her yet?"

Bridgette shifted forward just slightly and stood in the entrance to one of the stalls to get a better look at Ferringa and the other man who had just come into view. She studied the man as he lowered his gun to converse with

Ferringa. She noticed he held the pistol in his right hand and the flashlight in his left. Bridgette debated what to do next, but they took the decision out of her hands as the man turned toward the stable. Bridgette dove into the open stall, hoping she hadn't been spotted as she heard the man's footsteps approaching.

She backed up against the sliding door and waited. She could hear the soft footfalls of the man as he slowly walked forward and saw the flashlight playing on the floor and then on the roof, left to right, as he walked forward. She knew by the pattern he was checking each stall as he went. First on the left and then on the right before moving forward. Bridgette held her breath. She figured based on his current progress it would be only seconds before she was discovered.

Sunday - 9:10 P.M.

Bridgette withdrew the hammer from her jacket pocket and waited. A lump formed in her throat as she heard the man's footsteps grow louder. She looked up at the roof and saw a reflection of the light as the man moved forward, first checking the stall on the left and then the one on the right before moving forward again.

As she gripped the hammer tightly, she thought about his search pattern. There would be a moment when he would have his back to her. Bridgette had always trusted her gut instinct and knew this would be her only opportunity to strike with the element of surprise. She took a deep breath as she raised the hammer and silently pivoted on her left foot—timing would be everything. She looked up at the roof and watched as the reflection from the light moved closer. Bridgette held her breath as the man paused in the middle of the aisle again. She guessed he was no more than eight feet from her as she hid behind the stall door. As the light on the roof played to the left again, Bridgette rushed from the stall. The man was not quite in the position she'd hoped for when she struck with the hammer. She was aiming for high up on his back. A big enough target to see in the dark and hopefully vulnerable enough to get him to collapse on impact. But the man seemed to sense her presence and pivoted at the last moment, bringing his left arm up for protection.

There was no time to adjust or reset. This was the moment. Bridgette continued with her swing, bringing the hammer down with all the force she could muster. She heard a loud crack as the hammer struck the man's forearm. The flashlight crashed to the floor, and the man groaned in pain as he reeled back.

With the element of surprise gone, Bridgette knew the man's next move would be to shoot. The shock of having his arm broken would buy her seconds at best before he recovered enough to end it all with a bullet. Bridgette wasn't sure she could get the hammer up in time for a second strike and kicked the man in the groin with all the force she could muster. She heard the spit of his gun as it discharged, but the shot went wide. The man groaned again but quickly recovered. Bridgette swung the hammer again as the man raised his weapon. There was no time to hope or pray as she willed the hammer on through its arc. A fraction of a second too slow, and it would all be over. The sound of the hammer crashing into the man's skull was lost on her as she heard the second deadly spit from the man's pistol. She had no time to brace for the explosion of pain as she saw the tiny orange flash from the muzzle of the weapon. Her subconscious may have registered a tiny puff of wind against her left calf as the bullet passed close by, but this was lost on her as she watched the man collapse at her feet.

She heard the voice of Paul Ferringa call out, "Ryan?" as she reached down to pick up the man's gun. Bridgette could tell by the direction of his voice that Ferringa was still outside.

After switching off the flashlight, Bridgette moved back into the entrance to the stall. Ferringa called out again, and then everything grew quiet.

She debated calling out to tell him he was now on his own and that his henchman was unconscious, but she didn't want to give her position away.

The silence lasted ten seconds before Ferringa called out, "It looks like you got the better of my associate. Normally I would be angry with you for that, but you did me a favor… It means I get to kill you now…"

Bridgette held her ground as everything became quiet again. She thought through her options. She hoped Sterling had made the call to Vancouver Metro, but something in her gut told her that had gone horribly wrong. Bridgette peered out into the center aisle. She had a reasonable view of the stable doorway and in the darkness could just make out the silhouette of Paul Ferringa about forty feet away. She decided her best option was to sit tight. If Ferringa tried to enter, she had a good enough view to get several shots off. She glanced back quickly toward the window at the rear of the stable. If he tried to sneak in behind her, she was confident she would hear him and that would give her a chance to escape through the parking lot.

Ferringa called out again, "It's a pity we didn't get to finish our conversation. I would like to have known what was on that drive, but sometimes you have to cut your losses."

Bridgette frowned as she wondered what Ferringa meant by his statement. As she tried to figure out his next move, she heard the unmistakable sound of a door moving against a rusted hinge. *Why is he trying to shut me in? Surely he knows about the window at the back?* Bridgette knew the answer almost before she'd asked herself the question as she watched a small silver and orange object fly through the doorway and land in the first stall. The instant whooshing sound as straw caught on fire forced her to react. Bridgette stepped out into the aisle and watched with horror as the right-hand stable door began to close as well. She debated trying to put the fire out, but the flames quickly took hold, and she could see fire already licking up the outside wall of the stall. She had seen enough and turned and sprinted to the opposite end of the stable. With the gun held in her left hand, Bridgette was thankful she'd left the window open as she climbed outside again. She moved back about twenty feet from the building but at an angle that meant Ferringa wouldn't be able to see her unless he came around the corner. Bridgette raised Visontay's pistol in her left hand and used her right hand as best as she could to steady it.

With her arms extended and her body position in the Weaver stance, she focused on the rear corner of the stable, expecting to see Ferringa burst into view at any moment. The seconds ticked by, but there was no sign of her nemesis. The fire quickly took hold, and the entire compound became illuminated by an eerie smoky orange-blue glow. She barely noticed she was sweating from the fire's heat as she watched the elongated shadow of a man holding a gun moving down the side of the stable toward the rear corner. She glanced down and cursed under her breath as she realized she was also casting a shadow that would be partially visible to Ferringa. She debated moving back closer to the window but decided changing positions now was too risky.

The shadow stopped moving. She estimated Ferringa was about three or four feet from the corner of the building when he called out above the roar of the fire, "I know you're there. Nobody would be stupid enough to stay inside."

Bridgette wondered how long it would be until someone noticed the blaze and called the fire department. *Surely not long?* Refusing to be distracted, she maintained her stance and kept the pistol focused—chest high and about a foot to the right of the corner of the building.

Ferringa added as his shadow inched forward, "You realize this is futile. I know you're right-handed, and you've got two broken fingers—you can't possibly shoot straight now."

Bridgette wondered what Ferringa would do when he heard sirens. She hoped he would flee rather than risk being caught and tried to buy some time as she called out, "Why?"

Ferringa shot back, "Why what?"

"Why did you come back and put a dollar in your father's pocket?"

A soft laugh greeted her question. Bridgette glanced down at the ground again and noticed Ferringa's shadow continuing to inch forward. Now about two feet from the corner of the building, he responded, "His trustee overpaid my inheritance by a dollar. I couldn't stand owing him anything, so I paid him a visit and gave it back."

She heard the faint sound of sirens in the distance. "Why did you wait so long to kill him?"

Bridgette could see his shadow inch forward even further as he answered, "I figured eighteen months was a long enough…"

Bridgette tensed as she saw the shadow rush forward. Before she could react, Ferringa's arm reached around the corner of the building and blindly fired multiple shots in quick succession.

Bridgette felt her heart stop as she counted off four rounds in under three seconds. Ferringa had misjudged her position and fired well to her right, but this was her opportunity—a time to play for the camera or, in this case, the shadows. Instinctively, she slumped forward, lowering the gun slightly as she dropped to her knees. Ferringa rounded the corner with his gun not quite fully up in the firing position.

Bridgette raised her weapon again, just as she had done a hundred times before in training. But this time she wasn't concerned about her stance or worried about how she gripped the weapon or if her shoulders were relaxed. She thought of her mother and father, and Charlie Bates, and Roy Pepper, as she zeroed in on Paul Ferringa's chest and fired three shots in quick succession.

She dared to breathe as she saw the gun fall from Ferringa's hand as his shirt turned bright red. Ferringa stared at her with a slightly confused look for a good three seconds before his legs buckled and he collapsed on the cobblestones. She stayed in position with her gun still trained on his body as the sirens grew slowly louder. She felt no guilt or remorse for what she'd done.

Ferringa made no move to get up. Still shaking from what she'd been through, Bridgette got to her feet and walked toward Ferringa, the gun in her left hand still trained on his body, barely believing it was over.

She stood over him and kept the gun pointed at his face, and she watched blood begin to foam at the corners of his mouth.

Ferringa said, "Your shadow... I thought..."

"I got lucky."

"I hear sirens. Is that an ambulance?"

"I doubt it. Probably a fire truck and a couple of cop cars."

"You need to call an ambulance."

"Ambulances are for good people."

Ferringa hissed, "It's your duty."

She kicked Ferringa's gun away and then leaned in close. "You're not the only one who is cold and—"

Bridgette frowned and stopped mid-sentence. Tilting her head slightly to one side, she listened to the cacophony of sounds. Above the roar of the fire, the creaking of the stable as it began to collapse in on itself, and the blare of sirens, she heard a sound that didn't belong. She listened intently and turned toward the lower gate as she heard the sound again. The cypress hedge was well alight and closing in on the white van parked just behind the service gate. Ignoring Ferringa, Bridgette stood up and walked toward the van. The sound came a third time, this time unmistakable—the sound of a dog barking. Bridgette broke into a sprint.

Sunday - 9:25 P.M.

By the time Bridgette reached the gate, the dog was barking incessantly. She wasn't sure whether it was the smoke or something else that had caused it to panic, but she was now positive it was in the back of the van. She hoped beyond hope it was Spike, and his master too, as she looked up at the top of the gate. The vertical metal bars were spaced just over a shoe's width apart. Under normal circumstances, Bridgette knew she would be up and over it in under a minute. But with only one good hand and no cross braces to get a foothold on, it would take much longer. Bridgette looked at the gate's hinges. The lower hinge was about two feet off the ground and the upper hinge about five feet. She was confident she could get a foothold on each hinge as she removed her coat and placed the gun in her pants pocket.

After gripping one of the vertical bars with her good hand, she reached up her right foot and wedged it in the gap between the hinge and the brick column that supported it. Bridgette pushed off with her left foot and lifted herself up. With her head now parallel to the top of the hedge,

Bridgette coughed again as she inhaled more smoke. She turned to her right, alarmed at how quickly the fire was spreading. After shifting her right foot slightly to make sure it was wedged in firmly, Bridgette reached higher up the bar with her good hand and then raised her left leg in search of the upper hinge. Her hand slipped slightly, forcing her to grab at the gate with her right hand to steady herself. Bridgette groaned in pain and bit down hard on her bottom lip as sharp bolts of pain shot up her right arm. Despite the smoke, she breathed in and out heavily for about ten seconds until the pain became bearable. Reaching up again, Bridgette gripped the top of the gate and then felt around with her left foot until she located the top hinge. After getting a foothold, Bridgette climbed to the top of the gate. Amidst a coughing fit, she turned to her right again, barely believing how quickly the fire was spreading in the hedge. As the wind whipped up and she began to swallow smoke, she realized the van would be engulfed in flames within minutes.

With no time to spare, Bridgette straddled the gate and then dropped to the ground on the other side. She rushed to the van's side door and tried to open it, but the door was locked. She banged on the door and yelled in a croaky voice, "Roy, are you in there? Can you hear me?"

She heard nothing other than more barking and stepped around to the rear door. She tried opening it, but it was also locked. The driver's door was locked as well. Bridgette swore as she looked up at the fire, which was now spreading along the hedge consuming everything in its path. She figured everything around her would be engulfed in under a minute. Using her good hand, Bridgette pulled the gun from her pocket and fired two quick rounds into the driver's window of the van. The glass exploded as expected. After reaching in to open the door, she quickly hoisted herself up inside as the dog continued to bark. The driver's area was separated from the cargo area by a metal partition with a small glass window. Bridgette shifted her position and looked through the window. She strained her eyes as she stared into the dim cavern. She ignored the barking dog and focused on the form of a small man who lay still on the floor—Roy Pepper.

Bridgette was conscious of the van heating up. She turned to the dashboard and scanned the array of switches and buttons until she found the button for central locking. She pressed down on it hard and was relieved to hear the click as every door on the van unlocked as she tried to control another coughing fit. Bridgette jumped from the van and tried to head around to the rear, but the inferno had reached the gates, and the heat drove her back.

She raised her hands to shield her face and screamed, "No!" as she stared at the back of the van. The paint was turning from white to yellow and then blistering before her eyes. As Spike continued to bark, Bridgette jumped back up into the cabin in the hope of finding a spare set of keys. Now lathered in sweat, she admonished herself not to panic as she searched under the visors and in all the storage compartments she could find. When she came up empty, she shouted at herself, "Think!" as she stared out the front window at the smoky haze in front of her. The roadway that led up to the gates was almost level but not quite. With a glimmer of hope, Bridgette released the handbrake and moved the van's gear stick into neutral. Sliding out of the van and ignoring the pain from her broken fingers, Bridgette gripped the open door and the steering wheel and pushed for all she was worth. The pain in her hand was excruciating, but now running on pure adrenaline, Bridgette blocked it from her mind.

The van refused to budge, causing Bridgette to roar in frustration. She could feel her clothes and skin burning as the fire continued to take hold. After re-gripping the door and steering wheel, she pushed forward and pulled back in a rocking motion. She felt nothing more than a subtle shift in forward and reverse momentum, but she persisted, now barely able to see six feet in front of her as smoke enveloped the vehicle. As she began to cough and wheeze, she felt the van shift forward just slightly. Bridgette tried just pushing forward with all the strength she could muster, but the van rolled back under its reverse momentum. Keeping the rocking motion going, she continued pushing backward and forward again until she felt the van shift again. The searing heat burning her back and legs was almost intolerable, but she pushed forward again. At first the movement was almost imperceptible, but finally, Bridgette felt the van inch forward. Doubling down, she braced her legs and pushed forward for all she was worth until the van finally rolled forward. Now close to passing out, Bridgette closed her eyes and strained every muscle in her body to move the van to a safe position. Just a few inches turned into a foot, and then a foot turned into two as the van crept forward. Finally, she opened her eyes as she realized the van was now rolling down the slight incline on its own. Too exhausted to climb back into the cab, Bridgette let go of the van and stopped in the middle of the road, doubled over with her hands on her knees as she fought off exhaustion. She looked up and watched as the van crashed into the side of a building about forty feet in front of her at little more than walking pace.

Too tired to run anymore, Bridgette willed her body forward through the swirling smoke.

She zeroed in on the back of the van and was relieved when the latch worked and she was able to open the door. She ignored Spike who stopped barking as he jumped out of the van and focused her attention on Roy. He lay on his back with his feet facing forward and his eyes closed. With no discernible movement in his chest to show he was still breathing, Bridgette feared the worst as she reached in with her left hand and touched his pallid skin. She found his carotid artery and lifted her fingers until her index and middle finger were barely touching his skin. Tears formed in her eyes as she uttered a prayer for the second time that day. What she had been through seemed pointless if Roy didn't survive. She kept her fingers pressed lightly against the artery but felt nothing.

She whispered, "Come on, Roy," and closed her eyes. In an instant, her world became very small. Bridgette shut out the pain and exhaustion that racked her body and ignored the fire that continued to rage behind her. She no longer heard Spike's barking or the sound of the sirens. Bridgette no longer smelled the smoke or felt any connection to the world in which she lived as she moved her fingers imperceptibly to the right along Roy's artery. She continued to hold her breath but allowed herself a glimmer of hope as she felt a faint but steady pulse.

6 Weeks Later

Bridgette appeared in the doorway to Delray's office but decided not to knock when she realized her boss was on the phone. Delray caught sight of her as she turned to walk away. He motioned for her to come in and sit down as he covered the mouthpiece and murmured, "I won't be long."

She obliged but was conscious of the last time she sat in his office waiting for him to finish a call. It had been close to forty minutes before he finally got off the phone. As if reading her mind, he held up an index finger and mouthed, "One minute," before lowering his head to concentrate on the call again.

Bridgette smiled in response to her boss. It was good to see him well again after his medical incident six weeks ago. On the same night she'd had the harrowing ordeal in the NewFarm stable, Delray had been on his way to the hospital in an ambulance after collapsing at home. The hospital had run a series of tests before diagnosing low blood pressure. She was pleased he was back on his feet and fully functioning again. Delray hadn't been happy about the prospect of taking medication for the foreseeable future, but it was a small price to pay for his health, she thought.

To her surprise, Delray was good to his word and ended the phone call about a minute after she entered the room. After disconnecting, Delray said, "That was Cunningham's assistant. Looks like the hearing is going to be Monday next week."

Bridgette felt her gut tighten a little. Delray added, "There's nothing for you to worry about. You followed procedure—Sterling didn't—end of story."

"I'm not sure that's how Assistant Commissioner Cunningham is going to see it?"

Delray mused for a moment before he responded, "No, he'll be looking to blame someone like he always does, but the commissioner himself will be attending, and he knows you acted by the book."

Bridgette thought back to the night she had driven into the NewFarm Racecourse to meet Ethan Whitecross. "I still feel guilty about what happened to him…"

"Why? Because you're alive, and he isn't?"

"Kind of…"

"You've got nothing to feel guilty about, Bridgette. Before you got out of the car, you tried to contact me, and when you couldn't get through, you contacted Sterling. That's straight out of the ops manual—always let someone else know where you are and what you're doing. If Sterling had done the same, maybe, just maybe, he'd still be alive today."

"I guess…"

Delray pulled off his glasses and looked at her intently. "Tell me what you're thinking."

"I feel responsible. If Sterling hadn't shown up when he did, I'd be dead."

Delray nodded. "You remember when we were at the crime scene following Bates's murder and how Sterling was making an ass of himself?"

"Yes."

"I had a long talk with him after that—about his behavior."

"Okay."

"After I chewed him out, he opened up a little. I got the feeling he'd worked for Cunningham for too long and felt isolated from the rest of us. I almost felt sorry for him."

"I've never thought about it like that."

Delray shrugged. "It makes me wonder if he was second-guessing himself in the parking lot?"

"In what way?"

"Cunningham's not the kind of guy you call on a Sunday night. Maybe that's why he didn't call anyone else for backup... If he had, maybe you'd both be alive now?"

This was all news to Bridgette. She wasn't sure how she felt about Sterling now and would need time to think it through.

Delray chewed on the end of his glasses for a moment. "I shouldn't be telling you this ahead of the hearing, but the commissioner has told me he won't hear of any blame being apportioned to you. While he's gutted that we've lost an officer, he's not wanting to hang anyone out to dry for it, least of all someone who keeps getting results."

Bridgette didn't try to hide her relief. "Thanks, chief. It's good to know people here have got my back."

"Cunningham will huff and puff like he always does, but when he's finished, the commissioner will have the last word, like he always does." Delray seemed eager to move on as he added, "You know, Bridgette, we really haven't talked a lot about this. We've both spent time in the hospital, and things have been crazy since you got out."

Bridgette nodded. "It's been a roller coaster."

"We all know Ferringa, Visontay, and Whitecross had it coming, but that doesn't make it any easier... So how are you feeling?"

Bridgette thought for a moment. "I think I'm doing okay with it, chief. Considering I killed two men in the space of half an hour, I—"

Delray held up his index finger as he interrupted, "One man in self-defense. Visontay had smoke in his lungs, so he died in the fire, not from anything else."

"Well, considering I killed one man and almost another, I feel..." Bridgette got up and closed the door. When she returned to her chair, she added, "After I shot Ferringa and saw him lying on the ground, I knew he wasn't going to make it. I was surprisingly calm at that point. I didn't feel guilty...and I didn't feel elated either...I just remember thinking, 'It's finally over.'"

"This is something you've carried around for a long time. I'm no shrink, but this must give you a sense of closure?"

Bridgette nodded. "I no longer fall asleep wondering who killed my parents and why. I guess I'm finally at peace."

"Well, for what it's worth, Ferringa more than had it coming. After murdering your parents and God knows how many others and then wanting to kill you after he'd broken every finger and toe in your body..." Delray shook his head in disgust and then added, "The world's a better place without him..." Delray paused to put his glasses back on, adding, "Speaking of fingers, how are they mending?"

Bridgette smiled as she held up her right hand and

wiggled her small and ring fingers. "Almost as good as new. The surgeon checked them yesterday and wants me to continue with my physiotherapy, but he's happy with my progress."

"Can you drive yet?"

Bridgette nodded. "Yes, and just in time too. Roy is being released today."

"Well, that is good news, I really didn't think he was going to make it."

Bridgette thought back to the fire and how Roy had flat lined in the ambulance on the way to the hospital. "The doctors didn't either. The amount of Propofol he had in his system should have killed him."

"It's been a long, slow process for him."

"Yes, at first they thought he was going to suffer long-term organ damage, but Roy's a fighter. Each day he made a tiny bit of progress."

"So what's the plan?"

"I'm going to the hospital to pick up Roy first, and then we're going to pick up Spike who's been staying with a friend of mine."

"He must be looking forward to going home."

Bridgette nodded. "I visited him yesterday. He can't believe his boss has kept his job for him."

"Well, the guy deserves a break. After what he's been through, he deserves some good fortune."

"I think more than anything else, he's just glad he doesn't have to live looking over his shoulder anymore."

Delray nodded and said, "You can't even begin to imagine what that would have been like," as he reached into his top drawer. He pulled out a folder and slid it across his desk toward Bridgette.

"What's this?" she asked.

"A copy of the release papers from witness protection. I don't expect the hospital will have any issues with discharging Roy under his own recognizance, but seeing as how he was still part of the program when he arrived, this will stop things getting complicated for you." Delray half smiled. "So, are you taking a pool car or the Mustang?"

Bridgette smiled. "I'm surprised you have to ask."

"Well, delivering a witness home is considered official police business, so make sure you claim your gas money."

"Thanks, chief."

Delray looked at his watch. "I have to go up to level four. Cunningham wants to read me the riot act again."

Bridgette did her best not to roll her eyes. "What for this time?"

It was Delray's turn to smile. "Your new partner, as a matter of fact."

"My new partner?"

"His name's Levi Pearce."

"I've never heard of him."

"He hasn't worked homicide for close to eight years. He was working undercover until about nine months ago when a high-speed pursuit went horribly wrong and the perp's car hit a kid. Pearce took the boy's death pretty hard and is only now ready to resume work again. He doesn't want to work undercover anymore, which is understandable, so I've offered him a job back here. Cunningham's trying to overrule me of course, so I have a please-explain session with him."

Bridgette nodded. She had many questions but knew now wasn't the time to be asking.

As if reading her mind, Delray said, "He's a good guy, Bridgette—I think you'll enjoy working with him." As he rose from his chair, he added, "Let me buy you a cup of coffee tomorrow, and we'll talk about it then. Sound fair?"

Bridgette trusted Delray's judgment "More than fair, chief."

Delray put his coat on. "Give my best to Roy when you see him. Between your great detective work and his willingness to testify, we were able to flush Ferringa out, and I appreciate the risks he took."

"I sure will."

"The commissioner's planning on giving Roy a bravery award too. I don't know when yet, so don't mention anything until it's official."

"Okay, got it."

After saying their goodbyes, Bridgette stood in the office doorway for a moment and watched as her boss walked toward the elevator. While she was looking forward to having a partner again, she knew that would mean spending less time with Delray. She had enjoyed working closely with him and wondered if having a new partner would change their relationship. She decided it was something she didn't want to think about today and brushed it off by whispering, "Time to get your car keys, Bridgette."

Bridgette pulled the Mustang to a halt at the top of the gravel driveway. As she switched off the engine, Roy said to her, "I can't believe I'm home."

Bridgette looked up at the tiny cottage set amongst the trees. "Six weeks seems so long ago…"

They sat in silence for a moment enjoying the serenity of the rural setting as they listened to the tick of the engine as it cooled. "You know what's nice about coming home, Bridgette?"

Bridgette half smiled. "Surprise me."

"This really is home now. I don't have to run anymore..."

"That must be a nice feeling."

Roy nodded. "Life hasn't always been kind to me. I've tried not to complain, but finally, I feel like I'm getting a lucky break."

"And you deserve it."

Roy turned to Bridgette. "Thank you for all that you've done. I know if it wasn't for you, I'd have burned up in the back of that van."

Bridgette brushed it off by saying, "If I hadn't come here six weeks ago, that never would have happened."

Roy shook his head. "He'd have found me eventually. It was only a matter of time."

"You never have to worry about him again."

"And neither do you."

Bridgette let out a deep breath and said softly, "You're right, Roy, neither do I."

"I'm sorry about what happened to your parents. You've easily had as tough a time as I have."

"Thanks. But like you, now that he's dead, I have closure."

"Being able to put something like this behind you and move on is important."

They were silent for a moment before Bridgette said, "I've not really mentioned this to anyone other than my therapist, but up until now, I've never had a full night's sleep since I was seven. I started sleeping soundly in the hospital straight after the surgery to fix my fingers. At first, I thought it was just exhaustion, but as my body started to repair, I realized there was more to it than that... I still miss my parents and always will, but like you, knowing the man ultimately responsible for their deaths is no longer alive has brought me peace."

"Peace is a wonderful thing. Unfortunately, not many of us seem to have it."

Bridgette nodded as she thought about the tattoo she had on her inner left forearm. She wasn't a great fan of tattoos but had recently had the words "family" and "friendship" tattooed inside concentric rings as an everyday reminder of their importance. In the past week, she'd added the word "peace." She was about to share this with Roy when she felt a wet lick on her ear.

Bridgette smiled as she turned to the back seat and saw Spike pawing at her as he wagged his tail. "I think someone wants to get out?"

Spike responded with an enthusiastic bark.

Bridgette laughed and opened her door, which Spike took as his cue to escape the car.

Roy said, "And thanks for looking after Spike too."

"I didn't really do much. It's Connie that you have to thank. By the way, she was heartbroken when Spike left."

Before Roy could respond, the front door to his tiny cottage was opened by Blaine Kenmore. He waved to the car before bending down to pat Spike. Bridgette added, "I forgot to mention your boss said he was coming over to drop off some groceries and welcome you home."

Roy said, "That's very kind of him," as he opened the door.

"You go on up, I'll get your bag."

After retrieving Roy's small bag, Bridgette smiled again as she watched Roy hobble up onto his tiny front porch to the embrace of Blaine Kenmore. She recalled a conversation she'd had with Kenmore shortly after Roy had been admitted to hospital and how relieved he was that Roy had been found alive.

Bridgette exchanged greetings with Kenmore as she placed Roy's bag on the porch and then listened politely as he sincerely thanked her for everything she'd done.

When it was her turn to speak, Bridgette turned to Roy. "Well, Roy, I have a long drive in front of me, so I best be going."

Roy looked disappointed. "You won't stay for a cup of coffee?"

"I'm coming back this way in about three weeks to see a friend in Sanbury. I'd love to come and catch up then if that's okay?"

Roy beamed. "Of course. You know you're welcome anytime."

Bridgette nodded in Kenmore's direction. "Good to see you again, Blaine."

"Likewise, Bridgette. Have a safe trip home."

Bridgette waited for Roy as he hobbled down off the porch to say goodbye.

As Roy embraced her, he said, "I can never thank you enough for all you've done for me, Bridgette. You've given me my life back."

She felt warm inside as she responded, "You've helped me get my life back too, Roy."

They held onto each other for a long time. Bridgette found goodbyes awkward and simply said, "I'll call you in a couple of weeks," as they parted. She waved to them both as she headed back to the Mustang, feeling both happy that Roy was home and sad that she wouldn't be seeing him regularly anymore.

After climbing into her car and starting the engine, she

switched on her retro-style car radio and used Bluetooth to connect it to her smartphone. She scrolled through her playlists until she found the collection she wanted. Bridgette waved a final goodbye to Roy and Kenmore and then headed down the driveway. She started tapping the steering wheel with her index finger as the dulcet tones of Madeleine Peyroux filled the car. "Dance Me to the End of Love" was a song that always made her smile.

Next in The Bridgette Cash Mystery Thriller Series

vinci-books.com/cold-light

A decade-old murder. A body in the lake. Can Detective Cash uncover the mystery?

Detective Bridgette Cash faces her most perplexing case yet when the body of an unidentified man is found in a lake, with the coroner's report revealing a shocking discrepancy. The man has been dead for no more than a week, but police records confirm he was murdered a decade ago. With an innocent man wrongfully imprisoned for the murder, Bridgette must confront not only the dark secrets of the past but also her own beliefs and convictions.

Turn the page for a free preview…

The Cold Light of Day: Monday
3:40 P.M.

Bridgette paused at the top of the rise to take in the scene below. Despite her tall athletic build, she was slightly out of breath from her walk up the steep incline from where she'd parked her car. Breathing in deeply, she studied the paradox before her.

The serenity of the fir trees swaying gently on a light breeze at the edge of Lake Barnett was in stark contrast to the flurry of activity she observed below. Shielding her eyes from the late afternoon sun, she recognized one man instantly as the group of four worked together near the water's edge. She'd worked with him before and knew him to be a consummate professional. The other three people she'd never met, but she figured they were just as capable. Although she was out in the open and less than a hundred feet away, nobody looked in her direction. Their focus was entirely on a fifth man who was floating face down about fifteen feet from the water's edge. Partially obscured by a tall cluster of reeds, it was impossible for her to see anything more than a vague outline of the man's body from her current position.

Her boss, Chief Inspector Felix Delray, had told her the man had probably been dead for a week when he'd assigned her the case, but had conceded that was mostly a guess based on the sketchy details phoned in by the witness who had discovered the body.

Bridgette wasn't afraid of death. She had seen her fair share of dead bodies in her short career as a homicide detective. However, the smell of putrefying human flesh always made her nauseous. She'd come close to vomiting several times during her first murder case when she had watched the forensic team exhume the body of a young woman from a shallow grave. It had taken all her resolve to hold herself together and she knew today would be no different. She marveled at the stoic determination of the forensic team as the smell of the decaying corpse assaulted her nostrils as it wafted up on the gentle breeze. Bracing herself for what lay ahead, Bridgette withdrew a small tube of Vicks VapoRub from her jacket pocket and rubbed a liberal amount on her top lip. She waited a couple of seconds until the vapor was all she could smell before making her way down the slope through knee-high grass that was still wet from overnight rain. When she was about twenty feet from the water's edge, the four turned as one to acknowledge her presence as she passed under the police tape. Three of the team gave her a subtle nod. With their faces mostly hidden behind surgical masks, it was impossible to tell if their nods were accompanied by a friendly smile or not, but under the circumstances, she didn't think so.

The fourth member of the group, Doctor Ray Warner, was the Vancouver city coroner. Bridgette had worked with

Warner on previous cases and had enormous respect for his abilities.

Warner bent down and removed a surgical mask from a large plastic medical box he seemed to carry everywhere and handed it to Bridgette. His voice was clear enough as he said through his mask, "You have any trouble finding us, Bridgette?"

"No, Ray. The chief's instructions were good enough."

"Where did you park?"

Despite the Vicks, Bridgette found the smell of the body overpowering and waited until she had her mask fitted before she responded, "Back on the road behind your van."

Warner nodded once and then turned back to face the lake. They watched for a moment as the three forensic technicians fitted what looked like fishing waders over their white overalls before heading to the water's edge. One of the two women in the group carried a digital camera which prompted Warner to say, "We've been here about an hour and have searched and photographed the surrounding area but have found nothing significant. We'll take photos as a record of each step of the recovery, so this could take a while."

"Any idea of the cause of death?"

"Not yet. It looks like a drowning, but the reeds are making it all but impossible to get a good look at him. All we can tell so far is that he's a big guy, maybe six two or three. The uniformed officers here with us are searching around the lake's edge for any sign of a boat or canoe that he might have fallen from."

Warner pointed to a walkie-talkie he carried on his utility belt and added, "They'll contact me if they find anything, but I haven't heard from them yet."

They watched in silence as the technicians waded into

the water before Bridgette said, "The witness who called this in? Have you spoken to him yet?"

"Yeah, *she* met us at the road and then brought us down to the body but didn't want to stay, which I can understand."

Bridgette fought the urge to vomit. After regaining her composure, she responded, "She lives around here?"

Warner dragged his gaze away from the technicians who were carefully making their way through the reeds in about three feet of water and pointed south. "The woman's name is Julie Playfair. She brought her dog down here for a walk. That's when she discovered the body. She lives about half a mile further up the road. There are only a few houses on this road, and she lives in the last one on the left. You won't have any trouble finding it, so I told her to go home and wait for you."

Bridgette turned her gaze back to the lake and watched for a moment as the technicians continued their work. Their progress was slow. She estimated the dense clump of reeds at the water's edge was close to twenty-five feet in diameter. They were approaching the body from two sides, wading a single step at a time before stopping to search for evidence and take more photographs.

She said, "This recovery isn't going to be quick, is it?"

Warner shook his head. "We're going to be here awhile."

Bridgette closed her eyes for a moment. When she felt confident she could speak without heaving, she said, "This might be a good time to interview the witness."

"I expect it will be another hour at least before we get the body out of the water, so unless you see value in watching us work, go see her now."

Bridgette needed no more encouragement and said a

brief goodbye to Warner before heading back up the hill again. She kept her mask on until she reached the top of the rise. After removing it, she turned and looked back at the scene below, and zipped up her jacket to keep out the cold. Shielding her eyes from the glare of the sunlight that reflected off the lake, she watched the technicians progress through the reeds. She estimated they were now less than ten feet from the body but were still patiently stopping after each step to photograph and carefully search for evidence before moving forward again. Bridgette frowned. Already there was something about the scene she didn't like. She would talk to Warner about it when she returned, but for now it was time to interview Julie Playfair.

Julie Playfair lived in a two-storey white colonial at the end of Barnett Road. The house was set back from the road and partially hidden by mature trees in the front garden. After turning left onto the driveway, Bridgette noticed a late-model, gray two-door Mercedes coupe parked out front at an odd angle, almost as if the driver had been in a rush to get inside. As she drove up the driveway Bridgette presumed the car belonged to Playfair. The front door of the house was opened by a woman in her mid-fifties with a stylish bob haircut. Dressed in designer jeans, boots and jacket, the ashen look on the woman's face belied her professional image.

She made no move to leave her house watching Bridgette warily as she got out of her car and made her way across the gravel driveway to the front door.

When Bridgette was about ten feet from the front door, she said, "Good afternoon, I'm looking for Julie Playfair."

In a cultured voice, the woman responded, "You've found her. And you are?"

"Detective Bridgette Cash from Vancouver Metro Police," said Bridgette as she held out her business card. Playfair took it and said, "Let's go inside, it's much warmer there."

Bridgette followed Playfair down a short hallway into a sitting room on the right. Playfair motioned her to sit on a leather sofa and then said, "Can I get you a cup of coffee before we start?"

Bridgette politely declined and waited for Playfair to be seated in a chair opposite. "This must have been a big shock for you."

Playfair let out a lengthy breath. "It sure was..."

"Perhaps you could tell me in your own words what happened?"

Playfair nodded several times, almost as if collecting her thoughts before she answered, "I travel regularly for work and have spent the last three weeks at our head office."

"What you do for a living?"

"I'm a contracts lawyer. One of my firm's principal clients is acquiring another company which required my presence in Rochford. I normally don't like to be away that long, but sometimes you have to do what you have to do."

"And when did you get back?"

"Yesterday afternoon. I picked up Bonnie on my way home from the airport and then took her for a long walk as soon as we got home."

"Bonnie?"

"She's my German Shorthaired Pointer. She's actually the one who discovered the body. We were walking down by the lake when she started to bark frantically at something in the reeds. I thought it may have been a sick or injured bird at first, but when I got closer and smelled that smell, I knew it wasn't a bird…"

Playfair closed her eyes for a moment and then continued, "I didn't get too close. As soon as I realized what it was, I put Bonnie on her lead and came home and called the police. I went back and waited on the road and then led them down to the spot where he'd drowned. But I didn't want to hang around, so I came back here to wait for you."

Bridgette made a note to check Playfair's travel movements later. She could see by the distressed look on Playfair's face that she was probably telling the truth and gently asked, "Can I call you Julie?"

Playfair nodded.

"Julie, do you live here alone?"

"Yes, it's just Bonnie and me now. My husband and I divorced three years ago and he now lives on the other side of the country."

"You didn't notice anything suspicious before you left?"

"No, nothing out of the ordinary. Barnett Road is very quiet. We all look out for each other."

"How many people live on this road?"

"There are five houses on the road, but only four of them are occupied. Long ago they were all working farms, but over time the farmland got consolidated and the houses on this road got sold to city people like me who were looking for a quieter life in the country."

"So all your neighbors work in the city?"

"Mostly. Jerry and Nancy who lived next door are retired now, but they've been in Europe for the past two months."

Bridgette made another note to get a list of all Playfair's neighbors before she left.

Playfair commented, "Nothing like this ever happens here. It's one of the reasons I moved here."

Bridgette nodded politely and then changed tack. "Do you get much traffic on this road other than your neighbors?"

"No. As you can see out front, the road ends at my property."

"What about tourists or fishermen interested in the lake?"

Playfair shifted in her seat. "It's not a big lake and I'm told with all the reeds and silt, there aren't too many places to fish on this side. I've seen the occasional boat out in the middle when I've been walking Bonnie, but boats close to this side of the lake are rare."

"You haven't had any flooding in the lake recently?"

"No."

"What about currents?"

Playfair frowned. "Not that I know of. The lake is normally very still, so much so that at times the water around the edge gets quite stagnant. Why do you ask?"

"The water is only three feet deep where the body was found."

Playfair looked slightly confused as she replied, "I'm not sure what you're getting at?"

"When bodies are found in a lake, the normal assumption is the person has drowned. But this man's body was found in the middle of a thicket of reeds. It's highly unlikely the body managed to drift that far into the reeds, and it would also seem unlikely that a grown man would accidentally drown in just three feet of water so close to the lake's edge."

Playfair nodded. "I see what you're getting at. So you think he was murdered?"

The Cold Light of Day: Monday
4:48 P.M.

Bridgette spent another forty minutes interviewing Julie Playfair. Her suggestion that the man might have been murdered had shocked Playfair but had hardly surprised Bridgette. The rest of the interview had been as much about evaluating Playfair's honesty as it was about discovering additional information.

After studying Playfair's body language as she answered each question, Bridgette concluded the witness was unlikely to have been involved in the man's death, but she would still make the necessary checks on her story. After making her way back to the crime scene, she was glad she'd kept her mask as she descended the slope again. Stopping about halfway down, she studied the forensic team at work while she applied a fresh batch of VapoRub to her top lip.

The man's body had now been removed from the water and was currently resting face up on a flat piece of land about ten feet from the water's edge. As part of her criminology degree, Bridgette had taken several subjects in human anatomy and knew the bloated corpse was in an advanced stage of decomposition. She was reluctant to proceed any further. The swollen features and greenish-black color of the man's skin made visual identification all but impossible and while that made the man difficult to look at, it was the smell that was causing Bridgette to balk. She recalled some facts she'd learned about decomposition of bodies in water and how it was a perfect breeding ground for bacteria. And these microorganisms were now well on their way to dissolving the man's internal organs.

She descended the rest of the slope and stopped a few feet short of the team who were crowded around the body.

Warner looked up as she approached and said, "Good timing, Bridgette."

"What have I missed?"

The forensic photographer continued taking photographs while Warner moved away from the body. "White male, around thirty years of age, but I'll have a better idea after I've done a full examination. There's no ID on him and I'd say he's been in the water about a week."

"Cause of death?"

"Almost certainly gunshot wounds."

"He was shot?"

"He's got a bullet hole in his back."

"Did that happen here or elsewhere?"

"Hard to say. He was floating high in the water, which is usually a fair indication he didn't drown, but I won't know for sure until I've done a full examination."

Bridgette took a couple of steps towards the lake. "When I saw the location of the body in the middle of the reeds, I did wonder. It seemed hard to imagine a body floating that far on a current into such a dense thicket."

Warner stood alongside her. "Give me forty-eight hours and I'll have a lot more information for you."

"There were no signs of any drag marks around here?"

"No, but I wouldn't expect to find any anyway. They've had two overnight rainstorms in the last week and any trace would be long gone."

Bridgette turned and looked up at the rise she had just come down.

"It's a remote area. It's possible he was shot here, perhaps even as he hid in the reeds, but I think it's more likely he was killed somewhere else."

"I agree. This is as good a place as any to dump a body."

"What's the plan from here, Ray?"

"We'll be here for a while yet completing our initial investigation. If the uniforms don't uncover anything else, we'll bag the body and head back to town."

"How long until we can get a DNA sample?"

"I'll make it a priority. There's a good chance…"

Warner was interrupted by his forensic photographer. "Doc, come take a look at this."

Warner walked back to the huddle of technicians to see what they'd discovered. Bridgette reluctantly followed but stopped about eight feet away and watched as the photographer pointed to the man's short-sleeved shirt and said, "He's got a tattoo."

Warner moved in closer and said, "Where?"

Using a pointer that resembled a knitting needle, the photographer pointed at the man's right arm and said, "On his upper bicep."

Warner produced a tiny flashlight from his pocket and knelt down. After gently lifting the man's sleeve, he studied the marking for about thirty seconds. "This could help with identification."

Bridgette hadn't been standing close enough to see what Warner saw. "What did you find, Ray?"

"He's got what looks like a dragon tattoo. It's hard to make out because of the decay and mud that's covering his body, but we'll clean it up and photograph it again when we get back to the lab."

Warner stood up and then added, "With a little digital enhancement, I'm sure we'll get something we can use."

Bridgette studied the man's body for a moment. Now getting somewhat used to the smell, she noticed for the first time he was wearing a short-sleeved shirt, steel cap boots and work pants.

She noted, "He could have come straight off a construction site."

Warner nodded. "We'll have to trawl through Missing Persons records. Hopefully the clothing might help narrow down the search."

"I'll make a start on it when I get back to the office. It's not a lot to go on, but you never know."

"If I come up with anything else significant, I'll call you."

Bridgette took this as her cue and said, "I'm going to call in on each of the other residents before I head back into town."

She said her goodbyes to the forensic team and then headed back up the rise. Pausing at the top, she looked back at the setting sun which was beginning to cast an eerie orange shadow across the lake. Thankful that she could breathe fresh air again, Bridgette stood for a moment watching the forensic team setup lighting equipment to help them continue their work. The silence was interrupted by her phone vibrating in her pocket.

Bridgette retrieved it and checked caller ID hoping she

could let it go through to voicemail, but when she saw the number, she knew it was a call she needed to take.

"Hi, Chief."

"Hey, Bridgette. Just called to see how it's going out there?"

"Ray's team has just recovered the body."

"A drowning?"

"No. He's been shot in the back."

There was a pause before Delray replied, "Well, it looks like you just got your next murder case."

Bridgette filled Delray in on the sketchy details she had so far and then gave him a brief summary of her interview with Julie Playfair. Delray listened without interrupting and then said, "So what's your next move?"

"I'm just heading back to my car. I'll do initial interviews with the other residents who live on the road if they're home before I head back to the office."

"You could be hours."

"I guess."

More silence before Delray said, "I can't stay late tonight, I promised my wife I'd take her to the ballet ... but I did want to talk to you before tomorrow."

Bridgette had a fair idea where the conversation was heading but asked anyway, "What about?"

"Your new partner. He starts tomorrow."

Bridgette wasn't sure how she felt about having a new partner. Her first partner had been killed in a shootout while she was still on her first murder case. Since then, another officer had lost his life while working a case with her. She'd heard rumblings in the Homicide room that she was bad luck and trouble, and while she tried not to take it to heart, it played on her mind.

"You still there, Bridgette?"

"Yeah."

"I know what you're thinking, and like I've said to you before, homicide work can be dangerous and sometimes things happen that are out of our control."

Bridgette wasn't sure how to respond. As she watched the uniformed officers return to the crime scene below, pangs of guilt wracked her body as she thought about her two colleagues who were now dead.

Delray continued, "I know you start early, so let's meet first thing tomorrow morning. There are a few things I want to go over with you before we do the introductions."

Bridgette didn't know a lot about her new partner, only a few sketchy details that her boss had provided in a previous meeting. She knew his name and that he had worked most of his ten-year career as an undercover cop in narcotics. When she had asked why he wanted to join Homicide, Delray had been vague in his answer. She'd pushed for more information and had learned he was returning to police work after an extended sabbatical. When she'd asked why a relatively young officer needed a sabbatical, Delray had waved her off with a we'll-talk-about-that-later answer.

Bridgette was tempted to ask again now but knew this wasn't the time or place and made a mental note to bring up the subject when they met in the morning. Keen to get on with her interviews, she responded, "I'll be in around seven thirty, Chief. Do you want me to come straight to your office?"

"Yeah, do that. We'll discuss your new partner and then you can fill me in on the case."

Delray disconnected leaving Bridgette alone with her thoughts. She checked her watch. Now well after five PM, she hoped at least some Barnett Road residents would be home from work and available for an interview. As she thought about how she would approach them, she realized this might be the last time she got to work on her own.

With just over twelve months' experience as a police detective, she realized her new and more experienced partner would be the senior officer and would get to call the shots. She had no trouble taking orders and while she respected authority, many of the senior detectives within Homicide dismissed her because of her age and gender. Delray was the notable exception. He continued to encourage her with each case she solved. She hoped her new partner was more like Delray than her other male colleagues but wasn't counting on it.

She sighed, thinking, *You'll know soon enough*, as she turned and headed back to her car.

Grab your copy...
vinci-books.com/cold-light

About the Author

Trevor Douglas is a multi-award winning author and the recipient of the gold medal for best crime fiction novel, and the gold medal for the best overall novel in the 2024 Global Book Awards.

Trevor is married with two adult sons and when he is not writing, enjoys bushwalking, watching AFL and discovering the best coffee shops in Brisbane with his wife.

After a long and successful career as an IT consultant, Trevor now writes full time.